I0831907

MURDER BY TANGO

MURDER BY TANGO

MICHAEL T. GAMBLE

DOMINUS PRESS, INC.
New York

MURDER BY TANGO

A Dominus Book

Published by Dominus Press, Inc.

Book design by 1106 Design

Library of Congress Cataloging-in-Publication Data is available upon request.

ISBN: 978-0-692-75228-9

First Edition: 2016

10 9 8 7 6 5 4 3 2 1

Printed and bound in the United States of America

In memoriam
Carlos Eduardo Gavito
un auténtico milonguero

PART I

The Basic Figure of Argentine Tango

INITIATION

Leader:	*One step side (left). Close feet together.*
Follower:	*One step side (right). Close feet together.*

CHAPTER 1

DON LUIS DE GRANADA STARED down through bulletproof glass at his Argentine tango dance company. Its members lined the studio's main dance floor, as the final candidate auditioned for a coveted slot. World-class company dancers yawned, scowled. The young man's audition was doomed though it was hardly begun. Don Luis tugged the gnarled strands of his beard, thinking of Natalia. So young and talented, full of promise, yet her life had been doomed. His hard brown eyes strained from behind the one-way mirror. He scrutinized each face in turn. Was the killer among them? A source had said no. But Don Luis was a cautious man. And it was as though he could feel twisted energy permeating the entire studio. Like a sickness infecting everything, rising up to his second-story office where he sat wheelchair-bound.

There was unavenged blood on Don Luis's hands; he had not been held to account for his every wrong. He had forgiven most of those who had wronged him. But this was different. For this killer's transgression there must be biblical retribution: a life for a life.

The office, with its crossed dueling pistols, fencing sabers, and brain-tanned leatherwork, harked back to the Argentine pampas and their gauchos of the early twentieth century. The ground floor was elegant, more congruent with its neighborhood, Manhattan's Upper East Side. Six months of breakneck construction and countless bags of payola had produced the city's poshest dance venue. Don Luis had handpicked the Baccarat crystal chandeliers and black Italian marble columns. Crystal and perfect floor aside, the studio was an homage to one of Buenos Aires's hallowed tango venues, La Confiteria Ideal. The club where decades ago a young Luis found tango and lost his heart.

The wheelchair groaned when Don Luis shifted his bulk and refocused his eyes on the audition. He sighed, recalling the preceding months and all of the excruciating nightmares of Natalia's murder he had endured. In many dreams he had risked his life to save hers. Although he no longer awoke drenched in sweat, Don Luis was still heartbroken. Time had dragged. But reality had drilled its way into him slowly. Today, time had flown. He had spent hours on end watching immaculately groomed dancers vie to fill two positions. A New York City girl was favored to make the cut. It had been neither her résumé nor dance technique nor remarkable beauty that had impressed. Something impossible to identify had shone through. Don Luis noted it was approaching ten P.M., the conclusion of auditions. It seemed that a former champion ballroom dancer from Ukraine, now living in the United States, also would be tapped. Don Luis considered the Ukrainian as he began propelling his wheelchair toward the elevator outside his office. He muttered, "So much technique; so little soul."

The elevator's glass-paneled car was illuminated by myriad tiny lights boasting naked filaments. It seemed to twinkle, descending to the ground floor. The door opened with a hush and Don Luis exited, to caucus with the company's principals. He saw Jean-Luc, a stocky tango novice with olive skin and impossible-to-read dark eyes, talking animatedly to Candy, the company's sole blonde. She had brought him around the studio weeks earlier, before it had opened officially.

Jean-Luc, a French Canadian, was taking time off from his job as a private detective in Quebec. Already he was becoming a fixture at the studio. From across the floor, Don Luis observed them chatting near the foyer. Now where had Candy found him or vice versa? Anyway, Jean-Luc had turned out to be a man of many talents, tango the least of them.

When the door buzzer rang, Candy turned and hit the lock's release.

"*Perdón*," said a young man, brushing past Jean-Luc, hurrying to the unattended reception desk.

"Can I help you?" Candy asked in a mild Southern accent.

Don Luis noted the fellow's rumpled blue-and-white Argentina national *fútbol* jersey, boasting the number 10. He also sported roomy black training pants and sneakers! A worn backpack hung carelessly over one shoulder. Perfect soccer attire, but decidedly untangoesque—unless he was the Lionel Messi of tango. Don Luis took a longer look and considered that perhaps . . . he was.

"I am here to audition for the show," the man said to Candy.

"Oh, sorry," she replied half-heartedly, "but auditions are all finished."

Don Luis studied him, overlooking the stubbly beard and long, curly hair—again untango-like, except for its jet color.

"But it's very early," he said rapidly, checking his phone. "Is ten o'clock only."

"Everyone had to notify us in advance." She shrugged.

"But my flight, it couldn't leave Buenos Aires for many hours. And then it was diverted to Boston. I have been traveling for almost two days."

Don Luis heard Candy drawling, "Flying is a mess." He observed that the overhead halogen lamps had caught the boy's hazel eyes just so, revealing emerald streaks. They were uncanny, almost prepossessing.

Candy seemed mesmerized. "I'll see what I can do."

"Thank you very much, miss." He stood erect and perfectly poised, as elegant as a man could be in a jersey and track pants.

Candy went to Chaz, the company's principal male dancer. He shook his head resolutely. She returned to the young man and said, "All I can say is I hope you enjoy the rest of your trip. Sorry about this part not working out."

"There is no rest of my trip," he said. "I am here only to audition."

"All the way from BA just for this audition?"

His tone grew intense. "My word of honor."

Jean-Luc placed his shoes on the window ledge, freeing his hands. Arms akimbo, he stepped forward. "Sorry, man, the lady said you missed out."

Don Luis approached slowly. "Excuse me, Candy, is there a problem?"

"This guy came all the way from BA to audition but never contacted us." She turned and asked, "How did you hear about it anyway?"

"Advertisements at my milonga. You know, my tango club in Buenos Aires."

Candy's eyes widened. She glanced quickly at Don Luis. "Who targeted BA?"

"Oh, um, I took care of that," Don Luis replied. "On the outside chance some marvelous dancers might want to try New York." His face flushing, he added, "Looks as though we may have found one." Don Luis smiled kindly at the young man. He peered through vintage horn-rimmed glasses, holding the resplendent green eyes an instant too long. With a hint of an English accent, he said, "I am Luis Carlos de Granada, the show's producer."

"Mucho, mucho gusto conocerle estimado Señor Carlos de Granada."

"The pleasure is mine," he said, extending his hand. "Please call me Don Luis. And you are?"

"Miguel Andro Zanotto."

Don Luis's heart skipped a beat. His hand wanted to spring to his beard and tug as he absorbed every detail of the person. He grasped the wheelchair's armrests to still his nervous fingers and released his lower lip from his teeth's grip. Almost losing himself in the depths of those eyes, he plastered on a nonchalant expression and managed a courtesy. "Miguel," he said, "Allow me to introduce Ms. Candy Borakowski, a principal *tanguera*, and Mr. Jean-Luc Renard, an aspiring dancer."

Miguel dusted Candy's cheeks with kisses.

Don Luis noted Jean-Luc's eyes narrowing as he offered his hand.

Miguel shook firmly, sustaining the piercing gaze. "*Monsieur Renard.*"

Jean-Luc hesitated, before stammering in a thick accent, "*Enchanté*, Miguel."

"English, please, gentlemen," Don Luis said. He turned to face Candy. "I believe there is an audition in the offing."

"Good," she said, smiling at Miguel before heading toward the others.

"Thank you for the opportunity," Miguel said.

Don Luis nodded and then motioned to a man in a somber suit, who sat watching. "Kemal, if you please." The man sprang up, revealing his diminutive stature, and rushed to Don Luis. He whispered and Kemal rolled his master over to Chaz, who lurked listening, appraising Miguel.

Chaz looked askance at the jersey and sneakers, saying, "Some great dancers today. Is Renaldo here really worth our time?"

"Number 10 is Lionel Messi, the captain of Argentina's national *fútbol* team."

"Oh."

"And if we don't see him dance, we'll never know his worth."

"The girls have been here twelve hours," Chaz pressed. "We could've had more auditions if we'd started yesterday."

"But our studio is not open Saturday," Don Luis replied. "Oh, come now, Chaz, they're all young. And you . . . you, too, remain young at heart." He knew his tango star recognized that his orbit was ever so slightly beyond its zenith.

"Never felt fresher."

"That six-month hiatus worked wonders," Don Luis jabbed good-naturedly.

Chaz mocked the British elocution. "Let's give this chap a go, shall we?"

"Indeed. Now come introduce yourself."

Chaz approached Miguel with an easy gait. He wore a hand-pressed black suit and patent leather performance shoes. The collar of his crisp white shirt jutted up as if at attention. He extended his hand, saying, "Chaz Christianson, *primero bailarino.* Glad you could make it all the way from BA for our little audition."

"Hello, Chaz, nice to meet you. I've admired your dancing for a long time."

Chaz beamed. "And your name?"

"Miguel."

"That's great for a change." Chaz raised his voice slightly, adding, "No title is definitely a bonus."

"We have too many of those already!" Don Luis said, rolling toward them. "At least I don't ask to be called Professor de Granada."

Chaz rolled his eyes, stopping them dead on Miguel's sneakers. "Want to change your shoes?" He gestured toward a back corner. "The gentlemens' lounge is there."

"I would like that very much, but the airline lost my luggage." Miguel lowered his eyes and chin.

"Too bad, but I'm sure you'll be fine in those," he replied, smiling thinly.

"Chaz, perhaps you would be good enough to loan Miguel some shoes," Don Luis said. "You must have a dozen pairs about this place."

"Great idea, Don Luis," Chaz replied, "except I'm about half a head taller than Miguel." Chaz lengthened his posture, already ramrod straight. "Mine are too big."

"Come now, any pair of proper dancing shoes will be better than sneakers."

"I'll grab some." Chaz retrieved a pair of scuffed shoes from beneath a padded bench. "Frieds, from England," he said with a flourish.

"Thank you." Miguel nodded slightly as he turned toward the lounge. "Excuse me, please."

Once inside the *tangueros'* lounge, Miguel marveled at the polished lockers' rich wood grain. He pressed his feet into the dense wool carpeting. His eyes caressed the space, drank it in. So this was high-style New York City. He felt more foreign by the minute. He could see the shiny, perfectly clean tiled floor leading to the showers. Even more pristine than the best clubs in Asia and even Europe, where he and his sister had danced as tango stars. Miguel's heart welled with pain just thinking of her and then it was masked by a familiar rush of fury. He reined in the dark thoughts and walked toward the showers. No soap scum. No mold. Nothing like the shabby clubs in the home of tango.

Everything here was alien—just like him—save the artwork. Miguel stared at the gorgeous photos and posters from Buenos Aires's Golden Era of tango, the 1930s and '40s. He sat down on a bench between a row of lockers, studying Carlos Gardel's handsome face on the largest poster. Gardel seemed to smile at him, a comfort. Miguel escaped Natalia's tragedy for an instant, by stroking the shoe's thin leather uppers and teasing up the nap of their suede-covered bottoms. He used the activity as a pre-dance meditation, an opportunity to center his mind.

On a far wall, Miguel spied a poster of the most famous tango rogue of all, El Cachafaz, the rascal. The man grinned, intimately embracing a woman with a perfect heart-shaped face and flowing auburn hair. Miguel blinked. Blinked again. Her face resembled Natalia's. And her hair, although lighter in color, was styled similarly. His hands involuntarily clenched into fists. Miguel's brain felt suddenly as if it might explode with rage. He had waited too long, scheming, studying, agonizing. The old-time *milongueros* would have quickly avenged a loved one's murder. And those *milongueros* were not depraved men. They were sons, brothers, many of them husbands and fathers. But they understood when the authorities forsook the search for a villain or hardly bothered that justice must be in their own hands. And these *milongueros* recognized all too well that sometimes justice is just blind enough not to see a privileged person's guilt.

Miguel had seen no development in the case in months of scouring papers and the internet. The US authorities had always been reluctant to share anything with him. They probably considered Natalia an unlucky immigrant. Possibly she was thought to be a guest in the country who was up to no good, and got what she deserved. Miguel was there to find the bastard who killed her and exact justice, using his bare hands.

If only Miguel knew for certain who the culprit was, he would avenge her murder that very night. Odds were that he was in the studio right now, a member of the company. Soon enough, Miguel would strangle him, perhaps right there in the lounge. The killer would quake with fear and regret, until his final breath. He would feel the horror of dying Natalia's death of strangulation. Miguel looked away, trying to forget. He sought Gardel's friendly smile, but found a black-eyed glare. It was as though Gardel had seen her brutalized body lying on a pretty parquet dance floor. Miguel had read that after being strangled with her own scarf, Natalia had been slashed. He imagined gutting the killer. Miguel would watch the blood soil the shower's pristine tile floor en route to the drain, the murder's blood and soul heading to hell! His heart pounded. Miguel knew he must compose himself, prepare for the audition. He was not in the mood for tango, but for revenge.

Keep cool. Miguel took a deep breath and forced himself to focus on Chaz's flimsy English shoes. He wished for his Argentine dancing shoes, with their strong leather uppers and thin patch of rubber he had applied to the forefoot for maximum stability. He felt that he could grip the floor with his feet, like a powerful cat digging his claws into prey. Miguel had steeled himself into a predator, not only of tango, but also of man.

* * *

Don Luis called Chaz away from the others and asked, "With whom shall he dance?"

"We need a read on his milonga," Chaz said with just a hint of disdain. "Adriana hasn't danced much today."

"Adriana dancing milonga? He may not have a sporting chance." Don Luis recognized that by selecting an inappropriate partner, they would be guaranteeing Miguel's failure to impress.

"We agreed we need a guy for a milonga number and fill," Chaz said. "He'd better be good at that or—"

"The milonga dance, as you know, doesn't lend itself to imagination and creativity, not like the tango. Who knows, he might be an interpretative genius?"

"That's my job."

Don Luis said quietly, "She's Wagner's partner. He will smell a conspiracy."

"I was told the good doctor is at Bellevue, saving lives." Chaz grinned.

Don Luis muttered, "We'll see if he can save his own." He turned and observed Miguel's arrival. A smile replaced Don Luis's scornful expression. "Are you ready?"

"It's as if I've been waiting for this my entire life."

CHAPTER 2

Miguel Zanotto passed perfectly groomed and beautifully dressed dancers, arrayed around the margins of the main floor. Wrinkled sports togs, ill-fitting shoes be damned. He stepped confidently onto the honey-hued surface. Time began to slow. Miguel ceased to hurry. Felt his weight ever so slightly deflect the elastic planking. A charge of excitement jolted his heart, recognizing the floor's perfect finish. Miguel hoped that his performance also would be flawless. Embedding himself in this dance company was the first step in his mission of revenge.

Don Luis said, "Miguel, tell us something of your dancing."

"I have danced in big shows, and helped with choreography, too." He paused. "But for me, dancing tango in the milongas of Buenos Aires is the best. Like the old-time *milongueros*."

"What's your last name, again?" Chaz asked.

"Zanotto."

"There was a famous young Zanotto. But your hair, beard . . . different—"

Miguel said quickly, "Probably my cousin."

Don Luis asked, "Where did you say you are from? And where is your family?"

"I was born in La Boca, Argentina, just like tango." He added, with a slight edge, "Maybe we talk about something more interesting like *fútbol* or your family."

Don Luis eyed him steadily. "We shall indeed."

A willowy young woman burst in with an apologetic grimace. "Sorry to interrupt, but I think I left my cell." Her hands shot up and her head skewed to one side, highlighting wavy black hair. "I was so nervous today. I don't suppose any of you have seen or heard a stray phone."

"Well, Aggie," Don Luis said. "I believed we were going to have to wait to see you again."

Miguel stood motionless, processing his first impression of the bubbly young woman. He noted a gleam in Chaz's eyes.

Chaz said, "I'll look in the cantina for you." He hustled away.

"Aggie, allow me to introduce Miguel. Here all the way from BA," Don Luis said.

"*Encantada*, Miguel, Aggie Jacobs," she said.

"Ay!" Don Luis cried, smacking the arm of his wheelchair. "To help this motley troupe function as a dance family, we must speak a single language."

"Oops," Aggie snickered.

"Hello, Aggie." Miguel touched her cheeks with his lips.

"Aggie, come and sit by me while Miguel demonstrates the dancing style of a *milonguero*, like a man dancing purely for pleasure in his own neighborhood." Don Luis continued, "He will dance a milonga with Adriana, whom you met at your audition."

"Oh, great."

Minutes later the deed was done. Miguel and Adriana finished their lackluster dance and thanked each other for the pleasure, their eyes belying their words.

Slowly, Miguel approached Don Luis.

Chaz chirped, "Thanks very much, Miguel, for coming so far for the audition. We really appreciate it."

Miguel nodded. "Thanks for your shoes, Chaz. I appreciate that." He extended his hand toward Don Luis. "Thank you, sir. I'm sorry."

Don Luis's index finger jutted upward. "Miguel, about this *milonguero* dancing." He turned to Aggie. "My dear, what do you perceive to be the difference between a *tanguero* and a *milonguero*?"

Miguel focused, wondering whether this girl could possibly understand what tango meant to him.

"Any man who dances tango is a *tanguero*. But maybe *milongueros* are more passionate about tango," she said. "And I think they're more caring for the tango community, especially its, um, lesser members." She shrugged. "Maybe *milongueros* feel that all tango dancers are part of a big tango family."

Miguel was delighted. Aggie was not only lovely, but also had a clue about the essence of *el tango.*

Don Luis asked, "At the tango dance parties in BA, the so-called milongas, you danced with *milongueros* from the neighborhoods?"

"Oh yes! Their musicality came right from the heart."

"Would you be willing to dance a tango with Miguel?"

"Sure."

"Pray tell, Miguel, what shall the music be? How about Pugliese's "Recuerdo"? None better to stir profound memories," Don Luis asked, "Would you please dance a special figure recognizable from one of your maestros."

"With pleasure."

Miguel and Aggie embraced comfortably on the floor. Their bodies had melded already as the generous melody began to mount. Slowly, deliberately he moved himself toward her. She responded in kind, never more, never less than his lead.

The sweet embrace remained unbroken until the piece's frenzied crescendo when the two became a whirling torrent of sinewy legs and flying feet. Even then, the quiet of their melded torsos gave the impression of the calm eye of a storm of foot and legwork. At the piece's delicate conclusion, with torsos arching upward toward the sky, bound together in a majestic incline toward each other, they paused perfectly balanced, suspended in tango bliss.

Applause and catcalls rang out from company members. Miguel stepped back and gave Aggie room for a deep bow, applauding her with the others.

Miguel escorted Aggie toward Don Luis and Chaz, who extended a cell phone clad in pink plastic. He said, "Nice finale, Miguel, the famous Gavito Lean."

"Thank you, Chaz."

"It was wonderful," Aggie said, "really simple. Miguel is a true *milonguero.*" As an afterthought she said, "Thanks for finding my phone."

Chaz erupted, "But Aggie, in a show you have to impress people who know nothing about tango." He shook his head, adding, "They don't get this subtle stuff."

"Maybe, maybe not," Don Luis hedged. He cleared his throat and announced, "Let's call it a day. We shall resume rehearsals tomorrow afternoon, three P.M. sharp." He looked at Miguel. "Are you in a hurry? Can you spare me a bit of your time?"

Chaz interrupted hastily. "Don Luis, I'd like to speak to you privately."

Don Luis reached up a massive hand to grasp Chaz's fine-boned fingers. "I believe I know what you wish to say. You were superb today, both as a dancer and as a leader. I expect the same from you tomorrow. Please go home, get some rest, and embrace the Serenity Prayer."

"Which is?" Chaz sneered, "Unlike you, not all of us have a Ph.D. in religion."

"The operative aspect is to accept serenely that which you cannot change."

CHAPTER 3

DR. ERNEST WAGNER INSERTED the black obsidian blade near to the spine, just above the *patient's* L5 lumbar intervertebral disc. For once, he was not mulling Argentine tango while plying his medical trade. In fact, to hell with Don Luis and the auditions. This little demo was a building block to having the opportunity to do for the rest of his life exactly what he wanted. The time was now. And although Wagner shivered from the cold of the cavernous space, he concentrated on demonstrating the effortlessness of the incision. To stress this, he glanced up and smiled briefly to Dr. Rolf Thornblad, the eminent neurosurgeon, who looked on.

Dr. Wagner refocused on his work, squinting slightly in the dim light, encouraging himself silently. He recognized that while Dr. Thornblad was an accomplished surgeon, he was a mere pathologist, a bit of a lab rat in the eyes of some colleagues. So he was basking in taking a spin with one of his uniquely fashioned all-ceramic scalpels, proving its exceptional design and superior sharpness. With its ergonomic handpiece, it was simply a dream to embrace the Wagner Super Sharp Scalpel™. Dr. Wagner had been known to liken it to the comfort of caressing one's own anatomy.

A chiller grumbled to life, vibrating noisily overhead and sending a blast of near-Arctic air into Wagner's face. He steeled himself against the bone-chilling flux. "You see," he said authoritatively, "the lumbar laminectomy need never again be feared."

"Hmm," said Thornblad, raising his lab coat's collar.

"Oh, yes, just watch this." Dr. Wagner used retractors to pull aside the severed flesh, the fat and muscle, through which he had sliced to expose the lamina. Soon, a generous segment of the ligament supporting the spinal column was laid bare.

Dr. Wagner exhaled deeply and grinned again for effect. Squinting in the dimness, he took up a finer blade of identical composition, obsidian lapped by his own hand. He admired the instrument, twiddling it about. Its handpiece was even more delicate, enabling a finer feel. Now, to cut an opening through which to access the spinal column. He was unperturbed by a gurney's rumble on the rough concrete floor, only steps away. Even its crash into an enormous tub and subsequent low frequency drone, like an iron bell, could not compromise his concentration. Not even the didos of a pesky fly, zooming near to his face in a circular helix and then dive-bombing the incision. At last he achieved the bundle of nerve fibers hosting a swollen, compressed nerve and surrounded by what looked to be a mass of disgorged crabmeat, a ruptured disc.

"Ah, ha," Wagner gloated, "just as I suspected, Mr.," he glanced down toward the far end of the ancient gurney, "Auturo Diaz had ruptured his L5 disk." He sighed, "A source of lifelong pain and discomfort for many."

Dr. Thornblad nodded concurrence.

Wagner extended the handsome scalpel, asking, "Care to muck about?"

"Oh, no, thank you," Thornblad said, staving off the invitation.

Exhaling more freely, Wagner admired the tool's perfection. He said, "Just makes the process such a pleasure. Well, see here." He poked the tiny blade further into the spinal column of Mr. Diaz, who remained deathly still. Wagner twisted the instrument, carelessly plunging it deeper into the exposed bundle of critical nerves, hogging out a lump of disc meat. And then a pus-laden discharge spewed from the incision, its stench overpowering. Dr. Wagner poked in a finger to stem the flow, but it spewed onto the front of his pristine lab coat. In an instant of panic, he removed his finger and thrust a roll of gauze into the now-gaping hole. Wagner triumphantly held up the excavated disc material. "You see, absolutely effortless."

"I do see, Dr. Wagner. Looks like you've got something here."

"Delighted you concur. Shall we step away from the, um, patient, and chat for a moment?" He smiled amiably. "It's no secret that you have the ear of a board member or two at Profundum Medicus."

Thornblad blushed.

"I am in licensing discussions with them." Wagner kept his voice low. "I have always had the greatest respect for you and for your work, Dr. Thornblad."

The man's puny chest swelled.

"I could see a collaboration between us," Wagner continued cautiously, "should the capital for such a venture materialize."

"Well, yes, Dr. Wagner, turns out I have some particular research interests that have not been embraced by this hospital. It would be wonderful to explore them with an esteemed peer, like yourself."

Wagner's eyes glazed. Dr. Rolf Thornblad had called him a "peer," no, "an esteemed peer." He dropped the scalpel noisily onto the rude concrete, fracturing to pieces its finely crafted, yet extraordinarily brittle blade. Thornblad gasped. Wagner paid no heed, only removed a surgical glove and grasped the man's hand. "Thank you very much, Dr. Thornblad," he said. "And thank you for coming down here."

Thornblad barely parted his thin lips, smiling, his hand still shaking.

Before exiting the morgue, Dr. Wagner glared at the attendant. "Some fool left Diaz out for the flies. He's awfully ripe."

"What'd you expect for an unclaimed window-washer?"

Wagner shoved a hundred into the man's hand and strode away.

CHAPTER 4

MIGUEL AND DON LUIS ENTERED the elegant elevator. Miguel considered the futuristic vibe of the tiny lights jazzing up the cabin. He hoped his immediate future was about to be mapped out. The door opened to the second floor. Miguel eyed Don Luis, wheeling his way out and then crossing variegated white marble. A few strokes on a keypad, a soft buzz, and Don Luis forged through a hefty wooden door. Miguel followed.

They passed through a modern anteroom en route to Don Luis's office. It was as though stepping back in time. Miguel admired the office's darkly stained wooden furnishings with their well-patinated leather coverings. Massive brass fixtures and trappings suggested old-world gravitas and Argentine history. An enormous dictionary, its leaves yellowed by time and frayed by use, caught his eye. Don Luis's desk was deeply hued, apparently by ox-blood-stained leather. Such craftsmanship was an Argentine tradition dating back to the nineteenth century. An ancient coat of arms was affixed to a rough-hewn wall. Swords and pistols were mounted on a far wall suggesting an ancient fortification. Don Luis's office was definitely his castle.

Miguel hefted a high-backed chair and seated himself at a round table with finely polished brass belting and a squat piece of timber for a plinth. Don Luis rolled beside him. Miguel wanted to lighten his mood but the surroundings seemed to weigh heavily on him. He blurted, "This is fantastic, Don Luis."

"I'm delighted that you share my appreciation of old-world decor."

Miguel studied the coat of arms. He was sure he knew its red and yellow stripes and its roaring lion. It was as if he had seen it a million times. It sent a pang to his heart. But why? He concluded all Spanish crests were about the same.

"Thank you for speaking English, Miguel. You should speak it and speak it well." He nodded affirmatively. "When you command a language, any conversation, even a chat, can become artful, like a maestro on the dance floor."

Miguel had never considered speech to be nearly as important as movement. He said, "I will consider your point."

"That's a thoughtful response, Miguel. Perhaps you and I have the basis for something more than a trivial conversation."

"I don't know, sir. Chaz says you are doctor of religion. My philosophy is perhaps too simple for you."

"My mind is not so scarred from higher education that I cannot read the writing on the wall. That somber text becomes clearer day by day."

"I, too, have read it," Miguel said. "The end is tragic."

Don Luis cleared his throat and said, "I could use a bite to eat. How about you?"

"If you like."

He wheeled himself backward and turned to a wall-mounted intercom, pressed a button, and said, "Kemal." He eyed Miguel and asked, "*Jamon creudo* and Malbec, okay?"

"Sounds delicious," Miguel said, relaxing his face into a smile. He was famished, and loved Argentina's salt-cured ham.

Don Luis ordered a small feast and wheeled to the table. He laid a finger aside his nose. "Miguel, there is one more good reason to have the troupe speak English only."

"Yes?"

This is a tough business. Even the brightest tango stars in my lifetime have not ended particularly well. The ones who fared the best, I claim, are the ones who interacted well with the international press. It may be fine to be an enigmatic tango icon when you are young, but life moves along swiftly."

Miguel turned his gaze squarely on Don Luis. "So this rule is really for the individuals, not for the company as a family."

"Caught me up in a falsehood, have you?" He chuckled. "Unity is important, but this show will achieve its aim even if no one speaks to anyone else for months." His features settled into a brood. "But I assure you this company will be a living hell—a tango crucible."

"Why must tango be hell? Should be a release, yes. People suffer enough."

"There is some company history of which you are not aware." Don Luis settled heavily into his chair. "I took control after the tragic loss of our *primera bailarina,* Natalia Prafil. Now I have two objectives in life. And I will pursue them resolutely."

Miguel turned away, pierced by sadness.

"Ah hmm, regarding truthfulness," Don Luis said, leaning forward, causing his wheelchair to emit a metallic groan, "I must question yours this evening."

"Yes?"

"The virtuosic figure you danced with Aggie at the tango's conclusion, was it in fact Carlos Gavito's Lean?"

"It was the Bridge, you say?" Miguel's face reddened. "Sorry for my poor English." He added, "Chaz is a great dancer, yet he misunderstood."

"Carlos Gavito is a perfect example of a dancer who learned to communicate well with the international press. He became more famous and prosperous near the end of his life even than when he starred in the brilliant show *Forever Tango.*"

"Was fantastic, yes."

"Yes and no. But his Lean was always a backbreaking stunt for the lady." Don Luis continued, "Whereas Maestro Paiva's Bridge was subtle," his fingers expanded gently on an arc, saying, "a majestic human arch, never a human chevron. So, you studied with Maestro Paiva in Rosario?"

The question was more pointed than it seemed. Don Luis's eyes probed Miguel. "Oh, he used to come to Buenos Aires sometimes."

Don Luis drew a deep breath, as though bracing himself. "You said you have family in Rosario."

"Most of my family live in Buenos Aires, in La Boca." He shrugged. "You say in English . . . 'the poor side of the train tracks.'"

"There is a great deal of upward mobility from the bottom."

Miguel heard footsteps outside the door. Don Luis clapped his hands. Kemal pushed a gleaming serving cart into the room. Miguel noted his western suit had been replaced by antiquated Eastern garb. With his pencil-thin mustache, Kemal looked very much like the handsome British poet in his portrait where he wore an Albanian costume.

Don Luis said, "Looks rather like an Arab gaucho, in sultan's pants, doesn't he?"

Miguel nodded, observing that the man's trouser bottoms were tucked into the floppy tops of black leather boots. His colorful jacket, in red with white vertical stripes, was cropped short like the gauchos'. An emerald-color silk cummerbund winked underneath the jacket's margin. And from his hip dangled a jewel-handled dagger.

"Kemal, this is Miguel Zanotto, newly arrived from Buenos Aires."

"I am pleased to make your acquaintance, Mr. Zanotto," Kemal said, bowing.

"Pleased to meet you. Call me Miguel."

"Thank you, Mr. Zanotto."

"While in Egypt, I saved Kemal's mother's life. She gave him to me for life, to be my protector."

"Really?"

"I, myself, taught him fencing." He stabbed a stubby finger toward a display case bearing crossed sabers. "I used those while on Oxford's fencing team."

"Extraordinary," Miguel said, half believing the claim.

"When I became certain there was nothing he would deny me, I bestowed upon him his present moniker. *Kemal* means perfection."

Kemal bowed profoundly and said, "*Allah Kareem.*"

"Yes, Kemal, all gods are great," Don Luis agreed.

CHAPTER 5

AGNES NAOMI JACOBS BOUNDED into her father's spacious home office. "Pops, still up?"

"I'm just getting going here." He twisted around, blinking from the glare of the incandescent bulb in his old desk lamp. "What, no kiss for your poor old father?"

Aggie dodged a hefty hunter green leather wingchair, with its lawyerly looking tufted back. She raced onto the marvelous Bakhtiari rug, costing about as much as the entire contents of their previous home, and threw her arms around his neck, planting a big smack on the front of his balding head. "Love you."

"Love you, too, Honey. So how you doin'?"

"Super," she replied, thinking they may have moved to Morningside Heights, but her dad's Flatbush, Brooklyn—the real Dodger's territory—accent was never going *anywheres*. The brazen light illuminated endless columns of his account books and assaulted her eyes. "You were supposed to get a new lamp," she said. "LED bulbs are whiter and brighter and better all—"

"You going to go pick a few C-notes off the tree in the backyard?" He nodded. "Jakey and Mikey need braces. Got them Jacobi horse teeth. Not like you, all delicate."

"Pleeease."

"Did I tell you about great grandpa Jacobi in Italy, time the old mare was lame and he took a bit in his own mouth, helped pull the wagon to town?" He raised a fist.

"Pops, that's disgusting and untrue."

"I swear it, or my name ain't MoJo."

"Your name ain't MoJo. It's Morrey or Moe. And don't change the subject." Hands to her hips. "How long have I been back home?"

Aggie had to calculate the answer herself. Months had dragged by since she had returned to New York from a year abroad in Argentina. And she'd been slow to rekindle friendships she had enjoyed at NYU during her freshman and sophomore years. Now her life seemed overly full with working part-time for the family dry cleaning business and her tango obsession. Although she recognized that she was back in the world's most vibrant city, she couldn't help missing the European sensibility of Buenos Aires and the thrill of dancing tango onstage. Landing a part in the local company's show could help her on a couple of fronts. Her romantic life was DOA.

"You promised to replace this lamp," she said, peeking at the accounts. "Lots of zeros behind those sales numbers."

"You say." He hit the switch, extinguishing the irritating light. "Did I tell you about when I was saving up my stake and your mother and me was renting a room from them Mafiosos?"

"Yes, Pops."

"I swear if I didn't cross myself when walking past that makeshift altar they had in the living room, I could feel their heaters warming up. And it was hard for your uncle Dan, too. When he was clerking for that neo-Nazi judge downtown, he played piano in Harlem jazz bars at night for extra dough. Boy, when the judge got wind of it—" He shook his head as if jolting the horrid memory from his consciousness.

Aggie beamed, certain the mold broke after he was made. Probably because he dropped it. She noted the grayish stubble on her dad's chin and the deepening creases around his eyes. Success had taken a toll.

"Don't take this for granted, Naomi girl." His eyes roved the comfortable room. "Heck, when you're a doctor—"

"Pops, I'm not even enrolled this semester. But I'm going to help people, I just don't know how."

"The Peace Corps? How's your kids going to take ballet lessons and live abroad, the whole *schmeer*?" Her father rubbed together his thumbs and forefingers so forcefully Aggie feared they might ignite. "So what's up with this new tango bar, this tankeria?"

"It's a stunning *tanqueria*," she said slowly. "Marble columns, sumptuous draperies, huge floor, totally Upper East Side."

"The men, bunch a greasy guineas like Argentina?"

"Don't be racist."

"Hey, takes one to know one."

"They're mostly Argentines, except the principal male. Flashy, blond, probably West Coast."

"Guess I don't have to worry about him."

"There was one Argentine of Italian descent." She stressed the final phrase. "Looked like hell."

"What kind of language is that from a future doctor?"

"But the way he danced. . . ." Her eyes drifted upward slowly.

"Stay away from that one," MoJo said, before clearing his throat loudly. "Speaking of Brooklyn, guess who I ran into today, Seth Sheinberg."

"Huh."

"Sharp suit, shoes shiny as a mirror. Could brush your teeth in them."

"Great."

"Said he's working on something big."

"Selling time shares on Coney Island?"

"That kid could sell ice cubes to Eskimos. Reminds me of myself at his age."

"You've never been anything like him or any of his family." Aggie couldn't control herself. "If his eyes were any shiftier or squinty he'd be called Seth Snakeberg."

"Oh yeah, well while you was dancing the night away in BA, he was on the front lines with the Israeli Army." MoJo set his chin. "Went on his own free will, he did."

"Dad, he was probably cheating at cards or brown-nosing his commanding officer." She paused. "Front lines, pfff. He tell you that?"

"Don't like his humble roots, huh." MoJo crossed his arms across his chest.

She threw up her hands. "It's the way he *schmoozes* you and leers at me."

"Maybe he respects me, and thinks you're a dish."

"He just wants to be some super dealmaker, Gordon Gekko of Flatbush."

Aggie's eyes rolled two full circles. "Pops, I thought you despised his dad. Had bad dealings years ago, said he's in with the Mob—"

"Watch that. Their family is still together. None a them moved off to Patagonia."

"There're all holed up in that tenement because his dad's ill-gotten gain can't be spent on a decent home!" She was sick of this veneration of the Sheinbergs. "You always said that Mr. Sheinberg's money was dirty.

"Everybody's is. Wait till you earn some for yourself."

Aggie put her arms around her father's neck. "Pops, don't get angry." She enjoyed the moment of silence, a rarity.

CHAPTER 6

MIGUEL ZANOTTO SWIRLED MALBEC WINE, its purple hue cascading down the sides of the balloon glass. He admired its berry-laden aroma and soft tannins. The grape was Argentina's darling for good reason. Don Luis's generous treatment had buoyed Miguel's spirits, time-warped him to headier days he'd left behind. International tango shows, flying on the private jets and tasting the beautiful wines of rich clients were all things of his past. He was a new man, although he felt like an old man. His focus had changed, but dancing tango would be required to fulfill his mission of revenge.

Kemal had served the food and drink and then taken up a post near the far corner. He stood relaxed, hands by his sides, ridiculous garb on display, dagger at the ready. Miguel eyed Don Luis, who appraised his wine thoughtfully. It was the first lull in conversation and welcomed by Miguel. He used the time to calm himself and prepare for a continuation of the grilling. Although not good at talking and saying nothing, Miguel recognized that the stakes were too high for a misstep.

Don Luis moved the glass from underneath his nose and raised it. "I wish to propose a toast: to life."

Miguel steered his balloon toward Don Luis's. As they neared, he observed the tremulous unsteadiness of the older man's hand. It appeared to affect his entire arm.

"Life," Miguel echoed, and drank heartily. He wondered exactly what was going on here and what lurked behind those crafty brown eyes.

Don Luis said, "It is a great God who gave man the gift of wine." He paused. "Come to think of it, I should have used that in my disputes with colleagues in the religious studies department at CUNY."

"It's logical."

"Balderdash." Don Luis swiped a backhand as though shooing insects. "Those faithless bastards would repel even such keen insight."

"One of the brothers who taught classic literatures and bible at my school had many quotations in praise of God and wine. He really loved both."

"At which school?"

"Academia San Ignacio de Loyola de Rosario."

"So," Don Luis hesitated slightly, "you attended school in Rosario not BA."

Miguel's mouth fell open and he took a bite of the delicious cured ham. The blessings of letting food fill his mouth were twofold: he was starving and it kept him from disclosing things he hadn't intended. Miguel looked up and found Don Luis's eyes seemingly peering through his façade as handily as he peered through the scuffed lenses of his heavy-framed glasses.

Don Luis asked, "Are you a fan of books? Traveling professionally often means lots of time wasted in airports and hotel rooms, you know."

"Now, only one book interests me. You say, *The Count of Montecristo*?"

"Ah, a classic tale of revenge. Have you been wronged?"

Miguel tried to smile, adding, "Actually, I have little time for books."

"Are you so preoccupied with tango?"

"Family things," Miguel replied quietly. "How about your reading?" Miguel asked. "You have read thousands of books?"

"I'm afraid not. But I do have a few favorites, *Don Quixote* of course and *The Alchemist,* simple but meaningful."

"As a boy, I loved this one," Miguel enthused. "My sister read it to me."

"Your sister?"

"Yes, sir."

"Elder?"

"A few years."

"She dances tango?"

"Not any more."

"Is she well?"

"Better off than my mom."

Don Luis set his glass down heavily onto the starched white tablecloth. Color drained from his face. "Your mother is unwell? Is she going to—"

"She's going to be fine, one way or the other."

Silence.

Don Luis said, "I really appreciate a Columbian book called *One Hundred Years of Solitude*. Know it?"

"Only the title."

Don Luis shifted heavily in his chair, which groaned under his mass. "It's a family's story. Seven generations of a unique clan, the Buendias, are chronicled along with the history of a fictional village called Banana."

"Every family has a complex story," Miguel said thoughtfully.

"Thank you for the segue."

Miguel's head tilted.

"*Transición*," Don Luis said.

"Of course," Miguel replied, blushing.

"I know a terrific story of a family that easily can rival the intensity of the Buendias'," Don Luis claimed authoritatively. "And what's more it's true."

Miguel yawned. "Excuse me," he said. "I am very interested to hear your story, but have not slept much for a couple of days."

"I'll say just this much: my saga begins more than a thousand years ago in Tiberias, Palestine. A highly respected teacher and sage, Rabbi Aaron ben Asher, fastidiously developed and personally added the perfecting touches to what has come to be the most highly esteemed version of the complete Hebrew Bible, the Aleppo Codex."

"Jews?"

"That troubles you?"

"Not really. My family has had business dealings with them."

Don Luis sat erect. "Have these dealings not gone well?"

"I'm sure all businesses have their headaches." Miguel sighed. "Since Argentina's economy collapsed, our company is a problem. A Jewish lawyer, Mr. Marcovici, has caused our family some distress." Miguel shook his head in a silent rebuke. "I'm sorry. Too much excellent wine has loosened my tongue."

Don Luis nodded thoughtfully. "My saga is also a family tragedy. The Aleppo Codex, often called the Crown or *Keter*, contained all twenty-four of the sacred Hebrew books. While it was not the oldest complete codex, it was more perfectly elaborated and annotated than any other." He continued, "The lust for this Codex was pivotal in one particular family's intrigues and deaths for more than six hundred years."

"Sounds terrible, but fascinating. I love this kind of old story. Perhaps tomorrow, after I've slept—"

"It is old, but not over!" Don Luis declared, slamming his fist on the table, his face reddened with rage.

Miguel started, and then faked another yawn.

Don Luis appeared to shudder slightly before straightening out his face and collecting himself. He said, "So sorry, Miguel. Perhaps it is the wine."

"Is nothing," he lied, his senses reeling.

Don Luis turned and peered over his shoulder at a gilded clock, sitting near the ponderous dictionary. "I'll tell you straight away, company members are not allowed to stay in the guest rooms here at the studio. But I can make a call to my club; it's not far, Central Park South. I can arrange temporary lodging for you until you sort out your luggage and get settled."

"No, thank you, sir," Miguel replied. "I do not need charity. I have made arrangements for myself. A local friend helped." Miguel was not an animal, completely alone in the world, roaming helpless in a foreign city. At least he refused to admit it . . . to himself or others. And his supposed friend, who was actually a dance company member calling himself El Primitivo, was also off-limits for discussion just now.

"Of course you don't need charity. I just want you to be as comfortable as possible under the circumstances: international flight, detained luggage, unfamiliar surroundings."

Miguel had not meant to be abrupt, but his boundaries were firm. His whereabouts need not be known by his employer. It could be an impediment. "I do not mean to be rude, but I wouldn't inconvenience you further."

"Very well, I would like for you to be here tomorrow, ah, later today at three P.M., ready to rehearse. And believe me, there are plenty of discomforts ahead for this company," Don Luis said, narrowing his eyes.

Miguel tried to maintain a neutral expression, considering the ominous claim. He hardly heard Don Luis call out to Kemal. Miguel sat back absentmindedly as Kemal cleared away the light supper. He even withdrew his splendid dagger to scrape away breadcrumbs. Don Luis's office was like a Michelin-starred restaurant!

Miguel turned his gaze to Don Luis and began to speak. He felt a remarkable sting on the top of his right hand. "Ay!" Miguel yanked away his hand and glared at Kemal in astonishment. The man stood examining the dagger, fixated by a drop of blood hanging from its gleaming edge.

"What are you doing?" Miguel spat.

"Please forgive me, sir," Kemal said, turning toward his cart.

Blood rose along the surface of the slash. Miguel refused to wipe it away with his white napkin.

"Good heavens!" Don Luis exclaimed. "Kemal, a cloth, immediately."

Kemal handed Miguel a stark white, pressed linen napkin.

"I was scraping away crumbs and the blade uh slipped," Kemal said in anguish.

Miguel stemmed the flow and stood. "Good night. I'll see you tomorrow at three."

"Please don't rush away. Kemal can drive you wherever you like."

Miguel shook his head emphatically.

"Oh, come now, he said it was an accident," Don Luis said. "He'll even wear a western suit if you prefer."

"I refuse to burden you more," Miguel replied, looking down at the crimson line on his hand. "An important man like yourself must have very many things to do."

"To the contrary, in all of my remaining time, I have but two matters to resolve."

Miguel matched Don Luis's intense gaze and said to himself, "That's twice as many as I have."

CHAPTER 7

CHAZ CHRISTIANSON HASTENED toward the subway station at Lexington Avenue and Eighty-Sixth Street. He needed air. The lovefest between Don Luis and Miguel could last all night. The story of Chaz's life seemed to be on repeat: too much of the wrong kind of attention, not enough of the kind he needed. Anyway, he was tired. That was one reason he left the studio without voicing his objections to Don Luis's hijacking the selection process. And he was not having any success dreaming up a fantastic new number to wow audiences at the new show. Chaz exhaled forcefully, thinking that is the point of a show, amazing audiences with fantastic choreography executed by expert dancers. Although Miguel was a man of immense intensity, he was like a throwback to bygone days. The back rows would never get his *milonguero* mystique. Imagine trying to feel the passion of two people dancing small, intimate steps of a dance you've never seen, and can hardly see between a sea of heads in front of you.

If he had the money to run a company, every number would be sensational. That's what the public wanted, to be thrilled. Chaz recalled El Cachafaz, one of the first tango film stars. His outrageous exploits on the floor earned him fame and fortune. A smile overtook his face, thinking every tango dance era needed a flamboyant rogue.

A gust of moisture-laden wind mussed Chaz's hair, billowed his trousers. Rain would be a blessing, the heat during the past week having been oppressive. California summers were never this muggy. He recalled as a kid . . . then squelched the memory. Growing up is tough. He descended the station's gritty steps and sat alone on a cool metal bench. Even on the Upper East Side, sitting solo at night was never completely comfortable. Chaz eyed his phone and examined several direct tweets, semi-privates he thought of them. His expression saddened, reading the neglected messages. One particular direct message—a super private tweet—from @cut00 made him recognize afresh that growing up was tough for everyone, but hellish for some.

Chaz used username @cachafaz, and replied to CiiindyyyP, username: @cut00.
@cachafaz: "whyd u do it"

No response. He felt a rumble, not the train, but a truck overhead. He waited for the quiet bling of an incoming tweet.

@cut00: "had 2 im so stupid. Flunked math test again. #imadouche"
@cachafaz: "clean blade?"
@cut00: "eyeliner sharpener"
@cachafaz: "use antiB ointment. infection = hi Dr + million pills + psych ward"
@cut00: "WTF im soooo ugly nobody notices me until i screw up"
@cachafaz: "yeah . . . right. still bleeding?"
@cut00: "just stings. At least i no im alive"

Could he have been this messed up as a kid? Chaz shook his head, wondering how to help Cindy, really help. He bent to the tiny keyboard, thumbs tapping:

@cachafaz: "cindy: not good—cld get worse. pls tell ur mom"
@cut00: "WTF"
@cachafaz: "LOL pls try 4 me"
@cut00: "shes a reck. dads like 2 hard on every1 . . . her-me-him. f they split & shes alone for 5 secs she'll b suicidal again #myfamilysucks"

@cachafaz: "don't b2 sure. heard of munchausen syndrome? try surviving a mom w/ MS by proxy! #MunchausenSyndromeByProxy #sickmothers"

@cut00: "i hate drama n stress"

@cachafaz: "IKR some people love it. i was in the emerg room 20x b4 i was 2"

@cut00: "all my fault. should end it 2nite. stole her pills"

Chaz's heart burst, but what could he do? Maybe he should not mention using antibiotic ointment. Let the wound get infected, swell the leg, produce a fever, and maybe get Cindy to a doctor. Surely a medical professional would recognize her plight and force her parents to confront the truth. A shrink might be what she needed most.

The train's rumble was unmistakable. Chaz stood and paced the platform. He eyed a passing couple, arm-in-arm. Tall, blondish guy with a spunky brunette. Stale air gave way to her perfume's Oriental fragrance. And that guy, that could be him . . . someday. Chaz's thoughts eddied to Cindy. He was almost sorry that he had told her to get a vaccination when recently she began to follow him on Twitter. She'd been freaking out because she couldn't open and close her mouth and was looking for info from experienced cutters on how to zap an infection without going to a doctor. She had read his post to Bladerunr on how to get a Tdap shot for bacterial infection-induced lockjaw. He shook his head, thinking a bout of tetanus might save Cindy's life.

As the train ground to a stop, he tapped quickly.

@cachafaz: "get some sleep—betr daz ahead! sweetdremz"

Chaz boarded the train confident that Cindy would not kill herself. She, like other cutters—like him—was simply doomed to a long life of self-loathing.

CHAPTER 8

Ominous skies, gusts of wet wind, greeted Miguel when he took to the street. He paid hardly any attention to the weather. The unfortunate events at the evening's end dominated his thoughts. Being slashed by a menacing Muslim valet was unfortunate, but Don Luis's dramatic outburst troubled him even more. And not just the crash of his fist on the table, but his demonic glower and the intensity of his raised voice.

Miguel believed he could shake off some of his dread if he could just get to his hotel. Although he had arrived by taxi, Google claimed there was a subway station nearby on Lexington Avenue, but where? He'd walked for a block on Fifth, across the street from the Park, and was already disoriented. No wonder, what a night. The cut on the back of his hand throbbed. Miguel rubbed it lightly, scanning the neighborhood. He had the feeling that someone was watching him. Nonsense. He was rattled and perplexed.

What was behind Don Luis's passionate loss of control? All families had problems; Miguel's was a disaster. The rogue Marcovici had wrested away control of his mother's company and conveyed it to her sister, who had hardly done a decent day's work at the place in twenty years. But his mother was somehow beholden to her. It was one of several family topics never discussed. And Don

Luis's family saga was probably family fiction. The holiest Bible from one thousand years ago, haunting a desperate, modern-day family. It sounded fantastic. Miguel thought, what could it possibly mean to me, I'm not even Jewish. In fact, he was living a family saga of his own, and this was merely one juncture en route to its tragic ending.

Denser air. Blacker sky. A torpid gust tousled Miguel's hair. The humidity had risen, and he could feel the moisture permeating his clothes, dampening his skin. It was that stuffy, close feeling of the tropics. He had loved rain as a kid in Rosario. The smell of wet dirt. He would sit on the porch, playing by himself, imagining that his father would be coming home from work soon. The rain would stop and they would kick around the *fútbol* and then walk to Ramon's for ice cream. Yes, the strong, confident, and loving imaginary dad. He hauled the memory back and buried it deep inside, along with so many other pains and longings.

Miguel inhaled deeply, but smelling rain in the middle of a city was next to impossible. Battling nature's perfume were the secretions of wet asphalt, garbage, and exhaust. He heard a screech from across the street and quickened his pace. While the park was beautiful in daylight, it was ominous in darkness.

Lightning cracked; his nose crinkled. This was the same everywhere. But the smell of rain was not the same without the smell of earth. A drop, and then another, and then the bottom fell out. Miguel sought shelter under an awning, its broad white numerals and hunter green background billowing noisily in the wind. The bright storefronts were many blocks down and somewhat like tango shows: feasts for the eyes, not the soul. Miguel didn't care. He was no longer an entertainer, more machine than man. He sensed movement to his left, but didn't turn. Cut his eyes to track two figures moving toward him, faces obscured by drawn-up hoodies. He grasped firmly the straps of his pack and moved along.

Suddenly, from around the corner, a sports car turned toward Miguel, its bright lights blinding him. He shielded his eyes to try and understand the driver's intentions. The sound of squealing tires assaulted Miguel's ears. Scorched rubber smoke boiled into the night sky as the vehicle sped toward him. It must be a setup. The car nose-dived toward the pavement and its rear end curved toward Miguel. He wanted to escape the blow, but seemed rooted in the asphalt. The massive tires cried and evolved a fresh cloud of reeking, burned rubber that swept over him as the car's rear fender halted inches from Miguel's body.

Miguel released his breath, wondering what confrontation lay ahead. And then the driver thrust out his head from the open window; Miguel could hardly believe his eyes.

"Hey, Miguel, it's El Primitivo. Wanna ride?"

CHAPTER 9

"Assassination Tango?" the faded headline had once screamed. Just one of many sensational headlines the man had read, enticing readers to articles detailing the events surrounding Natalia Prafil's murder. This was a takeoff on the eponymous film, starring a gun-toting, tango-dancing hit man, used as a lead for the murder story. A greyish glow from the notebook computer's monitor illuminated the small, deeply scratched and disheveled desk. Paper scraps, chip crumbs, file folders, earphone wires, bread crusts, and insect traces all contributed to the mess. A cigarette smoldered in a tiny tin ashtray. Curvaceous clouds wafted into the claustrophobic room, reeking, until a damp gust from the open window cleared the slate. The man took up the cigarette, dragged heavily, then exhaled a noxious cloud. He fanned away the smoke from his face. It had obscured temporarily the vintage green and orange neon sign on the street below, advertising a hellhole of a bar where later he would meet his new biz associates.

A mass of newspapers and magazines lay before him. Their articles about the murder were chillingly absent compassion, but chock full of erroneous details. Her mutilated body having been found "naked and spread eagle on a parquet-patterned dance floor," was popular. The police report his associates had snatched for him claimed that she was found fully clothed in a red dress. Purple welts from strangulation, the official cause of death, were raised on her neck. Curiously, only her feet had been mutilated. But they had been slashed unmercifully with a small, razor-sharp blade.

For the press, this was just another sensational story, a mutilated tango whore. Puritanical message: Passion is dangerous! Stay at home or go bowling. Bridge maybe? Was it a comment on the insensitivity of the press, who glide so glibly through the waters of torture, warfare, mutilation, and death? Or maybe it was a scathing indictment of society, a world that has shut its eyes to tragedy, because empathy is so often ill rewarded. No black and white. Lots of dingy grey, thousands of shades.

He eyed a glossy mag called *USA Dancer*, stroking the stubble at his chin. He'd seen it a dozen times. But it was turned to a different section where a collage of photos confronted him. He didn't recognize the faces, but these were only the published prints. He noted the photographer's name on a stained pad before turning to the salacious article. Scant details. No leads. Lack of physical evidence cited. Total bullshit.

He dropped the smoke into the tin and grabbed the whiskey tumbler. Slammed down the booze, enjoying its burn. The A/C was on the fritz; and even the air was sticky. Thinking of sticky, he looked at Natalia's press photo again, evocative of a smoldering bitch. A real wildcat. So why hadn't she defended herself? He'd seen plenty of crime scene photos, had taken a few on the job. The meekest person fought hard to save precious life. Yet Natalia's long fingernails were not even broken. The coroner's report noted no trace of drugs in her system. What then, was she under a spell?

A grimace overtook his deeply lined face. This game of killing, he knew it well. Learned from experts out on *the farm* in Williamsburg, Virginia, a fine American euphemism. Most of his education had come from the Middle East version of the Company. Hit the cigarette again. Tossed back his head. Slowly, he emitted a thin stream of smoke through pursed lips. A cloud gathered against old-fashioned metal Venetian blinds. Some of its stench undoubtedly absorbed by the yellowed fabric straps to be reemitted tomorrow afternoon when struck by the searing sun. What did he care, this was not a vacation. He was here for the money.

He tapped the photo lightly with an index finger. As part of the high-stakes game he was playing, he had already made known his best guess as to the identity of the culprit. The old man, his auxiliary employer, had been dying to know. He told him it was the creepy doctor. A guess, really. But there was the incident of his wife's suspicious death at home. He had been a suspect.

The man might need to amend his claim. It didn't matter, the old guy was just going to stew over it and curse himself for his inability to actually do anything. He claimed he wanted the bastard dead, but he was old and rich and just crazy enough to forget after a month or two. Besides, taking him to the cleaners big-time was the real game. Investigating Natalia's murder was just the cover.

Despite this, the man actually wanted to solve the crime. It was not in his nature to be stumped. He had believed that he could see guilt in a person's eyes. But he was younger then, and had not yet realized that everyone is guilty of something. He examined Natalia's aquiline nose—not so different from his wife's—thinking this woman was not a slut, just a bitch. Another shared trait with the missus. Strangling such a beauty and slicing up her feet, the guy was a looney tune. The man was uncertain of the killer's identity, but was confident he was beyond redemption and would strike again.

Footsteps. The man ripped a small firearm from an ankle holster and listened. They passed and he relaxed. The yelling and screeching next door had also subsided. He assumed that by now they were either drunk or dead. Sure, he'd been in worse dumps than this Brooklyn rats' nest, but not lately. He'd been hanging out at Dubai's six-star hotel, the Burj al Arab. Impersonating a lowly waiter, but the joint was palatial. After that job, this was a good spot to lay low, cool off, and let his injured leg heal completely.

He puffed the cigarette before snuffing it out, thinking that the fringe benefits of this gig were going to be fantastic. He was looking forward to those pouty lips puffing on his dick. He blew a perfect smoke ring. It rose up, up, up toward the cobweb-encrusted ceiling. A blast of garbage-scented, balmy air destroyed it, before hitting him in the face. "Cool off, shit," he grunted, suddenly yanking the magazine from the desk.

The man shifted his position, trying to offload weight from his sore leg. The wooden chair creaked and he froze, wary of splinters. If this case were to be solved, before the next murder, it must be done by fathoming the killer's mind, making oneself at home in his insanity. That was the only way he saw to understand the sickness. The articles indicated that there were persons of interest, some of whom were members of the tango company. No shit. But he was going to get some handy photos. He'd decide the best way to use them, as case-solving aids or bargaining chips in his big-bucks game.

A follow-up article indicated that no one had been charged or arrested. Useful tabloid fodder: Public beware, a killer is on the loose. You could be next. Especially if you happen to be beautiful, young, extremely talented in dance, and performing in a certain NYC tango show. Make that a defunct tango show. But exactly like a phoenix, a new Argentine tango company—with the same dancers—had materialized. Didn't the old man recognize this was a disaster in the making? Anyone could see that the new show was rearing its beautiful head not from the ashes of the previous one, but from its grave.

* * *

The killer slept. In dreams, he saw vividly the crepe back satin scarf winding sinuously around Natalia's throat. She danced a circular figure around him, stepping back-side-forward-side, back-side-forward-side to the sensuous strains of golden-era Argentine tango. Crimson satin folds shrouded her elegant neck, supple and willing, while crepe caressed his steady hands. He was the axis about which the circular tango step, called *giro*, proceeded. Her head flung back, eyes closed tight—overcome by the ecstasy of *tangasm*—she was powerless to resist.

His biceps flexed; his gaze intensified, boring into her blissful face. He eased behind her, his languid artistry a perfect complement to the melancholy strain. Suddenly he tightened the scarf and their silken movements became a rhythmic rant, physical dissonance. His expression darkened. Her long fingernails scraped at the fabric constricting her throat. He heard her unproductive scratch, watched her writhe fruitlessly, eyes bulging. His muscular forearms expanded and the veins of his straining neck engorged. Half a minute later, Natalia lay dead. He searched his pocket calmly for the knife.

Ankles slashed and toes whittled, the metatarsals, the essence of a tango dancer's balance and the mediator of the love affair with the dance floor, were last to be slit. He recognized what he'd done—but was unconscious of exactly why. The killer rose and walked away, leaving Natalia Prafil desecrated on the floor.

He awoke in a sweat, having relived the hideous deed, turned over, and fell fast asleep.

CHAPTER 10

Brooklyn's Fontaine Bleu Hotel was not exactly what Miguel had expected, although it wasn't the worst place he'd ever spent a night. He had specified an economical place, but this joint looked seedy, not to mention dirty. Oh well, he was prepaid for weeks. Might as well ignore the smell of stale booze and the blare of a televised boxing match from the hotel bar around the corner from the front desk. He filled out a registration card. No questions. No eye contact with the sullen clerk. He took a corroded key and his suitcase, dropped off intact by the airline, and headed for the elevator.

Miguel was soon in his room, flinging open the dusty windows, seeking fresh air. He noted a pulsating orangey-red and celery-green sign across the street, hawking Sarge's Bar. At least on this floor, Miguel mused, gunshots could be hardly heard. He dropped heavily onto the spongy bed, running his fingers through his hair in disbelief. Eyes closed, he tried to blank his mind. Miguel couldn't help reflecting on the day's events: the audition and Aggie, the peculiarity of Don Luis, the unlikely nicking of his hand by Kemal, and last, but certainly not least, his wild ride to Brooklyn with El Primitivo. Omens? He hoped not.

After a few minutes, he abandoned the bed and hefted his suitcase. It seemed twice as heavy as before. Miguel yawned and lugged it over to the armless desk chair.

He dropped it onto the well-worn seat with a bang. After dialing in the lock combo, he threw open the top and ran his hand through carefully folded clothing. He found a sharp rectangular edge and paused. It was late. He was exhausted. Could he do this?

Miguel withdrew the wooden frame gently from the case. He closed his eyes and exhaled completely. Reopening them, he stared at the photo. Three smiling faces. It was December 18, 2014, his mother's fiftieth birthday. Miguel's mouth began to quiver. He felt sick to his stomach. He touched the glass, tracing the faces. His heart melted.

Miguel had tried to forge his heart into an unfeeling, metal lump. But it grew, swelled within his breast. It was as though he could feel his ribs cracking with the volume, a nearly unbearable strain. The hardness of steel, pumping his blood like a creaky, rusted iron lung. It must have actually encroached on his lungs, because Miguel found that he could hardly breathe. His entire body sagged under the psychological load. Then suddenly his mouth drew into a cut across his face. Miguel thrust the frame back inside the case and rifled to the bottom where he grasped cold, hard metal. He yanked out the knife and depressed the thumb stud. It flicked open with a whoosh that spiked his pulse.

Miguel examined the blade's razor-sharp edge. The Ti-Lite, Japanese-made switchblade was brand new. Flawless. Its AUS 8A stainless steel blade gleamed in the room's rude lighting. The forged, ventilated, 7075 aluminum handles shone. Yes, a ten-centimeter blade would be ample. No pocket clip. No quillon. No *nada*. It was a single-purpose implement. Miguel envisioned himself an angel of death and this was his sword.

He closed the blade until it clicked neatly into place within the frame. Not bothering to undress, Miguel turned off the bedside lamp and in the darkness stretched full length, his feet extending beyond the end of the double bed. One thing was sure, he was going to be part of that company. Even if he had to scrub and polish the floors of the studio or the toilets in the elegant lounges. And he would vet every dancer, manager, secretary, delivery boy . . . until he found Natalia's killer. His thoughts flew back to Don Luis and his improbable welcome supper. The old guy was up to something. Had to be. But what? And the remainder of the company, at least Chaz and El Primitivo, ditto. He slid the back of this hand across his face, the whiskers pricking the stinging wound, thinking, deceit, unlike tango, was a game for more than two.

CHAPTER 11

Don Luis had forsaken brilliant morning sunshine to cram himself behind a smallish, antique writing table, located in the bowels of his ritzy four-story building. The arms of his wheelchair abutted the center drawer, forcing him to bend unnaturally at the waist in his studies. His back ached. And the expensive LED lamps he had installed himself had never illuminated his work optimally. He ignored the ghosts and shadows. His life was crowded by them already. The greyish vault with its rough masonry walls, never painted, felt damp and close. Restricted airflow and flooding years ago caused by Hurricane Sandy produced a nearly intolerable reek. It was a poor environment for precious diaries and manuscripts, and a poorer one for humans.

In a gloved hand, Don Luis held open lightly a page of text. In a bare hand he held a small flashlight. He examined the relative placements of the carefully penned characters—calligraphic characters—on the double-sided leaf. He had noted everything that he could on each side, regarding the sequences of characters, the frequency of certain characters, their positions relative to each other. Brow scrunched low. Owlish eyes nearly shut from concentration. This was all there was left to consider, the relative positions of characters on the front and reverse of one leaf. Was there not one single clue here? How could one elude him? Possibly because he was no master of Kabbalah. In fact, he had been an atheist for most of his adult life. Hoping against hope that the saga was untrue, he squinted his eyes tighter, concentrated harder. The type matched perfectly, line for line. There were no variations, no illuminating patterns; there was *bupkis*.

Perspiration beaded on his broad brow. Don Luis dabbed it with a damp hanky. More airflow was needed into his inner sanctum during these summer months. Perhaps he could manage a small fan, holding it in his lap as he descended in the tiny elevator. Truth was the cell had been prepared when he purchased the building decades ago as a stronghold for his ancestors' diaries, precious manuscripts, and the *Keter*. But now, the feeble draft of fresh air, generated by a compressor located two floors above, at ground level, seemed only to tantalize him. It was as though he were taunted by the possibility of real refreshment. Exactly like the fragile leaf he held so gingerly. What profound mysteries, what secrets of the ages were at his fingertips if only he could decipher them!

Don Luis inhaled deeply. His face reddened and his grip tightened. The flashlight wavered, hardly stabilized now by a trembling hand. "I will find it," he muttered to himself. "I will—" The ancient parchment gave way to his overly fast grasp with an anguishing *riiiip*. He gasped, nearly traumatized by the awful sound of the tearing leaf. Don Luis sat petrified for a long time, staring at the torn fragment. A tear welled and fell. And another formed. He lay down the volume with utmost care, smoothed the wounded page, and closed his eyes. Where was this infinite mercy? He could not imagine it, even in his most transcendent of dreams. Life was hard for everyone, sometimes devastating. And respite all too rare.

What Don Luis felt was familiar and quite real. It was as though they were glaring down at him, pronouncing more powerful curses while shredding their garments. Not only was he not enveloped in mercy, he was ensnared in the curse. His family had been for centuries. He could almost see its hideous head rearing. Don Luis slumped in his chair. The metal frame of his wheelchair groaned pathetically, seeming to express his unvocalized pain. He had sworn to himself that he would never part with his most precious treasure, the legacy of his forefathers. But as time passed, he recalled the warnings proffered by the ancients in its preamble: "Blessed be he who preserves it and cursed be he who steals it, and cursed be he who sells it, and cursed . . . and cursed. . . ."

The buzzer on the control panel near the table's left-hand side roused him from his gloom. A small cluster of video screens had come to life, showing a visitor at the street level entering the studio's front door. Don Luis saw a man of average height and build, a tad on the slim side, carrying a bulky aluminum case. He was overdressed, in a sport coat and tie, as though making a sales call. He knew the man well and the fact that he was selling something. Don Luis glared at the screen, thinking, the man had been lucky, but his good fortune was running out. He imagined the man convulsing in his death throes. But then Don Luis realized that he was in the presence of the *Keter*, and must keep his thoughts pure.

Don Luis depressed an intercom button and said, "Good morning, Dr. Wagner." He watched the man start. "Please give me a few moments before coming up," Don Luis added. "I'll be in my office in a jiffy." The man's jaw stiffened and his head shook imperiously. Don Luis banged both legs of the writing desk with his wheelchair's frame, extricating himself. He rolled across the concrete masonry floor into a claustrophobic lift, depressed the button for the second floor, and jolted upward. The door opened and he exited into his office. Don Luis rolled along an unassuming bookcase, stopping to depress a switch hidden in its woodwork. The bookcase slid silently, concealing the lift's existence, as he wheeled behind his enormous desk.

Some moments later, after composing himself and drawing an easy breath, Don Luis neutralized his expression and propelled himself outside his office door to the glass balustrade. He called out, "Dr. Wagner, you may come up now." Wagner sprang from a *banco* like an overdone Pop-Tart. Pompous ass, thought Don Luis.

Wagner entered the office and stared at Don Luis, who understood his facial expression to be one of a person who counts the faults of those who make him wait. But did Wagner's patients when delayed have an equal opportunity to scorn him? Then he recalled that Wagner had no patients. He was a pathologist, kept chained to a desk in a dank Bellevue basement.

"Good morning, Don Luis."

"Do come in, Ernest, and have a seat. Coffee?"

"No, thank you," he replied, seating himself.

Don Luis watched as Dr. Wagner rested his burden on an exquisitely woven silk rug, one thousand knots per square inch of love and care. Jabbing his thumb toward the case, Don Luis said, "This is the very best."

"For portable analysis, yes. Far better than the toys used in the field by Homeland Security. Not everyone can walk out of Bellevue Hospital carrying one of these."

Don Luis assumed the pregnant pause was intended to allow him to reflect on Dr. Wagner's exalted status as a pathological surgeon—um, surgical pathologist. "And you are completely competent in its use."

"While such analyses are generally relegated to technicians, I am conversant with the process." Dr. Wagner sat tall in his chair. "Given a suitable sample, standard chemicals are used to extract the DNA from it. The next step is to amplify, if you will, DNA fragments into a sufficient number of copies to analyze, using the PCR technique. For statistical accuracy, you see."

"Yes, but is it absolutely accurate?"

"No."

Don Luis's owlish eyes narrowed, drilling Wagner.

"Nothing is," Wagner snapped. "It is better than one in a million for determining parent-offspring and sibling relationships." Wagner's eyes widened questioningly.

"I have an incidental interest in understanding the relationship, if any, between DNA samples from three persons."

"As it happens, Don Luis, geneticists are making startling discoveries regarding the complexities of DNA. There have been recent research papers, published in journals such as *Nature* and *The Journal of Neuroscience*, detailing experiments where lab mice and even humans have had genetic switches manipulated permanently."

"Quite fascinating. Now—"

"Epigenetics, the research is called." Wagner took to the edge of his seat; his voice rose perceptibly. "Type 2 diabetes was induced in a male mouse by feeding him a high fat and high sugar diet. Although he was not genetically disposed to the disease, he transmitted it to multiple generations of daughters, all of whom had diabetes-free mothers. The effect is called epigenetic transgenerational inheritance."

"No diabetes in my line," Don Luis replied, disinterested.

Dr. Wagner raised the case and placed it atop an occasional table. He unfastened the latches and split its halves wide-open, exposing lackluster contents: an LED screen, a few elongated syringes, and a probe attached to a harness of colorful wires. He pulled on surgical gloves, snapping them at his wrists with an air of superiority.

Wagner commented, "The *Times* coverage of epigenetics was credible. But there are so many tacky come-ons for articles aimed at lay people, "What Happens in Vegas Stays in Your Family Forever" and "Sins of the Father Are Visited on Everyone." He chuckled. "Turns out, physical and mental abuses are not wiped clean from generation to generation." He tugged at the margins of his gloves for a second time. "Those abuses go right down the line, compounding when succeeding generations are subjected to the same stress factors."

Don Luis started. He fought to maintain his composure. But his mind buzzed, considering the ramifications of epigenetics. He was suddenly nervous and struggled to maintain an expression of detachment. What could it mean to him or to his people?

"Ready to begin?" Wagner asked. "Are these the specimens?"

Don Luis nodded.

Wagner lifted a white cloth covering three specimens on a nondescript metal tray positioned beside the instrument.

Fingers to beard, Don Luis could not expel his somber thoughts. Epigenetic transgenerational inheritance was disturbing. There might be no diabetes in his line, but there was a generous pile of abuses, physical and mental, from generation to generation. And not just his line, but those of his tribe. He must understand how this new research differed from his elementary understanding of inherited genetics, and what it implied for the serially abused. As much as Don Luis hated to push Wagner's PLAY button again, he asked, "Dr. Wagner, about this, what did you call it, transgenerational—"

"Epigenetic transgenerational inheritance. Fascinating research."

"Quite right. And which researchers in the field do you most admire?" Don Luis noted Wagner was as keen as a housecat for the question.

"Michael Skinner is certainly talented. And the entire ENCORE project is well respected in the community." Focusing his laser-like gaze to a point between Don Luis's eyes, he asked, "Anything of particular interest?"

Don Luis cast down his eyes to a writing pad on his desk and scribbled, resenting the good doctor's scrutiny.

"What have we here?" Wagner muttered, whisking away the cloth covering the specimens. He eyed two glass vials, both of which contained strands of hair. One, containing a wiry, gray mass, not unlike Don Luis's mangled beard, the other bore a fine lock of smooth, black hair, corded by a baby blue band. He could not help but gawk at the jewel-handled dagger's crimson tip.

Don Luis's hand shot across the desktop. He grasped Dr. Wagner's dainty wrist in a meaty vise. Wagner gasped. Don Luis said, "Per our agreement, this little inquiry will be kept absolutely private, yes."

Dr. Wagner recoiled, his eyes no longer sedate. "Have you reason to doubt me?"

"Not in the least." Don Luis released the delicate wrist and sat back in his chair.

"And per our stringently binding verbal agreement between gentlemen," Dr. Wagner stressed the term, "you will honor your word when the time comes."

"I pledge to you, on my honor and that of my family, that you will be elevated to *primo bailarino* for the opening of the coming season."

"Perfect timing." Wagner's razor-thin grin nearly cut across his entire face in an instant of bliss. "I am engaged in a transaction that will enable me to reduce my medical schedule substantially."

Don Luis's mien darkened as he thought, *Should you live to see the day.*

CHAPTER 12

Miguel heaved himself from bed. He'd tossed long enough. Showered and in street clothes, that differed little from his tango attire, black pants and white shirt, he was prepared for his first full day of New York. He stashed his case under the lumpy bed and slipped his weapon into his right hip pocket. Coffee time. What he really wanted was a *café cortado*, the espresso-based coffee preferred by Argentines.

In his travels, Miguel had learned many expressions for *cortado*, suggesting a cut of the espresso's acidity. This cut was accomplished by the addition of a small amount of warm milk. More *latte* than an Italian *macchiato*, but less *lait* than a French *café au lait*.

What is the phrase in English? Had he ever known it? The French he knew well. *Noisette* actually meant hazelnut, but in a French coffee shop it was understood how much milk should be added to the espresso. Unfortunately, in a European slaughterhouse, as in BA, a *noisette* was known to be a specialty cut of meat taken from the rib or loin of beef and lamb. Miguel quickened his pace, fixed his vision ahead. His eyes burned to examine his hands, to see that there was no blood or gore from brutally slicing the animals apart. He held his breath involuntarily to ward off the stench of rancid meat that soiled the entire plant where he had worked, parting away *noisettes*, ribs, intestines, organs, and everything in between.

Miguel was not ashamed of his slaughterhouse job, just disgusted. While the wreckage of his past seemed to haunt him constantly, Miguel was proud to have supported his family when they needed him most. When the US and European economies had faltered, Argentina's totally collapsed. Miguel sighed heavily, acknowledging that the most *milonguero*-esque thing he'd ever done had nothing to do with dancing tango. He had supported his family using a knife.

He considered that his labor there had been more honorable than working for a cousin in La Boca as a snoop for divorce lawyers. He hadn't lasted six months. An ex-cop, his cousin thought the jobs were manna from heaven. Miguel found them hellish at best. Training with his cousin—learning police brutality—had made Miguel strong, his muscles hard. It was essential later, when he thrust his hands and arms inside bleeding carcasses to grab out vital organs and parted away precious pieces of meat to help pay his mother's bills. Miguel stuffed his hands into his pockets. He believed that his fingers, nails, and cuticles were no longer blood-stained, but he couldn't be sure. He dared not look.

From Noah's Bagels, the aroma of freshly baked goods and coffee wafted onto the sidewalk. It lifted Miguel's spirits. He took his *café* and pastry to a small corner table, where a page of discarded newspaper caught his eye. An advertisement for a sexy sports car, a Lamborghini, sent his mind racing back to the previous night and his wild ride in New York City. He considered whether it had all really happened. Absentmindedly he stroked the back of his hand. Yep, Kemal had sliced him well. And El Primitivo had a fantastic car.

Miguel recalled pretending to know El Primitivo well, but he wasn't very convincing. But it hadn't mattered: El Primitivio had been loaded on drugs. There was a burning joint in the ashtray when Miguel entered the car. And El Primitivo frequently twitched and shook his mane of hair out the open window, citing the need for more air. And his laugh was way over the top. It accentuated his wide-set eyes and oversized teeth. The entire scene was surreal, but real.

Miguel had asked, "What are you doing here so late?"

"I hit the gym at the studio after the auditions." He smirked, "Didn't want to bother the principal dancers. A candombe *schlepp* like me."

Miguel got the meaning of what he said, if not the particulars. The African rhythm-dominated dance called candombe was always overdone into farce in tango shows. And unlike milonga, sometimes it was omitted altogether. The guy was clearly no tango star. Miguel didn't know him at all, except for a single phone call arranged by Miguel's cousin and doppelganger Miguel Andro. It became clear that El Primitivo and Miguel Andro had been close, very close.

Miguel had said, "I'm going to the Fontaine Bleu Hotel in Brooklyn."

"I know that. I rented the place for you, remember?" He snickered slightly and then added, "It's no trouble. Got a gig over that way myself."

"Is the Fontaine Bleu French?"

"Ahhh, no." El Primitivo had cut his eyes to take in Miguel's rumpled track suit, before adding, "But, it's going to be, um, just fine for you."

Miguel asked, "Is it convenient to go over the famous bridge?"

"Sure you ain't a tourist?" El Primitivo asked before wiping a grin from his face. "Check this out." In an instant the car heaved and the rear end dithered back and forth as the sound of squalling rubber overwhelmed the cabin, deafening Miguel. Smoke from burnt rubber nearly choked him and he grasped in vain for the window control. El Primitivo's maniacal laughter evoked an image of Don Giovanni as the car jetted forward into the tempestuous night.

Jet lag took its toll and Miguel almost nodded off. He barely heard El Primitivo say, "Weird thing, Miguel Andro and me was really close. And I wasn't sure if I knew you. You're about two inches taller, and more handsome."

Miguel let the remarks slide. Tomorrow this guy wouldn't recall a thing.

El Primitivo chuckled again. "Remember when we were blitzed at the Cactus Club? Took that little *señorita* back to my place. That was sooo wild."

Miguel's eyes popped open. The Cactus Club was BA's most progressive gay milonga. It was mostly for foreigners. He'd been there only once, and it wasn't with this guy. Unsure what to do, Miguel had said, "Oh, yeah, really wild." He sounded to himself like a talking robot.

"And after we tired her out. . . ."

Miguel felt El Primitivo's hand squeeze his leg. Oh shit, he thought, this cannot be happening. He placed the errant hand back on the wheel. "You'd better concentrate on driving or you'll crash your fancy car." Miguel began to doze. They banged along as though the car were a pothole-seeking machine. El

Primitivo had opened his window completely, admitting wind and rain. Miguel didn't care. He had slept only a few hours in the past fifty. *Blam*! The car hit a crater-sized hole in the pavement. Miguel was stunned back to reality.

"Here's your bridge." El Primitivo goosed the throttle and fishtailed.

Miguel peered up at one of the most iconic edifices in the United States, the entire world: the Brooklyn Bridge. It spoke of a bygone era, as did BA's Alvear Palace Hotel and the iconic *tanqueria* La Confiteria Ideal. He wondered why Don Luis had painstakingly recreated that particular bar. He had no doubt there was a compelling reason. Crossing the rusty old bridge, Miguel felt its cultural significance, and began to think of La Boca. Just like the port's colorful houses, this bridge was photographed endlessly and used for travel advertisement and postcard fodder, more trivialization of Western civilization.

"So, the old guy likes you. Kept you upstairs half the night."

"Don Luis?"

"Tough to figure, Old World royalty and all that." El Primitivo shook his head thoughtfully. "Something's up with him. Now Wagner, he's a dick weed, but harmless."

"Oh."

"And Chaz, the tortured tango genius." He stared off into space, looking out his open window.

"Watch out!" Miguel warned, now wide awake.

El Primitivo jerked the wheel, and the car darted from the opposing lane. "They always are, you know. Life's tough for them."

El Primitivo's tone suggested that he knew personally of what he spoke.

"Now me, I ain't no tango genius, but I'm good with numbers. Got it from my old man, bond trader on Wall Street. Worked eighteen hours a day for twenty years and got a heart attack at forty-nine. Never fully recovered. Not good numbers."

"Hmm."

"Got everything from him, including his name, Perseus Panopoulos." He rolled his hand, saying, "How passionate is that? Now you get the El Primitivo *shtick*."

Miguel forced a smile. What he would give to have lived such a story.

"Your dad teach you dancing?" El Primitivo had asked. "I saw your audition from the back of the studio. You move like you were born on a tango floor."

Miguel tried not to stiffen. "My mother was a beautiful dancer," he said casually.

"She stopped?"

"She's not well." Miguel was thankful for the ensuing silence.

"Not working myself to death," El Primitivo spouted. "I want to make my bundle quick and get out."

The line spoke volumes. A couple of Miguel's cousins had been keen to make a quick bundle on the heavy tango traffic in BA, selling lessons, taxi dances, and party aids to rich *turistas*. Unfortunately, when the crowds stopped coming and they were no longer paid to dance with tourists, too often the cousins consumed their party wares themselves. The results were ugly. It would have been an easy road for Miguel to take when his world collapsed, but he had chosen to harden his heart and strengthen his body instead of weaken himself with drugs. It was to the slaughterhouse for him. Miguel could almost smell its stench blowing in the car's open window.

El Primitivo smiled. "We all have our secrets, huh, Miguel Andro."

Miguel might have fooled ICE, sneaking into the United States using his cousin's passport, but El Primitivo was too street smart. He knew and was playing along, but why?

"*Pow*!" A loud noise outside the bagel shop startled Miguel into the present. Customers sitting at window tables began hitting the floor in a scramble. He looked out of the front window and observed a passing jalopy; it backfired again. Miguel thrust back his chair. He had to do a little shopping. He had researched a company online and believed that their goods were just the ticket for his investigative task. Exiting the shop, Miguel's eyes were open wider than before entering. The scene of urban squalor: graffitied, bombed-out buildings; scattered refuse; panhandlers and sidewalk sleepers gripped him. Another backfire and he might hit the pavement.

CHAPTER 13

THE PURPLE CHRYSLER BOMBED down the Brooklyn-Queens Expressway. It smoked like a chimney, not only from the exhaust but also from the passenger windows. Gusts of morning air buffeted the backseat passenger, who held down his cigarette to keep ashes from blowing into his thick beard and impenetrable eyes. He was a watchful man. And was confident that his hosts, in the front seats, were giving him grief for no good reason. He had marked it in his little black book, the one with notches on its spine.

A cigarette stub stuffed between thick lips, the driver swerved onto the Broadway exit. It was not too far until the cross streets of the thirties and he intended to make the smoke last. Pulling into the smallish asphalt parking lot of the Safety First Security Company, the land-yacht ground to a stop. The driver threw a look over his shoulder and said, "You gonna have about five minutes to memorize whatever you need." He took on the man's cold stare, and barked, "And no pictures."

"Nonsense." The man shook his head. "No one will know." Pointing to his clunky-looking wireframe glasses with an embedded prism in the corner of one lens, he said, "All I have to do to snap a frame is blink."

"Walk in wearing those and they'll know you're a *glasshole*."

"These are not Google. Yissum Research from Israel. Totally different."

"I don't care if they came down from Heaven on a bolt of lightning."

The man in the front passenger's seat thrust a stubby finger toward the guest. Through stained teeth he said, "You agree or we'll fuckin' take you right back where we found you. I ain't getting fingered when you leave them glasses on the bar at some strip joint and the cop who's tailing you picks them up and downloads your pictures."

The man sneered, "Remember, I found you."

"We all know *how* you found us, through one of our guys in Brooklyn. Now, no pictures?"

He removed the glasses.

"Let's go," said the driver. "Hey you, follow my lead."

Exiting the front seat, the passenger smirked, "Genius superspy, huh."

The driver brushed down his face toward his chest. "Yeah, a real master of disguise."

They cracked up, but stifled their laughter at the entrance.

Once inside the shabby office, the men stood at a counter. The portly driver said, "We're here to see Mr. Guggino."

A frail-looking woman of forty with straw hair, wearing a dowdy dress said, "Can I tell him who's calling?"

"Yeah, tell him it's Woody Bono of Bono Brothers Electronics." He grinned.

"And can I tell him the nature of your business?"

"I'll, uh, relate that to him when I see him." He pulled up his coat sleeve and eyed a corroded watch whose expandable band was stretched nearly to breaking.

The bearded man trailed his chunky hosts into a dingy office with faded furnishings and yellowed paint. He observed Mr. Guggino, a nervous fellow, who squirmed, sitting at his ancient Steelcase desk. Standing too quickly, he knocked his knee on the half-open middle drawer. He winced, indirectly looking over the menacing trio.

The bearded man listened as the passenger worked over Mr. Guggino. Access to the man's private files didn't appear to be a sure thing. He supposed the stories about New York's Mob having at least one finger in every pie in the state was not strictly true.

"We already discussed this yesterday," the driver reiterated. "We got to examine the layout of the security system. Mr., um, Beard here," he gestured, "is an expert in identifying possible failures and opportunities for upgrades and stuff, you know, improvements in the current systems and so forth. The area is still substandard, you know, after the hurricane and all."

Mr. Guggino smoothed his wrinkled tie. It looked as though it was coordinated with the dilapidated office. He sort of squeaked, "The Upper East Side substandard?"

"That's what I said. Now we have lots more appointments today."

"Well, strictly speaking, no one outside the company or without written permission from the central office is allowed to see security system plans."

"You told me." The passenger leaned over the desk toward the man, adding, "And remember what I told you?"

Mr. Guggino began to cough uncontrollably. He grabbed up a chipped cup with a stained teabag string dangling down its side. He held it to his lips and gulped and then whispered, "But I could lose my job."

The passenger growled, "Your nasty little habit is going to cost you a lot more than just your job. Now get in there and get out them plans."

Mr. Guggino's eyebrows knit and he clasped his chin with one hand while the other reached around his back to scratch. He appeared to wrestle with himself.

"The Upper East Side is a dangerous place. The building could be in jeopardy right now," the passenger sneered.

Mr. Guggino said, "Okay, but only Mr., um, Beard can have access to them. And his signature will be required."

"No problem. Get a move on."

* * *

"Dreaming of dancing tango, huh," Candy said to Jean-Luc, closing the studio's front door behind them. She hit the lights and the place sparkled. She never tired of coming to work here. They sat side by side and changed into dancing shoes for the lesson.

"It was strange," Jean-Luc continued. "I was dancing great and then realized that I'd forgotten to put my pants on. I tried to be cool, dancing over to the men's room." He chuckled. "To soak my head, I guess."

Candy laughed, showing unnaturally white teeth between naturally pouty lips. "Have you never performed for an audience? Didn't you give presentations for work or something where you had to, um, expose yourself?" She worked her eyes.

"I usually work behind the scenes," he said. "Just a small-time PI in Canada. Not much happening there." He smiled, removing his sport coat and draping it over the back of a nearby chair with a thud.

She stroked the beautiful floor with her forefoot, hardly feeling the steel toe in her teaching shoes. It wasn't really steel, but that might not be a bad idea, she mused, when teaching Jean-Luc. "All performers have had that recurring dream," she said. "You get over it." She disappeared into the music control booth saying, "Get used to it, anyway."

Candy cued tango music and strutted onto the floor. She twiddled her fingers beckoning Jean-Luc, blue-red nails fluttering. "Recall the basic—well, really there is no Argentine tango basic figure." She nodded. "I've been calling this simple collection of movements, these seven foot placements, the basic figure. It's useful to develop a sense of posture, embrace, intention, and breathing while dancing tango."

"Yeah, make fun why don't you. Dancing and breathing is not that easy."

Candy smiled.

Jean-Luc looked sheepish. "And embracing you always takes my breath away."

"Keep breathing; it relaxes you and your partner. A woman wants comfort and ease in the embrace and the dance. She might prefer things a little rougher later."

Jean-Luc's eyes popped. He hesitated, then asked, "Know what I really want?"

A perfectly contoured eyebrow arched.

"I want you to show me what Miguel did yesterday. The profound *milonguero* thing." His hands shot out toward her. "You said it was simple, but so elegant."

"Simple, yes; easy, no." Her hands went to her hips. "Besides, I thought you wanted to dance like Chaz: lifts, *boleos, saccades* . . . all the tricks. Make up your mind."

"I don't even know what those are."

"We'll explore them, don't worry. Now, the basic step: side left, two steps outside on my right, and pause, leading me into my *crusada*, where my left foot is crossed over the right."

"Did I hear my name taken in vain?" Chaz asked, amiably.

"Eavesdropping? Your devotee is having second thoughts."

"That so?" Chaz posed, leaning against a column. "Let's see what he's got."

Candy stepped in front of Jean-Luc. He embraced her nervously, wrapping his right arm too snugly around her back, pulling her toward him. She felt the crush of her breasts on his expanding chest. It would have been a fine position to begin making out, but it was not going to work for dancing tango. Candy was so far forward that when Jean-Luc lunged with his chest it sent her nearly toppling over backward, with a single step.

"Whoa, cowboy," Candy laughed, freeing herself.

Jean-Luc's face reddened. "I'm sorry," he stammered.

Chaz approached and said quietly, "It's all about the legs. Not the action leg, but the standing leg." He demonstrated. "Go forward with the action leg, send it first, show it, but keep the weight and the balance longer on the standing leg. Once you begin to transfer your weight, feel the luxury and balance of the middle of the step—when your weight is shared on both feet for an instant—and then take all of your weight on the action leg, quickly collecting the trailing leg."

Jean-Luc said, "That is so clear, Chaz. You must have done this all your life. Where did you grow up?"

"He was an amateur ballroom champ in California," Candy said.

"I'm not surprised. Who was your partner, Chaz?"

"I had so many." He half-smiled. "Can't possibly recall them all."

"Sure you can," Candy prodded. "There was Donna Richards. She went on to represent the United States as a pro in Viennese Waltz in Vienna, and won!"

"Impressive," Jean-Luc said. "Whatever happened to her?"

"She was always very impressive," Chaz said. He turned and headed stone-faced toward the cantina.

Jean-Luc shot a look to Candy, who shrugged. She noted the keenness in his eyes when he asked, softly, "Where exactly did Chaz grow up?"

She whispered, "He'll tell you Beverly Hills, but it was really Alhambra. And his mother Regina is a total whack job." She screwed a temple, adding, "Munchhouses Syndrome or something. She apparently hurt Chaz when he was a kid so she could rush him to the hospital and be a drama queen."

"Hmm."

She shook her head. "Don't know how he coped, but it worked out."

"Well, it was nice of Chaz to explain the movement to me. He's helpful."

"Not always."

"What's he like otherwise?"

"He was the star of the previous company. I showed up from Miami, busted and divorced." She grimaced. "Chaz and his former partner Natalia had a love/hate relationship. Not sure who loved and who hated the most. But they both ignored me."

"I understand that ended badly for Natalia."

"Ohh, I don't like to think about it. A company full of *milongueros*, *tangueras*, and egomaniacs I can stand, but a killer, that's too much."

"Don't you think the killer is a company member, just waiting to kill again?"

Ashen-faced, she said, "Don't joke about that. Sometimes after rehearsal, when I take steam, I'm scared half to death."

CHAPTER 14

THE CAB RIDE DOWN Brooklyn's Gowanus Expressway had been a memorable adventure for Miguel. He couldn't help but wonder how much more devastating for the human spirit it would be to live in Kabul, Afghanistan, or Aleppo, Syria, the war-torn ancient city dear to Don Luis. Miguel recalled that exiting the taxi in full daylight and then walking past the Sunset Park he'd reached back twice to verify that his weapon was at hand. Reflecting, he recognized that the threat level was no greater than in La Boca, Argentina. It had just been unfamiliar territory. But there was something a little unnerving, he had to admit, about strolling up a place called Dead Man's Hill.

His newly acquired goods were stashed in his backpack. The transaction at the seedy store had been much like registration at the Fontaine Bleu: short, sweet, no chit-chat. And now, what had been a twenty-minute cab ride was going to be ages on the Green train, heading uptown to the studio. Miguel was jostled along in a relatively clean, sparsely populated subway car. People wearing business suits had boarded at the previous stop. BA could learn a few things from New York City about public transportation, he thought, allowing his shoulders to slump and relax.

It was hard to admit to himself, but Miguel was becoming attracted to the city's energy. BA was exciting, but not like this. He closed his eyes, again recalling the previous night's wild ride with El Primitivo. How they had raced over the Brooklyn Bridge and bombed down rutted side streets. It was too bad that El Primitivo had seemed a nervous wreck one minute and then completely composed the next. Miguel recognized this sign of addiction taking hold. He had seen one of his tango heroes act this way before finding a too-early grave. He missed the man.

The train banged over an uneven section of track, reminding Miguel of his joy ride to Brooklyn with El Primitivo. He had slowed his supercar and called out in a mechanized cadence, "Beautiful Brooklyn; Flatbush stop ahead."

"Where is the Fontaine Bleu?" Miguel had asked.

Ah, the Fontaine Bleu," he cackled. "You definitely are going to need some protection. Maybe not this much."

Miguel looked on in surprise as El Primitivo pulled an enormous pistol from under his seat.

"Lotta pop in a .357 magnum," he had said, waving the piece.

Miguel swallowed hard. "Flatbush is not so bad, you said." He eyed the weapon's massive barrel, which appeared to be about a foot long.

"It's not, but you're going to need some protection."

"*Dio proverrá*," Miguel murmured one of his mother's religious expressions.

"It's okay in the daytime. But it ain't a friendly Italian neighborhood no more."

Miguel nodded and reached for the door handle.

El Primitivo produced a pencil and scrap of paper from the console; he scribbled. "Here's my cell. I do some business over here. Call and I'll give you a ride to the studio."

"Thanks."

"Otherwise, take the Lex train and get off at Hunter College." He grinned. "Fantastic ass there; it's worth the extra walk." He nodded. "And those kids will do anything for an eight-ball of purple meth. Anything—"

How sad, Miguel thought.

El Primitivo added, "I know the cook. Can get you a few eights pretty cheap."

He stuffed the scrap of paper in Miguel's hand and pulled him close. Miguel braced for the kiss. Rain splattered the windshield, sounding like a blast from a fire hose. He tried to withdraw, but El Primitivo held him fast, whispering, "Don't worry, *amigo*, your secret's safe with me."

Miguel had scrambled out of the door. He waved good-bye as the car heaved upward and then with a deafening cry rocketed forward.

He turned toward the entrance of his dismal new home, but looked back down the street. Curiously, El Primitivo's car's distinctive brake lights illuminated the glossy, oil slick of a street like a psychedelic contrail. The car began a power slide before turning into the first drive on the left, underneath a faded sign for Sarge's Bar.

Miguel roused from the recollection at the subway car's noisy halt. From the window, he saw "68th Street Hunter College" displayed in bold block letters on a royal blue and onyx mosaic background. He jumped up, grabbed his pack, hit the door.

CHAPTER 15

CANDICE BORAKOWSKI STRUTTED toward the studio's front door. From outside Miguel could see her through the window. The generous hemline of her black tango skirt swayed as her legs switched neatly back and forth, feet on a single track. She neared the lock release and her blonde hair, done up on the back of her head with a few silky strands dangling, and clear blue eyes came into focus. She smiled at him with full lips. She buzzed him in and strutted away. Miguel watched, pretty sure there was no rounder ass than hers on the entire Hunter College campus. He entered the door thinking, too bad El Primitivo didn't go for her.

She turned. "Miguel, right. I'm Candy. Have a seat. I'm finishing up a lesson."

"Thanks, Candy," he said, approaching the practice floor.

"You met Jean-Luc Renard."

"Hello, Jean-Luc," Miguel said in clipped speech.

"Jean-Luc asked how you did the Lean thing," Candy said. "Thinks maybe he should be a *milonguero*."

Jean-Luc turned away, his smooth cheeks reddening.

"Got a minute? Want to show him?"

Miguel doffed his pack. "I have dancing shoes today. I'll change."

He headed toward the lounge and changed quickly, taking just a moment to smooth the leather of his worn shoes and to express his thanks to God, or whatever, for this opportunity. He stowed his pack in a locker and returned to the small practice floor where he saw Jean-Luc and Candy in an uncomfortable leaning posture. Each appeared to strain not to topple the other.

"That looks a bit like, uh, Gavito's Lean, but this is not the best posture, Jean-Luc, for beginning dancers," Miguel said. "It can hurt the lady."

"The man, too," Jean-Luc said, separating, rubbing his lower back.

"You want to make dancing nice for her, to protect her," Miguel said. "Never forget that tango is not about dancing steps. It's about taking care of a woman."

Jean-Luc focused beady eyes, suspicious or possibly uncomprehending.

"And the essence of *milonguero*," Miguel continued, "is not just taking care of the lady, but also your friends, and your family."

Jean-Luc's focus strayed. He appeared to be dazed by the words and asked, "Just how can I do that?"

"In this instance, maybe you use the *volcada*." Miguel smiled. "It, too, is an off-axis figure, a lean." He turned with a serious expression, saying, "Is a figure requiring great trust. The woman gives her weight to you, here." He pressed a flattened hand to his chest. "You must support her, so that she can embellish, you know, play using her feet, enjoy her femininity, while you care for her."

From the corner of his eye, Miguel saw Candy lick her lips.

"C'mon, Miguel, lead me," she said, raising her arms slightly, welcoming him in to her fully opened chest.

"Front or side *volcada*?"

Brows arched, she replied, "I like both."

Miguel embraced her intimately.

Candy turned to Jean-Luc, "As with all of these inward-leaning figures, *volcades* and the Bridge, *el Puente*, our torsos must be in firm contact and we both exert a slight upward pressure there. It keeps you tall and elegant, and helps the lady not to collapse her lower back. That's painful and ugly."

Miguel stepped back, bringing Candy's body tilting toward him. Restoring her uprightness, he said, "Is the idea, okay." Then Miguel stepped around Candy to his left and quickly torqued his chest from side to side, prompting Candy's free foot to swing up behind her from the floor in a flick. Then he walked around her in an elliptical path. She leaned on him as he inscribed an arc. Her foot swept the floor in front of her leaning body. Miguel righted them again.

"I like that," Jean-Luc cheered. "Now what did I just see?"

Candy said, "The first one was the most basic, a simple tip of my weight toward him. He moved backward while keeping his chest forward and high toward me. This put me directly in front of him and into a leaning position: *volcada*."

"And the second?"

"The second one was fancier. He stepped left and torqued his torso clockwise, which had the effect of winding up my body. Then he turned his torso counter-clockwise, which caused me to unwind quickly and sent my back leg kicking into the air: a *boleo* or *voleo* it's sometimes called. He circled clockwise around me from a slight distance, taking me into an angled lean toward him on an arc: side *volcada*."

Miguel marked Jean-Luc's worried expression. He nodded encouragement.

Jean-Luc said, "But you could've fallen."

"No way, I trust him."

"Trust what, his tango—his face; his motives? You don't even know him."

"Miguel's a *milonguero*," Candy said. "He'll take care of his lady and his family."

Miguel smiled and started toward the cantina only to find Aggie and Adriana watching. Surprised, he said, "*Hola*, um, hello."

Aggie clapped her hands quietly and crinkled her nose. "*¡Eso, milonguero!*"

CHAPTER 16

MIGUEL ALMOST HAD TO PINCH himself to believe this was real. He looked down from the elevator car onto the studio, evocative of La Confiteria Ideal. Although this studio was fancier and immaculate, his heart skipped a beat. It was well before three P.M. and he planned to thank Don Luis for supper. There was no way he was going to screw this up. When the door whisked open Miguel heard raised voices from inside Don Luis's closed office. He exited the elevator and listened.

"Ernest," he heard Don Luis say, "please."

"I demand to be heard."

"You have been heard. But the gritty business of selecting company members has been concluded."

Miguel's ears pricked up. Sounded like his position had been challenged.

"Did you video each candidate as I requested?"

"Not exactly, but there is good news," Don Luis enthused. "The new members are certain to be credits to the company. A *tanguera* as fresh and lithe as spring and, as I told you, a solid young man with the soul of an old *milonguero*."

Miguel wanted to scream with joy. He punched the air, biting his lip to keep silent.

"So I'm being dismissed like a nonentity."

"Ernest, the company management is delighted to have access to your dance talents but is in no way in need of your directorial expertise."

"Well, when I'm *primo bailarino*, I expect—"

"When you are, we shall have a different conversation."

Miguel heard the door handle rattle. He could not imagine encountering this Dr. Wagner, coming from such a heated discussion. He would have to thank Don Luis later. Quickly, he darted around the corner, and found an interior stairwell. He descended at once, hardly paying attention to his footfalls. He scampered face to face with Jean-Luc, heading up the private staircase.

"*Perdón*," Miguel said, startled. "I didn't expect to find someone here."

"I, um, is there a men's room up there?" Jean-Luc asked. "I usually use the one by the cantina." He forced a smile.

Miguel noted the nice face Jean-Luc was making, but found his eyes ice cold. "Maybe the closest is in the *tangueros'* lounge, downstairs," Miguel replied.

"Thanks," Jean-Luc said, turning back, rushing down.

* * *

Aggie Jacobs practiced *ochos*, figure eights, in the fishbowl, a glass-enclosed practice floor. She used a ballet bar as her partner. They were well acquainted. In fact, she often considered that self-service was her specialty. While both forward and backward *ochos* enable ladies to show off the swiveling sensuality of their hips, they were also important as links and transitions into and from various figures. They were essential elements of Argentine tango whose perfection could not be overlooked.

She saw Miguel in the mirror, walking past the fishbowl, peering in. The tango music playing softly in the background seemed to swell. She waved. He opened the door and entered.

"Ready for rehearsal number one?" Aggie chirped.

"We will see very soon."

"I really enjoyed our tango yesterday. It was moving, authentic."

"Me, too. Much nicer than the milonga." His smile turned upside down.

"The milonga wasn't bad," she said. "All things considered: new partner with whom you'd never danced, new studio, and the pressure of all eyes on you."

"Does it bother you when all their eyes are on you?"

"It's exciting, but a little nerve-racking, I guess." Aggie blushed.

Intensity possessed Miguel as he said, "Take the energy from spectators: the good, bad, in-between. Let it energize you to reach a higher level."

"Is that what you do?"

"I try. Usually it works; unless they hit me when throwing things. That disturbs my balance," he said, laughing and wobbling on one foot.

For the first time, Aggie noticed the honesty of Miguel's smile, the whiteness of his teeth against his lightly colored, smooth skin. And then she was mesmerized by his splendid eyes. She gazed at them, disappearing for an instant into the hazel parts, driving deeper into the green flecks.

"Shall we dance, to warm up?" Miguel asked, reassuming his perfect posture. "This music is nice, no. Maestro Troilo's classic, 'Soñar y Nada Más.'"

"*¿Porque no?* er, why not?" she teased.

Miguel's facial expression assumed the semi-serious mask of social tango before he caressed Aggie lightly. He exhaled and began to subtly shift her weight from side to side, wrapping his right arm farther around her slender back, their torsos approaching.

Aggie could feel her breath quickening, although she attempted to relax and be supple. Tension built in her spine and her legs. Finally even her neck was stiff and unyielding. "Just a minute," she said, relinquishing the embrace and stepping back.

"Something is the matter. Is too close for you?"

"No, the embrace was fine," she said, adjusting her skirt. "I just, um, I think I'm a little nervous, maybe." Her eyes found the floor and she felt like smacking herself.

"Nervous? Is just you and me in this little room." He smiled kindly. "There are no prying eyes. Not even *el custodio* is mopping close by."

Aggie was relieved that Miguel had missed the point completely.

"We go slowly. No tricky steps," he promised. "Embracing and walking, like the old *milongueros* on La Avenida Corrientes, seventy-five years ago in Buenos Aires."

They embraced and began to move through space in perfect synchronicity. The clarity of Miguel's lead, the intention with which he endowed each minute movement, was reassuring. They walked, *caminar*, and then he led backward *ochos*. Aggie could feel her breasts scrubbing against his protruding chest. Her nipples hardened and her eyes closed. She passed again, arching her back to bring her torso closer to him. Her forehead tilted forward and lightly touched his forehead. She knew it was bad form, but the music sprang to life, filling her soul, nearly bursting open her tender heart.

How she wanted to grasp the nape of his neck and run her fingers down its length, show him how she felt. The hair on her arms tingled. She pressed herself against him and felt his right arm, which encircled her completely now, snug tighter. She relaxed her lateral muscles, filling his cupped fingers with her back. The embrace felt relaxed yet secure. So intimate, as though they were one. Aggie arched her sternum, fully opening her chest, giving herself to Miguel. Suddenly he stopped. She had missed the song's punctuated conclusion, her head thrust backward and eyes shut tight in tango ecstasy.

Chaz poked his head inside the door. "Well, looks like you two have danced together for ages. I hope you dance that fluidly and passionately with your new partners. The public loves that bullshit look of authentic tango bliss."

Aggie was embarrassed to be caught having a tangasm. She'd had them a couple of times in clubs at two A.M., but never, ever at rehearsal. And she'd never before felt like a tango whore, but maybe it was high time.

CHAPTER 17

THE MAIN FLOOR BUZZED with dancing and dissention, even before the rehearsal began. Miguel watched and listened to the familiar scene. Frowning and carping seemed to be a part of the creative process. Getting it right. Honing it to be better. He would be out there soon, doing the same thing.

His mind suddenly went into overdrive, thinking the killer was there. He could feel it. How much intuition or gut feeling was sufficient to end someone's life? He needed time to observe everyone and to build a case. Proof is what he wanted most. Hopefully his newly acquired spyware would yield that fruit.

Miguel took particular interest in Chaz, who was strutting, observing, instructing. He barked, "Tony, the floor, the floor. Go into it and she won't feel heavy."

"It's like dancing with a hundred-pound sack of potatoes."

"*Ratoncito*," fired his partner, turning away, crossing her arms. She emitted a mousy squeak, reinforcing her claim.

Chaz called out to a couple across the room, locked in a contortionist's pose. They admired themselves in a ceiling-high mirror. Miguel hardly recognized El Primitivo, his ebony curls parted in the middle of his head and pulled into a tight ponytail.

"What do you want?" El Primitivo asked. "We nearly perfected that line."

"I apologize. I'd like for you to dance with Aggie Jacobs. She's local. Maybe you know her." He motioned for Aggie to come over.

Miguel grinned to himself, thinking the new girl was going to be subjected to candombe, the worst dance. He got a big surprise, hearing Chaz say, "Ingrid, show Miguel your milonga routine, please." So the new guy is in the same boat!

"Hello, Miguel. I'm Ingrid."

"Hi, Ingrid." Miguel smiled. "So, you like to dance the milonga?"

"Not really, but I guess that's what we'll be paid to do."

"But maybe we can have some fun. Jazz it up here and there."

She continued, "Roberto and I perfected a routine last year for the show."

"Roberto?"

"Moved to San Francisco when the show was cancelled. You're his replacement."

"And the music?"

"'El Choclo'. I danced it all over BA when I was a girl playing with tango on the side." Her chin rose ever so slightly, adding, "While studying ballet at Teatro Colón."

Miguel tried to appear impressed, hiding his despair at having to dance milonga with a ballerina—a failed ballerina. He asked, "Should we get some music to our speakers and try a milonga, to feel our connection?"

"There's a video of a perfect performance on the studio's computer system. You can watch it in the kiosk by the cantina."

"Didn't Chaz say—"

"He said to show you the routine. There's no room to dance."

Suddenly, Ingrid winced and grabbed her upper thigh. "My psoas major. Better stretch it out." She turned and floated toward the wall-mounted ballet bar.

Miguel headed to the cantina. He nearly bumped into Candy, entering.

She asked, "Burned out on milonga already?"

"My partner prefers a wooden rail," he said, shrugging.

"I know her lame routine. Come on, I'll teach you."

"Where?"

"There's plenty of room." She smiled. "I thought you *Portenõs* could dance tango on four tiles of a crowded floor."

"On one at midnight! But not a whole routine."

Chaz chided Miguel for disobeying his command to dance with Ingrid. So dance they did. By the five o'clock break, Miguel was disgusted and tired. He wet his handkerchief and squeezed out the excess water before seeking a quiet place to drape it over his forehead. He slumped on a *banco* away from the main floor, bottle of cold water in hand. He took a sip, considering this was the big-top of Don Luis's tango circus. Miguel sensed motion and whisked away the cloth from his eyes. Don Luis sat inert in front of him, his keen eyes and expressive face a mass of florid flesh.

"Don Luis, something is wrong? Can I help you?"

"Yes, and possibly yes." He sighed. "I was hoping to speak with you privately after rehearsal, but I'm afraid—"

"Please, tell me what's wrong?"

"Oh, a late night. And a small problem." He managed a smile, asking, "May we meet for luncheon tomorrow? My treat."

"With pleasure."

"Leave your address for me up front. I'll pick you up at eleven. And bring your pack. We'll come directly to the studio for rehearsal."

"If you like," Miguel stuttered, "I can meet you somewhere."

"Heavens no. And do take care, my boy." He added, *sotto voce*, "There's more at stake than you know."

With that, Don Luis turned away his chair and slowly wheeled himself toward Kemal, who raced up, taking the handles and the helm.

Miguel sat slumped, knees apart, wondering what to do. He was determined to maintain a certain amount of privacy, hopefully without offending his employer. Lost in thought, he didn't notice Aggie's arrival, *café cortado* in hand.

"Thinking great thoughts? Should I not interrupt?"

Miguel dabbed his face with the wilted handkerchief, saying, "Please do."

"I stole a peek at your milonga. It's completely different from your tango." Aggie brushed a curl from her face. "You're deep in the floor. Earthy as I've ever seen."

"Is not a difficult routine."

"I was thinking," she sipped, squirmed, "maybe you could teach me milonga?"

"Maestros teach, I just dance."

"What you said in the practice room was insightful."

"Was nothing."

"Then I won't call it teaching." Aggie winked slyly. "Maybe before rehearsal, you could make a comment or two."

"Well, maybe Friday."

"The fishbowl, at two?"

"You really want to dance milonga?" Miguel's brows knit together when he said, "Milonga sounds playful, but it is a serious business. Is like a knife fight, you know."

Aggie recoiled, her coffee cup rattled in its saucer.

His voice lowered in pitch and his speech slowed. "The real *milonga* is low and quick . . . and very, very dangerous. Is like a fight with the knife, and one partner is always killed."

CHAPTER 18

How many ways could Miguel say that he was sorry for everything that had happened and that he prayed daily for his mother's recovery? He was wiped out from jet lag and rehearsal, but sitting in the computer kiosk afterward, Miguel was trying his best to concentrate. He typed the message slowly and carefully, using the studio's communal computer. This was not a throwaway text. This was his most visible form of moral support for his dying mother. He wondered if his communications—or his prayers, for that matter—had any impact at all. And if she were still drifting in and out of consciousness, she might have no idea who he was. Miguel wondered why as humans we are tasked to place so much faith in the unseen, the unheard, the unwitnessed, when the disappointments from doing so are often visible. It's as though the universe rubs our noses in our failed faith.

His fingers fell dumb at the keyboard. Perhaps the message would arrive too late. Miguel sighed and ran his hands over his hair, before resting his forehead heavily in his palms. It had been a long, unsatisfactory afternoon spent learning Ingrid's milonga routine. He raised his chin and looked around the kiosk. Like everything else, it was a bit too perfect. The equipment, lighting, seating, all top drawer. He fluttered the collar of his damp white shirt, fanning air-conditioned breeze that cooled his chest. He bent to the keyboard, hurriedly finishing the message. Another unsatisfactory event complete.

Miguel sat listening to the silence. He wanted to understand its meaning. Dancing the silence was the pinnacle of tango, according to Maestro Gavito. The croon of tango that had permeated the air for the previous six hours had hushed, as had the gnaw of the coffee grinder's burr nearby in the cantina. If someone were working out in the exercise room, and he doubted that very much, or taking a relaxing steam, more likely, and decided to check e-mail before leaving, he could hear them approaching on the polished wooden floors. It was time for him to act.

Miguel withdrew his backpack from under the table. He unzipped it and plumbed the bottom for an opaque plastic bag. From the bag he removed a tiny flashlight and a small plastic cylinder, a little black pinky with electronic connectors on each end. There had been two options for him to keep tabs on his tango colleagues' computer use, software or hardware. The little plug that he admired was the latter. While it could be spotted by someone checking out the CPU, located underneath the glossy tabletop, it had the advantage of not being detectable by a computer's spyware detection software, common on newer machines. Besides, who in the glitzy confines of Don Luis's tango circus would be crawling around on the floor looking at a CPU? Who but him?

He snagged a tissue from the desktop container and polished the little gem, removing his fingerprints, just in case. Next, he energized the penlight and stuck it in his mouth, before squatting low and thrusting his head underneath the tabletop. He observed a container of computer cables and odds and ends, all tidy and neat, shoved back into a—gasp!—dusty back corner. He half-smiled, causing the light to skew before he hefted the CPU, turning its back panel toward him, exposing communications ports and power connections. He located the keyboard's cable and traced it to the CPU's input and immediately dropped the penlight from his gaping mouth.

Miguel stared into the darkness, his heart racing. There was already a keylogger in the circuit. Who indeed would be prowling around underneath a finely polished computer desktop, seeking information on the company's computer use? Was that a footfall? Miguel banged his head on the table's undersurface and leapt up into the comfy chair, massaging his bruised head and cursing under his breath. He pretended to study the blank screen and began to type gibberish on the keyboard, wishing that he'd never used it to write to his mother. He stopped. Jibberish could draw someone's attention to his usage, when examined. He listened. Nothing. Miguel waited a long time before continuing.

He eyed the keyboard, staring intently at the thin, gray cable that emanated from its side and snaked down a tidy hole, lined by a rubber grommet, located in the far reaches of the tabletop. Curious, Miguel turned the keyboard around and observed an output on the opposite side, a convenience feature of a pricey product. He nodded, before ducking under the table, grasping his penlight and going hunting in the computer cable snake pit, a term of art for stagehands. Light in mouth, he connected one end of the cable to the keystroke recorder and lodged it away from the CPU, between the tabletop and the fabric-covered partition it abutted. Before coming up for air, Miguel forced the cable connector up through the cable penetration hole in the tabletop. He parted the cheap plastic runner, used to gather all of the cables coming up through the table, and embedded the new grey one deep inside the bundle. Finally, he connected the cable to the unused side of the keyboard and tucked it around its margins.

Miguel launched Google Maps and searched the Flatbush neighborhood of Brooklyn. He scribbled the address of the Travel Inn on a notepad and logged off immediately, without researching anything on the computer's hard disk. He would save that for later, not directly after having sent email from his address. Miguel reminded himself that every single keystroke was being recorded, and not only by him.

CHAPTER 19

INTENTION IN EVERY STEP, as though on the dance floor, Miguel strode from the subway station toward the Fontaine Bleu Hotel's entrance. It was not a neighborhood for sauntering. The rain had stopped and the air was acrid, metallic, from the exhaust of cars, grease from ovens, probably from chemicals volatilized in meth kitchens. Puddles on the pavement of his new home-away-from-home reflected the unnatural bluish light cascading from a streetlamp and the yellowish headlights of passing junkers.

When moving through a city in the evening, walking with intention, as though you know exactly where you are going, was key. He understood that when dancing *el tango*, your partner feels more secure believing that you know where the two of you are going and that you are confident to get there. Miguel supposed that humans are wired to respect focus.

Across the dimly lit street leading to Sarge's dive bar, the outdated neon flickered depressingly. Miguel recalled El Primitivo's erratic entrance onto the rutted dirt trail and wondered what he was up to in such a place. He had actually felt relief when El Primitivo disappeared immediately after the rehearsal earlier tonight. Raindrops began to fall. Dense air. Damp wind slapped Miguel's face.

He tucked his chin and hurried into the hotel's dark entrance, as welcoming as a dank cave on a blustery winter's night.

There was no sign advertising the hotel's nightspot, so Miguel followed his nose and the noise around the front desk. He would have a congratulatory beer on making the company and a bite to eat. Maybe hold a strategy session with himself. The small detail of discovering another spy in the company needed some thought.

He passed the front desk and saw glossy black hair cascading down a slim back, as though pointing toward too-tight leather jeans. His mind on other things, Miguel didn't tarry, but followed a short, darkened corridor to the bar's entrance.

Burnt cooking oil and stale whiskey replaced the metallic smell from the street. Longshoremen or union roustabouts laughed uproariously, swilling beer as their heads flew back, exposing snaggletooth grins. He imagined they were planning new capers, certainly recalling old ones. Miguel approached an unkempt barman wiping with his spotted white apron the interior of a scratch-laden tumbler. The man looked blankly at him. Maybe he should take a look inside Sarge's? It was good enough for El Primitivo, and he drove a supercar. It wasn't like the health inspector was going to shutter this place tonight. Tomorrow, maybe. Miguel exited briskly.

"Was it something I said?" A soft voice asked in accented English. "Or maybe our bar's too cool for you?"

Miguel turned to find the desk clerk standing in the shadows. "Ah, no," he said.

She stepped forward and fixed her doe-eyed gaze on him. A bright smile lightened her face. She stood tall—all five feet of her—holding a thin sheaf of papers. She wore a cut-lace top, sporting an intricate pattern, resembling leaves floating on her taut torso. When she brushed back one side of her hair, draping it over her shoulder, she revealed just sufficient shape to win accolades in Brazil.

"Beer," Miguel blurted, "I was thinking to have one." A throaty roar from the bar filled the hallway.

"Drink there, you get them. Drink here," she gestured toward a corner grouping of chairs, "you get me." Her smile widened, demonstrating a mouth full of small teeth, set off by flawless olive-colored skin.

"Sounds good."

The young woman turned and disappeared around a corner. Miguel considered that it was not her small stature or hair, blacker than black, or even her dusky skin that set her apart from BA's leggy *porteñas*. One thing seemed clear, the girl was the polar opposite of his ex, Patricia, who was tall and slender with light skin and hair. This young woman's look was reminiscent of the other side of *los Andes*, perhaps Chile.

But of all the dancers in BA, the truest, Geraldine, looked like her. Geraldine was not, and had never been, a willowy *bailarína* in a ballet company. She was, and had always been, an earthy *tanguera*. But Aggie, leggy and lean as she was, had felt to him like a *porteña*. Quivering, subtle, and fragile, while capable, confident, and expressive. The best of both worlds; the woman-child. He shook his head, knowing that he had to forget her. Miguel could not risk corrupting his resolve with real intimacy.

The clerk escorted him to a corner seat. She said, "I'll call a waitress for you. You want beer right away?"

He adjusted his position, breaking eye contact. "Yes, please."

"How much body do you like?"

Miguel's eyes panned her from head to toe, half joking.

She relaxed her weight onto a single curvaceous thigh as he proceeded.

He looked her in the eyes and said, "The beer, maybe not too strong."

"My name's Heather. Let me know if you want anything else."

Miguel's head skewed, saying, "Pleased to meet you . . . Heather."

She tensed, her tanned cheeks turning ruddy. "It's my professional name."

"Fine."

"*Me llamo Ina Gonzales*," she confessed. "But please call me Heather."

"*Me llamo Miguel Angel*," he said, smiling genuinely. "Please call me Miguel."

"Calling you *Angel* would be *un poco mucho*." Heather turned away, smirking.

Miguel intuited that she was clever and possibly fearless. Heather had probably inherited the former and no doubt earned the latter. He cast down his eyes to the tabletop, followed a rough cut set of initials with a slender finger. She was probably the opposite of Patricia, a spoiled society brat. Patricia had inherited her handsome father's looks and mediocre brain. He was hardly capable of performing as a government functionary and counting her mother's abundant money.

A waitress brought a pale ale, menu, and setup, complete with placemat. A wink at civilization, he assumed. The tenderloin steak called out to him from the menu, *bife de lomo* it was called in Argentina. But it was twice the price of meat in BA, and he had to be careful with his money. If he were terminated from the dance company, then he would have to depend solely on his cash on hand. A fontina cheese sandwich and fries cost $14.95. He assumed that in the United States, fontina was very precious.

Heather interrupted Miguel's thoughts, asking, "What do you think?"

"Maybe just the beer."

She exhaled forcefully. "The ribeye's not bad."

Ribeye. Miguel thought of it as the *ojo de bife*, one of the tenderest muscles of the cow. He'd parted out thousands of them at the plant. He slid his hands under the table. His knuckles tightened and his fingers involuntary contracted. He questioned whether it was the memory of the blood of beast or man? He just wanted to forget that his hands had been stained by both.

"Everything is okay?" she asked.

"Sure. The turkey sandwich sounds tasty." For $18.95 it should be, he thought.

Her tucked chin and widened eyes seemed to suggest disapproval.

"Even Argentines get tired of beef sometimes."

"Huh, Puerto Ricans never tire of rice and beans." Her face creased harshly. "Another good reason to be here."

He sipped his beer.

She asked, "Good?"

Looking up at her, he self-consciously wiped foam from his upper lip and nodded.

Heather seemed to be lost in his eyes. She blinked and turned to go.

Miguel became lost in his thoughts, wondering who was monitoring the studio's computer. Don Luis was the most likely candidate. After all, it was his device. But there were easier ways for him to do it. He wouldn't need a keylogger.

Soon, a waitress brought Miguel's food. The turkey was dry and the bread stale, so he cast off the bun and slathered coarse-grain mustard on the meat. He glanced at his phone. Still early for BA. But he felt tired from his travels and the pressure of rehearsal.

Heather sauntered by a while later. "Dessert, coffee?"

He nodded and patted his stomach, as flat and firm as a board.

"Showing off?"

"I'm a dancer. It's not good to be too heavy on the floor."

Heather's cheerful cheeks paled and her lips turned down at the corners. "I danced in some music videos," she said, "for the rapper Killshot. Know him?"

Miguel shrugged and said, "*Soy milonguero del tango Argentino.*"

"*Ah, sí, el tango,*" she said, her eyes again shiny. She spoke rapidly, "*Sabia que tu no eres un caco.*"

"Sorry, English, please. I must improve it for my new job."

"Oh yeah, me too, for acting." She raised her chin slightly.

"You just said that you knew I'm not a caco."

"Gangsta."

He laughed quietly and shook his head, closing his eyes in surprise. He opened them to find two men in his peripheral view. They stopped near the far side of the front desk, illuminated by dingy pools of overhead light. One was a tall, skinny board, the other a fireplug. Both wore hats, dark glasses, and long black coats, even though it was still warm outside. Skinny panned slowly from side to side, without removing his moonglasses. Pudgy lifted his glasses onto his forehead and slewed his eyes rapidly. He appeared to sniff the air, like a feral cat, as though he could smell trouble. Miguel had seen plenty of the type in La Boca. Heads too hard to crack open; skin too leathery to pierce. Better avoided.

Heather turned to see the men and gasped. "Oh, my agent. Gotta go." She turned and hurried away, hair whipping her back like a lash.

Miguel drummed the scuffed tabletop with his fingers. From the corner of his eye he observed Heather addressing the stocky man. He stood with his feet apart, arms folded on his up-thrust chest. His chin jutted forward aggressively, like a vicious dog. Heather waved her hands and spoke rapidly, finally resting her hands on her hips.

The man leaned toward her and poked his stubby finger in her face. Miguel turned away to admire the dusty overhead lamp fixture and faded plastic chair upholstery of the grouping where he sat. He tried not to, but couldn't help training his eyes on the chubby man, who had grasped Heather's arm and was nodding menacingly. Miguel closed his eyes, thinking his plate of revenge was overly full. He needed no more violence. Everyone had problems; obviously, Heather had hers. He peeked and saw the man had drawn back his fist. Heather stood defiant.

CHAPTER 20

KICKING OFF HER FLATS at the front door, Aggie Jacobs raced to the kitchen to find a heaping plate of pasta and red sauce awaiting her in the warmer. It smelled delicious. She dived in. Halfway through her feeding frenzy, footsteps sounded on the living room's smooth maple wood floor. She recognized the gait.

"Lookie here," MoJo said, "my favorite daughter, returned from dancing the day and night away." He walked over to her, scaled a few ribs. "What's this, no meat?"

Aggie shook her head, still chewing.

"You're not, you know, puking up your food like them sick models?"

"Not me, Pop. I love mom's cooking too much to part with it like that." Poking his paunch, she added, "But maybe you should consider it."

Aggie watched her father peer off into space, a rare reflective moment. He was not an intellectual by any means. But he was sharp, in business, especially. Used to say his cousin Benny taught him everything. Aggie was pretty sure he was a fictitious person, but she seemed to recall a man known as Uncle Benny or Cousin Benny when she was a child. Her dad looked glum, so she said, "Tell me about Cousin Benny."

Just a neighbor." MoJo shrugged. "You the star of that outfit yet?"

"There are some really good dancers. My first partner was obsessed with perfection. I knew him from ballroom. Maybe he just can't handle criticism. The guy from Argentina, on the other hand," her fork fell lax, "there's something about him." She fell silent, then added, "Dignity or something."

"So, what's this kid's name?"

"Miguel something."

"Don't you think you should know some guy's name before you go all goey over him? I mean, who knows, he may be one of Argentina's most wanted."

"He sure is." She beamed.

"Well, he may not even be from Argentina. Maybe he's on the lamb, you know. Like Uncle Benny used to tell people he got all them scars on his face being attacked by lions when he was a doctor in Africa. You just never—"

"Got it." She stood up straight. "He's the most gentleman-like, sincere, intense. . . ." She sighed. "And his last name is not Jacobi or Jacobs or Jacobstein."

"Whoa, where's that coming from? I said nothing about a particular last name."

"Right, Pops, it's a subtle thing I've noticed my entire life. Like if you hear something enough or if you say it a million times, then it's supposed to become true."

"We're your family and want the best for you." He rolled a hand. "One day you'll be a doctor and have a bunch kids and you'll understand."

Aggie watched MoJo growing more excited. She figured soon he'd be dancing and singing about when she's a gray ol' *bubbie*. "You want the best for me, but what a tragedy it would be if I didn't end up with a nice Jewish boy from Brooklyn, right."

He looked shell-shocked for an instant.

"No matter who I marry, my kids will still be Jewish. It comes from the mother."

"*Oy vay*!" MoJo viced his head between his hands. "Your mother and you, the both a yous couldn't cut a deal for day-old bagels with a blind baker."

"Pfff."

Pinching up a hairy patch of weathered skin on his forearm, he said, "And see this skin and this *schnoz*, this is the real thing. Your mother's whole family looks like Prince Charles's cousins. Like you. You could draw blood with a nose that skinny."

"If you're saying mom's not as Jewish as you because she's Sephardic—"

"Not a hook on the bunch of them. And you, all starry-eyed over a tango bum."

"Could you just have some faith in me."

"I got faith in you, Naomi girl." MoJo's eyes glittered and he said, "Maybe this Miguel would like to teach me some tango. The guy could use extra dough, unless he makes a whole lot more than you ever did dancing."

"Oh no, Pops!" Aggie said in amazement. "I'm not even sure he'll teach me."

"I thought that was how these studios make it. Bunch a people see the dancers and want to take lessons. The house gets a hefty cut. Who's this old guy running the game?"

"Don Luis de Granada," Aggie said with a flourish.

"That neighborhood where he's put his studio costs a fortune. Betcha he's hot for a few extra shekels. I'll go see Don tomorrow. Do a deal."

"Dad, that's crazy. Everyone's working hard on the new show. And from the looks of the place, Don Luis isn't going to be out panhandling anytime soon."

He wagged a finger. "Appearances are real tricky."

"All right, Pops, I'm convinced. Now, I've got to shower." Heading up the stairs Aggie tried to envision Don Luis panhandling in front of his tango palace on the Upper East Side. No way. She giggled thinking of her dad . . . totally *Meshugga*.

CHAPTER 21

Miguel's pulse raced. He watched the stocky man's drawn fist, ready to destroy Heather's beautiful smile, knocking out her pearly white teeth with one punch. Miguel slid his right hand toward his back pocket. Nothing. He eyed his pack, sitting zipped on the floor. His plate looked like a battleground. The serrated blade of his dinner knife dripped yellowish mustard like blood. He grasped the cracked wooden handle and pinched the bloody blade with his napkin, drawing it through. Then he stashed the weapon in his back pocket and rose, clearing his throat loudly. Both men turned to glare at him.

A couple of steps forward; Miguel felt his heart rate accelerate. Heather turned and faced him, her eyes wide with warning. He approached closer and the man's hand fell to his side. His face distorted into a snarl. The accomplice pulled back his coat, revealing a handgun that reflected a dull incandescent glint. They smelled like they hadn't bathed in weeks or like they worked in a brimstone refinery. Miguel said, "Excuse me, miss, I asked for my check a while ago. Could you please see what is the problem?"

"Go see yourself," the shorter man spit, jerking his head toward the hall.

Miguel did not move. He leveled his gaze at the man.

Heather wrenched away from the man's grasp and turned. From the scant cleavage of her forested bosom, she produced a cache of folded bills. She thrust them forward. "*Aqui, Gordo.*"

He snatched away the money with purple-tinted fingers as quickly as a cobra strikes. Heather strode toward the darkened hallway. Gordo elbowed his cohort; the coat dropped closed. Gordo ticked cautious glances in all directions, taking extra time to focus on Miguel, who stood relaxed. Gordo raised his hand, formed it into a make-believe pistol, and mouthed, "Bang."

Miguel managed not to flinch. It was a great bluff, he thought, watching the pair exit. He retook his seat and placed the knife in his plate. Heather brought his check and a tiny cup of espresso. She faked a smile, setting the cup on the table with a shaky hand, spilling half into the saucer. Miguel covered her trembling hand with his. Their eyes met. Moments later he left fifty dollars on the table and headed up to his room, feeling right at home. There was little difference in the human tragedies of a maligned little port *barrio* like La Boca and a bad neighborhood in the Big Apple.

Miguel pushed through the rickety door to his no-tell hotel room. He dropped his pack to the floor with a thud. Atmosphere, close; scent, musty. He shook off the place's dismal vibe and removed his shirt. He hung it on the door handle, using a misshapen metal hanger. Then he opened the pack and withdrew his dancing shoes and blade. He tossed the knife onto the bed and carried the shoes to the window. Although far from new, they were precious. Like old friends that never let him down.

At the risk of having to battle mosquitos again, he cracked open the window and thrust his face toward it. Ah, not so fresh air from the street. Better than the stale room. He put his shoes on the windowsill to freshen them up and noted the glow of a faded neon sign across the street.

He collapsed onto the bed. His heart ached. As if Miguel's grief and longing had settled deep inside, in spite of his efforts to harden himself against the pain. So much for what was supposed to be his improved, stony heart. No denying it, he missed his family, his city, his life, his former life. This was his new so-called life.

In the bathroom, over a stained basin, Miguel washed his face. He glanced in the cracked mirror, wondering who that faithless old man leering back at him was. And how did he get here? Suddenly, El Primitivo's face appeared in the mirror. He laughed at Miguel. It was he who actually had chosen this hellhole. Miguel knew there were better low-cost accommodations around New York City. Why here, of all places? He wondered what El Primitivo was up to in this neighborhood. Miguel grabbed a towel from the rusty rack. The cloth smelled like chlorine. Better than the alternative, he thought, burying his face in it, trying to wipe away his dread.

Miguel sloughed off his trousers and folded them over a nearby chair's back, thinking that again today he had failed to call or even email home. And what was the use now? His mother was probably asleep or unconscious. And if they actually spoke? He recalled his last phone conversation with his sister. She had said, "It's urgent! We have to talk. Please come!" He had asked her just to tell him on the phone. She had refused. What was he to do, jump on a plane every time there was a news flash from New York? It would have been his last opportunity to see her. He exhaled forcefully. Maybe he should have come. At least he had told her that he loved and missed her—

He vowed to try and make contact with his mother tomorrow. Miguel closed his eyes to rest, but visions of his childhood in Rosario played in his head like grainy homemade movies. He squeezed his eyelids together tighter. Still he saw his mother caressing his face, kissing him. He saw his sister's awkward smile, from under mother's raised arm. A portrait of simplicity and love, just like the photo in his suitcase.

An odd family? For sure. Outcasts? Not really. Their small textile company hummed along. Sometimes Miguel was amazed that the Spanish market for Argentine bric-a-brac never wavered. His mother and cousins created no masterpieces, but payment for their wares was certain. Family life had a veneer of happiness, even though Miguel was *fatherless*, owing to an unfortunate episode that his mother never discussed. According to his cousins, it was a matter of theft. But whatever the truth, his father had to leave Argentina in the middle of the night, and was never heard from again.

Still, Miguel was not without father figures. Maestro Paiva, creator of the majestic tango arch, and Esteban Prafil, a boat captain on the run from an unjust government, a survivor of the dirty war, were good men. All in all it had been more real than his life of stages, international travel, and now tragedy, Natalia's death. And so much finer than his unreal life in New York, the sole purpose of which was to track down her killer.

A flood of grief washed over him. Miguel clamped down hard on his emotions. And then, in his mind's eye he saw Aggie's face: its delicate structure, determined eyes. He had felt her pent-up sensuality dying to escape, desperate to find a vessel to fill with her passion. To overflowing, he imagined. She was too good, too pure. Perhaps she would forget performance tango and find a real life. He hoped so.

"Knock it off, fercrissakes!" resounded a voice from the other side of the paper-thin wall. "Fuck you!" sounded a muted reply.

Miguel clutched his blade and listened for escalation. Squeezing the handle, he recognized that he must numb his feelings and not release his emotions until he had watched someone, who desperately deserved it, die by his own hand.

Lights out, time passed. Miguel tossed. It was hot and his room's air conditioner did not work. He sprang up and marched toward the window. Down in the street, the neon sign advertising Sarge's blinked—or was that a wink? He forced the window open wider and noticed an array of LED brake lights, like those on El Primitivo's hot car, turn into the dirt road leading to the bar. Did he go there nightly? What was up with the place? Miguel paused to consider his friend El Primitivo—his cousin, Miguel Andro's friend in reality. Definitely strange, but strange enough to be the killer? Miguel's investigation of company members had to begin with someone. He spun from the window and grabbed his trousers.

CHAPTER 22

MIGUEL GRASPED Sarge's grimy door handle. He paused and felt for his new blade before pushing inside. He tracked the wall, not getting too close to avoid being scratched by peeling paint. His eyes adjusted gradually to the low-light, smoky den. It must be against the law in New York to smoke inside a place of business. Miguel assumed places of funny business were exempt. Even the milongas of Buenos Aires for years had been smoke-free. It had been a saving grace, enabled him to quit. Miguel's eyes watered, scanning the room. He didn't recognize anyone in particular, but he'd seen them all: coworkers at the meat packing plant, *vatos* at the milongas, thieves lying in wait in the shadows of La Boca. So far, no gay tango dancers.

Speakers near the pool tables blared Tito Puente's music. Miguel liked the hot Caribbean vibe but wanted to be away from them. He strained to see a vacant two-top near the back corner. A deathtrap in the event of trouble. And Miguel assumed the place saw a lot of that. He approached the bar and ordered a beer from a dull-eyed, half-dressed girl. Miguel nodded thanks and slugged warm suds.

Although midweek, the place was nearly full. It struck Miguel as a waiting room for the Caribbean penal system. He rubbed the chipped mug's greasy surface, thankful the alcohol would kill the germs. Turned and eyed a table where a chunky man with slicked-back black hair wearing a sports coat, completely out of place, sat with others. The guy's tall ears reminded him of a rabbit, a *conejo.* Apparently he had not gotten the memo that this *used to be* an Italian neighborhood. Miguel did a double take and recognized El Primitivo half-hidden behind the guy's outstretched arm, his finger poking toward the face of a man of color. Miguel made for the wall and wended his way toward a vacant table within ear- and eye-shot. From there he saw that although *el Conejo* looked funny, his expression was not one of amusement. Miguel heard him preaching about wanting stuff of higher purity, the highest on the East Coast. He said that calling it Purple Passion was a good marketing *shtick*, but he stressed that maximum purity was key.

The man replied in vulgar terms, in Puerto Rican slang, that he was doing his best. Miguel had danced two years earlier at a fancy Puerto Rican resort. He recalled the local's accents and peculiar slang. *El Conejo* raised his voice. Miguel froze when he heard the warning: "Gordo, you're about to get that smart mouth stuffed with something you're gonna miss."

"*¡Bugarrón!*" A homophobic slur from across the room grabbed Miguel's attention. The crack of wood set him on his guard. He slewed around his head to face the action. A pair of threadbare men went at it in the corner. One was stretched across a pool table with the other trying to choke him with a broken cue stick. A third restrained the aggressor, holding him back, grimacing. No one else seemed to notice or to care. Typical *barrio* rage, they may have thought.

Miguel closed his eyes to block out the brutal scene. And then a lamentable facet of tango exhibitions overtook his mind. Desperate immigrants lashing out at one another was an oft-romanticized element of the beginnings of tango. Every tango show had the obligatory barroom brawl number, complete with macho men in striped suits, wearing fedoras and drinking heavily. They flirted with loose ladies, who inevitably fomented trouble among them, probably trying to experience some sense of self-worth.

Miguel had to look. He glanced toward the pool table fracas. The pitiable faces represented their grim reality, and it was nothing like tango show depictions. No champagne glasses, suits, sexy dresses, and certainly no silk stockings. These ragged men of color acted out their rage on each other in reaction to loneliness and lowliness. That was the kinship this place shared with the birth of tango.

Suddenly he felt the heart-wrenching disenfranchisement of these people. Here in a cruel *barrio* of a huge city, they held their isolation at bay by drinking and attacking any viable target, including a best friend. Sometimes just to reaffirm their existence. They may have no family here, no loving support group to reassure them they are valued. In tango terms, theirs was a hell of desolation and endless melancholia called *¡tanguidad!*

For the first time in his life, Miguel identified with their plights of alienation and isolation. When he had danced in Europe and even as far away as Asia, he had taken the love of his family with him, nestled it safe in his heart. He was alone often, but never before had he been lonely. So much beauty lay in his past, yet his future seemed bleak. His was a hell of loss and revenge: *¡tanguidad!*

Miguel had only his miserable mission to guide him. He slugged the bitter beer, thinking he would track down Natalia's killer and destroy him, if it were the last thing he did on Earth. No silver-tongued lawyer would represent the bastard as a nice person who got a little mixed up or had a bit much to drink. No jury would deliberate his fate and decide he deserved a tidy cell with three meals a day and all the pot he could smoke. And no early parole for being a good boy and snitching a lot. The murderer's fate would be dictated by old-world justice. A man receiving a just sentence for pure evil. It was true that revenge would not bring Natalia back. But her soul hopefully would rest more easily once avenged. Miguel knew that his soul would, even if it were required of him in the act.

Miguel heard El Primitivo laugh and say, "I'm tellin' ya, the old man loves him." Miguel wondered if he was being discussed. *El Conejo* said, "I wonder if Big Benny knows who this kid really is?" Then another person whose back was to Miguel said, in thickly accented English, "I agree. The old man's got a thing for him. I saw it."

Miguel recoiled.

The man continued, "He may be useful to me. So don't hurt him . . . for now."

Miguel stared disbelieving. This was serious. He drained the beer, beginning to understand that he was mixed up with some deceit he knew nothing about. It was pretty clear that El Primitivo was not Natalia's killer, but his cohorts could be lethal.

Miguel sneaked a peek and saw the rabbit slam down his glass hard on to the table. He asked, "You running this show now?" Then he turned to Gordo, asking, "You still here? Get the fuck out and cook me up some dynamite shit. And keep your cool. That hot head is gonna put you under."

Miguel spun the empty mug on the table, searching his brain for answers. There were none. When he turned his face back toward the distant table, hungry for more info, a bulbous belly overlaid with black leather dominated Miguel's view. The smell of rotten eggs and ammonia assaulted his nose. Rolling his eyes up, Miguel met Gordo's glare.

"Fucking cop?" Gordo asked.

"No."

"What're you doing here snooping?"

Miguel pointed to the mug. "Having a beer."

"Maybe you have your beer somewhere else."

"Maybe you mind your own business."

Gordo opened his coat, showing Miguel his nine millimeter. "Gotta problem with me?"

Miguel locked eyes with Gordo. He exhaled slowly, regulating his breath, wrapping his hand around the heavy mug. And then a couple of noisy patrons approached. A man slapped Gordo on the shoulder. Gordo yanked out the pistol and spun around angrily. The man threw up his arms and paled. His *amigos* doubled over with laughter. Miguel heard one of them ask, "*¿Tienes Purple Pasión*?" Gordo gave Miguel the stink eye, before shoving the pistol into his pants. He turned toward the exit and spoke to the couple, "*Vamos*."

The back door slammed shut. Miguel drew an easy breath. He hit the front door a moment later, feeling only slightly more soiled than when he'd entered. The sky had cleared and the breeze had died, but the air was acrid. Miguel held his breath against the stench of rancid cooking oil, mixed with the scent of burnt rubber, a by-product of meth production. He picked up the pace, contemplating his beloved tango and how it mirrored his life: a combination of the elegant and the tawdry, each battling constantly for supremacy.

CHAPTER 23

BROOKLYN'S TRAVEL INN looked pitiful to Miguel. He hustled under its dilapidated porte cochère to await Don Luis. It had been a long slog to get there. His eyes darted everywhere. It was a shabby part of town, soiled by gang-related graffiti. Still, it was better than the rattrap where he was holed up. He had El Primitivo to thank for that, and heaven only knew what else.

Miguel turned and stepped toward the hotel's constrictive circle drive, but his progress was checked by the arrival of an enormous limousine that pulled up right next to him. Gleaming silver and black paint reflected the morning sun like a giant, bug-eyed penguin, a wealthy penguin. Really, this car at this dump. The limo stopped at the curb. Miguel stepped back and turned away, only a quarter turn so that through his slanted eyes he could admire the occupants. A smallish man exited, dressed in a black suit and chauffer's cap. He rounded the car's rear and opened the door.

"Good morning, Mr. Zanotto," Kemal said. He swept his hand toward the interior.

Miguel rubbed the back of his hand, and feeling the dagger's snick he hesitated.

Don Luis craned his neck and smiled. "Do come in, Miguel."

He entered cautiously, nervous that his shoe soles would soil the pristine ivory-colored carpeting.

"Okay place?" Don Luis asked, jabbing a thumb toward the hotel.

"I don't stay here. Close by."

"Good. Back in my day this was the Quality Inn. Positively dreadful."

Miguel ignored the denigration, running his palm over the supple upholstery. "This car is really fantastic." He concentrated for a moment. "I recall in England, I saw something similar."

"Similar, perhaps, but this is American, a '33 Cadillac *Sixteen*. Like me, it's old but still goes." Don Luis chortled.

Miguel smiled and nodded, settling deeper into the luxurious leather. He was delighted to find color in Don Luis's cheeks and light in his eyes.

"There's much to know about America, much to admire," Don Luis said. "And New York is the perfect place to begin getting to know her."

It was a strain for Miguel to assimilate this aspect of his new employer, the one where he cruised the *barrio* in a chauffer-driven antique American limo.

"In fact," Don Luis continued, "there is no better place to start than here in your *hood*, as they might say in this vicinity."

Miguel looked askance at so many boarded-up windows. He felt embarrassed for the place and for being associated with it.

Don Luis eyed his watch. "It's just about lunchtime. We can pop over to Junior's for a sandwich and a tiny taste of the world's most delicious cheesecake."

"No, thank you. *Café*, perhaps."

"There'll be no time for food later," Don Luis said. "The company will convene at three." He added, "A few extra pounds on your frame wouldn't hurt."

The remark impressed Miguel not as critical but fatherly. He wondered how often Chaz had been coddled this way. Miguel really wanted to end the pleasantries and get down to business, to better understand this guy's game. And to make an initial inquiry about Natalia. He asked, "The decision on the new members is final?"

"Yes. But there is a spot of bother about that. We'll discuss it."

Miguel nodded. Dr. Wagner's bother was more like a mountain than a spot.

"Aggie and you will need to fill out a bit of paperwork for Barbara, the business manager," Don Luis said. "She will assign your computer account. She's also responsible for travel reimbursements, the building's security, things like that."

"I, um, accessed the computer last night," Miguel said timidly, cutting his eyes to gather Don Luis expression.

"But you will need access to the company's files, and some disk space to store your music, dance clips, and so on," he replied flatly.

"Hmm." No hint there.

Don Luis depressed a button and spoke toward a smallish black grill embedded in the glass panel separating the chauffer from the rear compartment. "Kemal, Junior's."

"Yes, sir."

"Earlier in life," Don Luis said, "I expounded the gospel according to me. I was a college professor and spent a good deal of time just south of here at Brooklyn College."

"Really."

"At first all I could see is that it wasn't Oxford, but I came to love it."

"Things are often this way. Love grows on you slowly." Miguel seemed to detect Aggie's fresh scent, perfuming the car.

"Well, the deli I love most is in Midtown, the Second Avenue Deli," Don Luis's face darkened. "Poor Abe, the former owner, was murdered years ago, '96 I believe." He sighed. "The city can be dangerous."

Miguel had figured that out, but said nothing.

"The Second Avenue Deli." Don Luis's scowl softened. "Abe's nephews carried on the tradition. That's a must." He balled a fist, punctuating the point. "That's why it's still called the Second Avenue Deli although it's moved to Thirty-Third."

"My mother taught us to respect tradition," Miguel replied.

Don Luis's expression became pensive until he said, "Ah, Miguel, I expect you wonder why we are here, other than to enjoy a fine luncheon together."

Hallelujah!

"Let me say that your dancing is impressive on a variety of levels. Your bearing, confidence, connection—I could go on—all splendid. You would be a credit to any company. But I would like to clarify a few things."

"Thank you. And I would like to better understand a few things, too.

"There was some slight opposition to selecting you. Chaz, whose style is quite different from yours, favored another dancer. Perfect technique, flamboyant, probably impossible to direct, only mildly deranged."

"Chaz is this way?"

"He's like a tango god when he's on: ingenious, thrilling, a superb showman. You will never dance quite like Chaz."

Miguel's neck stiffened.

"It's like controlled madness, a frenzy of pent-up passion and pain he's trying to express." Don Luis searched his beard. "The *tangueras* recognize his genius, but don't connect with him. And the audience feels that. They sense the futility of it all." He sighed. "Perhaps, if he slept with the *tangueras*."

Miguel understood the difference between dancing with someone you don't really want to be dancing with and dancing with someone for whom you burn. Everybody can see and feel the difference. He also understood the perils of the latter.

"And then there's Dr. Wagner, the perfectionist. Completely sterile, but very ambitious, and possibly dangerous."

Miguel kept his face neutral, but the info intrigued him. This lunch was paying dividends already.

"The crux," Don Luis said, "is that you will be required to work harder than anyone in the company. And I don't mean perfecting your bits for the show."

"What, then?"

He tugged the beard and spoke with authority, "This represents a unique opportunity for you. I threw myself into the breach, and I shan't see you squander it."

Miguel believed that Don Luis spoke the truth. But why? Why had this man bothered? His ruminations were interrupted when the big car slewed almost sideways, tires crying out, avoiding a collision. Kemal deftly maneuvered the behemoth around the stalled clunker and righted it without incident. Miguel was impressed. Kemal drove with the skill of Miguel's cousin, the private snoop.

"Now where were we? Never mind. Did you attend university at all?"

"My sister started university and enjoyed it, so I went part-time."

"Did she finish?"

"No. Was difficult for both of us, dancing, studying, and some issues at home. I stopped after the second year and worked some jobs."

Miguel could feel the color of his cheeks reddening. He was thrown back to the slaughterhouse and its stench. But that had been better than listening in to private phone calls, installing spyware on computers, and sitting night after night with his cousin in a car, waiting to photograph some errant husband or pervert. And his cousin's cop stories were despicable. The only good part of the work was when Miguel got to practice get-away driving in his cousin's beefed-up car. It was a beater, really, but with a hot engine. At night in La Boca they would practice late breaking, power slides, 180s, you name it.

After the collapse of Argentina's economy and his mother's business being stolen away, money was critical. And to think that his mother continued to pay her sister, Palmira, even when there was no money. Marcovici! He couldn't help thinking of him and how he had eventually stolen away the business. The name invariably conjured up the same image: sly, squinty eyes; mean, narrow lips; stringy, combed-over hair; flaccid pale skin and long dirty nails. But the voice, soothing and measured, was a disgusting asset. Miguel squelched his emotions before revealing how emotional he really was.

"There are many campuses of the City University of New York, CUNY, where I taught," said Don Luis. "Somewhere, on the Brooklyn College campus, there is an auditorium dedicated to yours truly."

"Very impressive. You were professor of religion?"

"Yes and no. I taught in the philosophy department. But there wasn't even a degree program in religious studies back then. There is now, of course. And I did spend a great deal of time telling wide-eyed undergraduates that there is no God, and no need for one." He sighed, adding, "I played as though I had all of the answers. But, I, myself, was searching, groping for truth."

"And now?"

Don Luis turned to face Miguel squarely. "Should there be even one chance in a trillion that there is an architect of this vast universe, and should It be willing to enter into a relationship with mankind, anyone who didn't spend the majority of his days trying to establish such a relationship would be, in my opinion, an utter fool."

CHAPTER 24

JUNIOR'S RESTAURANT TEEMED with life. Patrons talked, laughed, gobbled massive sandwiches, plunged forks into sinfully delicious-looking desserts, and swilled beer and cocktails. Miguel found it different from BA's best delis. Electricity seemed to fill the air. One could seemingly be shocked just by touching the handles of the glass doors. The buzz of people, the blare of the music, and the *ca-ching* of the cash register all contributed to the ambience. Don Luis and Miguel sat at a corner booth, reddish-orange and green-striped fabric with a white tablecloth and napkins. Enough mirrors to rival a funhouse. An array of pastry display cases, the aroma of your grandma's kitchen, and the human comedy lay before them. At Don Luis's urging, Miguel ordered a pastrami sandwich with onion rings while Don Luis opted for corned beef and cabbage.

Beautiful raven-haired women, some dressed casually and others suited up for business, men in working clothes and business suits: they all ate, drank, came, and went. The energy in the place was fantastic. Miguel wondered if it was just a Brooklyn thing, or did Manhattan have scenes like this? Kemal, having parked the car, approached the table and spoke quietly to Don Luis. He pointed to a far table of swarthy-skinned gentlemen wearing little skullcaps. Don Luis nodded and Kemal headed their way. Miguel was taken aback by the fact that the men sat beside—nearly shoulder to shoulder, really—to men in long black coats with big black hats and curly sidelocks. America was indeed a melting pot.

But this aspect of American life was not so different from BA, Miguel considered. After WWII, Jews escaping persecution and Nazis escaping prosecution both emigrated in droves to Argentina, many to BA. Turned out, they both enjoyed *wurst, saurkraut,* Riesling wine, and many other foods and drinks that brought them together at restaurants all over the city.

Lunch was delicious, and the scene at Junior's something from the movies, but Miguel could wait no longer to ask some questions. His eyes roved the space as he searched for the right words. And then he caught sight of a man wearing a ball cap, white coveralls, and prominent metal-framed eyeglasses. The man entered hastily and made tracks toward a far wall. He turned toward a staircase and his profile looked so familiar.

"Is something the matter?" Don Luis asked.

"No, Don Luis, please forgive me for changing the subject, but perhaps you can tell me a bit about the history of your company." Miguel paused. "About the tragedy."

Don Luis's mirth deserted him. His cheeks seemed to sag and his keen eyes dulled. Miguel's gaze never wavered from Don Luis's face.

"Did you know Natalia Prafil?" Don Luis asked.

"Yes. We danced in Buenos Aires."

"She was murdered, you probably know, while debuting a show for the press. More than half a year ago." He sighed a deep expression of despair.

"The police, what do they say? There are suspects?"

"I dare say everyone in the company is a suspect. But I don't know how hard they worked the case." He clucked his tongue. "A foreigner, not in the country very long—"

"She was a person like any US citizen." Miguel insisted. Although his pulse reverberated in his temples, he had to remain calm. "Do you think it was a company member?"

"I, um . . . no one knows," Don Luis replied. "The investigation is ongoing."

"Is it?" Miguel said, "Well, I believe there is a shadow over the company so long as this is unresolved. I, too, am Argentine." He observed Don Luis's reaction.

It betrayed nothing. "If I'm slashed to death at a rehearsal, I hope there will be more interest."

"My boy," Don Luis said, "this is neither the time nor the place. But I assure you that I have not forgotten Natalia. And I never will."

Don Luis's sincerity impressed him. But Miguel's mind was muddied. He excused himself to the restroom. En route to the stairs, Miguel studied the patrons, hunched over sandwiches or leaning back in ecstasy, devouring impossibly tall tranches of cheesecake. A new phenomenon: cheesecake-induced tangasm!

Climbing the stairs to the men's room, Miguel hoped for another glimpse of the man wearing metal-framed eyeglasses. There was something about the little hitch in his walk. Miguel opened a door and stumbled into a congregation of unfriendly faces. It was not the toilet! Two of the men made moves to the inside breast pockets of their bulky sport coats. Miguel's hands shot up to chest level, fingers spread open wide. He stammered, "Excuse me, gentlemen."

Miguel backed away slowly toward the entry, his eyes capturing the scowl on each and every swollen, doughy, or chiseled face. The most menacing expression was that of the man sitting at the table's head. He had a pock-marked face, lumpy and brown as an overcooked hamburger with a whopper of a pitted, dill pickle nose. *He must weigh three times as much as me,* Miguel thought, averting his gaze. It was only then he saw the man wearing white coveralls. He snapped his chin to his chest, avoiding Miguel's glance. Did he recognize him? Was it possible he had seen him before?

A younger man, dressed in a nice-looking gangster suit, dark with white chalk stripes and a burgundy polka dot tie, sat beside him. He stared insolently at Miguel. The guy looked to Miguel like a kid modeling dad's suit and taking it very seriously. One thing was certain: Junior's was like a real-life film noir. The big man at the table's head barked, "Hey, time for you to leave."

One of the chunkiest goons stood and headed toward Miguel. He said, "I'll take care of him, Big Benny."

Miguel squeaked, "Sorry," and banged out of the door, smacking his elbow's funny bone on the molding. Grasping his stinging arm, he hurried to the opposite end of the hall, to the gentlemen's room door, with more urgency than before.

Miguel's nerves were on high alert returning to the table. Halfway there, Don Luis called out, "Miguel, come quickly. We must go."

They hustled toward the door. Miguel asked, "What's wrong?"

"A robbery at my building." Don Luis clutched his chest, his face as pallid as a corpse, saying, "If it's stolen, I'll die."

CHAPTER 25

THE SKULLDUGGERY AT THE STUDIO continued to distress Miguel even after reaching the welcoming arms of the Fontaine Bleu. Home, sweet home, he thought, grasping the grimy door handle with his shirt cuff. His head spun with ideas of intrigues, robbery, and, of course, murder.

The question of who had been spying at the studio had dominated Miguel's thoughts the previous night. But now, he was preoccupied with the greater mystery of who had vandalized the place—at midday. Were they connected? You could bet your *burro* on it, he believed. Miguel learned in the car, heading back to the studio, that Don Luis owned the entire building. And the fancy security system had been disabled by the thief, who shot straight to his target in the basement. But how? Had it not been for Barbara Reed calling the police after hearing banging noises underneath the *tangueras'* lounge, something of great value would have been lost.

He considered suspects: Chaz was in charge when Don Luis was absent. But he had passcodes to the building; why break in? Killer Kemal was with them all morning. Besides, he was legs and arms for Don Luis, who Miguel thought had it in somehow for Dr. Wagner. And it wasn't just the fiery discussion that Miguel had overheard. He had noted contempt for Wagner in Don Luis's eyes when mentioning him in the car. Candy, El Primitivo, Ingrid—oh God, not her. And for what? Who else in the company was devious enough to make the attempt? Miguel had had many different types of experiences at tango studios, some circus-like, but never had his head spun so fast trying to understand this. Could he sort it out, a beer would certainly help.

When Miguel neared the front desk, he could hear the din from the low-life bar growing louder. Near the end of the darkened hallway, a familiar voice, said, "¡OMG, *es mi salvador*!"

Miguel turned and faced Heather, standing outside the front desk with a huge purse hung from her slight shoulder. She sported a fitted purple dress with an asymmetric hemline and tall black pumps. When coupled with the big black purse, and its interlaced white C's, the ensemble suggested that she was off to a midnight fashion show.

"How are you, Heather?"

"Yes, English," she said, approaching and planting a smart peck on each of his cheeks. "Very well," she replied, wiping away her lipstick from his face. "And you?"

He dithered his hand and cocked his head. "Going out?"

"Just finished my shift." She craned her neck to peek down the hallway to hell and cupped a hand behind one ear. "Staying in?"

He shrugged. "Got to be better than Sarge's."

"You learn fast," she said. Casting sideways glances, she added, "*We're* going out because *you* deserve it." She put a finger to her ruby lips and then turned and walked toward the front desk. She bent over and ogled a bank of closed-circuit TV monitors.

Miguel's eyes started at her slender ankles and inched upward. Her's was a build for candombe dancing. The physique was not so different from *las porteñas*, but it was quite different from Aggie's slender, elegant shape. Miguel's fingers flew to his hair, brushing fallen strands away from his face. Aggie, he must forget her. There was no time, and besides, she was far too lovely.

In an instant, Miguel's mind blocked the offensive smells of burned oil and spilled liquor in favor of the aroma of Aggie's perfumed hair. He checked himself, thinking, it must not happen. Besides, she was not a real *tanguera*; she was a big-city girl playing a forbidden game. But she played it so sincerely, like—

"You still here?" Heather waved her hands in his face. "I can't tell if you're thinking about heaven or hell, but it's one of them."

"Both, perhaps."

"New woman or new job?" She paused, before adding, "Both, perhaps?"

"So you're a mind reader."

"Great," she said deadpan. "Wait here a few minutes. I'll go out this side door and get a cab. I'll hold it at the intersection. You take a left out the front door. See you in five minutes." She winked and hustled away.

Miguel smiled to himself, thinking, man-eater, maybe; pocket rocket, positively.

They streaked through Brooklyn's mean streets, Sinatra singing an American classic on the cabbie's radio. The entire world knew the song. In fact, a *tanqueria* owner in BA had played it to death during the afternoon setup. The only way to get him to stop was for Miguel to tease that he was developing a tango routine to it. Miguel never dreamed he'd be this close. And until now, he'd never understood the power of the line, "If I can make it there, I'll make it anywhere."

The spray of moisture, hissing off the tires outside, was a backdrop for the wipers keeping perfect time, like the rhythm section of an unseen band. Miguel tried to turn off his brain, to be in the moment. Heather caressed his hand, squeezed it. Miguel squeezed in return. No idea where they were going. In the back of his mind he was pretty sure they were going nowhere. It seemed a safe place.

To ditch his negativity, Miguel turned to Heather to speak, but their mouths engaged instead. He put his hand to her neck and felt the strong beat of her heart. He had never doubted her prowess as a woman. Soon they were sitting close in a cozy corner booth in a Queens Borough bar, El Paradiso, slightly more upscale than the dives of their Brooklyn hood, and Heather proved him right.

Suddenly Heather sat up and released his face, brushed away curls that now stuck to one side of her hot, moist face. "Oh, I love this song," she said. "You rumba, no?"

"Easy steps only."

"Come on," she said, standing, pulling him from his seat. Her eyes seemed to drink him in. "Glad to see you're up for this," she said, smiling naughtily.

Miguel held her gaze. On the floor, they were comfortable in each other's arms. Heather had a nice sense of rhythm. Miguel didn't care a bit for showing off or whether anyone else was in the place. Their dancing was real. It was a rare moment of tranquility and confirmation that he could relate to another human being. His mind was finally at peace and for that he was grateful to Heather or Ina or whatever her name really was.

On the cab ride back, Miguel could scarcely keep his hands off her. He was determined to treat Heather with as much respect as she wanted in public and with as much intensity as she could handle in private. Back at the off-Flatbush Avenue hellhole, aka the Fontaine Bleu, Miguel paid the driver while Heather made a cell call.

Afterward, she smiled. "Having friends owe you a favor is a good thing," she said. "Even crazy friends like Lexi. Well, she prefers Lexi Lexus." Her eyes rolled.

"We Argentines say, a friend who needs your help is the best friend."

"Wanna come up for a night cap or something?" she asked, provocatively.

"Definitely."

"Give me ten minutes. Room 213."

"You have a room here, too?'

She nodded, shook a finger. "And be quiet."

CHAPTER 26

CHAZ CHRISTIANSON WRITHED on his sofa. His back ached. Hopefully it would help to settle deeper into the comfy cushions. Newly opened snail mail slid from his lap to the floor. He enjoyed his well-appointed modern apartment in the not-so-modern, but posh Meatpacking District. Clunky, low-rise red brick structures that once housed bleeding beef, pork, and lamb hung up on meat hooks, now accommodated hipsters, reality TV hopefuls, and dance divas, hung up on themselves.

Ah, much better. His back was comfortable at last. He assumed an expression of repose and closed his eyes. An incoming tweet pinged. He grabbed his eyeglasses and glanced at the smartphone with one eye. The blissful expression evaporated from his thin lips as he groaned, "Crisis management time."

@cut00: "OMG saw coolest flic ever"
@cachafaz: "vampires—wizards—demons—all 3?"
@cut00: "by a swiss guy—ingmar berman no im?"
@cachafaz: "Bergman was Swedish"
@cut00: "duh, im so stupid. hes sooo deep ya no"
@cachafaz: "very cool, dpresssing tho"

@cut00: "LOL he totally gets me—Cries & Whispers had 3 sisters: 1 dying of cancer, 1 an actress liv ulman? so awesome—1 desperate sister, feels like total shit, a nervous reck.

@cachafaz: "yeah—is about relationship of the sisters"

@cut00: "ah man remember at dinner she breaks a glass and bastard husband glares—like fu bitch. she takes giant piece of glass & staring him in the face in front of everybody slashes her . . ."

@cachafaz: "LOL been so long ago—don't recall that. Seems they all suffered differently n tried to help 1 another"

@cut00: "self rejection of 1 sister was totally real. after ripping herself she wiped blood all over her face at the table. like in yur face f'ed up husband! WOW she cut back in 1800s totally emo!!"

Chaz collapsed back into the cushions. He emitted a long sigh that fogged his eyeglasses. First, his aching back and now foggy glasses. The universe reminded him constantly that although his social media friends and followers, like Cindy, who was born in 2000, were mostly teens, he was by comparison an old fart. And while it had been almost twenty years earlier, in college, that he'd watched the film, he was certain that Bergman had not created an emo—originally a euphemism for a hyperemotive, disenfranchised punk rock music lover—classic twenty years before that. Cindy had viewed the film through a warped prism of poor mental health and desperation. She needed professional help.

Chaz reached for the glistening surgical steel paring knife that he'd used as a letter opener. He grasped its steely handle. Held up the four-inch blade for inspection: heat-treated, ice-quenched, deathly sharp. Slowly Chaz dragged the edge across his left wrist, over the scar, almost completely concealed by time. But, indeed, an indelible scar remained on his mind. Poverty, social injustice, and alienation—on both sides of the societal divide—were typical grist for the mills of cutters.

Ping! He dropped the knife and grasped the phone.

@cut00: "u there?"

@cachafaz: "so many + films out there. *Billy Elliot* is great! seen it?"

@cut00: “whats it about?”

@cachafaz: “tru story: poor kid dreams 2b ballet dancer & does! makes lifetime friend. ur mom wld luv it 2 . . .”

@cut00: “cool—btw whatdyano abt german movie guru Werner Fastbinner?”

CHAPTER 27

MIGUEL RACED UP THE STAIRS to his room, unwilling to wait on the hotel's poky, claustrophobic elevator. It was the only European aspect of this fleabag. He checked the time on his phone again. Minutes dragged by. It was strange; he was not an aficionado of the music of Maestro Astor Piazzolla. Not that he didn't know the maestro's melodies, they just never seemed to meander through his mind the way those of Miguel Calo and Carlos di Sarli did. But amid a quick grooming, Miguel became caught up in the melancholic Piazzolla masterpiece, "Oblivion."

No denying—whether one considered "Oblivion" a danceable song or not—it captured the essence of *tanguidad*, that inexplicable melancholia that stabs at the heart of every tango dancer, regardless of creed or origin. *Tanguidad* is the very depth of longing for something you're confident will never be yours. A relationship, a union that you know will never be realized; aching for an all-consuming passion that will consume you and your *amor* at the height of ecstasy, before you part the bitterest of enemies. In the throes of *tanguidad*, you crave the utter destruction of the impenetrable defenses you have erected around your heart to keep it intact and free from the insensitive smashing blows you are destined to sustain from the one you would love.

Miguel glanced at the phone and hurried out the door, failing in his haste to set the lock, on his way to room number 213. The heart-rending strains of "Oblivion" played counterpoint to his desire to be with someone, to open his heart, if only a crack for an instant. He reentered the stairwell and nearly tripped over a janitor leaned against a rough-finished wall, smoking, admiring his mop bucket. "*Perdón,*" Miguel huffed, not looking back, taking the cement stairs two at a time.

Once inside Heather's dimly lit room, Miguel proceeded slowly. This could be a setup, he thought, as he slipped a hand to his hip, finding the blade. She led him toward a furniture grouping. He broke the eerie silence saying, "My luxury suite comes complete with lights."

"Shsssh," she whispered before gently pushing him down onto a loveseat, holding a finger to his lips. She whispered, "Want something to drink?"

"Water." Miguel had no wish for more alcohol. He wanted his senses to be fully alive to feel every inch of delight with this wildcat.

Heather returned from the kitchen to the living room with two plastic cups of bubbly mineral water. She sat next to him and they toasted. Heather admired Miguel soulfully while running her fingers through his thick hair. Blood coursed powerfully through his body. He loved its enlivening effects. The veins of his temples began to bulge and pulse, almost making him dizzy. His penis began to swell. Heather smiled as she playfully reached between his legs and massaged his growing cock. She encircled its head through his pants with her supple fingers and then began sliding her wrist up and down its growing length, coaxing it ever harder. He slid forward and projected up his pelvis, demonstrating an impressive bulge for her consideration.

Miguel leaned toward her and gently cupped her breast in his hand. He scrubbed his palm against her firming nipple. And what a nipple it was. It grew broader and bulged under the friendly friction, its delicate nerve endings responding to the titillation. He caressed the nipple more firmly and kneaded it between his fingers. Heather's eyes closed and her playful massage waxed more insistent.

It had been a while, but Miguel recalled the next step. And he wasn't waiting for an invitation. In a single smooth move, he thrust his hand between Heather's muscular thighs, separating them while lifting her chic dress until he found the upper margin of low-rise panties. He slipped them down her silky thighs, dancer's thighs, exposing a perfect slice of paradise. Slowly, and with the skill of an artist, Miguel slid his fingers underneath the closely cropped muffin and grasped Heather's entire cunt in the palm of his hand. He stroked her clit with the heel of his hand in a firm, side-to-side motion. She moaned and melted into his palm.

Heather whispered, "This is going to be great."

"I can't wait."

She stood and waved him into a cramped bedroom, before easing the door shut. She pressed the lock, making a slight face at its noisy click. They went at it in record time, but then slow motion set in. Every caress, stroke, lick, flick, and wail was unhurried. Miguel was inspired by Heather's confidence and capability. They loved like the Latin dance bolero: deliberate, passionate, and penetrating. After she climaxed for the second time, Miguel was ready to liberate his pent-up emotion. He thought if all of his hurt and frustration were released in one orgasm, it would be earth-shattering. But he had a subtler goal in mind: to experience release in the arms of a woman. One he didn't know at all, it was true, but who cared enough to ease his pain and penetrate his isolation, if only for a while.

Carefully, he maneuvered her away from the flimsy oak veneer headboard, to spare both of their heads. Miguel focused on the dark skin of her neck and breasts as he thrusted. Her generous nipples stood erect, crowned by delicious domes of chocolate candy. He took tiny bites as he drove ever deeper. Heather took the pounding. She pulled him into her more forcefully, contracting her vaginal muscles, gripping him tighter with each succeeding thrust.

She locked on his eyes, her face shiny with perspiration. Lips bared by the intensity of the moment. And then, the dizzying vastness of space, the unfathomable depth of the ocean. In ecstasy, Miguel gripped her shoulders viselike as his mouth opened to scream.

Heather jerked a hand free and muffled the sound as he laid into her mercilessly. And then, like awakening from a dream, he lay atop her, gasping for air, their sweat-drenched bodies melding perfectly.

Time died.

Miguel held Heather close enough to feel the rhythm of her rock-solid heartbeat. It helped calm his wildly beating chest. For a change he synced his heart to a woman's. He felt her fingers play on his shoulders. Then downward, massaging his lower spine, finding his buttocks.

Grasping a hand full of glut, she squeezed. "I like this," she said.

"And I like this," he replied, fingering her glistening, dusky neck.

Heather massaged his neck gently and stroked the back of his head. Her heart, metronomic. She cooed, "*Che, acabé maravilloso.*"

"Me, too."

"*Mi Dios,* I'm making Argentine love to you. Why you are saying *Inglés*?"

Miguel burst into laughter at her pouting face. "I have to. My mentor, the producer for the show, is very strict." He could hardly believe what he had said.

Her dark eyes hardened. "He just wants to know if you plot against him."

"He is a Spaniard."

"Why is he your mentor? These producers are druggies, scumbags, perverts. They're only after what they can take."

"He's a rich man, old." Miguel said, sitting up. He leaned against her. "Right away he treated me like family."

Her passion boiled over. "Why does he let you stay at this *aduana*?"

Miguel tried to conceal his feelings, but he couldn't help his chin lowering. He set his eyes on her, imagining the emerald tarnished. The business relationship Heather shared with Gordo was now clear. He considered all of the nasty things that had been said in BA about his aunt Palmira and her favorite—bastard—son, Miguel Andro, named for his presumed father, Count Andro of Croatia. The difficulty of their lives when his father was killed tragically had been a constant worry to Miguel's mother, who seemed somehow to feel responsible. Miguel considered that at least Heather seemed to be trying to make it on her own. Or was his bill the next thing to come? Miguel receded before posing the question in a measured tone, using common Spanish. "*¿Gordo es su chulo*?"

Heather's tone was thick with sarcasm, saying, "A desk clerk doesn't need a pimp." Her hard, shiny eyes burned into the void.

"But he used to be, right?" Silence. Miguel asked, "What is he now and why is he around here?"

"A jealous brute," she said. "Now he, uh, cooks across the street."

Miguel recalled Gordo's stench. It was meth, not rancid oil. "Sure, he's a chef."

"I said he cooks." Heather pointed at the door. "Just go, please."

He lifted her face; moist eyes met his. "I have a better plan. If you can handle more of me, I'll take you for breakfast afterward."

She stroked his face and gave him a delicate peck on his cheek. "First, tell me about your woman."

"You are the first I have found for a while." His eyes roamed uncomfortably, admitting, "I have not really been looking."

"Is better to have no partner than a bad partner," Heather said. "I just learned this year." She stared into the distance, adding, "But can be lonely sometimes."

"Uh-hum."

"This world is a meat grinder and we," she poked his chest, "are the meat."

He drew a deep breath and exhaled forcefully. "No man at all in your life?"

"I pay for this place," she said, "and only one man comes here, *El Jefe*."

The door jangled. Heather shuddered, staring at its rattling handle.

Miguel leapt to his feet, snatched up his pants. Quickly he accessed the blade and opened it with a whoosh. A menacing glint shone on the blade.

CHAPTER 28

Dr. Ernest Wagner bent to his work, his eyes and mind focused. Was the edge of his new scalpel prototype sufficiently sharp? An overhead hemispherical surgical lamp shone down harshly on the blade's multifaceted fracture planes. The room was filled with scientific equipment and medical paraphernalia. Rows of vessels containing specimens lined the walls. An ice bath was close at hand. Dr. Wagner studied the blade, twisting the sensuously curvaceous haft. Tango music wafted softly on the air of his little shop of horrors, as his deceased wife Helen had referred to it.

He exhaled lightly and continued to admire the piece. This was the fruit of a decade of arduous labor. Wagner approached a conventionally lighted microscope, a Carl Zeiss STEMISV8. He recalled his first attempt at percussion flint knapping. It was clear that his exceptional motor skills and hand-eye coordination were ideal for it. Not long after, compression knapping and reproducing credible replicas of ancient bifaced points was within his grasp. He progressed quickly to eastern fluted points. Helen had teased him about wasting so much of his time making small rocks from big ones, a euphemism for chain gang labor in the old South where both had grown up. He squeezed the scalpel, squelching the memory.

Having secured the blade on the microscope's table, for observation of the edge near the tip, he cranked the magnification up to 640X. At this high magnification, a steel blade would demonstrate a crenulated edge—appearing much like a serrated saw blade—the obsidian edge, even after several uses, remained incredibly smooth and amazingly sharp. It appeared as straight and regular as an interstate highway does from thirty thousand feet. Using a photographic digitizer, he could measure all the little peaks and valleys of a blade's edge and statistically compare two edges for closeness to perfection.

Dr. Wagner clicked on the digitizer and pressed start before turning to a powerful computer workstation, bearing a statistical analysis program. Minutes later, the results were in. His homemade obsidian blade, even after multiple uses, continued to be more than nine hundred times sharper than a new Swann-Morton steel scalpel blade, used at Bellevue and just about everywhere else in America.

One thousand times sharper was his goal. And Wagner was confident that it was attainable. Given his superior craftsmanship, expensive high-technology equipment, and access to abundant rare base material, perfect African obsidian, it was obtainable indeed. Because he had purchased for a pittance most of the African obsidian available, there was a higher barrier for competitive entry. For Dr. Wagner, African obsidian was simply another type of blood diamond.

"And now for the acid test!" Wagner crowed aloud. He whirled around and removed the meaty contents from an ice bath. He dried the specimen before placing it on a wooden cutting board. He held it down forcibly with a single hand and reminded himself that he was an artist, no matter what the world thought. Meticulously he began to slice, all the way to the bone, no cheating. One, two, three incisions; his breath more rapid; four, five, six; his grip grew tighter, the mealy musculature looser; seven, eight, nine; his hand slippery from gushing gore, one more. . . . The last incision executed, his work was complete.

Dr. Wagner mounted the limb on the table of a Zeiss Axiotron Reflected Light Microscope that he had purchased online for a song. Great addition to his home workshop. He examined the incisions at 500X. They bore a perfect forty-five-degree bevel that was so precise under powerful magnification it was possible to ascertain that his scalpel had cut between cells rather than tearing them as did other so-called state-of-the-art steel scalpel blades. He had used his most sensitive motor skills, fine fingertip manipulation of his ingenious scalpel. And he had cut in continuous motion, producing an incision so clean that bleeding would have been insignificant and healing time dramatically reduced in a live specimen instead of a squishy day-old cadaver.

CHAPTER 29

"MOMMY, MOMMY, I'M SCARED. Let me in, please," came the muted cry from beyond Heather's bedroom door. Miguel relaxed. He forced the glinting blade into the knife's aluminum handle, eyeing Heather. She gathered a fluffy terrycloth robe about her as he pulled on his pants. Heather opened the door and slipped out. Moments later, she reentered leading a tyke wearing New York Yankees pinstripe pajamas. Miguel, now completely dressed, stood disbelieving.

"Hector, I want you to meet mommy's friend, Miguel."

Hector buried his face in his mother's robe.

"Come on, now, what do you say?"

"Hi."

"Hello there, Hector," he said, approaching the boy, squatting, a hand extended.

Hector retreated further into the robe's folds.

"*Pobrecito,*" Miguel said.

"*Él no es pobrecito,*" Heather snapped. "Hector, don't be a baby," she said firmly. "You are *El Jefe*, The Boss! Now, shake hands like a gentleman."

His fearful face lifted toward Miguel. Hector cautiously extended his left hand, little fingers curled under like tiny seahorses.

Miguel caressed three little seahorses, shook them gently, saying, "*Hola, Hector.*"

He broke into a toothy grin, returning Miguel's infectious smile.

Miguel's heart burst open for an instant before he clamped it shut. He saw shades of himself in the boy's fear and uncertainty. Miguel's life had gotten off to a rocky start and now he was back in another quarry. He regarded Hector fondly, noting his sincere dark eyes, olive skin, and thick, wavy hair. He was a beautiful little boy. Such promise his life could hold.

Miguel kissed Hector on the brow and watched as Heather guided the little fellow out of the door. Miguel sighed, recalling that he had planned to have lots of *bambinos*. Had been determined to be the father that he never had. He stood around for a few minutes and prepared to leave. His mind was clearer. He certainly was more relaxed. Miguel had missed sex more than he allowed himself to admit. And Heather, she was the bomb in bed. But tomorrow was going to be another busy—

Bang! Bang! The front door resounded. "Open up, goddamit." *Bang! Bang!* "I know you're in there, Ina, you bitch. Open the fucking door, or else!"

Miguel froze. He recognized Gordo's raspy Puerto Rican accent. And it didn't sound as though he was dropping by to tell Heather about an early morning audition. Miguel felt for his blade and found it secure. He scanned for a bigger weapon, anything he could swing.

Heather burst in, her face a portrait of fright. "I'm sorry!"

"Is okay. I can fight."

"No, don't. They are two and have guns." She pointed to the window. "You must jump, *mi amor*."

He nodded. "If I break my legs, my life is over anyway."

Tears began to stream down her smooth cheeks. "Please, do it for—"

The doorframe screamed, *crack*, giving way.

Gordo's voice resounded through the small apartment. "Fucking whore, I'm gonna kill you."

Miguel hardened his gaze. He raised the puny knife.

Heather sunk to her knees and through chest-heaving sobs said, "I beg you."

Miguel stood his ground, clutching the knife ever tighter. He looked into Heather's terrified eyes, hoping to convey to her the rigors of the *milonguero* code. There was no time to speak. And words would prove insufficient. He had tried to live by what had been called a code of honor among thieves. It had been difficult. Even his countrymen had not understood. But now, with his heart racing and his pulse clanging in his head, Miguel knew that it would be easier to die a *milonguero* than to live as one. Perhaps this was the secret the old *milongueros* knew. Their sole comfort. However challenging their lives, they were constantly prepared for their deaths.

Miguel took a step toward the door. Heather lunged and grabbed his leg.

She cried out in a desperate prayer to him, "Oh, God, leave now, please."

"But Hector?"

"He won't hurt him. He's his fa—" She broke off and hung her head in shame.

It was like a stab to Miguel's heart. Hector's beautiful prospects seemed to vanish. But Miguel was the odd man out, the third wheel. His defenses tumbled like the walls of Jericho. He gnashed his teeth, wondering why he could never reinforce them sufficiently not to fail. Miguel shucked Heather from his leg with a violent jab and flew to the window. He raised it and thrust out his head. The wet wind jetted into his hair, assaulting his face. He could hardly see anything on the ground. Cars and vans raced past. An asphalt parking lot welcomed him. There was no safe place to jump. He hesitated, and then he heard the shots. Heather screamed, "Jump, please!" and ran out of the room toward her doom.

Miguel teetered on the windowsill, wind buffeting his body. He watched the movie of his life. Frames sped past with perfect clarity. He danced tango with his sister, receiving step-by-step instructions, in minute detail. Her raptor eyes taking in everything at once. He saw his mother's youthful face, smiling as she bent down to kiss him. The locket she always wore around her neck, dangling on a golden chain, its enameled crest so clear, a perfectly distinct coat of arms. Oh God, it was the exact one in Don Luis's office! More shots rang out. Miguel twisted his head toward the open window and saw its curtain billowing in and out like a Halloween ghost. And then the film continued, Aggie's eyes shown before him, their light honest, pure. But the projector jammed, the film scorched, and the show was over when he saw the muzzle of Gordo's pistol pointing at his head and heard the round sizzling toward him. An instant later, Miguel tumbled into oblivion.

PART II

The Basic Figure of Argentine Tango

CROSS

Leader:	*Two steps forward. Close feet together.*
Follower:	*Two steps back (left then right).* *Cross left foot over right.*

CHAPTER 30

BRILLIANT SUNSHINE STREAMED through Don Luis's bedroom windows, yet he was hardly able again today to disgorge himself from bed. He had passed the entire night in his dungeon, figuratively lashed to his reading table. The remainder, the larger part of the whole, of a complete English breakfast, dutifully served by Kemal hours ago, sat neglected on a bed tray. The *New York Times* languished. Its coverage decried Iran's progress toward perfecting nuclear weapons while condemning the violence in Syria. Don Luis believed that while these were clear and present dangers to many in the region, the greatest threat was to his people. And he believed that threats from within exacerbated threats from without.

Don Luis's research had confirmed that transgenerational epigenetic inheritance was more than a theory; it was fact. The sins of the father and grandfather and on and on were indeed passed forward to future generations in their very DNA. And so were grandpa's fears, prejudices, and paranoia! It all piled up over centuries, over millennia, reducing the opportunity for clear-minded decision making, having a negative impact on the probability of self-preservation. Concrete-minded politicians and irrational religious factions made damning decisions for an entire people. It must stop.

In his cell he had pored over the sacred text the night through. Of course that occupied his mind in full, kept him from obsessing over Miguel's unexplained absence at the studio. No call, no word of any kind. Don Luis had reminded himself hourly that he was not Miguel's mother, although he was something very near to it. He had labored over the Codex seeking a Kabbalistic clue regarding how to alter the course of what seemed otherwise inevitable. If only he could determine the very best use of his bargaining chip, if it was proper to speak of a verbatim copy of the world's most perfect sacred text as a chip.

His flea-bitten morning coat, fabricated of sumptuous *vicuña*, now derelict with age and neglect, cocooned Don Luis. It hadn't been cleaned or mended for at least a year, since Carolina's passing. He cinched the belt, fingered its ragged seam, thinking of the day she had purchased his and hers robes on Madison Avenue. And while he had seldom objected to her frivolous extravagance, Luis had expressed shock at the price and demanded that she return them. But how she loved her robe. And he owed it to her. Owed her everything, because she was so giving and he was unable to give to her that which she wanted most, himself. Don Luis sighed heavily, thinking, it was a different world, old New York, and I was a better man. He coughed and slouched further into bed, brushing aside the depressing papers, hoping to do likewise with his gloom.

There was a singular ray of hope. He had one shot remaining to get desperately needed help in preparing a plan and executing it before it was too late. Time was an enemy, one of many. If he waited too long or did nothing, there would be no reason to launch nuclear weapons and face retaliation. The goal of driving a people into the sea could be achieved by overpopulation on every side, political subterfuge, or superpowers invading the region, guarding their economic interests. And if a peace process was infeasible because of genetic resistance to trust or to reasonable deal making, then his bargaining chip must make the difference. Israel must continue to wrestle with its God—as its name declared—but endless conflict with its neighbors was unproductive and ultimately would be its undoing.

Don Luis believed that his family had an important role to play, influencing his people's struggle for peace. It was, for him, an affair of the heart and head. He would see to it that it was not botched again. He reached for the phone. "Kemal, come up at once." Hanging up, he muttered, "Someone's got to save them, who better than me?"

CHAPTER 31

Aggie Jacobs moped across the practice studio's floor toward the ballet bar. She couldn't help herself; she ached for Miguel. He hadn't been to the studio for rehearsal for two days. She sighed heavily, extending her fingers to the wood. Slid down her hand a goodly length, seeking the bar's pulse, trying to connect with its energy. Aggie raised and lowered herself slowly, activating her core and recalling Miguel's last meaningful words to her: "The real milonga is low and quick . . . and very, very dangerous. It is like a fight with a knife, and one partner is always killed."

A tear wended its way down past Aggie's nose to the corner of her lips. She tasted salt, saw Miguel's face. But what if she had never before seen him? When Aggie had danced in Buenos Aires, there were many handsome men who tried to catch her eye at milongas, to invite her to dance. The *cabeceo*, from the Spanish word *cabeza*, or "head," is an invitation to dance by nodding the head. While unorthodox, it is discreet. And the woman is capable of an equally shrewd acceptance or denial of the invitation. Aggie found it strange at first, but in time understood the importance.

It had been surprising to see a man across the most crowded dance floor catch a woman's eye and jerk his head toward the floor, to invite her out. From the distance, the woman would invariably meet his gaze squarely, question if it was she who was being asked by tilting down her head slightly, and he would reply by nodding yes or no, without embarrassment. If yes, they rose from their seats and converged together on the floor.

Perhaps even more impressive was seeing a woman who wished not to dance with a man standing directly in front of her, only a few feet away, make it impossible for him to catch her eye. She could look everywhere except at him, with such confounding skill and composure all the man could do was drop his head and leave her alone. But these rituals transform the atmosphere of the milonga and further differentiate it from other dance experiences. Except for the lilt and croon of tango music, the milonga is silent. On the floor, couples convey a world of things with their bodies: passion, accessibility, wounding, vulnerability, melancholia, while never speaking a word. Those who are not dancing want to desperately. They are watchful for the eyes of a suitable partner, longing either to escape or to embrace *tanguidad*.

Women in BA do not go to a milonga to chat with other women. And while the dancers are listening intently with their bodies, those sitting are listening visually with equal focus. But how could she ever feel about it as she once had. She had been transformed as a *tanguera* and as a woman, and there was only one man with whom she burned to dance.

* * *

Miguel trudged into the studio looking much like something a cat might drag inside, sorely abused and barely alive. It was nearing half past two, and he was thankful that it was Friday, the day of the shortest rehearsal, according to Chaz. Miguel's left eye was purplish and nearly swollen shut. That was complemented by a good-sized bump on the left side of his head that ached almost as much as his left shoulder, upon which he had landed in his death-defying dive from Heather's window.

The springy aluminum roof of the tour bus on which he'd landed absorbed most of the crash. Miguel was certain that it looked it, too. Dented to hell, ruined. But he had been happy to scurry away from the scene without a broken leg or being shot. Muzzle flashes from Gordo's gun, extended out from the second-story window, had energized his getaway. The rounds had either whistled past him or struck the RV with a harrowing metallic ring.

Miguel stood outside the fishbowl where Aggie was stretching. The lights were low and a soft glow radiated from the blond floor. It was as though Aggie was a figment, dancing in Miguel's dream. It was much more soothing than his horrific reality. Even his apology and made-up story were odious to him. Although lying had never been Miguel's strong suit, it seemed now that his entire life was one big fib. He told himself that he wouldn't do it if it weren't necessary. Aggie had one foot caressing the wooden floor and the other extended, perfectly straight, in a point toward the ceiling. Her body was as limber as a willow branch. And he was about to find out how flexible her mind was.

Miguel tortured himself as Aggie stretched. He winced at his wrinkled shirt, seen clearly in his reflection on the glass. It had been clean and pressed a week ago, when he stuffed it into his suitcase. He sighed. How could he face her? Even his lie about being mugged would just draw her closer. And there was no way he could tell her the truth. The sordid event was so far beneath her. He should just go. Hurt her a little now so as not to hurt her much more later. Miguel turned and took a step.

"Whoa, look here, the elusive Miguel!" said El Primitivo. "This is priceless."

"Thanks."

"Tell me the other guy got the worst of it," he added, pointing to the shiner.

"I, um, didn't do much more than save my wallet," Miguel replied. "I fell running away." He shrugged, noticing the man's sunken eyes and swollen face.

"Son of a bitch, I told you to watch out in that neighborhood." El Primitivo shook his head. "No worries, I'm taking you to your place after rehearsal."

Miguel shook his head involuntarily.

"I ain't taking no for an answer." He patted Miguel's left shoulder.

"Ay!"

"Sorry, man." He pointed toward the lounge entrance. "I'm going to take a little steam before rehearsal. Hard night for me, too." He winked and hustled away. Turning back, he said, "Man, you look terrible. Go lay down or something."

"Thanks again."

Miguel glanced through the glass door and saw Aggie racing across the floor, head cradled in delicate hands. He thought she was going to cry, and then she did. He felt lower than a La Boca wharf rat, but was determined to dance this whole mess behind him, for a few hours at least.

CHAPTER 32

A HELL OF A DAY . . . and not so great a night. Miguel slumped against the elevator's glass panels, descending to the ground floor. After the murderous rehearsal, Don Luis had been keen to try and patch him up with ibuprofen and Malbec. They had helped somewhat, but he was still a human repository of aches. And he just had no temperament or compassion or whatever—for the man's enumeration of his family's torments and his obsession with their tragedies and how he could end them. It had been exhausting. The session confirmed to Miguel what he had learned in recent months, that a man is never so blind as when he seeks to see into the depths of his own soul. He rested his head on the cool glass and wilted.

His eyes closed, Miguel could hear Don Luis say, "I recall when possessing some knowledge of two great countries, Spain and Argentina, I thought I knew the world. But I moved to North America, to New York City. I made mistakes. People running this city in my day were called Giuliani, Grasso, Sonsini. You must embrace them and learn to deal with them," he'd said.

Miguel had interjected, "I already dealt in Buenos Aires with Marcovici. *Basta!*"

Don Luis's eyes had borne a glint of malevolence when he replied, "I will make him pay dearly for his sins."

Miguel was sorry he had gotten a bit irritated and replied that he was from La Boca and knew lowly people not lawyers and politicians. He had said his *milonguero* associates were true to their hearts and spoke the street language *el Lunfardo* and used a stiletto when necessary. But Don Luis had countered by claiming that those *milongueros* whom Miguel venerated had invented their argot, *el Lunfardo*, to raise a veil between themselves and the law. They even sought to distance proper society, precisely because they were mostly Jewish immigrants from Iberia and Italy, who had been persecuted and felt more secure with both a secret language and code of honor.

Don Luis had claimed that an outsider would call himself *un lunfardo.* Together the outcasts were called *Los Lunfardes* or *Lunfardim*, a Hebrew plural form! They had twisted together Italian, Spanish, and a Sephardic Hebrew argot called *Ladino* to make a street language insulating them from society and potential oppressors. He claimed that many of the *Lunfardim* were miscreants and forgotten to history, yet some had prospered.

Miguel had been stunned. Could Don Luis have been correct? Were those *milongueros* of Avenida Corrientes in tango's golden era really Jewish immigrants, fiercely caring for their tango and cultural families? It was hard for him to absorb. He had looked intently at Don Luis, whose face had assumed the kindly, insightful composure of a maestro. Of what mastery, Miguel was undecided. It was possible that he was merely a master of deception—

The door chime sounded again and again. For how long he'd been glued to the glass he couldn't say. Miguel unstuck himself and noticed the greasy mark on the otherwise perfectly clean glass. Story of his life, screwing up every beautiful thing he touched. He was more determined than ever not to touch one particular beauty. She didn't deserve to be soiled by him.

CHAPTER 33

HAD MIGUEL EVEN LEFT the studio, he wondered, entering the door at minutes before three on Monday. His wounds felt no better and the blood bruises were now in full bloom. Midway through rehearsal, his arm dangled when not embracing a partner and he clenched his teeth when he did. He needed something to kill the pain. During a mini-break, El Primitivo sidled up next to him and offered booze from a hip flask, along with a handful of oxycodone. It only served to heighten Miguel's uneasy feelings about his new friend. At five thirty, Don Luis ordered Miguel out of the lineup. Half an hour later, he tossed fitfully on the sofa in the *tangueros'* lounge. He lay on his back, feeling soothing air from an overhead air-conditioning duct. He wore only grey midrise briefs. His arms rested easily at his sides, their least painful position, with his well-differentiated biceps snugged against flared pectorals. Miguel didn't move when he heard the outer door swing open. Surely even El Primitivo would not make a move on him in his pitiful condition. He closed his eyes, feigning sleep.

The footfalls on the hardwood floor were too faint even for a skilled *tanguero.* Interesting thing about skillful dancers, Miguel considered, their street walks were usually not *elegante*, not quite gorilla*gante*, more like sloppy*gante*. The expensive carpeting hushed the footsteps, giving Miguel an instant to enjoy his

Spanglish joke when perfume gave her away: a distinctive fragrance, a delicate floral bouquet. He had considered it a strange selection for someone embracing the role of a bleached blonde bombshell. Perhaps the delicate peach and citrus notes reflected a demure little girl trapped inside her. Maybe that chubby little person had not been seen or appreciated, so now the *femme fatale* thing was being overdone. We're all fallible, he thought, before wondering what Candy was up to.

Miguel cracked an eye. Candy was standing above him, red lips parted in a mischievous grin. Her crystal blue eyes drank him in. Although not a prude, his first response was to cover his genitals for decency's sake. But Miguel sensed this was a standoff of sorts. And he was the male of the species, so he remained on display and completely at rest. Candy's feet were spread wider than shoulder-width apart, affording an excellent view of the apex of her curvaceous thighs, from under her fringy practice skirt. He didn't dwell on the pleasant scenery, but met her twinkling eyes with his.

Candy descended slowly. She glided downward so smoothly, without the slightest hitch in her movement, until her torso dominated his view. She leaned forward until her breasts reached Miguel's forearm. She eased into a 180-degree split and appeared to sit comfortably, the full weight of her bosom now resting warmly on his arm.

"Candy, can I help?"

"I was going to ask you the same thing," she replied in a more sultry drawl than usual. She extended a hand to his forehead and asked sincerely, "Does it hurt here?"

"No."

She slid the hand down searchingly to his torso. Made a slight swirling, massaging motion, asking, "Here?"

"No."

She slid the hand down his smooth abdomen and grinned extra-wide when a full six-pack involuntarily jerked up from his previously relaxed belly. Her pretty fingers raised the margin of his underpants. Peeking, she said, "I bet it's there."

"This is not a good idea," he said, grasping her wrist.

She used her free hand to simulate a wardrobe malfunction. "Oops," she said, exposing an ample breast with no trace of silicone, just a perfect tan line above a smallish, rosy nipple.

"I understand that I'm the new guy and you're a sex goddess. But this is no good. We have to work together. There would be bad feelings sooner or later."

She pouted. "I'm sorry you feel that way." Suddenly, she thrust her hand down his pants and grasped his firming cock. She squeezed it. "Feels good now, though, huh."

He regripped her wrist and began to withdraw her hand. She tightened her grasp on his wad.

"Bad idea. You may need this when you get well."

He was surprised by her strength. Only then did he realize that Candy could strangle a person to death. He eyed her cautiously, yanking her hand away.

Her eyes narrowed. "Guess you've already set your sights on Skinny-Mini." Her mouth twisted with sarcasm, adding, "She looks kinda dry to me."

Miguel pushed Candy's hand away and released it. Her balance in the split position was unstable and she began to fall backward. Both arms propellered for an instant as her mouth and eyes widened comically. In slow motion, Candy tumbled, landing on her back with a thud of her head. She lay there stunned.

Miguel couldn't have imaged she would fall so hard. He sprang up from the sofa and extended his hands to her. "I'm sorry. Let me help you."

"I don't need help," she seethed, standing.

"So what was coming here all about? This is a terrible time for me."

While restoring her wardrobe, and adjusting its contents upward and outward, she said, "Skinny-Mini's dad, Momo Jacobs, whatever . . . called you. His number's by the phone in the cantina." Rolling her baby blues, she added, "Says it's important, pfff."

"Look, Candy, I'm sorry—"

"Don't be. Ain't my first rejection." She turned to leave, but couldn't resist a parting shot. "Good luck, but I think you and her take different holidays. That makes a big difference in this town."

As the door closed quietly, Miguel considered the episode. While Argentine women could be aggressive they were usually certain of the outcome before they threw themselves at a guy or another girl. He had to admire Candy's courage for just giving it a go. Her last statement stuck in Miguel's mind. He hadn't even considered Aggie's religion. Was it really important? Maybe it was just one more reason not to get closer.

Rest time over, Miguel dressed and headed back to the floor. Don Luis called him over and asked to speak with him after rehearsal. He felt Candy's eyes weighing heavily on him. She leaned on the ballet bar, arm in arm with Chaz. She appeared to be chewing his ear. His head was thrown back and he was laughing and gesturing with both hands. Miguel caught her eye. She smacked a kiss to him and returned to devouring Chaz's ear.

Miguel panned the room. Dr. Wagner danced a profound tango with Aggie. She was either enthralled by his prowess or supremely bored. He was in full *tangeuro* flight: flawlessly erect posture, stable frame, crisp footwork, pinky of the right hand extended directly away from her back. What! Miguel looked away. He couldn't bear the over-gentrification of his *barrio* dance. He headed for the cantina, thinking that something was definitely up with Wagner. Something he did not like and would investigate.

CHAPTER 34

NEWS AND IDEAS FLOWED FREELY from Don Luis when he cornered Miguel after rehearsal. Miguel tried to be attentive, but he really needed something to kill his shoulder pain. In the background, Miguel saw El Primitivo motioning toward the gym. He pointed to his wrist, suggesting later they could carpool to the other side of the universe.

Don Luis informed Miguel that Aggie's father, who called himself MoJo, had called and invited both of them on the following Saturday evening to Aggie's sort-of-surprise birthday dinner. "It is sort of a trendy place, Buddakan, in the meatpacking district. Apparently Aggie used to enjoy going there with friends."

Miguel's stomach did a backward flip. He felt nauseous. The last place he wanted to be—much less eat—was near a meatpacking plant. He refused to glance down at what he was certain would be his bloody hands and crimson cuticles.

"What's the matter, my boy?" Don Luis asked. "Don't worry, I'm certain this place is as elegant as Aggie herself." He paused. "We'll scout it."

Miguel stared blankly, thinking this was the opposite of his plan not to get closer to Aggie. He said, "Please apologize for me, but I don't think I can make it."

"Really?" Don Luis's hand flew into his beard-nest.

Miguel was lying again, and hating it.

Don Luis looked at him thoughtfully. "This show is going to come together faster than you can imagine. You'll require many things for the PR *shtick*. Tell you what, I'll pick you up tomorrow morning. We'll tackle some of the impasses to this momentous event. See if we can't get you squared away." He smiled broadly.

Miguel nodded cautiously.

"Kemal will take you to your place. You needn't worry with public transport tonight." He arched his bushy brows. "Not looking and no doubt still not feeling swell."

"Thanks, but I have a ride."

"Very well. I'll see you at the same place and time tomorrow morning."

On the ride to Brooklyn, El Primitivo asked more questions than old maids quilting in a *conventillo*. Miguel recognized that his friend was loaded again. Fresh from an arms workout, he kept flexing and demonstrating his bulky biceps, pretending to smell his armpits with savage relish. He drove like a maniac. Miguel's desires were simple: he wanted to get up to his room and get to bed, without crashing or getting shot or arrested.

A police cruiser was parked outside the Fontaine Bleu. Nervous, Miguel asked to be dropped off by the side door—the one Heather disappeared from that fateful night. He declined the offer to take the big pistol from under the driver's seat, but accepted two oxycodone pills. When Miguel promised to call El Primitivo if he needed his help, his words had rung empty, like a rusty tuna tin. More lies.

The metal door was locked. Miguel obsessed over going through the front door. Even Heather didn't like doing that, without cops crawling the place. Climb the fire escape? Too suspicious and a last resort, given the pain in his shoulder. Miguel grimaced and knocked. Nothing. He knocked a bit louder, the metal rang. Nothing. Exasperated, he banged on the door, it resounded.

A tall man in a rumpled white shirt, who smelled strongly of cigarettes and alcohol, opened the door and thrust out his head, asking, "Whadaya want?"

"I, um, want to get back to the bar."

"Get back? I didn't see you before." He hesitated. "But I know you, don't I?"

"No, just checked in. Went out to call a friend."

"Go around front. This door's for employees."

"Look at me." Miguel pointed to his eye, black with a purple halo. "Can't you see I need a drink bad."

The man nodded, moved aside.

"Thanks," Miguel said, slipping past and moving into the darkish hallway leading from the bar. He wanted to get a look behind the front desk, maybe catch a glimpse of Heather. He dared not ask for her. Maybe he would call down from his room. Bad idea. Maybe he should use a house phone, if the dump had one. Ouch, his head began to throb. He had to get to his room ASAP.

Miguel darted from the hallway around the corner. He approached the elevator, pressed the call button, and stood close to the door. The space seemed as bright as the beach at midday. Head lowered, face nearly in his collar, Miguel wanted to peek behind him, hopefully to see Heather's big smile. He could hardly bear up. What was keeping the lift? This was New York, not Europe.

The door opened and he tried to duck inside, but a trio of people, two wearing policeman's uniforms, charged out. Each of the cops bore a big black trash bag. Their faces were etched with gloom. The gloom brigade, Miguel thought. What were they doing? It was pretty clear that Heather was not behind him at the desk, but now he had to look. Miguel spotted a familiar face. It was Gordo's accomplice; he stood near the furniture grouping where Miguel had first been seated by Heather. From over the top of a newspaper, the accomplice watched the cops depart. Newspaper, sure. He, too, was a member of the gloom brigade. He and his boss caused the gloom whereas the cops cleaned it up. An all-around gloomy picture.

Uncertain whether he'd been spotted by the spotter, Miguel entered the elevator and depressed buttons for the fourth, fifth, and sixth floors. The doors rattled shut and the cabin ascended with a jerk. He stepped out on the fifth floor. No sign of the gloom brigade, but it was far from cheery. Stained chocolate-colored carpets led to dingy doors with grime-encrusted hardware. This was worse than the second and third floors, he thought. He made for the stairs and raced down. Opening the fire door, leading to the posh third floor, it creaked ominously. He stood dead still and listened. His pulse ticked up into his temples, assaulting the left one painfully. No voices; no footsteps. What he heard was the throb of his heartbeat pulsing into his head.

Miguel's room was at the far end of the dark hall from the elevator and stairs. He moved deliberately, taking slow, quiet steps. He walked metatarsil to metatarsil, heels never touching the floor. He evenly transferred his weight with each step.

Tension built in his arms. His hands began to quiver slightly. Suddenly he was a young *tanguero* again, not accustomed to dancing with stars.

He clenched his shaky hands into fists, recalling ten years earlier shaking nervously the first time he had embraced Mia, Buenos Aires biggest tango starlet. She whispered in his ear to calm him. It had been a nightmare that had stayed with him. A few years later when they danced an exhibition together, she smirked when reminding him of the event. He acted as though he'd forgotten, but then he danced her heels off that night. He had dragged her, literally, the diagonal length of the floor. While the drag is a valid tango position called *arrastre*, it is the most *machismo* maneuver of all, depriving the follower of both stability and posture, while holding her powerless. To make matters worse, it was not part of their routine. Mia was limp and furious when exiting the floor. He recalled having smiled at her and having given her, alone, the extra bow at the performance's conclusion. She had earned it.

Room 316 was there in front of him now. That memory had been a valuable distraction. Miguel pulled the key from his pocket and unlocked the door handle lock. He turned the handle and pushed. The door held fast. Miguel's entire body became an antenna for motion and sound. A million thoughts rushed through his mind, first and foremost that something was wrong. It had always opened easily. He had not locked the dead bolt and the maid had not locked it before. He listened to the drone of a TV from his left. Caught an unmentionable shout from his right.

Miguel nestled his ear to the door. Nothing. It was time to make a move. Another curse from down the hall. He sighed. Life was too short for this, or that. He unlocked the bolt and thrust the door open firmly. He waited. Took a deep breath, before reaching around the wall and flipping on the lights. His cell was quite clean; his bed was made; and his possessions appeared intact. Miguel closed the door and bolted it, before falling onto the lumpy bed. He shoved the two oxycodone tabs in his mouth and swallowed them dry before turning over for a fitful night's sleep.

* * *

Chaz nestled more deeply into the comfy cushions of his expensive sofa. He felt responsible, just a little bit, for Cindy's upbeat frame of mind. No one knew better than he how hard it was to hang on during the tough times, making yourself believe your lucky break is just around the corner. He was glad she had met someone and was on cloud 9. He direct-tweeted Cindy, curious to learn something more about her new beau, Bo:

@cachafaz: "c i told u 2 nevr give up. Life is worth it!"
@cut00: "coolest day of my hole miserable life"
@cachafaz: "great! what's Bo like?"
@cut00: "he's totally on lacrosse team"
@cachafaz: "is he a + person?"
@cut00: "has a car! will no more after date!! luvya gotago :):):))"
@cachafaz: "me 2—2 work :("
@cut00: "no way—go get laid. ha a rime. cya"

Even the positive feeling of providing faith and counseling to a young person desperately in need of both was insufficient to soften the edge of Chaz's reality. He wallowed in his plush sofa, finding its comfort disgusting. His eyes narrowed, looking around his chic apartment, at his *cool* possessions. The remark had slit his delicate underbelly open wide, "Just like the bad ol' days," he murmured. And why's that so important anyway, he thought. I'm a professional at the sexiest dance in the world.

Chaz felt like smashing his costly phone, like destroying something. Instead, he inserted his earbuds and scrolled down the fancy phone's music folders leaving the sultry tango behind in favor of some vintage death and depression tunage, maybe by The Smiths. It was tucked away in the folder marked Emoshit. Once in the folder, he opted for a cutting classic by the Goo Goo Dolls, "Iris." He murmured a line from the song, ". . . you bleed just to know you're alive."

CHAPTER 35

SHOWERED, SHAVED, AND DRESSED, Miguel exited the Fontaine Bleu in daylight without fear. He wended his way through light rain down Flatbush Avenue, using a now-soggy newspaper as an umbrella. He neared the Travel Inn and ditched the paper. He wondered if Don Luis would be in the Cadillac limo. Perhaps something a bit more exotic would please him today. The sun peeked through low, leaden clouds. A slight breeze warmed. Miguel's spirits were higher already, wondering what excitement lay before him. There were surely reasonable answers to all of his questions. He just needed time to pose them and sort out the responses.

"That's him!" Someone yelled from inside a vintage pink Lincoln Continental, lowered to ride inches from the ground. Tires squalled as the big car did a uey. It jumped onto the curb, landing with a bang, and headed straight for Miguel. He ran toward the hotel, certain he could outrun or at least outmaneuver the junker for a couple of blocks. The engine roared ominously close. Surely, he could make it. He shot back a glance and saw the hot pink Lincoln racing down the sidewalk, gaining. Gordo hung out of the passenger's window, his arm pointed straight at Miguel.

Miguel heard a handgun's report. He zigged and then zagged, but it used too much time. If not shot, he was going to be run down any second. He veered left, headed toward an alleyway formed by two bombed-out buildings.

Tires squalled. The awful firing continued. Windowpanes in front of him burst into chards. This was insane; it was broad daylight. Miguel achieved the corner of a dilapidated brick building and rounded it. For the first time in more than a day his shoulder didn't bother him. Now his thighs burned like fire. He could dance tango half the night and then make love until sunrise, but he hated running. If ever he made it back to the studio, he swore he was going to start using the treadmill . . . at least once per week.

Miguel began to fade as he neared the rear entrance. Two men carrying a load of trash held open a service door. Miguel straightened his posture and smoothed back his hair. He entered at a leisurely pace, his legs like jelly and his heart pounding wildly. The lobby realized, he glanced casually from behind a structural column out to the circle drive. No classic Cadillac, but an ebony Mercedes Benz occupied a prominent spot.

The car gleamed in the summer sunshine. It had hardly been spotted by the rain. Miguel noted his cell, 10:05; he was late. It must be Don Luis. He stole a glimpse of himself in a decorative mirror, wiped perspiration from his brow onto his sleeve, and stepped authoritatively toward the entry doors. Something told him not to do it. Not to go outside. He ignored the extrasensory perception and opened the glass door. He strode to the automobile and tapped the dark glass of the rear passenger's window. He waited anxiously, wanting to duck behind the fender, at least to cover his head in the event a hail of bullets erupted. He slewed his eyes left and right. Nothing. Finally the window lowered and Don Luis exposed a mirthful smile.

"May I get in, please?" Miguel asked.

"Oh, yes, yes, but I'm having a bit of difficulty with my seat belt. Do hold on."

Miguel rocked from foot to foot. Finally, the door unlatched and he barged in, shut the door, and slammed down the lock. He exhaled as slowly as possible, allowing his breath to salve his raw nerves.

"My goodness you are in a state," Don Luis observed. He spread his hands. "It's plain daylight. No need to stress."

Miguel forced a smile, and closed his eyes.

Don Luis stared out the window at the squalor. "If only they could understand that they harm themselves when they harm this community." He clucked his tongue. "The poor pay a very high price indeed for their ignorance."

Miguel didn't contest the point, although he wanted to say that he was pretty sure the poor paid the highest price for being powerless.

Don Luis spoke to the little black grill, "Kemal, Marty's place on Varet Street. Take Bushwick Avenue, please."

Once inside the ancient building in East Williamsburg, Miguel supposed that Don Luis was in the market for clothing. Don Luis moved deliberately using his stick. "Good morning, Señor de Granada," said a lady carrying a bulky bundle of colorful cloth. The shop was like a hornet's nest, people racing up and down aisles filled with fabrics, mannequins, and cubbyholes. It was a feast for the eyes and the nose. The smells of freshly steamed fabrics pervaded the air. This shop could have been in BA, in the old days, Miguel thought, fingering a bolt of sumptuous camel hair fabric.

A sandy haired man of sixty approached them. He adjusted his spectacles and tugged the margin of his waistcoat, saying, "Señor de Granada, always a pleasure."

"Toddy, delighted to be here." He extended his hand.

"Maybe Dad can come out in a bit. He's not doing so well today."

"Perhaps best not to trouble him," Don Luis offered. "Toddy, turns out we're in a spot of trouble. But first, please, meet my, um, my associate, Mr. Miguel Zanotto, a tango maestro."

"Pleased to meet you, Maestro Zanotto," the man said genuinely.

"Call me Miguel, please." He took the man's hand and said, "Beautiful shop."

"Forgive me," Don Luis said. "This is Mr. Todd Greenfield, proprietor. His father worked here as a young man and ended up owning the place. A great American success story, compliments of a hardworking European family." Don Luis smiled.

Todd blushed. "Please call me Todd, Mr. Zanotto." He straightened out his face and asked, "How can I help?"

In no time at all they were hailing Kemal. Miguel carried a box, bearing his new shirt. A made-to-measure coat and pants from a rack were to be ready on Friday afternoon. It was like magic.

After crossing the Brooklyn Bridge and snaking well up FDR Drive, Miguel recognized the studio's elevated neighborhood, the Upper East Side. Instead of turning onto Park, Kemal continued to Madison and drove for several blocks. He stopped in front of an unassuming storefront between East Seventy-Second and Seventy-Third streets.

"Shall we," Don Luis said, smiling.

Miguel looked at him, puzzlement etched on his face.

He glanced down toward Miguel's scuffed street shoes. "Don't you think it's time for a new pair?"

There was no seat bottom in front of Miguel for him to plunge his shoes underneath. He said nothing, walking underneath a bright red awning bearing the name Silvano Lattanzi. Miguel and Don Luis were buzzed into the intimate salon and greeted warmly by a sales assistant. Don Luis spoke to the man, but Miguel was stopped dead in his stride by the intoxicating aroma of the salon. Images of the Comme il Faux workshop in Buenos Aires and of the cobbler's shop of his childhood in Rosario, where his small family's tango shoes were mended, danced in his head. But this was different; this shop was extraordinary.

Don Luis shook hands with a sturdy man sporting a classic blue blazer and salt-and-pepper grey hair. He said, "Miguel, please meet Mr. Silvano Lattanzi. He is seldom in New York. He prefers the tranquility of his workshop on the Adriatic coast of *Italia*."

"*Certo*," said Lattanzi, extending a meaty hand to Miguel. "Here, I am only in the way. And there is where the magic is made."

"Silvano, we need some serious magic," Don Luis said. "Miguel is in need of a new pair of shoes for the coming weekend. He needs something already made up. He can return some time later and order the world's most marvelous bench-made shoes."

Don Luis continued, "In fact, a trip to the workshop for Miguel would be a brilliant idea. Miguel, you could meet *la bella signorina*, Silvano's younger sister, and Mama. She's on the floor, sewing all day long, leading by example."

Miguel couldn't shake the spasm that squeezed his heart. Silvano's sister was alive and well and awaiting his return to Italy. If only Natalia were alive in Argentina. Miguel would run out of the shop that instant and catch a cab to the airport. Home he would go, to his small family, to the ones he loved so dearly, and who cared for him.

In the ensuing flurry of activity, Miguel regained his composure—measuring, trying candidates, selecting the perfect shoes for him. The winners were glove-soft, calf leather lace-ups with a muted black finish. The toes were capped and just slightly elongated. Miguel determined them to be classic yet distinctive, an appealing combination to a *milonguero.*

There was no talk of money. Again, Don Luis scribbled on a sales receipt, neither paper nor plastic changed hands. This time, Miguel felt no pang of poverty, although he suspected that weeks' worth of his wages had probably just been spent.

Silvano said, "These must be polished frequently when breaking them in." He thrust up his mitts, clenched like a boxer's. "With the bare hands."

Miguel turned away. In his hands, he held a shoebox, covered in *fleur-de-lis*. But he had that sickening feeling, as though the gore from the plant had permanently stained him. He had blood on his hands; there was more to come. Lattanzi's destiny was to use his strong hands to produce the world's most wonderful shoes. Miguel's was to use his bare hands to destroy the son-of-a-bitch who had killed his sister.

CHAPTER 36

AGGIE WAS FRUSTRATED at the conclusion of Adriana's Friday morning dance technique class. It had bothered her that she was the newest member of the company, only a couple of weeks' tenure, and suddenly raising her level of dancing technique was seen as a necessity. But when Adriana had asked her to attend, Aggie was all smiles, tapping it into her phone's datebook.

Not at the top of her game, physically or mentally, Aggie's lower back was killing her. Once in the locker area of the lounge, she wished she could hold her breath against the reek of Candy's cigarette breath. And to make matters worse, she could've sworn that Candy snubbed her. She'd hardly returned Aggie's greeting when they met face to face entering the studio. Aggie smiled at her a couple of times, but was ignored. Candy was not in a bad mood with everyone, though. Chaz, who had apparently been in the gym working out, passed the floor, all sweaty and pumped. He had made a goofy face and Candy responded by blowing kisses to him. Had she offended Candy somehow? Aggie wished she knew.

The highly polished bench stretching in front of the lockers seemed a perfect place to contemplate actually doing some exercise. It had been obvious in class that Adriana was a lot stronger than she. Aggie glanced down at her bird legs and sighed. She comforted herself thinking that Adriana's Argentine thunder thighs were powerful and shapely now, but maintaining them would be a lifelong, uphill battle.

Aggie grabbed her towel and a spongy floor mat and marched from the lounge to the fishbowl for some stretching. Her hand was already on the studio's glass door handle before she saw Candy staring daggers at her from across the floor. Too late to change venues, Aggie took the positive approach, an opportunity to clear the air.

She stepped inside the studio and headed for Candy, who was in full stretch on a yoga mat. "You're so flexible," Aggie said, thinking, but not voicing, *to be so chubby.*

"Not like you," Candy replied, extending her fingertips another inch.

Aggie hoped that the quiet would help her center herself, but it just gave her more time to consider what might be Candy's problem. It was too early to be making frenemies in the company, especially for no good reason. She decided to make another try.

Aggie stood and rotated her torso independently from her waist. She held the stretch, looking directly at Candy, who didn't make eye contact. Aggie said, "You didn't seem to have any trouble with the movements or holding the positions today."

"Yeah, it's the same stuff she's done before. The stronger the core, the better." Candy raised the lower margin of her top and tensed her abs.

"Nice," Aggie said. "I had a stronger core when I danced ballet every day."

"Hum."

"That was years ago. I can't believe I'll be twenty-three next week." Aggie looked up to the ceiling, shaking her head in disbelief.

"So, you're a virgin."

Aggie's head halted and her eyes snapped to Candy's, her mouth agape.

"Oh, my God!" Candy cut her eyes away and cast her hands about unnaturally. "I meant Virgo the, um, astrology, you know." Her palms landed up.

"Oh, yeah, sure. Uh-huh."

Candy nodded.

"Virgo the virgin, that's me," Aggie said, recognizing how stupid it sounded as the words escaped her mouth. She tried to laugh, but her facial muscles felt as though they were frozen in the expression of the man in Edvard Munch's, *The*

Scream. She pushed her arms straight down by her sides to keep from grabbing her temples, in a case of life imitating horrific art. Okay, lotus position, I really need you now. Aggie closed her eyes. Don't squeeze together the lids as tightly as possible, that won't block out the entire world. Nothing will, unfortunately.

She didn't hear Candy exit. Just as well, it'd be difficult to explain to any woman over eighteen years old that the right time/guy/situation had never materialized. Even for someone who had danced tango all night long in Buenos Aires and experienced tangasm! She had been sure it was going to happen, but didn't want to force it. Time had passed. Screw them if they couldn't understand. Screw all of them.

Exasperated, Aggie stood up and grabbed the mat and towel. She dragged them behind her rudely. Candy would probably forget about it, stupid cow. Suddenly Aggie realized that a *café cortado* was the answer. And if not the entire answer, a vital part of it. Tired of schlepping around the mat and towel, she dropped them in the floor and moped toward the cantina. All she needed was a little pick-me—oh, oh . . . voices. Whispered voices in the cantina. Aggie stopped mid-step, paralyzed. Straining, she heard Candy speak gibberish and then, "I said, oh my God—" Aggie didn't have to strain, but very nearly collapsed when Chaz replied, "Are you serious?"

CHAPTER 37

Miguel fought his demons, sitting quietly listening. Don Luis expounded en route to another of his favorite restaurants, the Second Avenue Deli, which apparently was located on East Thirty-Third Street. When could they explore what *he* wanted to, Miguel wondered. Now there was another topic high on his list: how to repay Don Luis for the fabulous new clothes and shoes. And what was with this crazy idea Don Luis had about God cursing his family? The poor old man certainly believed it. His cheeks had gone pale and his booming voice was often squelched to a whisper talking about it. Miguel wondered if such a thing was even possible? The Bible said so, but. . . .

Miguel also wondered what it would be like to have a family where one was willing to take life-threatening risks for the remainder. Willing to endure a curse for the benefit of others? It was not the kind of family he had known, apart from his mother and sister. His aunt and cousins had seemed more interested in playing on his mother's sympathy than trying to achieve anything for themselves, much less others. Was it his mother's fault that their real father had been killed in cold blood? Had he been a *porteño* out slumming instead of some Croatian count or baron—or whatever he had told them he was—it would have been considered life, um, death as usual. Just like the demise of Esteban Prafil, a decent man and the closest thing Miguel had known to a father.

If Don Luis liked sad family stories, Miguel had one. A real tearjerker, complete with loss, insanity, and murder. Talk about a cursed family, he could make a pretty good case for his own! Miguel clenched down hard on his mind. It was useless and infuriating to contemplate this stuff. He should just focus on Don Luis's wretched tale. It was killing the old guy. Perhaps speaking it aloud would be his salvation. There he goes again, "Ohhh, a family accursed. Despised by the Almighty! And why?" He paused, lapsing in contemplation or perhaps just too overwhelmed to continue.

The car inched along in Manhattan's lunchtime traffic. Don Luis continued, saying, "A presumably pious man copied verbatim the most monumental parchment ever penned." He tugged his beard. "Documents describe this man as tall and light-skinned with arresting green eyes. A veritable genetic aberration for his kind. But you need some background to really understand. We must backtrack more than a millennium."

Miguel creased his forehead, thinking, the traffic jam was not that bad.

"More than one thousand years." Don Luis tented his fingers, eyes closed in concentration. He desperately wanted to get it right. "The background: this pious man's family had moved from Palestine to the north of modern-day Syria. They settled in a town called Aleppo, which was a bustling place then, not the war-ravaged hell it is today. In fact, it was about eleven hundred years ago, circa 900 AD. About the time our villain, um, shall we call him an antihero?"

"He may be a bit of both. Maybe we call him *villero.* Sounds Latino, yes."

"Very well, about the time our *villero's* ancestors moved to Aleppo, in say, 915, back in Palestine, in Tiberias, on the Sea of Galilee, a famous scribe and an *über*-grammarian and teacher, Rabbi Aharon ben Asher, created a colossally important work."

"Galilee sounds familiar."

"Yes, about a thousand years earlier a Nazarene from nearby walked upon the Sea of Galilee and churned up the entire region." He added, "Neither has settled down."

Miguel nodded.

Don Luis jabbed a stubby thumb skyward for emphasis. "Our episode begins about four hundred years or so after the move in 915, which lore has it was for religious reasons. Apparently, Jerusalem was a difficult place to be pious during the 1300s, so the family clan moved far away to Tiberias, Palestine."

"Is like me moving from BA to Rosario to learn really how to dance *el tango*. In BA there is so-called authentic tango," his eyes rolled. "But many people, even some famous ones, are so fixed on dance theater they never actually felt a connection with a partner, which is the essence of *el tango*."

"Interesting analogy, Miguel," Don Luis replied. "Anyway, during 1099 Jerusalem turned out to be unlivable, figuratively and literally. The marauding Crusaders misappropriated Aharon ben Asher's masterwork, along with hundreds of other sacred texts. Later, they ransomed them to the highest bidder. His text was not a book but a codex."

"What is the difference?"

"Fundamentally, a book consists of pages bound along an edge. A codex is a collection of unbound leaves, called *folios*. I shall use book and codex interchangeably."

"Fine."

"So, the book was ransomed by a wealthy Egyptian community living in al-Fustat, an ancient capital of Egypt, near the modern-day capital, Cairo. It's sometimes called Old Cairo. There is an inscription by the scribe who received it from the Crusaders by way of ransom."

"*Los Cruzados* ransoming a holy book?" Miguel shook his head in disgust.

Don Luis shook his in turn. "My boy, you have no idea."

Don Luis broke the painful silence. "Now, we come to one of the most important moments for the book. There was a scholar, physician, lawyer, poet, philosopher genius called Moses Maimonides. There exists a namesake medical center for him in Brooklyn, in fact." Don Luis smiled. "I like his nickname. It's an acryonym for his title, Rabbeinu Mosheh ben Maimon." He spelled it aloud, "Rambam."

"Rambam! I like that too. Fortunately, I have not visited his hospital yet."

Don Luis looked askance at Miguel's purple eye. "Now, Maimonides or Rambam was truly the most gifted Jewish philosopher of all time and he lived in al-Fustat, now called Old Cairo. Originally from Andalusia, from Córdoba, he was, of course, a very fine Spanish chap. But he worked in Cairo, where he was the court physician, attending to the Kurdish Muslim ruler Sultan Saladin."

Miguel glanced out of the window to find a sea of yellow taxis swimming in canyons of skyscrapers, their triple black Mercedes limo a shark among baitfish.

Don Luis touched Miguel's sleeve. "Do listen, my boy," he said. "So, the man, Maimonides, left Spain—made uncomfortable by *reconquista*, and all that—with his family, circa 1170, lived in Morocco and other places, finally assuming a post at court when he was in his mid-thirties. Maimonides served at court for almost forty years, and he always commuted to work." Don Luis nodded. "Quite progressive."

Miguel jibed, "Even a short camel ride is a big pain in the—"

"Ah hum, actually he was rowed to and from work on the river," Don Luis claimed. "Turns out, he was associated with the Jewish congregation in al-Fustat, where the marvelous book that had been ransomed was kept. Immediately he assumed an intense intellectual interest in it." Don Luis laughed. "He had intense intellectual interests in many things. He wrote a book entitled, *On Sexual Intercourse*."

Miguel snapped his wrist, flicking his fingers, saying, "My man, Rambam!"

"Almost all of his writings were in Arabic and he lived his entire life under the aegis of Islamists. *Aegis*, suggesting protection, but really meaning control."

"Amazing," Miguel said. "But was he a member of this family you were telling me about? The *villero* who wrongly copied the great book?"

"Oh, no," Don Luis said, shaking his head. "The tyranny of words. But, not to worry, I've written it all down, every last detail. While so many of my colleagues at university were publishing poppycock, I scrupulously, in the manner of Moses Maimonides and Moshe ben Avraham recorded this history precisely. It is preserved for future generations in my, um, library."

"Who is Moshe?"

"Thank you. Moshe ben Avraham is none other than our scribe, our *villero*!"

"Ah ha. Tell me."

"So Maimonides's most important work was a legal compendium entitled *Mishneh Torah*, the most revered code of conduct ever written. With its exact delineation of the rules for writing sacred scrolls of the Torah, *Hilkhot Sefer Torah*, the *Laws of The Torah Scroll*."

Miguel said slowly, "So this is a really important Jewish book."

"It is a vital, sacred Hebrew text."

Miguel was taken aback by Don Luis's passionate revelation. He didn't know much about Judaism, but he knew that there were so many important books about religious rites, laws, and customs, even more than ones about the greatness of the culture. Miguel noticed Don Luis squinting at him. Trying to read his thoughts, perhaps. Miguel said, "This is incredible, and complicated."

"This is quite credible and scrupulously true," Don Luis said, as he twisted and torqued his beard as though in agony. "And the main resource Maimonides used for his master work, entitled *Repetition of the Torah*, was what he called, 'The book that has illuminated the darkness of the world.'" Don Luis raised a finger, saying, "And that book, my friend, is Rabbi Aharon ben Asher's codex or Crown, as it is sometimes called, that our *villero* copied verbatim almost two hundred years later in Syria. By then, it had remained in Aleppo for so long it was known as the Aleppo Codex or the Crown of Aleppo. It has come to be referred to simply as the Crown, or in Hebrew, the *Keter*."

Miguel said nothing. He tried to grasp what he had heard.

"Over a period of a year, fourteen months actually, he copied the book completely, down to the most minute Masoretic detail," Don Luis said. "It is, in fact, the details that are most important. Every pen stroke, the placement of each accent, and each of the copious explanatory margin notes, every single one is a direction from the Divine."

Miguel said, "So, the Aleppo Codex, or Crown, is incredibly important."

Don Luis looked as though he might burst with rage or passion, when he said, "The Aleppo Codex was the most perfect example of the complete Hebrew Bible, all twenty-four books, ever created."

Miguel was floored. He said slowly, "But Moshe didn't steal anything. In fact, the book's inscription said the one who saved it would be blessed. Before, you said he actually saved it, but you never said just how. And you just said the Crown *was* the most perfect Hebrew Bible. I believe there is a problem."

"Not a problem, but a tragedy, a shame, and a blight on my people." His trembling hand found Miguel's knee. "The Aleppo Codex has been partially destroyed by its caretakers. It will never, ever be made whole."

Don Luis broke into profound sobs, as gut-wrenching as a man losing to fate the love of his life or a woman losing to disaster her beloved child. Miguel wondered silently if the crime of Moshe ben Avraham, resulting in a six-hundred-year family curse, had actually been the salvation of the Crown. He tried to suppress the question of why a divine intelligence would ever be a party to such an unjust scenario, even on this pitiful planet.

CHAPTER 38

Aggie exited the *tangueras'* lounge, her mind a jumble of recriminations. She mumbled, "How could I have ruined my life already? I've never done anything wrong, hardly done anything at all . . . never even done *it*." She was sick of her flat, although not cut, abdominals and her boyish hips, which she was hopeful would be spread by childbirth or maybe chocolate cake.

She slowed her pace and cut her eyes to the fishbowl, where Chaz danced with Candy. They were apparently working on a new-style tango routine, called *nuevo* tango or neotango, featuring lots of open embrace dance figures and lifts. Candy oozed sex on the dance floor. Aggie understood there was more to one's appeal on the floor than the sum of body, face, technique, whatever. The most popular girls at milongas were not necessarily the prettiest or the best dancers, although either or both of those traits would assure you some dances every night. They finished the number and Aggie heard applause and a thickly accented voice say, "Bravo," as Jean-Luc stepped from the shadows.

Oh, him, Aggie thought. There was something she really didn't like about that man. He reminded her of mean old Mr. Schwartz from the synagogue. Always smiling to everyone's face, scowling to their back. She saw him open the fishbowl door and heard him add, "That's how I want to dance."

Chaz replied, "I thought you wanted to be Don Quixote or a *milonguero*, same thing really."

Aggie noted the big jab directed squarely at Miguel. She sensed more than a hint of jealousy. No wonder, Aggie thought, they were both marvelous tango dancers, although Miguel had Chaz by at least ten years. And what of Chaz's little breakdown earlier in the year? If the *tanguera* grapevine had been accurate, it wasn't so little, and perhaps not the first. Better not to stray off one's medication.

CHAPTER 39

MIGUEL WAS STUFFED with the Second Avenue Deli's delicious food. Never before had pastrami and onion rings been so tasty. He had to admit that while Junior's won the cheesecake award, the gangster count at Second Avenue Deli seemed much lower, a big plus. But the deli had been so lively and loud that he and Don Luis had sat in relative silence. That, too, was not such a bad thing. Don Luis had been able to compose himself and Miguel took the opportunity to better assimilate Don Luis's groundbreaking revelations. He still did not understand how or why the caretakers of the most important Hebrew Bible ever created, the Aleppo Codex, would partially destroy it, but he wanted desperately to know.

Cozy in the car, Don Luis depressed a button and spoke toward the intercom. "Kemal, home, please."

"Yes, sir," Kemal replied.

Miguel and Don Luis shared a smile, during which Miguel could almost see Kemal's toothy grin, piloting the limo to *his* home as well. As though Don Luis had read his mind, he said, "I think I owe you a little story, don't I?"

Miguel suppressed his desire to request the story that was eating him alive. He settled into the firm, contoured seat and listened.

"When I was on the grand tour of Europe and the Near East, as a young man, I encountered extraordinary women, some quite wise. That is how I came to have Kemal."

Miguel jerked his head to attention.

"Poor choice of terms. But, in fact, his mother did give him to me when he was a boy. Out of gratitude for my saving her life."

"Really?"

"Oh, yes. She was a beautiful widow who refused to marry her brother-in-law. She and three sons worked day and night baking sweets and bread to sell to passersby to pay debts to her brother-in-law accumulated by her deceased husband. I saw them on the streets of Cairo several times. One morning just outside my hotel, I saw the woman being lashed with a piece of rope by a stern-looking, stick of a man wearing a filthy *gallibaya*." He stabbed at the air, saying, "A long, dress-like thing."

Miguel nodded.

"I was young, strong, and stupid perhaps. A head full of ideas about the equality of the sexes, races . . . the extinguishment of oppression. Fresh off a philosophy degree from Oxford, you see. So I snatched away the rope from him."

Miguel delighted in Don Luis speaking not like an aristocrat but a caring man.

"He vanished and I insisted that my guide ask the woman about the problem. The debt was only a couple hundred dollars. So I gave her a wad of bills and departed."

"You risked a lot for a strange woman."

"Big risks for women, yet seldom sufficient—" Don Luis cut himself off abruptly.

"What is life without risks? Perhaps the risks we take define our existences."

"I have risked much, and lost. But one must risk while one is able."

"Yes!" Miguel said, unable to check his enthusiasm.

Don Luis continued, "She delivered to my rooms the brightest, most honest of her three sons. A shrimpy, peanut of a boy. She called him Seleem, meaning peace. She stated that she could not support all three by herself so she was giving him to me to be my servant for life, per tradition."

"This story is fantastic," Miguel said, hardly masking a measure of disbelief.

"Her sole condition was that although I was probably a Christian, I must not force him to alter his religion. She said he was special to God."

"So, you took him away?"

"I had no intention to take the boy. I paid for him to go to a boarding school away from the city, in hopes that one day he would elevate his impoverished family. The mother died—accidentally burned to death in the kitchen, while cooking for a new husband. Once finishing school, Seleem refused to return to Cairo. Philosophical scholar that I was, I devised a test of free will for him."

"Playing God?" It slipped from Miguel's mouth.

Don Luis's eyes narrowed slightly. "I sent him to Rome where he underwent a program of study in philosophy and religion. He learned well; his mind is sharp. But he remained steadfast in his Islamic belief.

"Was that a problem?"

"No. I hired him to work in my family's import/export business in Spain."

Miguel smiled.

"When I met my wife, who died not so long ago, I had Saleem trained as a chauffeur and bodyguard, mostly for her benefit."

"But you call him Kemal."

"Whereas Seleem means peace, after his education and proving his loyalty to my family, personally I taught him fencing." He added enthusiastically, "Foil, rapier, even halberd. He's quite lethal, actually, and obeys my every command."

Miguel frowned, wondering how a master of blades could accidentally nick his hand with a fancy little dagger.

"It was then," Don Luis said, "I gave him a new moniker, Kemal, perfection!"

"This story is fantastic," Miguel said.

"True in its entirety," Don Luis snapped. "I'm looking forward to hearing more about your family, Miguel."

"Would be less exciting, maybe even depressing. My family is not like yours."

"Maybe, maybe not." Don Luis extended his meaty hand. "Let's make a pact to share our stories truthfully, then, however fantastic or depressing they may be."

Miguel grasped the hand, gave it a solemn shake. Now, he could pose his questions and trust Don Luis's responses, with only a hint of skepticism.

The studio was completely quiet on the Friday afternoon. Perfect for Miguel's little errand. He proceeded toward the computer kiosk and just before entering he was surprised to hear a flurry of keystrokes. Momentum seemed to carry him into the doorway. Jean-Luc sat, staring fixedly at the monitor, typing furiously.

"Sorry," Miguel said, "I, um, didn't know you were here."

"Sometimes I have to think too long before typing. I end up sitting in front of computers more than using them." Jean-Luc smiled good-naturedly.

The words made sense, but the smile was odd, Miguel thought. "I'll just have a *café*; care to join me?"

"No, thanks, I've got to get going. I have a dinner date tonight."

"Anyone I know?" Miguel jibed.

Jean-Luc looked surprised, then shook his head.

Waiting for the Italian-made espresso machine to build pressure, Miguel chewed the interaction. Was every student allowed to use the company's computer? Was that Don Luis's intention? Where was his teacher, Candy? The analog pressure dial crept up past nine bars and Miguel began to salivate, thinking everyone certainly could enjoy the wonderful *café*. After he enjoyed his, he planned to check up on Mr. Renard's computer usage, in case he turned out to be as sly as his name suggested—

CHAPTER 40

DON LUIS WAS SWATHED in his flea-bitten vicuña bathrobe. Papers lay scattered about his bed and a television droned quietly from the far wall. He ignored these distractions and contemplated the good day. And this night had the potential to be even better. He reflected on his conversations with Miguel. A bond of trust was developing, and he liked what the boy had to say. Pithy accusations aside. Don Luis considered that perhaps it is true that when a person and that person's family members are healthy and happy nothing else matters. He had heard it was impossible for some *good* mothers to be happier than their most miserable offspring. He hoped that was untrue.

There was not time to burrow into the claustrophobic confines of his *sanctum sanctorum*, struggling to unravel the *Keter*'s deeply hidden secrets. He needed to be in his office by eleven. Don Luis plopped into his wheelchair, which groaned as though in pain, and headed downstairs. Entering the office, the heat seemed stifling, so he left the door cracked open to admit fresh air. The phone buzzed softly; its fourth private line blinked. Don Luis tensed his shoulders, his natural response to stress, and eyed the open door before grasping the receiver. "Yes?" He rasped, his free fingers diving into his beard. He listened and then asked, "Is it done?" Don Luis paused an instant, before screeching, "And why not?" He grasped the phone's cord, twisted it between stubby fingers, whose pads oozed oil and perspiration.

Don Luis's blood pressure and core temperature skyrocketed. "You said he did it!" Don Luis insisted. "All of your research, the deceased wife and all. . . ." He strained to hear every word. The caller was nearly drowned out at times by mariachi-sounding background music. "A new prospect who was definitely in Los Angeles when she was killed, you say? Who?" He listened. "But, how could you possibly find that out? Are you CIA? I'm warning you not to play games with me." The minute-long confrontation ended abruptly after Don Luis seethed, "Don't think I can't finish him off. I've done it before."

Don Luis slammed down the receiver. He flicked up his eyes toward the open portal and asked, "Who's there?" He turned his chair abruptly, banging his shin on the massive desk, turned in the opposite direction, doing likewise. Grimacing, he yelled, "Show yourself, I say!" A cool breeze wafted in, rustling the curtains.

CHAPTER 41

BUDDAKAN WAS GRAND, and teaming with energy. Miguel had to admit to himself that in all of Argentina there was no equal. His eyes were pinned to the ten-meter-high ceiling from which hung majestic chandeliers whose lights evoked flaming torches. They flooded an enormous dining room with eerie illumination, reflected in gigantic mirrors hung on filigreed panels lining the walls. The room's centerpiece was an enormous table, seating at least thirty, on whose surface the primitive ember-like light danced. The vibe was Genghis Khan does Versailles.

Miguel arrived at Aggie's table for eight. A busboy hurriedly removed two place settings, making for a spacious arrangement for six. He introduced himself immediately to Aggie's mother, Ruth. Miguel shook Don Luis's hand. He brushed his fingers across the sleeve of Miguel's sumptuous new jacket and smiled broadly.

MoJo greeted Miguel and introduced him to Seth Sheinberg, indicating he was a longtime family friend and an up-and-coming businessman. Seth wore standard-issue Wall Street navy blue with chalk stripes. He sported slicked-back, black hair and overly eager eyes. The look struck Miguel as a *Lunfardo*, an old-fashioned Argentine mobster.

Seth's stiff posture and cool greeting suggested they might be rivals. Miguel lamented that it would have been orchestrated more deftly in the Latin world where men snub each other warmly, as an art. It seemed impossible to Miguel that he would have met this man; he knew no one in New York. But something about his weasel-like face was familiar. And coupled with the look of disdain in his eyes, he was memorable.

Aggie, the birthday girl, looked lovelier than ever. She wore a flowing dress, off one shoulder and snug at the waist, accentuating her perfect shape. Her hair was unrestrained by clips that she used at the studio, and it fell gracefully past her shoulders, curling in lustrous ringlets. Miguel whispered, "*Muy hermosa*," nipping her cheeks with kisses, before taking up his exile at the table's far end. He could swear that he had felt the slightest cling of her fingertips when he released her.

Miguel took his seat, noticing Aggie's call to a waiter and her empty martini glass. The smile had deserted her face. Miguel was not in the mood for alcohol; he was nearly drunk on ambience. Exotic spice scents swirled about him: curries, peppers, and saffron, his favorite. Servers bore huge trays of artistically prepared edible art. So many young people, wearing everything from tuxedos to tunics, from dashikis to destroyed jeans. Miguel had felt self-conscious dressing in his expensive new clothing. Now he understood and appreciated Don Luis's efforts to help him dress appropriately. There was much to learn about this city.

Ruth asked, "Are you enjoying New York, Miguel?"

"Yes. But it can be a bit overwhelming."

"Hopefully Don Luis is helping you to find your way."

"He is a great mentor."

Don Luis waved off the comment. "Miguel has danced and traveled widely in the capitals of Europe. He's very much at home here." He added, "We hope to have him with us for a long time." He squinted slightly, continuing, "Ruth, I must say that Aggie and you share a striking resemblance. Both quite ravishing."

She blushed.

"Where I grew up in southern Spain, in Andalusia, there were women whose features and skin tone were exactly like yours." He paused. "And men who looked very much like Miguel."

"Well, actually I have relatives in Spain," she said. "A good many members of my family lived there previously."

"Not at all surprised to hear that."

Miguel wondered if Don Luis was molding the conversation to some end? If so, why bring him into it?

"All countries make mistakes," Don Luis said. "Spain is no exception, I'm afraid." He raised his hand gently. "But there was a time, a golden age, when no place on earth was as cultivated and as civilized as Spain. Everyone was welcome to participate in commerce, land ownership, religious freedom."

"You're right," Ruth said. "Do you still have family there?"

Miguel noted Don Luis's searching eyes. This was a first.

"My only brother passed just last year. We were not as close as brothers should be." His head shook. "Perhaps I was a bit in his shadow." Don Luis continued, "Now that he's gone, it's as though I miss the shade."

"Many of my relatives passed there," Ruth said. "Will you go back there to live?"

"No, my life is here. I have minimal business interests in Spain." He sighed. "And Spain's *faux pas* regarding the return of the *Anusim* is regrettable."

"Absolutely!"

Miguel saw Ruth's posture relax and her eyes widen in acceptance of Don Luis, perhaps a bit more of him, too, by association. She immediately took up the thread. Miguel was not sure who or what the *Anusim* were, but the pair had struck a deep chord.

Aggie drained another pinkish martini. Her eyes met Miguel's and she hurriedly lowered the glass. Seth bragged to MoJo about a recent negotiation. Aggie rolled her eyes. Miguel's heart went out to her.

After the meal, Miguel saw Aggie wobble away from the table. He feared the worst. From his pocket he produced a small white box, bound in a delicate red ribbon, knotted with a bow. He placed the present on the table for her to find.

Seth laughed. "Don't you think a ring's premature?"

Miguel smiled thinly.

"So, Miguel, how does this compare to Buenos Aires?" Seth asked, mispronouncing the city's name as though it were part of the zodiac.

"Buenos Aires is often called Paris of South America." Miguel's eyes roved, adding, "but we don't have this."

"Yeah," Seth sneered, eyeing the little box with envy. "Moe," he said, "I'd like to offer Aggie a distinguished dessert wine, if I may?"

"Go ahead. She'll be thrilled."

Miguel frowned, thinking another drink might drown her.

"What's wrong, Miguel?" Seth asked. "Don't like dessert wines? Me neither." He raised his chin. "But Chateau d'Yquem is special. French, from, um, one 'a the best wine regions, Burgundy, right bank, you know."

"Wow," said MoJo, regarding Seth with admiration.

Miguel turned toward Ruth, but heard Seth's comment to MoJo, "I'm working on something huge."

The bottle was ordered and poured before Aggie limped back to the table.

Seth made a grandiloquent toast to the birthday girl. Afterward, he looked down the table. "Miguel, isn't this the most wonderful thing you ever tasted?"

"Seth, this is a delicious Sauterne."

Silence.

"Yeah, Sauterne, that's what I meant," Seth replied, his eyes narrowing.

Seth nicked the little box from Aggie's fingers. He lifted it to his ear, shook it.

Aggie snatched it away. "That's mine." She thrust it under the table, her complexion assuming a shamrock-like green.

Ruth motioned to MoJo, who called for the check. Moments later, she began to rise. Miguel smoothly stood and helped with her massive chair.

Seth spewed, "How gallant, Miguel. You learn that from the tango bros in the *barrio* of BA?"

Miguel found the comment mean-spirited. It jarred his memory. Bros . . . that weasley face . . . the recollection dropped on Miguel like a bomb. He replied, "Excuse me, Seth, but the crowd you lunched with in Junior's backroom looked more like bros than billionaires. In fact, they looked a lot like the Sopranos."

MoJo's sparkling eyes leadened. His mouth fell ajar, staring at Seth. Miguel sensed that the *kibosh* was on the bromance.

Seth squinted. "I'll do you a favor and forget you said that."

"Thank you, but I don't need any favors from you."

Miguel nodded his appreciation to MoJo and Ruth. Before departing, he bid a listless Aggie a very happy twenty-third birthday.

CHAPTER 42

WAS IT A BLACK NIGHT, or possibly just his state of mind? The man lay alone at home with only the flickering video illuminating his bedroom. Ghostly shadows from the screen's reflected light swept across the ceiling. Stealthy. Menacing. He watched her obsessively. The focus of the surveillance video softened as he slowed down the playback speed. She moved gracefully, yes, but then so did many others. But there was something that earlier he hadn't noticed, how could it have escaped him? Perfect innocence.

He slowed the sequence even more, zoomed in. Finally, Miguel was out of the frame and he could observe her without distraction—full view, side angle, bent backward, as effortlessly as a young reed in the wind. Hold it right there. He smashed the pause button. He recognized her ecstasy. And in broad daylight. He emblazoned the expression on his warped mind. That's just what she would look like in the pangs of passion with him. He could feel it. Taste it. And, oh, was he going to feast on it.

He closed his eyes, squeezed rhythmically, awaiting a response. So that's what he'd wanted, and hadn't even known. It was so arousing, yet his frustration only grew. This little problem must go away. Now he had a fantasy that he would make reality. He promised himself that this time it wouldn't get out of control. He knew how not to be overcome by jealousy or passion. After all, Aggie's footwork was not as perfect as Natalia's. Nothing about her dancing was uniquely wonderful. And she was pure, so what was there to be jealous of or intimidated by?

Exasperation set in. Pulsing, teasing, cording, stroking . . . nothing. He threw back his head, ran sweaty fingers through his hair. And he was supposed to feel lucky that his medicine didn't impair his balance. What man would feel lucky to live like this? At least he was alive . . . but he intended to be more alive still. He leapt up from the bed, stormed the medicine cabinet, and flung it open wide.

* * *

Aggie awoke with a splitting headache and searing thirst. She cracked open an eye, nearly two A.M. She saw the small white box she had placed with care on her nightstand before crashing. It wasn't Tiffany blue or Cartier red, but who cared, it *was* the correct size. There had been no need to open it right away. Why not fantasize until morning. But the little present bore witness to that fact that not all of her recollections were dreadful nightmares. There had actually been a birthday dinner. Just how hideous she was uncertain. She'd dreamt of downing numerous cosmos, vomiting in Buddakan's ladies room, and having to hold onto her mom's arm getting to the car. Her stomach did a double flip recalling it. She took a deep breath and recoiled. If it hadn't really happened, why did her hair smell of puke?

She turned to her side and curled up, drawing her knees as close to her torso as possible, crushing a pillow into her churning stomach to calm it. If it were true, then on the way home her mom did go on and on about Don Luis, and how brilliant and sophisticated he was and that he was probably Jewish. And that made perfect sense, her mom had said, because he told her that the most important issue facing mankind was establishing world peace. Aggie recalled her dad's reply and had to laugh, although it made her stomach hurt more. He said that Don Luis was certainly too old, fat, and ugly to be Miss USA, so if he said that, he must be a Jew!

Her mom ignored the jab. She said that Don Luis knew a great deal about the Jewish diasporas. He had spoken about the Sephardim, Mizrahim, and Maghrebi Jews, including how the Babylonian Jewish traditions differed from the Palestinian ones of the Ashkenism. Her dad had countered that maybe that was because he was a former professor of religious studies at CUNY and because he was a Syrian Jew by blood. Okay, so dad really did say that. But why in the world did he say that Seth had told him? That's ridiculous. Oh, she didn't want to think now. Her head throbbed and her stomach churned. She was afraid of being sick again. Aggie cracked open the other eye. The little box was still there. Beyond, the wall began to spin. She shut both eyes tight. How would Seth know anything about Don Luis? They'd never met, as far as she knew. But how much did she really know?

Regarding Miguel, her mom had pointed out that he'd handled himself much more like a gentleman than Seth. And then what her mom said . . . oh, oh, the headache was a real ball-buster now. What a vulgar term. Aggie recognized that she had never thought that before. To distract herself from the pain, she focused on recalling the next snippet of conversation that she'd heard, lying down in the backseat, wishing for sleep.

Oh yeah, her mom told her dad that his plan had backfired. Huh, Aggie thought, his plan? She surmised that the whole wonderful-birthday-dinner-with-friends *shtick* was a setup to discredit Miguel and promote Seth. Suddenly he's showing up everywhere, at the cleaners, bumping into her dad and such. Aggie didn't trust him. He'd never been her good friend and he was never, ever going to be her lover. Aggie wanted only Miguel, and she would be his.

Aggie rolled to her stomach, smashing the pillow deeper into herself. She felt sick and exhausted, but could not control her mind. It was in a free-association mode. And what was that crack Miguel had made at dinner about Seth lunching with *mafiosi* at Junior's Deli? That had pissed Seth off big-time and sent her dad into a tailspin. Then when her mom had mentioned it on the way home, he'd clamed up. It was like *omertà* kicked in. Aggie tried again to blank her too-busy mind. Bing! About Madonna standing on top of their table singing "Like a Virgin" to her, that was not real—just a nightmare!

CHAPTER 43

"HEY, MAN, WAKE UP, and get your ass down here," the caller gruffed.

Miguel shuddered, wondering why he'd bothered to answer his phone in the middle of the night. Wasn't the Fontaine Bleu hellhole bad enough without some maniac dialing random numbers? "Look, you got the wrong—"

"Miguel, it's El Primitivo. Don't hang up!"

"Hold on." Miguel wondered what mess his buddy had gotten himself into now. It was inevitable, the way he'd been living. Miguel yawned and stretched. He looked around the darkened room, seeing only stray light from between the poorly fitted blinds slashing the walls at dramatic angles like so many machetes. The stripes crossed his chest like wide lash marks or an old-fashion prison shirt. "Okay, now what do you want?"

"Brush your teeth, douche? 'Cause I need for you to get down to the street ASAP to help me save your miserable fucking life."

Miguel shot bolt upright. "Don't tease me like that."

"No teasing. And don't bolt out the front door. Exit by the bar."

"Yeah, okay."

"I'll be in my car near the end of the building, on your right."

Miguel managed a smile; the guy was so out there. This was probably not nearly as serious as El Primitivo pretended, but he'd better play along just in case. Minutes later Miguel had slithered out the side door and was inside the El Primitivo-mobile. He stared at his friend. El Primitivo looked completely wigged: eyes encircled in black; hair a veritable packrat's palace; and skin as ashen as a snuffed pyre.

Miguel asked, "So what's the—"

"Shhh, let's get outta here first." Five minutes and as many miles away from the no-tell hotel, El Primitivo blasted, "You been holding out on me, huh. Yeah, I'm a sucker, a sweet guy." He turned and faced Miguel, pushed a stubby finger into his chest. "And what do you do, you fuck me up."

Miguel pushed the daring digit out of the way and grabbed the wheel, steering the car back onto the road from the shoulder. He was determined to remain calm, at least until he understood what El Primitivo perceived to be the major problem. He asked, "What have I done to you exactly?"

"So you got a little action on the side. How's that going? Seen her lately?"

Miguel squirmed. The luxurious seat suddenly felt like a cauldron. "Heather?"

"Yeah, Heather. Well, guess who got a call from her phone today." He thumbed his chest.

Miguel sank into the seat and a big grin spread across his face. He knew she was okay. Probably in hiding. Now she was relaying love notes to him.

"You like that, huh. Well, she was asking where to find you? Asked if all tango dudes had ten-inch dicks."

Miguel crossed his legs involuntarily and laughed. "Hopefully you assured her we do." This was getting funny. He knew Gordo didn't have the guts—

"No, I didn't. See it was Heather's phone, but it wasn't Heather."

Miguel ate his grin. "So, what are you saying?"

"Because Heather was shot dead days ago, *schmuck*!" He paused. "And the cops got no leads or witnesses. But somebody figures you know something pretty important and they want to have a chat with you." He sighed. "But I'm pretty sure you won't live through it."

Miguel's leg began to quiver. He cuffed his thigh to stop his foot from dithering. "You're sure about this?"

"It's been in the papers. Other day the hotel parking lot had so many of Brooklyn's finest, looked like a scene from *Die Hard*." He laughed. "Die . . . *hard*, get it?"

Miguel was not amused. "Gordo?"

"Bada bing," El Primitivo said, his smile fading. "Cops know he did it, but there's no proof. Don't suppose they're going to find your prints in that apartment?"

"If yes?"

"You'd be looking like a real good fall guy. They may be getting some moola on the side from Gordo's boss, so you'd be very convenient."

Miguel's knee jerked and struck the bottom of the glove box. Cinched his thigh tighter. His mind raced back to Heather's warmth, Gordo's intrusion, and poor little Hector. What would become of him, Miguel wondered, forgetting his own plight for an instant.

"Not too interested in the next move, I see. Or you the quiet type?" El Primitivo looked over at Miguel and steered the car onto the shoulder.

Miguel grabbed the wheel. "Look, man, you're too loaded," Miguel said. "Let me drive so you can think. We need both of our brains to figure out a plan."

"Lucky for you, I already have one."

Miguel's eyes popped.

"You got to face Gordo before he snuffs you or the cops nab you."

Miguel's jaw dropped.

"You got to assure him, and I mean a blood oath," he grinned, apparently liking the sound of it, "your lips are sealed. And you're blowing the country now."

Miguel shook his head. He couldn't see how he would survive it.

"Okay, then get that pea-sized brain of yours all pumped up, and come up with something better. Gordo's in the kitchen, behind Sarge's, right now."

"Even if I make peace with him, you say the cops will make me for the killer." Miguel shrugged. "Either way, I'm screwed."

"I'll be your alibi for that night. Your prints could've been left there anytime."

"And if they're not the prints of Miguel Andro Zanotto?"

"We know the answer to that. But there's plenty of illegals in this place."

Miguel wondered why the man had been playing with him. He'd known all along. It was not time to be embarrassed by being an exposed liar. Besides, it had been out of necessity. Miguel looked out the window at the squalor of some neighborhood he'd never seen. Shopping cart people, vagrants lying on the sidewalk . . . their lives were more valuable than his. At least by living, they had a chance to improve their lots. A chance—a really tiny one—to win the lottery. It was as though he'd just lost the biggest lottery, the lottery of his life. Miguel could not be Natalia's avenger if he were locked up in jail. In an instant of frustration, he said quietly, "Okay."

El Primitivo crushed the brakes. They skidded to a stop. Grit and debris cascaded over the car and shrouded the brilliant headlights in a bluish fog. "Okay, what?"

"I will face Gordo now."

* * *

The man leaned against a dusty automobile, parked in the hotel's lot, across the street from Sarge's. He took a long drag on a cigarette, exhaled toward Sarge's dilapidated neon sign. Smoke blew back into his beard. He turned his face to avoid it. He hated wearing this thing; at once it smelled like a garbage disposal and ashtray. He spotted the gibbous moon, nearing fullness. It was beautiful and there really was no hurry. It was pat. He could write a book on how it would work. Shit, he could write a book so thrilling and bizarre it'd make Seal Team Six taking out bin Laden look like a fairytale. Actually, he knew beyond doubt that it was—

A couple stumbled arm in arm from the Fontaine Bleu's entrance. He didn't turn away his face for fear of being seen. Dark raincoat, dark beard, dark trousers, dark shirt, dark shoes; he was invisible. The couple stopped and leaned against an opposing vehicle. They kissed; he watched. His heart rate dropped a point or two. Had experienced much and was trusted by some very powerful people, but he had missed that. Strolling with a lover. Smooching in open air. Caressing her breast, feeling its heft in one hand while grasping her neck with the other. Not his story.

His mate had been chosen for him. And there had been precious little kissy face even in the beginning, none in as long as he could remember. But as long as he did what his employer asked, she and the kids lived relatively safely—as safely as you can live in a veritable war zone—while he roamed the world playing spy games. Roamed and played. Played roles and games. Mind games, dangerous games. The objective was usually to watch, learn, and protect or kill before being killed.

He usually played on a team, but tonight he was playing solo. He despised his overstuffed contacts, but they had been necessary. He hit the cigarette again, his eyes closing slightly from the harsh tobacco he'd grown up with. Parting his eyelids, he noticed the scene was brightening. A pale bluish filter colored the brightening landscape. The intensity grew and the spectrum whitened, turning onto Sarge's street. Pebbles and glass crunched underneath bulbous tires. There were few such cars in this part of town. He snuffed out his smoke, ditched it down a sewer grating. Unbuttoned his coat, recognizing it was time to play.

CHAPTER 44

Miguel eased the car up to the retaining wall, protecting the entrance of Sarge's. It was a low, crumbling block structure probably installed to keep loaded losers from driving through the front door. El Primitivo's job was to go around back to Gordo's *kitchen* and prepare him for a civilized talk. All Miguel had to do was wait in the car until he signaled him to come. Then Miguel must grovel a little and assure Gordo that he was splitting town. Then get the hell out of Brooklyn, prepaid room be damned.

Miguel watched El Primitivo kick the car door open wide. He wanted to speak, but couldn't find the right words. His mouth was so dry, saying anything was a chore. El Primitivo had insisted to go in alone. That was final. A spark flashed in Miguel's mind. He rummaged around under the driver's seat and withdrew the humongous handgun. Miguel thrust it toward his friend.

"What, you want to get us killed?" El Primitivo waved away the weapon. "I told you this guy and I got some common business interests, the same partners." His hands were juggling again. "We can talk. Just wait for my signal."

"I can't tell you how much—"

"Shut the fuck up." Pointing an unsteady finger, he added, with a mischievous grin, "But you definitely owe me."

Miguel nodded profoundly. He watched his buddy staggering up the concrete path and around the side of the dive. He shoved the piece under the seat, thinking, *Why is he involved with these people? He's from a good family, he's funny, he can dance. Why is he throwing it all away on drugs?*

Miguel thought of Heather. She was history and Hector was not going to have much of a chance. Gordo would probably raise him up to be a vile whoremaster. And Lexi Lexus, heaven only knew what she was like or how long she would live, working mean streets. Miguel's heart ached for these people. He sighed for them, forgetting himself for a merciful instant.

Before Miguel could save the world, he had to save himself. And of all his performances, tonight's would be the most important. After all, he'd danced on some big occasions, but never to save his life. Miguel tried to lean back and lose himself in the luxury of the driver's seat. It was humid and he was sweaty. The shirt clung to his back and his hands perspired. They were sticky like when he was a kid at the fair, eating *copo de azúcar*. He imagined tearing away a fluffy strand of pale-colored spun sugar. What was it called in English? No clue. He must improve, assuming that he lived through the night.

The crack of gunfire jolted Miguel from the refuge of his childhood. A staccato sequence of three shots. He scanned the ground leading around Sarge's right side but saw nothing. His mind raced. What to do? More shots rang out. Miguel threw open the door and dropped to the ground, peering around its sculpted margin. From the side of the dingy building, out from the darkness, El Primitivo burst into the light. He raced toward the car, his face filled with terror. One arm flapped ghoulishly as he sped, the other cutting the air trying to pull him ahead faster. Miguel told himself to stay calm. Both of their lives depended on it. El Primitivo was in front of Sarge's, running toward the low concrete barrier. He appeared not to see it and ran square into the wall at full speed. It caught him at his knees. He howled in pain and fell backward.

Miguel screamed, "Primo, you can do it!"

His friend looked up and emitting a horrible cry, stood to his feet and took a step toward the wall.

"Come on!" Miguel shouted. And then he saw the muzzle flashes from beside the building. A flurry of bullets screamed past, close by him, glancing off the car's fender. Miguel quivered and then yelled again, "Primo, come on!" His friend stood. And then Miguel heard the sickening squish of rounds drilling live flesh. El Primitivo bounced like a gruesome marionette. He grabbed his chest, his mouth flew open wide, and he fell face-first over the decrepit barrier. Miguel looked on in horror as the muzzle flashed again, closer this time. The shooter was coming in for the kill.

The night air reeked of burnt gunpowder; grease; ammonia, sulphur, and pseudoephedrine. And Sarge's had done a booming business, a big Saturday night for immigrant urchins and the men who would abuse them. The heavy moon shone, its sterile light illuminating the just and the unjust, exactly as rain falls on both. *Is there any point in being virtuous in this vile world?* Miguel asked himself. He had no answer.

Miguel cowered behind the sleek door panel. His knees dithered; they knocked together like an anxious school child's. Is this the way a *miloguero* meets his fate, he wondered. Pissing his pants, hiding while his friend, who was trying to help him save his skin, is shot down like a dog. What a hypocrite. Had he always been so weak? Had he only kidded himself that he was a true *milonguero*? It was clear that he had become nothing more than a poser.

If he was willing to hide and watch his friend perish in the mud, then he possessed no soul. He should stand and take the next round himself, maybe two or three. Miguel considered that if he was a blight on the face of Earth and could never face himself in the mirror after this, why bother to save his neck. The world did not need another taxi-dancing *tanguero* . . . another tango whore.

Miguel didn't want to be a killer. The role had been thrust upon him. He had read that for some greatness is thrust upon them, but for him it was his destiny to kill. He grabbed up the giant handgun and stood. He sighted his objective, a rather tall person advancing slowly. Miguel squeezed the trigger again and again. The muzzle of the pistol flashed blindingly. Rounds seemed to explode from the chamber, kicking up the barrel as each screamed toward the moving target. A few shots later, he didn't know how many, an agonizing scream could be heard coming from the target's direction. The flashes ceased, as the man retreated, leaving behind deathly quietude.

Miguel stashed the pistol in his belt and rushed to El Primitivo. Miguel picked him up with seeming superhuman strength and carried him to the car. He lay down his friend gently in the passenger's seat and closed the door before racing around and entering the driver's side. Miguel scanned for the ignition. No key. No nothing except window controls on the console and a sleek touch screen, completely blank. El Primitivo slumped unconsciously in his seat, gushing blood onto the buttery leather. Miguel frantically began to push the screen. The stereo began to blare jungle music, a candombe classic. He tried to turn it off. Nothing worked. His friend groaned and Miguel patted the man's face, trying to rouse him. He would die soon if Miguel couldn't get him to a hospital. The music was deafening.

Uncertain how much more he could tolerate, Miguel said, "Primo, wake up. Start this thing!" He shook his buddy, feeling a growing sense of dread. Miguel turned and stared out of the windshield. They had to get away. It was a death trap.

The music ceased. Miguel snapped toward El Primitivo, who had a bloody finger poised over the screen. "You're going to be okay," Miguel said.

"Sure of that?" El Primitivo said weakly. "If you don' get us out of. . . ." A violent cough overtook him. His chest reddened with each spasm.

Miguel put his hand over the hole to stem the outflow. He couldn't control his emotions. He screamed, "How to start this fucking thing?"

El Primitivo raised his hand to assist, but it fell limp on the console.

Miguel took up his friend's hand; he tried to feel an impulse, direction. It was less definitive than a Ouija board's triangle.

Miguel continued to futz with the high-tech car's dash to try and start it.

"Mob's bad, but Mos—worse." El Primitivo coughed up a mouthful of blood.

Miguel looked on in horror. He had to fix this mess, and quickly. His friend was dying. He racked his mind for answers, patting El Primitivo's shoulder. "We are going to be okay. I won't let you down."

Another frantic stab at the dash and the instrument panel sprang to life. "¡*Esso*!" Miguel shouted and fingered the car into reverse.

His friend grabbed his arm with a death grip. He struggled to speak.

Miguel thought he said, "Mos dad at the studio. They know . . . the book."

Assuming he was delirious, Miguel turned to look over his shoulder to back up.

El Primitivo said in a tortured voice, "I'm sorry, I set you up—"

Miguel's face snapped toward El Primitivo, whose eyes were filled with tears.

Suddenly the windshield shattered in a hail of shards. A barrage of bullets drilled straight through to the rear window, blowing it clean out of the frame.

Miguel jerked around the doorjamb to see the continuous flashing of an automatic weapon advancing from the side of Sarge's building. In the dim lighting, Miguel recognized Gordo, carrying what was probably his favorite toy, an assault rifle. He walked upright without fear, like an action hero. Another fusillade. Miguel ducked into the floorboard. Bullets pilloried the car's exterior and the seat above his head. It was like a violent hailstorm banging an old tin roof, only louder, and lethal.

His heart pounded inside his chest. Miguel reasoned that the closer Gordo got, the more certain their deaths. He grabbed the massive pistol from his belt. Without hesitation he sprang sideways out of the open door and rolled to its outer margin. He looked up to see Gordo outside the small retaining wall, advancing for the kill. Miguel aimed at his chest and fired. The pistol bucked uncontrollably. It was a monster. Gordo ducked and fired from the hip. Miguel rolled behind the door, bullets hammering it. They pierced the thin metal, seemingly aching to penetrate him, to drill him dead. Miguel was half deaf from the clamor, and almost completely numb from fear.

Miguel realized that their lives soon would be over. He may have one chance in a million to shoot Gordo before Gordo wasted him. The bullet barrage ceased for an instant. Now was the time. Miguel drew a deep breath and tumbled out past the car door into the moonlight, crunching glass shards as he rolled. He stopped on his belly and thrust the mighty handgun in front of him with both hands. He looked up to find Gordo standing on the crumbling wall, ten feet away. Gordo sighted his weapon, smiling fiendishly.

CHAPTER 45

DON LUIS ROUSED from fitful slumber. His neck throbbed. He had passed the last several hours resting his head on the rickety writing table of his *sanctum sanctorum*. He clutched an antique dueling pistol in his right hand. Bulky. Weighty. And as deadly as the day he used it to dispatch insolent Count Andro—an excellent day and a doughty deed.

What nightmares. Such tragedy. He could not help himself after waking, fearing for the safety of his precious books, particularly for the safety of the *Keter*. He had come down in the early morning hours to ensure their safety, to maintain a vigil in their defense. The recent robbery attempt had been unsuccessful but unsettling. He believed it had been an inside job, but how? No one knew of his secret cell, not even Kemal, his most trusted ally. He had even denied access to electrical contractors after Hurricane Sandy. Yet the power to so many magnetic clutch locks had been cut and the labyrinthine passageway leading from the outside to the bowels of his building had been navigated expertly. He had seen the footprints. Could see them now, leading from his small desk. Save for a bulky chain and padlock, his priceless relic and key to the betterment of his people would be gone. Don Luis tugged and twisted his gnarled beard until his face ached. Who was he kidding, his secret was blown. It was time to act, before another disaster, altering his DNA beyond repair.

Don Luis had been altered by strife. There was no denying it. Epigenetics had proven that everyone is changed by prolonged adversity. And no family had suffered more than Don Luis's for over half a millennium. His bitterness had evaporated into a willingness to try and persuade his people to save themselves. Ah, but they were a population steeled by millennia of hardships, pogroms, and near annihilation. Now, perhaps genetically unfit to navigate the treacherous waters of a peace accord with neighbors, their very DNA altered by excessive trials and tribulations.

He rose and stood on unsteady legs, fortifying his stance using the little table. Don Luis nearly stumbled over his wheelchair. His emotions bottomed as he considered the imperative, 'Physician, heal thyself!' Don Luis's head swam; his thoughts eddied. He was no master of Kabbalah and certainly no oracle like John of God. He was simply a man . . . a man who feared for his people and desperately sought to help them find their way to peace, before it was too late.

CHAPTER 46

MIGUEL TRAINED THE HANDGUN on Gordo's chest. Perspiration hampered his vision, but he could see the automatic weapon's muzzle lowering toward him. Miguel fired. Gordo dodged and was thrown off balance. Miguel squeezed the trigger again, the massive gun clicked. Frantic, he pulled and pulled the trigger only to hear the futile clicking of the firing pin.

Gordo righted himself and trudged forward. The smile was replaced by a menacing scowl. All was lost. But Miguel was not going down without a fight. He leapt up and screamed a battle cry, racing toward Gordo, who stopped dead in his tracks, glowering. Miguel did not hesitate. He rushed forward faster. Nearing Gordo, he heard two faint pops, something like a child's cap gun. Gordo began to waver. Then he dropped his weapon and fell to the ground face first, like a Goliath, landing with a splash in the mud. Miguel looked down to see Gordo's head, spilling blood onto filthy ground.

Miguel jerked his eyes in every direction. He saw no one, heard nothing. He collected himself enough to think of getting El Primitivo to a hospital. He raced to the car, closed the door, and hit the accelerator. No response. The stench of smoke had filled the cabin. He smelled melted electrical insulation. Although it was an electric car, it could still explode. "Hey, man," he shook his friend violently, "we got to get—" It was then that he saw El Primitivo's face: eyes open wide, completely still, lifeless. Miguel felt the neck for a pulse. Nothing. Miguel had never been particularly religious, but he carefully closed his friend's eyes and whispered a prayer for his forgiveness.

Shocked and uncertain what to do, Miguel saw that on the console, in El Primitivo's open hand, lay a cell phone. Strange, it hadn't been there before. And it was as though he were offering it. Miguel heard the first wail of sirens. Cops closing in. He was going to be taken into custody and if not tried for murder at least deported for immigration violations. Could this be the end of his quest?

No! Miguel grabbed the phone, dropped the pistol to the ground, and shot away from the car like a human bullet. As he disappeared into the night behind Sarge's dilapidated façade, he heard an explosion and turned to see El Primitivo's supercar engulfed in a super-fire. Miguel shivered and crossed himself for his friend, trying to will him into heaven. Then he ran like hell.

PART III

The Basic Figure of Argentine Tango

RESOLUTION

Leader: *One step forward (left). One step side (right). Close feet together.*

Follower: *One step back (right). One step side (left). Close feet together.*

CHAPTER 47

Don Luis shoved away from his cluttered desk and wheeled toward the lift. He had to have some fresh air, a break from his claustrophobic cell. Wheeling himself through gritty stink, he recalled a rare book dealer in the Hasidic community in Williamsburg, Brooklyn. Decades earlier, the man had offered a fraction of the missing Torah for a million dollars. Don Luis had read the dealer's identity in 1990, shortly after his untimely demise in a Jerusalem hotel room. Don Luis had only recently used shady members of the same congregation to float a quiet offering for the Aleppo Codex's entire missing Torah, the Pentateuch, the five books of Moses. Given the explosion of the art and antiquities market, he decided to be taken seriously he must ask for one hundred million dollars. He had floated his trial balloon with the help of a Brooklyn businessman, aka Mafia associate, Mr. Sheinberg. The man still lived in Flatbush, although it was rumored he had made plenty helping out the Mob. Don Luis had gotten his name from an antiquities dealer, who said that Mr. Sheinberg could bring his offer to the attention of big shots in the United States and Israel. Don Luis was now a believer. He had attracted the attention of a dangerous organization, more dangerous even than the New York Mafia, the Mossad.

Even if the word of his possession of a priceless relic were out and if it were his undoing, hopefully something could be achieved. Perhaps his plan to motivate Israel's leaders to engage in meaningful negotiations with their neighbors would be more successful. He believed in the power of the sacred text that he possessed. And, further, he believed it could make the difference between war and peace, prosperity and extinction.

His office secure, his mind bubbling over with thoughts, Don Luis rolled toward the hallway to the building's internal lift. He glanced down with pride at the honey-colored floor, radiant in morning sun. But the sun didn't usually shine that far into the studio's recesses. And it was not soft morning light flooding the space, endowing it with an aura of dew-kissed honey, it was an incandescent bulb, wasting electricity!

He mounted the fancy lift and descended, swearing to himself that he was going to review the tapes from the security cameras and determine who was responsible for this senseless waste. Someone must be admonished. Alas, he hated those cameras. In a country that had managed to retain some semblance of civil liberties well past 1984, he would be the last person to erode those few remaining liberties. But with mass surveillance of the populace on the rise, society was headed toward totalitarianism anyway. And that was exactly why he would not spy on the undisciplined tango company. Human rights and human dignity mattered.

He exhaled forcefully, propelling himself from the lift and rounding the corner leading to the switch panel. "Damn," he muttered aloud, seeing a faint wedge of light bleeding onto the floor in front of the door for the *tangueros'* lounge. Were timers the answer? He threw open the outer door and made to flip the light switch. The inner door was not well sealed, held ajar by a clump of black canvas. He rolled closer, examined the baggage. He thrust open with his hand the door and blocked its recoil with the chair's footrest. It was Miguel's backpack. And there, scrunched on the hard travertine stone flooring, Miguel lay smeared in blood.

Contorted into fetal position—no, curled even tighter—Miguel lay motionless. Don Luis gasped, seeing the handsome face muddied, bloodied. Miguel's shirt was shredded, mired by gore and sinew. His skin and clothing glittered in the lighting as though bodily he had rolled on the floor of a filthy glass factory.

Don Luis understood that Miguel had chosen a tough neighborhood. He apparently had to learn of the savageness of those streets the hard way. But why must it be so? Don Luis collapsed from his wheelchair to his knees and wept for all the misery in the world, including Miguel's and his own.

CHAPTER 48

AGGIE JACOBS METICULOUSLY PULLED the interior dough from her toasted bagel. She sat at her father's desk at the drycleaner's main office in Williamsburg, Brooklyn. Ignoring the water stains on the lower walls and the glare of fluorescent lighting, she focused on her breakfast. She was inured to the traffic noise from the raceway on the street outside. These were comfortable surroundings. Aggie had *schlepped* a couple of boxes full of documents for bookkeeper Anna from their home office. En route, she'd snagged a fresh poppy seed bagel with a half-helping of full-fat cream cheese and a newspaper from the shop just off Broadway.

When Aggie arrived at the office early Monday morning, she was delighted to have her head feeling normal again. Yesterday's hangover had been a bear. And while she was still not okay with her dad's happy birthday prank, she found it difficult to be angry with him for long. Aggie ignored the open *New York Times*, taking another sip of coffee, wishing for an Argentine *café cortado.*

A burly man with grease-stained hands, wearing soiled khaki work clothes, stopped in the doorway. "Hey, Aggie, good to see ya. Where's MoJo?" The man smiled at her, a deep slash on his cheek compressing to a sickle.

"Your guess is as good as mine, Sammy. What's up?"

"Got a problem with the P-47 cleaner at the Bronx store. Unit's ten grand." He nodded solemnly. "Want me go see about it?"

"Better ask Dad. I'm just the help, you know."

"You're the princess, I know," he said, smiling.

"And you're the enforcer," she said, in all mock seriousness.

He plastered on a frightening scowl. "Used to be."

Sammy disappeared around the corner. Aggie scanned the newspaper and noshed the bagel. She spied an article about a shooting in a not-so-far-away Brooklyn neighborhood over the weekend. There'd been an unsolved shooting there a week or two ago, she recalled. She scanned the article, until her eyes stuck on a name she recognized, Perseus Panopoulos. She ceased futzing with the bagel. Her mind filled with disbelief as her eyes welled with tears, reading of the brutal demise and the charred, nearly unrecognizable remains of El Primitivo.

Aggie drifted into a daydream, recalling the first time she met Percey, about ten years earlier. The faded grey walls of her dad's office turned cheery, festooned with blinking lights and tinsel, like the Brooklyn ballroom dancing studio where they had met. They were hardly teenagers, well before either danced Argentine tango. Long before he grew his hair out and dubbed himself "El Primitivo." Aggie recalled how he'd fallen for his Latin dance instructor, Christopher. The guy wasn't even gay, just a ballroom dandy.

She dabbed at her eyes with her napkin, noting with interest that the police were seeking an unknown assailant responsible for the death of Jose Roberto Diaz aka Gordo, a drug peddler and pimp with ties to organized crime. She knew that Miguel and El Primitivo had been seen together recently, but surely Miguel wasn't mixed up in the mess. Miguel respected women. Sordid Mob business was just not him. She read that the US Open Tennis Tournament was in full swing. Hadn't been for years, but it was a good time, she recalled, scrunching the last bit of bagel.

Aggie penned a brief note to her dad and rested it on top of the paper and exited. Something inside her was anxious to finish her company errands and change her clothes. She would feel better once at the studio and she could see Miguel's face. And who knew, maybe they would dance a song or two before rehearsal.

CHAPTER 49

THE SENSATIONALIZED ACCOUNT of the Bloody Brooklyn Gun Battle, as it had been proclaimed by the media, disgusted Don Luis. He sat in his office, feeling revulsion similar to what he had experienced when reading the lurid coverage of Natalia's murder. It was not yet midday. Miguel had been attended by a private physician more than twenty-four hours ago, but was still sleeping. The family friend had said that although Miguel was not seriously injured, he was in shock and should be sedated lightly. Don Luis had known the doctor for decades and had no fear that he was going to become anonymous fuel for the blogosphere. Why bother with this, he wondered, looking up from the glaring screen. He needed to compose himself and prepare to face the company.

Don Luis drew a line across an elongated sheet of yellow legal paper, on which he had penned remarks. He would speak from the heart. Say that the company would survive this loss, just as it had survived Natalia's. Don Luis's chest heaved. He was trying not to go there. His blood began to boil with rage, alternatively slacking with dolor. Initially, her loss had almost killed him. Now, it had stolen his legs and his lust for life. If unresolved much longer, it could drag him into an early grave.

No, this company would not be spared the hot poker of trial. He insisted to increase the heat. And he, himself, would be the agent of destruction, if necessary. Don Luis clenched the paper in his fist and ripped it from its binding. He crushed it to a tiny ball and jammed it into the rubbish bin. His head swam. Hand to his carotid artery, where he felt his heartbeat thump. He must calm down or risk not making it to rehearsal at all.

Don Luis was trying to relax when the phone's studio line rang. The caller's identity was blocked, so he listened for a message.

"Señor Don Luis de Granada, I know you're there. Pick up the phone."

Don Luis snapped forward. He stared at the phone. A computer-altered voice, deep and grating. Not the call from the police that he'd expected, something worse.

"I will not ask again. I think you know what's at stake."

He grasped the receiver and spit, "Who are you and what do you want?"

"To trade a codex for a life."

Don Luis's hand trembled as he stared into space. The massive desk overwhelmed him. He felt very small, like a kid at his daddy's desk. This call or something similar had been contemplated. But he had not expected it today, not while Miguel lay sedated upstairs, having been through torment over the weekend. Was there ever a good time for a horrifying call? He had courted this insane interaction, claiming to be in possession of a priceless article of Judaica, and had welcomed all bidders. Was this a repercussion for not having defined the coin of his realm more clearly? Perhaps the bidder understood Don Luis's value system better than Don Luis had gauged he would.

"Sorry," Don Luis replied, "but I haven't a clue what you're talking about."

"The *Keter* for the boy. He's a killer. I got the murder weapon with his prints."

A tidal wave of dread surged over Don Luis. "I'm hanging up now."

"When you come to your senses, turn on the studio's street light. Let it burn tonight. I know you hate wasting electricity, but I think it'll be worth it."

Don Luis flinched. How could he know that unless he was an insider?

"Put the *Keter* in an old grocery shopping bag. I'll call and tell you where to leave it. Don't bother calling the cops. No light and I'll take care of that."

At rehearsal, a pall of dread pervaded the dance company. El Primitivo's absence was a tragedy, Miguel's a mystery. Don Luis faced the group, slumped in his wheelchair, hands inert in his lap. He found himself assessing each member's response to the news. Everyone, including Wagner, seemed to have been shocked. Chaz was the exception. He arrived late, looking like the juxtaposition of a vagabond and something that a cat might have dragged in. Chaz's face was whiskered with days of neglect, his eyes redder than bloodshot, and his hair more stray than spiked. Don Luis realized there was no loss of love between El Primitivo and him. But he recalled that Chaz hadn't bothered to show up last time the company assembled to mourn a slain member, Natalia. He took off for California sun to visit mommy immediately after the incident. It would perhaps be doubly on his conscience, should he have one, once again not to be respectful of the dead.

The previous time this company met to discuss a member's untimely demise was before Don Luis had acquired the company outright. He had not been a financially invested party, but his personal investment in Natalia could not have been overstated.

Don Luis found himself telling his crew to be strong and tough. He eyed Wagner, was he smirking? He would pay soon enough. And Chaz, he wanted to drill through Chaz's unconcern, gouge his soft underbelly. Don Luis roared, "This will be a tango crucible!" Their faces had disfigured, muttering translations: "*Este será un crisol del tango.*" He squeezed a fist so tightly that it could have drawn blood from a vegetable. And then he surprised himself. The ladies gasped and the men gawked when Don Luis cast off his squeaky chair and stood on quivering legs.

Don Luis reminded them that membership in his tango troupe could have unanticipated health risks. He assured them that he would fathom this irregularity and ultimately deal it a crushing blow. He gazed at every face in the troupe, examined every eye. Time stood still— And then Don Luis announced the new show's name, a macabre combination of mortality and sensual dance: Murder by Tango. Whispers of disbelief. Amazed whispers. "*¿Muerte por el Tango? Sí,*" and "*¿Muerte por el Tango? No.*"

CHAPTER 50

MIGUEL AWOKE IN A STRANGE ROOM to musical bombast. Head woozy, eyes blurry as if he'd been drugged. A bedside clock indicated that it was after four P.M. The room was like a modern-day castle with a soaring ceiling, sumptuous draperies, and antique, darkly stained wooden furniture. Tango music wafted up from below. But not the syrupy golden-era outpouring of passion he adored. Modern tango music, so-called *el tango nuevo* or neotango. The orchestra was known as the Gotan Project. *Gotan* was Lunfardo for tango, the syllables reversed. The track blaring below was from a disk called *La Revancha del Tango*, hugely popular in Argentina a decade earlier. The music was thunderous, without the elegance and refinement of golden-era violins plucking your heart's strings. The song was particularly dark, as the title suggested, "Una Musica Brutal" . . . brutal music.

Miguel panned the elegant room. A large closet housed his entire wardrobe, all four outfits. Oddly enough his clothing was pressed and more neatly hung than ever before in the history of his ownership. He dressed quickly and located stairs just down a lengthy hall hung with elaborate portraiture of what appeared to be a noble European family. The music waxed louder. He followed its increasing volume and found a heavy bordeaux-colored velvet curtain concealing a staircase.

He parted it and walked onto a curvaceous glass balustrade whose sweeping arc led him outside Don Luis's office.

The main dance floor lay directly below. Ghostly shadows danced by faux-torch light. The company danced to the macabre music as though performing some satanic rite. Miguel crouched, although his thighs burned, and watched with amazement. His head, groggy from drugs, couldn't fathom the scene, and his heart, heavy with loss, only grew sadder. Miguel clasped his hands to his ears and shut his eyes.

"You call that passion!" Don Luis screamed over the din. Miguel opened his eyes and ears and saw that Don Luis spoke to no one in particular.

The dancers lunged, thrusted, and whirled more wildly than before. "More," Don Luis shouted, his walking stick banging the floor with resonant strikes. "Give me more!"

Miguel recoiled. He turned away his face, wondering whether Don Luis had gone mad. Although the scene was unsettling, he turned back. The stars were dancing with different partners. Don Luis had caned his way over to where Dr. Wagner danced with Flora, a second-rate *tanguera*. Don Luis put his hands to his hips and stared stern disapproval. He shouted, "Come on, Ernest, try to thrill her. You can't be completely detached from humanity, can you? Even after what you've done!"

Sweeping the space with his gaze, Miguel eyed Candy embedded in Claudio's groin. They didn't bother to dance, only titillated. Was that their idea of passionate *el tango nuevo*? For him, it was a bastardization of *lambada*, a sexy Brazilian dance from the '80s. He searched and found Aggie locked in Chaz's embrace. He gyrated his entire body, like a samba dancer. His pelvis thrust rhythmically toward and away from her. His protruding chest, smeared on hers, crushed her pert breasts and menacingly dominated her space. Miguel believed she wore a professional mask. He understood that she was new to the company and it was important to dance well with the *primo ballerino*.

Chaz seemed to exult in their confining embrace. It was as though fueled by the frenzy and Don Luis's urging, he ravished her. Chaz stood tall, dipping Aggie low. Miguel's pulse quickened and his blood warmed as he watched Chaz slide his ankle up her exposed leg, past her calf, up to the inner thigh, and beyond. Chaz gloated, an expression of superiority and dominance overtaking his face. Miguel gritted his teeth when he saw the anguish in Aggie's eyes when they met his.

Suddenly, Aggie hauled herself upright. She pushed away Chaz, who jerked his head and shoulders as though awakening from a trance. She ran under the second floor's overhang and called out, "Miguel, are you okay?"

"Yes."

"I'm coming up," she said, disappearing underneath the balustrade.

Miguel watched Chaz protesting loudly to Don Luis, who looked toward Aggie and shrugged. But when Chaz turned and took a step in Aggie's direction, Don Luis grabbed his lagging wrist, held it firm. The expression of indignity and malice on Chaz's face was disturbing. Miguel recognized the man was certainly an egomaniac, and perhaps something more.

CHAPTER 51

Aggie lay on Miguel's bed. He stretched full length beside her as she stroked his brow with her delicate fingers. She believed that nothing could mar this moment of bliss. Nothing else in the world mattered to her now. Not the strangeness of the grand guest room or the luridity of Chaz's dancing; not even the humiliating disclosure of her sexual inexperience. The latter could be dealt with in short order, she thought, continuing to soothe him.

"I'm so glad you're safe," Aggie whispered. "I'm sorry for Percey, but—"

Miguel's brow creased deeply. "I couldn't save him. But I was a *mensch*."

Aggie's jaw dropped and her heart leapt, thinking, if only.

"I swear it. But, my effort was not good enough."

"Shhh." She caressed his cheek and touched his neck on the way to his chest. "I shouldn't stay too long. You need to rest."

Silence.

"You can get undressed and get under the covers. I'll help you." She began to unbutton his shirt, robotically, at first, wondering how this really worked. She understood women, kind of, but men, this was all new to her. A while ago, it was as though Chaz would have deflowered her right there on the floor. And he definitely knew. Miguel's shirt was finally off, revealing innumerable scratches, and a bandaged gash on his torso. Suddenly Aggie felt as though she was forcing herself on him and getting no response.

To her surprise, Miguel unbuttoned and unzipped his pants. He began to slide them down, exposing incredibly muscular legs, with sparse hair and perfectly differentiated quads. Aggie felt flush. His pants put away, Aggie could see the outline of Miguel's penis, lying relaxed and pointed upward toward the margin of his black briefs. He was not excited, but she was. She tried to speak, but her lips were dry. She moistened them with saliva, looking intently at Miguel's masculine physique. She wondered what the hell she was going to say, anyway. Just go for it.

Aggie started to reach out to touch his penis, but Miguel pulled up the covers to his chest and turned to his side to face her. He half-smiled and reclosed his eyes.

Was he rebuffing her? She was just about to grab it, for chrissakes. Had he heard? Oh, no, she obsessed, he's heard that she doesn't do it and he wasn't even going to bother. Aggie's heart rate rose as her libido fell. And then the question she hated most pinged into her head: "What would Candy do?" Probably just rip off the covers and jump right on top of him. Hoarsely, she said, "Miguel."

"Yes, Aggie," he said lazily, slowly opening his eyes and looking directly at her.

Oh, my God, she was suddenly a puddle. The emerald flecks of his eyes sparkled in the afternoon light. How she burned for this man. "Is there anything I can do for you?" She paused. "To make you feel better." Now, there it was, ball(s) in his court.

"I'm glad you're here," he said. "Sorry I'm not more—"

"I understand," she said faintly. "It'll be fine."

Okay, so he's not more . . . but I am, so this will work. Her cup overflowed. Maybe she should take off her shirt now? Why bother, bust was not her strong suit. Her plan, like the show tune advised, was to "Accentuate the Positive." She quickly undid her skirt and slid it, along with her sheer panties, down her long, smooth legs, thanking her lucky stars that she'd worn a dancing skirt, something she seldom did. She scooted under the covers and faced Miguel, drawing up close to him. If the sensation of bare legs touching didn't do it for him, it was certainly going to send her into orbit. Just a little friction, high enough for him to feel her lush bush on his thigh. As though a magic wand was underneath the covers, they began to rise.

In a minute, Miguel went from dud to stud. He caressed her torso and hugged her to his chest, kissing her passionately, his tongue alternatively filling and withdrawing, teasing her hungry mouth. He massaged her clit gently, yet firmly, just as she imagined he would. Aggie was in heaven. She stroked his girthy cock. It felt like warm steel in her grasp. She was really doing it! Aggie was delighted with herself.

It was time for the main event, painful though it might be. Aggie maneuvered to her back and pulled Miguel atop her. His penis projected well past her belly button. Hopefully, there was not going to be a problem accommodating it. Aggie tried to relax, wondering would he drive it home? She didn't really care, so long as he enjoyed it.

Miguel regarded Aggie tenderly and she returned his soft gaze. She could feel herself tensing up. She wished he'd just hurry up and do it. He licked her dry lips. She pulled him toward her.

"Are you sure you want to do this?" he asked seriously.

He knew! But she thought every man wanted to deflower a woman. Why be dramatic? Why hesitate? He awaited her response. Perhaps it was a matter of etiquette the first time. *Maybe in Argentina you had to ask? Then maybe I have to give permission.* She was confused. Her mind raced. Aggie's palms began to perspire, feet began to feel chilly. And the love faucet was off. Could he sense her discomfort? Aggie burst out, "Yes, I want to, buuut, I'm not very experienced." She tugged at Miguel, forcing a seductive smile on her wan face.

"What I mean is, I don't have a condom." He skewed his head.

Aggie felt like a perfect idiot. She froze.

Miguel lifted his weight from her, supported himself on one muscular arm, asking, "Just how not very experienced are you?"

Tongue tied in a massive knot, Aggie could have died as a tear welled in her eye.

"Oh," said Miguel, "this is, um, not possible." He gently rolled off of her and lay on his back, facing the ceiling.

Aggie stared at the sheet, forming a tent . . . the big top. "C'mon, it's okay." She had never been much of a salesperson. Never had to. "How do you like it?"

"Ahh."

Aggie's voice broke and tears flowed, pleading, "It couldn't be that bad."

"No, no," he said, pressing a finger to her lips. He pressed his face deep in her black curls and whispered, "*Creo que es maravilloso.*"

"I don't feel marvelous. I feel like shit," she stammered, surprising herself.

"Me, too." He released her slightly. "But when we feel better, we'll talk then."

She nodded.

"You know, Don Luis may come up to check on me at any moment," he said. "He may be wondering what are the children up to." He worked his eyes at her.

Aggie managed a half-smile. "I better go."

Miguel touched her cheek with warm lips. She slipped from the covers and primly searched the floor for her skirt and undies, feeling naked and ashamed.

CHAPTER 52

Miguel awoke, wincing. He felt as though he were burning with fever. Was this how it would feel to be a witch on a spit? He knew exactly how he'd felt after Aggie's departure, like a heel. But what could he do? No matter how much he secretly cared for her, his life seemed more in jeopardy each day. It wouldn't be fair to her. No one knew the future, but his seemed especially bleak and maybe brief. The man who claimed her virginity, as unlikely as the whole scenario was, should be alive to call her the next day.

And if he were alive tomorrow, Miguel had pressing business, neglected business. He had lost sight of his primary objective, but the previous night had brought it back into focus. He would be remiss no longer. *I sound like Don Luis*, he thought. But maybe that was not entirely bad. The man was highly educated and very smart. Too smart, perhaps.

Another turn, another flap of the covers. This was hell, he thought, hearing a faint knock at the door. He answered, "Yes?"

Don Luis's muffled voice asked, "Miguel, are you sleeping?"

"No."

"May I come in for a bit?"

"*Momentito.*" Miguel sat up and turned on the bedside lamp. He thrust his arms into the sumptuous sleeves of a silken robe, draped over a bedside valet.

"Sorry for disturbing you," Don Luis said, from the doorway.

"No, no, please come in."

Don Luis gestured toward an array of prescription medications on the bedside table. "The white ones, not certain what they're called, will help you sleep, the doctor said. I think the pink ones are Xanax, for, um, anxiety. Just in case."

"I am not anxious," Miguel tapped his temple, "just too many thoughts."

"I, too, have too many thoughts." Don Luis sighed deeply. "Miguel, do you recall how you got here?"

"You brought me, yes?"

"Not to this room, but to the studio last night."

"Taxi."

"Do you recall what happened?"

"Yes." He lowered his eyes.

"And do you recall a gunfight? Did you shoot someone with a handgun?"

"Yes, but he was killing El Primitivo. Two of them." His hand shot up. "They tried to kill us both." He spoke rapidly, "And one had an automatic rifle."

"Yes, yes, of course. Do settle down."

Miguel balled his fist. "I was scared, but did not desert him—"

"Where did you get the pistol?"

"El Primitivo. I think he had some rough business associates." Miguel's eyes moistened, saying, "But he was trying to help me. To talk with one of them for me."

"Help you?" Don Luis squirmed. "You know these people?"

"Yes, I mean, no. Not really. You see, there was a woman—"

"Always." Don Luis nodded sympathetically.

Miguel skewed his head in surprise as Don Luis's eyes welled with tears.

"Always a woman, and a family." The old man's chest heaved. He exhaled a long, heavy sigh. "Sometimes even a cursed family."

"You really believe in this thing, don't you. Can people not ask forgiveness?"

"They could, should they recognize and rectify their sins." He raised a hand adding, "Consider the preamble to the precious *Keter*. The inscription says, ". . . cursed be he who steals it, and cursed be he who sells it, and cursed be he who pawns it."

"But the man, our hero or *villero,* what was his name?" Miguel asked.

"Moshe ben Avraham. And actually the inscription begins: "Blessed be he who preserves it!" Don Luis smiled. "And preserve it, perfectly, he did."

Miguel said, "He didn't try to sell it so he must have been rich."

"No, educated, but poor. He was also pious, but corruptible."

"Which is to say he was human."

"It was the only thing of worth this man could transmit to his heirs. It made him proud that he possessed it. He believed that it would make his son proud to receive it. And that perhaps eventually it will make his family important—not rich, but significant." Don Luis nodded. "So he does not right the wrong of secretly copying it and therefore he cannot repent and be absolved."

To Miguel it sounded as though a different Divine was judging Moshe than the one he had learned was merciful and long-suffering.

"Thus begins a vicious cycle of terror reigned down on his line from almighty God," Don Luis boomed.

"I have to ask if you can be more specific about the wrong committed and your certainty that a curse actually exists?"

"How much time do you have?"

"More time than money," Miguel said, smiling.

"And I'm the opposite," Don Luis replied, his face solemn.

* * *

Minutes after leaving Miguel's room, Aggie was in the *tangueras'* lounge sitting on a bench, searching her soul. The baudy music had long died away, the company members had vanished, and she had failed. She wiped her eyes for the last time—she swore—as she slipped from the lounge and out the front door. A wet blast in the face greeted her. The dark sidewalk and empty street welcomed her. Would she ever again find the strength to face them all? Miguel? She didn't know.

Rain spit into Aggie's face as she hurried toward the subway station. Was it too soon to give Miguel a call? She grasped her phone. And what was up with that article she'd read about so many mammals being more selective of sexual partners than men. Falsely bolstered hopes! She walked on considering that when she had read the piece she never connected herself with the expression, 'bitch in heat.'

Near the block's end, a car was parked curbside. A man in the driver's seat lit a cigarette, attracting her attention. The car, American made, no dents, clean and shiny, was definitely a rental. He looked up and blew smoke from the side of his bearded mouth. He glanced at her through unfashionable metal-framed eyeglasses. Then suddenly, he ducked down his head and grabbed up a newspaper, flicking the freshly lit cigarette onto the curb. Her mind was far from clear, but it was as though he'd recognized her. Aggie stopped and lifted her phone. The man cranked the car and jammed it into gear. Aggie snapped photos as he bounded over the curb, screeching away.

Her nervous system went on high alert. Her hands shook. Aggie quickened her pace toward the subway station, thinking, *What if he makes the block and comes back to get me?* Her heart skipped two beats. If this were a life-threatening situation what would Agent Willows do? She wouldn't let the bastard abduct and kill her and get away with it. She would leave some clue.

Aggie noted the still-smoking cigarette on the sidewalk. She didn't want to walk backward. Too much drama for one day. Who was that guy and why did he avoid her? She turned and walked briskly toward the subway station. She was no crime scene investigator. She was a scared young girl who hated conflict. And she definitely didn't want to lose her life—just her virginity.

Headlights ahead. A car was turning from a side street. It hugged the curb coming toward her. Aggie flew toward a building entryway, seeking a place to hide. A gust of wind blew past, chilling her already shaky legs. She glanced surreptitiously out to the street and watched the taxi pass slowly, its driver slumping in his seat. Aggie eyed the smoldering cigarette on the ground. She had seen enough episodes of *CSI: Crime Scene Investigation* as a teenager that she was sure she could perform a mass spectrometry analysis if needed. And now, she knew exactly what Willows would do.

Aggie scurried back and scooped up the butt, using a damp tissue from her pocket. It seemed exceptionally stinky, more like the stench of a cigar. She rolled it in the tissue and stashed it in her bag, before strutting quickly toward the corner, quite proud of herself. With this new sense of willpower, Aggie was confident that she could make her way home safely and perhaps cry herself to sleep.

CHAPTER 53

JUNIOR'S BACK ROOM WAS ALIVE with persuasion and pasta. Big Benny sat eyeing his minions, wishing for a break from their *kvetching*. The death of a subcontractor was not monumental, unlike the huge slice of cheesecake looking up at him from the table. Running drugs and hookers was a bit dangerous, Benny had said, especially if you were not a made man. Benny had also expressed the fact that the guy wasn't a member of their family. Maybe a part of nobody's family.

"Big Benny, you're not hearing me," said Vinnie Rabbit Ears. "I'm gonna look like a fucking creampuff. Some kid smokes my man and I sit on my hands." His face shot toward the ceiling. "Just what we don't need right now."

"I'm hearing you too much," Benny said, slicing down with his fork into four inches of heaven.

Vinnie dropped his spoon loudly into a plate of fusilli pasta and clam sauce. It splattered onto his necktie. "Shit, now look what you made me do."

Big Benny's eyes cut into him.

Two fullback-sized goodfellas in cheap sports coats and sauce-splashed ties flanked Vinnie. They rubbed the speckled tablecloth with their palms.

"Sorry," Vinnie said. "Look, this kid took out my guy. Now there's about to be a turf battle with Dominic. He says he should have been running that hood all along. And who's gonna cook the stuff? I got nothing to sell."

"That's a bunch a crap," Benny said, saving a bite of crumb crust from the napkin, recalling days when he couldn't afford anything. "Waste not, want not" was the motto then, same as now. Benny stuffed a giant bite into his pie hole and said, "I fixed things up with Dominic, see. So you got no problem with the action in Flatbush."

"Bull!"

"You talking to somebody?" Big Benny asked.

Vinnie waved him off.

"And he wasn't your guy. He was a crazy piece of work, from what I heard. Offed his girlfriend for nothing. Family don't do that." Benny shook his head. "And the baby?"

"Just 'cause he was a beaner—"

"I don't care if he was Eskimo," Benny said loudly. "He wasn't family, see. Besides, he blasted our kid."

"The dancing faggot."

Big Benny stood and all three hundred and fifty pounds reverberated when he stamped his foot. "That faggot was family."

Vinnie's palms shot up. "What? He was Greek or something."

"A beautiful Argentine tango dancer, besides." Benny stabbed his fork at Vinnie. "Something you don't have enough class to know anything about." Benny plopped into his chair, sending a seismic shockwave across the room. "Your psycho trashed a member of this family . . . an artist."

One of the goodfellas said, "You know, Big Benny, Vinnie's got a point about showing strength." He hesitated. "The other families are wondering what's going on with this *glasshole* showing up, jerking us around. It ain't like driving Ms. Daisy, *schlepping* him all over New York."

The other fellow goodfella nodded.

Big Benny said, "Don't screw with him. He'll cut off your *schmeckle* and stuff it in your mother's *mezuzah* at midnight and ring the doorbell.

Vinnie bowed his chest. "Yeah, tell him to come and get it."

"Maybe you should stuff food in your face," Benny said. "I know what I'm doing, here. You got no idea how much moola is behind that guy, or what he's after."

Vinnie pressed. "All I know is he showed up on the coattails 'a that smirky college kid, don't know dick. I knew his old man for thirty years. Never could trust him."

Big Benny let it slide. He called out to a waiter, who entered the room as though showing up late to Mass. "Joey, I'm going to need . . ." He rolled his hand suggestively.

The man took away the empty plate. "Right away, Big Benny."

"I've done a lotta things for this family," Vinnie said. "I should be able to talk to a guy when I feel it's important."

"Talk, yeah; whack, no," Benny said.

Vinnie pursed his lips, moved his hands as though see-sawing a slinky. His tall ears wiggled in time. "Goddamn druggie faggot dancer."

Big Benny said calmly, "Tango dancers are not faggots." He hesitated. "Well, this Primo was a little confused, I'll admit."

"And he's dead, but the one that nailed my guy right between the eyes is alive and kicking, on the Upper East Side." His disdain was thick. "He's up to something besides tango, shooting like that."

"I told you," Vinnie said. "Tony got the scoop right from Shaft, from the Holy Land. He came up right after it happened."

Big Benny gave him the stink eye.

"Said he saw the kid play dead, then plug Gordo in the noggin. All for no reason." Vinnie widened his hands. "Maybe he's Argentine Mob."

Big Benny was silent. Withdrew a toothpick from his shirt pocket.

"Just want to chat with him, that's all." Vinnie smiled as harmlessly as a shark.

"Tell you what I'm going to do," Big Benny said. Then he cut off his response abruptly when Joey entered with his second piece of mile-high cheesecake.

* * *

Unable to constrain himself, Don Luis reached toward the curtains and drew them open slightly. He craned his neck and looked down to the darkened street. There was hardly a light visible, not a moving body of any kind. He gazed straight down to the studio's darkened door and caught his breath. He stood wondering what tomorrow would bring. Would the caller be true to his word? Did he really believe that his proposal would be accepted? Don Luis released the draperies and recalled Shakespeare, who understood that with men the fault lies not in their stars, but in themselves, if they are miserable.

CHAPTER 54

A NEW DAY DAWNED FOR MIGUEL, one that he hoped would see improvement in his body and mind. He had slept much better. The bedside clock indicated that it was past ten. He stretched and felt a slight pang of hunger, a change from his constant pangs of pain. He wondered how breakfast worked at Don Luis's luxurious convalescent home.

Miguel reached for the colorful silk robe. The house phone rang, but he assumed it was not for him. It stopped, but then began to ring again. He answered and found Don Luis on the line, asking if a light breakfast in Miguel's room would interest him. Shortly, Kemal arrived dressed in a dark suit rolling his shiny cart, bearing an assortment of fruits, breakfast breads, spice cake, fresh-squeezed juice, *café*, and tea.

Don Luis took a dainty sip of his tea. Almost instantly, the man's expression darkened. Miguel took the cue. "Don Luis, I hope that you will tell me a bit more about this interesting family, now that my mind is fresh. I'm sorry last night I faded away." He sipped *café*. "The last thing I remember was that the book had been saved, ransomed from good Christians." He shook his head in shame.

"Transferred by the right of redemption from the spoils of Jerusalem. . . ."

Miguel asked, "How did the cursed family come to be in Spain?"

"The golden age of Muslims in Europe lasted about three hundred years, 750 to 1050 AD. The Umayyads, meaning sons of Umayya, came from Mecca in Saudi Arabia. They shared a common ancestor with Mohammad." Don Luis continued, "The Umayyad Caliphate was quite just. They ruled the fifth largest contiguous kingdom the world has known. It included much of the Middle East, Northern Africa, Asia Minor, and Iberia."

Miguel fetched a generous piece of spice cake.

"The Islamic rulers of that day ruled tolerantly. They allowed religious worship, official offices to be held, professional capacities to be occupied by Christians and Jews."

"This I knew," Miguel said.

"As I mentioned, the great thinker, physician Maimonides—"

"Rambam!"

"Indeed! He lived his entire life under Muslim rule, yet he flourished."

Miguel said, "The Greeks who came before the Romans who came before the Muslims had knowledge of medicine, science, art . . . so many useful and beautiful things. It is silly for every empire to reinvent wheels."

"Quite a good point, Miguel." Don Luis mused, "Makes one wonder why there is so little tolerance for the *other*, who may be able to teach you much."

Miguel found himself nodding emphatically. He was enjoying his new friendship with Don Luis. He wanted to trust him, but there were important unanswered questions.

"Shortly after our *villero* completed his unauthorized copy of the *Keter*," Don Luis said, "there was a great rift within the Aleppo congregation in which his clan were teachers. Circa 1360 they were essentially driven," he wagged a finger, "by their tribesmen from their home of hundreds of years. They moved to Seville, Spain. The golden age for Muslims having been a golden age for Jews, too. And there was still a tolerant attitude toward Jews by the Spanish monarchs of the early fourteenth century."

"So our *villero* was not simply Jewish, he was a rabbi?" Miguel asked.

"Exactly. But when he and his clan moved to Spain, they acquired shops and became prosperous shopkeepers, although he taught Hebrew on the side."

"Industrious," Miguel said, reaching for the strawberries.

Don Luis brooded. "Oh, conditions for Jews deteriorated rapidly in Spain over the following three decades, but the clan was unscathed."

"Perhaps our *villero* thought he was entitled to a bit of divine protection, being the keeper of this ultra-sacred codex, no?"

"Possibly." Don Luis sighed. "Well, they were protected for a time. And then on July 6, 1391, thousands of Jews were slaughtered in Seville's *Juderia*. Almost all of the inhabitants of the Barrio de Santa Cruz were massacred. And, of course, the synagogues were looted and burned. Of the entire clan, only our would-be hero and a single son survived. This would be a pattern for centuries."

"I'm sorry," said Miguel. "There are many dark chapters in the book of human history. This must be the darkest and saddest for Spanish people."

"Take heart, my boy: the story worsens. The man and his son, destitute and alone, were forced to convert to Christianity and were paid to help rebuild the synagogues and convert them to churches where they worshipped as *Marranos*."

Miguel bristled at the word for pig. It was cruel and one of the most unfortunate mistakes of his ancestors to persecute and label other men as animals. He was beginning to wonder if his personal story really could rival Don Luis's woeful tale. His family had experienced tragedy, but nothing like this.

"Converted Muslims were referred to as *Mariscos*," Don Luis added, "not exactly complimentary, given that shellfish are a forbidden food for Muslims."

Miguel cast down his eyes and scratched his chin, trying to ward off more shame.

"Although all else was lost, the *Keter* survived intact." Don Luis laughed. "Our would-be hero hid it among the Christian texts from which he taught catechism to new converts. That tradition was followed in Seville for generations." He fell silent before saying, "And then came Tomas de Torquemada, the Grand Inquisitor."

"*¡Caramba!*" Miguel said, recognizing this really was becoming a horror story.

"Oh, yes, our anti-hero, the chief rabbi, cum chief *priest* came under suspicion by Satan himself." Don Luis shook his head as if disbelieving his own account.

"Which was he," Miguel asked, "rabbi or priest?"

"Both, actually. More on that later." Don Luis half-smiled. "So, in 1485 the Grand Inquisitor visited this priest's humble Christian church. Our man's diary states that he was not completely convincing in his Catholic ruse, but was unmolested for a time."

"Great."

"Well, there was a price: the loss of a son and the man's death." Don Luis sighed. "His eldest son was a strikingly handsome young gent, appearing completely different from his immediate family. He was quite tall and bore gemlike green eyes, similar to his progenitors from more than a hundred years before. He was spied by Torquemada's cousin Augustina Olivia de León, who was visiting Seville from Granada." Don Luis counted on his stubby fingers. "She was beautiful and rich, and a Christian zealot."

"Sounds like she would fit very well in Buenos Aires."

Don Luis's expression turned severe.

"Sorry." Miguel asked, "But wait, isn't there some law of genetics that says you cannot have just any eye color or hair color, that it depends on your parents?"

"Classical genetics says so, but there is an emergent field called inherited epigenetics that explains physical traits that recur for generations, and appear to be lost, only to pop up again. It also suggests that in one single generation, an abused person's DNA can become profoundly altered in very negative ways."

"Really? I thought maybe each baby gets a new chance. Only seems fair."

"Fairness, *fey*. The damaged DNA is propagated down the line indefinitely." Don Luis shook his head. "This is especially horrible news for people who have been abused for millennia." Don Luis's lips began to quiver. He worked his eyes, trying desperately to focus. "Unless there's something sufficiently valuable to change the course of their history and someone brave enough to dare to use it," he boomed, "catastrophe for my people is inevitable!" He lapsed, wild-eyed, as though out of his body, and his mind.

CHAPTER 55

MIGUEL'S INITIAL FORAY up to the building's fifth floor was fraught. He helped Don Luis along slowly, after exiting a richly paneled, antique elevator, past a sprawling formal dining room. There were darkened chandeliers, tapestry wall coverings like those in European castles, and a lustrous table with at least twenty chairs. Miguel felt a lump of unworthiness form in his throat. What was he doing here, in a silk morning coat of all things? They turned into a modern kitchen, with stainless steel everywhere; even the glass pantry cabinet doors were faced in brushed metal. Don Luis flipped a bank of switches and light glinted off every grime-free surface.

"Perhaps some cold water, from the refrigerator," said Don Luis, poking his stick toward a refulgent door. "And Miguel, a bit of water in the kettle, too, please."

"Certainly."

"For how long was I out?"

"A few minutes only," Miguel said nervously, underestimating the time by half. He was bewildered. One minute Don Luis had been raving; the next minute, he was out cold.

"Now where were we? Oh, yes," Don Luis continued calmly, after taking a refreshing sip. "Soon enough, the son in Seville, who was being groomed to follow the family's religious tradition and also to be keeper of the sacred text, was lost to Granada."

"That's a pity."

"Hell, Torquemada even attended the wedding, which was performed in a grand cathedral by the boy's dejected father."

"*Mala leche*." Miguel bit his finger knuckle at the family's rotten luck.

"Bad luck, no. It was the curse! You had asked how I was so certain of its continued existence. Well, there is a genetic aberration that presents itself as a reminder of the family's sin and of the curse that has yet to be lifted. That boy possessed the marker and was made an example. The ones who bear it always are—"

"How can you say this for sure?" Miguel asked. "What happened to him?"

"The boy moved to Granada and was thrust into a world of Christian bigotry and fanaticism beyond what he could imagine. Within a month, his father, disconsolate and bedridden, called him to Seville and conveyed to him the story of his ancestors. He also told him about the Codex and charged him to keep it and pass it down the family line. That tortured boy became an even more tortured man, according to his journal. He was torn between his duty to his father and his ancestors and his wish to destroy the Codex and to free himself and his offspring from its curse."

"What did his brothers and sisters say? How were they affected?"

"Oh, they never knew, although they suffered equally. Only one male child per generation, the eldest typically, was told that they were what has come to be known as crypto-Jews. That was a curse in itself. Condemned to the loneliness of knowing the truth about one's family and unable to unburden oneself, even to siblings." Don Luis shuddered. "It is a hell on Earth."

Miguel recalled the closeness he had shared with his family. He could not imagine enduring such awful isolation from them. It would be torture.

"There has been an interesting alteration in relaying these family truths over the centuries," Don Luis said. "For instance, these crypto-Jews who live in the New World—Monterrey, Mexico, and Santa Fe, New Mexico—to this day they maintain the practice of telling the truth to only one offspring." He thrust out a finger. "But, often it is not the first son, but a tight-lipped daughter."

Miguel smiled and nodded. His sister had always been a rock, but she could not really keep secrets. She would not be a good crypto-Jew. Regarding himself, he had only one thing in common with them . . . something to hide.

"I'm delighted that you agree, Miguel, because so do I. In the family of this story, however, only one son ever survives and so he must be told." Don Luis's tone was firm, and his delivery more than definitive.

Miguel shuddered, thinking, *What has it to do with me? I have my own wretched story of death and loss and heartbreak. This is not my problem.*

"Anyway," Don Luis said, softening his eyes and speaking more naturally, "with Isabella and Ferdinand in control, there were many indictments of Jews, well, former Jews called *conversos*, for conjurations, blood libels, any excuse to take their money and land."

"The money," Miguel echoed. "Perhaps it is the root of evil."

"The worship of it, possibly," Don Luis countered. "But wonderful things can be accomplished with generous material resources. It's up to the holder to master them, and not to be mastered by them."

"I'll try to remember when I win the lottery." Miguel giggled and grinned.

"I believe you will do quite well," said Don Luis, matching the expression.

Miguel noted Don Luis's apparent misuse of English: "will," as opposed to "would," the certain, opposing the theoretical. It was an unusual mistake by a master of the English language.

CHAPTER 56

DR. ERNEST WAGNER STARED LOVINGLY at his creation, the Wagner Super Sharp Scalpel™. He ignored his cluttered office and dilapidated surroundings. What difference would a new, state-of-the-art pathology lab possibly make? The analyses and determinations he produced here were irreproachable. He couldn't help thinking how abashed his jealous colleagues Popov and Johnson would be when he was granted the patent for his new lithic processing technique. And when his devices were certified for official use at Bellevue, well, he would be vindicated and his sterling reputation restored.

Wagner bristled recalling they had dared defame him. And when he was at his lowest point, how they had testified against him in court, nearly costing his medical license and freedom. All after his almost unbearable loss. But the last laugh, his, would resonate in their ears for the remainder of their miserable lives. The Wagner S-Cube, as he thought of it, was revolutionary as was its name. A more creative moniker than Katalyst Surgical, LLC's, Keratome Super Sharp blah, blah Knife. His was much more easily pronounced and it was ingenious, not some marginal innovation. He was a master of traditional techniques, like hand-lapping ceramic surgical blades—almost a lost art form—just as he was a maestro of traditional Argentine tango.

Suddenly, he was gripped by that gnawing thought. Had Popov purchased his medical credentials from the Russian academy from which he claimed to have graduated? Although Dr. Wagner had tried on multiple occasions to explore the details of his tenure at certain Russian centers of medical excellence, he could never determine satisfactorily whether Popov was a bona fide physician. He vowed to reopen his researches into the matter as soon as he had distanced himself from him. And that wouldn't be long.

"Damn it," he muttered aloud, turning to face the cavernous, morgue-like lab, "why is he still full-time and I'm moderated?" He gritted his teeth and raised the knife menacingly. Even if he had been injudicious, everyone makes mistakes. Suddenly, Don Luis's words from the recent rehearsal resounded in Wagner's ears, "Come on, Ernest, try to thrill her. You can't be completely detached from humanity, can you, even after what you've done!" But how did that pompous Spaniard know? So, he'd done some research of his own, but could prove nothing. Oh, Helen, Wagner thought, *mea culpa*.

And then the searing flashback began to play in his mind. He could not turn it off. He stood over her, holding the scalpel, uncomprehending as her scarlet blood oozed onto the wet wooden floor.

Wagner thrust down the weapon, without fear for fracturing its painstakingly worked blade, and dove for the supplies closet. A panic attack! Just like that night—. He was only human; he was not made from stone, like his blades. He rushed past sealed jars filled with human and animal organs and tissue samples. He tore through every kind of glassware desperately seeking escape. And then he thrust his hands and arms into the closet fully, where he shoved aside amber bottles of formaldehyde and clear bottles of muriatic acid until grasping an unopened liter of ethyl alcohol. He ripped away the top and chugged a quarter, before slumping into his rickety Steelcase desk chair. Oh, how her sliced flesh gaped and oozed, right in front of him. He put the opening to his lips and turned the bottle skyward, vowing to finish it off then and there.

CHAPTER 57

Miguel summoned his strength to make a foray out into the neighborhood, walking toward Fifth Avenue for lunch on his own. The Upper East Side was the equivalent of Buenos Aire's Recoleta neighborhood. The famous cemetery where Eva Peron was buried, the Alvear Palace Hotel, and innumerable designer shops were Recoleta's glory. It was not Miguel's hood. He never felt completely comfortable there.

On Seventy-Third and Lexington, Miguel spotted a little place called the Organic Avenue. Their portobello Reuben wrap was delicious and well complemented by an arugula sprout salad. He had actually been able to free his mind of dolorous thoughts until he had seen a guy who could have been El Primitivo's brother. It was then the negative cycle began anew: Why did it have to happen? How much of it was his fault? Should it have been he who was shot to death and burned?

En route to the studio, Miguel considered the ultimate fate of the green-eyed boy in Don Luis's tragic family history . . . family horror story. The boy's end was probably not at all pleasant. Reflecting on his own eyes, Miguel considered that they were nothing like gems, but even green streaks were an aberration for his family. No one else had them. Of course, in his family there were some mysteries, not like Don Luis's mysterious clan, but his paternity had been questioned, and it bothered him more than he had ever acknowledged. His mother would only say that his father had to leave. Badgering her about it, Miguel believed, would only salt her wound.

His cousin, Miguel Andro, whose passport he had used to enter the United States, had had a noble father, his aunt always said. But similar to Miguel, neither father had bothered to lend his name to the offspring. How noble was that? Still, the nobleman's untimely fate seemed to fuel Miguel's aunt's anger for his mother. The two beautiful Zanotto sisters, had always been the Zanotto sisters and would always be—even with four kids between them! Sure, there had been whispers about his aunt's mores, about his mother's, too. But when he and his sister and mother had moved to Rosario and were embraced by Maestro Paiva, they were embraced by everyone. It was then that Esteban Prafil became his mother's companion and offered his embarrassed sister his name. Natalia had been a perfect *porteña*: hard and intimidating as diamond on the outside, putty at the core.

Miguel entered the studio, planning to head straight up to Don Luis's office and drag the complete story about the green-eyed boy out of him. Ha, as though that would be necessary. He decided that *café* was in order before more doom and gloom from Don Luis. He walked past the *tangueros'* lounge toward the cantina. Candy and Jean-Luc talked, standing on the practice floor. Their voices were faint, but audible. When he heard Candy speak his name, Miguel stopped to listen.

"Miguel, are you sure?" Candy asked Jean-Luc.

"Yes, he's working with Aggie on a milonga routine."

"Shit! I'm the one who taught him Ingrid's pathetic routine. If he teaches Skinny-Mini some variant, I'll pick it up in no time, maybe dance it with her for exhibition."

"Oh là là."

"People can't seem to get enough of two women together." She reared back her shoulders. "I'll stuff these in her face."

"Sounds like heaven. And you could be more famous than Natalia ever was."

"Bitch!"

Miguel couldn't believe his ears. He bent low, crept closer.

"I think Miguel would prefer to dance milonga with her and headline the show dancing tango with you." Jean-Luc set his chin.

"Hey, why not? What's Steph got that I ain't?"

"For one thing, an insecure star who constantly has to watch his back."

"Chaz is really good at what he does, though."

"I think everything about Miguel tells Chaz that what he *does* is not really tango."

"Ouch!"

"Lucky for you, Chaz knows you're not angling for his spot," Jean-Luc said. "And don't let on. I've got a feeling that could be dangerous."

Miguel considered the possibility that Jean-Luc might not be so stupid after all. But why was he filling Candy's head with ideas? Or was her head already full of them, just waiting to be expressed?

Candy said, "Then Wagner better watch out. He's not really hidden the fact that he's gaga to be the *primero bailarino*. Especially since," she quieted her voice, "Chaz's little hiccup earlier this year."

Miguel strained to hear. He inched closer to the corner. Peeked around.

She said, "After Natalia, Chaz totally disappeared for six months. Now, Wagner says he's more dependable than Chaz, and a better dancer."

"Wagner told you this?" Jean-Luc looked doubtful.

"The walls have ears. And Wagner's technique is the best of all. He's just so uncreative." Her head wilted, like Dr. Wagner's creativity. "He's also got another little problem." She raised her eyebrows. "But Wagner cut some kinda secret deal with Don Luis. If Chaz bails or doesn't hold up, Wagner gets his spot."

Jean-Luc caressed his chin. "Why would Don Luis do such a thing?" he asked. "He's pretty sharp and he loves Miguel."

Candy said, *sotto voce*, "Yesterday, it was like he wanted Chaz and Wagner to go at it. The tango crucible thing." She quoted the term with her fingers.

"Where murder by tango is distilled or revealed." He smiled broadly.

Candy paled. "But Don Luis is sharp. He's a sharp dancer, too."

"You saw him?"

"He's only been in that wheelchair since, you know, Natalia." She nodded unflinchingly. "I tell you, when Natalia was here, he was all over her. And she was trouble, but he liked it." She raised her nose. "Could smell it a mile away."

"Sugar daddy?" Jean-Luc asked, leering.

"Only the best for her," Candy rasped. "But she's dead, and I'm moving up."

Miguel seethed. Why hadn't he seen it before? He was too busy keeping his *verga* in his pants to spot Candy's treachery. He had already found out that she was physically strong enough to kill. Yet, his intuition had led him astray. It would not happen again. Creeping back toward the cantina, Miguel's head ached, but his mind was eased, believing he was closer than ever before to justice.

CHAPTER 58

A BOMBASTIC RANT AWOKE MIGUEL. He had planned to close his eyes for a few minutes but an hour had elapsed. It was a mixed blessing. He was reliving the horrific events at Sarge's from a few nights earlier. The Tex-Mex rhythms that filled the bar had now morphed into a syncopation with the vocalist continually using the Spanish slang word *narigón*. The song "Narigón" was a *neuvo* tango classic sung by a failed Argentine rock star. The lyrics depicted a cocaine-addicted *barrio* rat, the big-nose. The song was painful to hear. Miguel's body ached. He eyed the pill bottles confronting him from the nightstand. El Primitivo had been the most recent *tanguero narigón* to die. It was too soon to play that song, even to crush the dancers in Don Luis's tango hell.

Miguel pulled a pillow over his head. Bass boomed in the mattress, jarring his temples. The syncopated rhythm of the guitar opposed his heartbeat and set his nerves on edge. Miguel bolted up and grabbed his trousers. He was beginning to have concerns about Don Luis's methods and motivations. Standing back from the mezzanine balustrade, Miguel surveyed the main dance floor. Narigón was being looped and had begun anew. Don Luis, stick in hand, prowled the floor shouting, "Pain . . . *narigón*! Disillusionment . . . *narigón*! Death . . . *narigón*!"

Miguel observed that same-sex couples danced, a fairly common practice exercise everywhere in the tango world, except Argentina—. He understood the theory: every leader becoming a follower and vice versa was bound to produce more empathetic partnerships. The overwhelming tasks of navigating the floor and leading interesting steps while interpreting the melody of tango music only could be appreciated by attempting to lead. And the near-impossible demand to listen and respond to every nuance of a leader, and to embellish whenever possible while not interrupting the leader's flow, all while being absolutely seductive could only be fathomed by following.

"Change!" Don Luis demanded. Miguel saw each couple's embrace change, leaders become followers and vice versa. Don Luis shuffled toward Chaz and Dr. Wagner. He bellowed, "Well, Ernest, shoe on the other foot? How does it feel, like Cinderella . . . unclean, abused?"

Wagner reddened.

Don Luis snarked, "Now, Chaz, don't pinch the good doctor's bum, no matter how much you may be inclined."

Chaz stumbled, throwing off a high *sacada*. "Don't rush your footwork!"

Don Luis grinned and plodded away.

In the far corner, Miguel sighted Candy leading Aggie. No fancy footwork, no separation, they were stuck together. It was like the ebb and flow of a tango tide, their bodies undulating, moving in unison like waves. Aggie concentrated. Candy was at ease leading. But what was she really leading up to, Miguel puzzled. Had she motivated the exercise? Otherwise, how could she have had it on her mind just an hour before? Maybe Don Luis was boiling both the women and the men in his tango cauldron.

Don Luis propped on his stick and admired the couple. Miguel could only wonder whether he had been privy to the rivalry and rancor that Candy had felt for Natalia. Was he purposely rekindling Candy's dangerously jealous spirit? If so, to what end? Miguel bristled, glimpsing Aggie's compliant expression. He resolved that Candy would have to go through him to harm her.

CHAPTER 59

The Milonga loomed on Saturday morning. Don Luis furrowed his brow and plowed into the morass under his chin, considering the long day and night ahead. He had risen at seven and met the setup crew from David's Perfect Parties. Kemal scurried about in a work outfit, a khaki shirt and trousers, heeding Don Luis's every command. Even Barbara the bookkeeper, who had come in to get a jump on her accounts, had left her post at his request. Well before evening the space would be transformed into a 1940s *tanqueria*. Don Luis had promised local contacts that his new show would be the most arresting *espectáculo de tango Argentino* in New York's history.

Miguel was missing, although the previous day he seemed to have felt much better, almost normal. Don Luis caned himself around the studio level, considering whether David was depicting New York's '20s, à la Gatsby, or Buenos Aires's '40's, à la Gardel. Only when large-scale, framed posters of Gardel, di Sarli, and Pichuco were relocated from the lounges and raised to the studio walls was there no doubt.

Don Luis glared at the front door standing open wide. Energy lost, money wasted. He plodded doggedly toward it, recalling that there was something he had failed to do. Oh, Barbara needed to cut a deposit check for the trappings. He turned and saw Miguel. "Good afternoon, sir," he quipped.

"Trying to get my BA mojo back." Miguel smiled warmly. "I thought sleeping through lunch would put me on track."

Don Luis clapped Miguel's back. "Sounds like you're even better today."

"I feel sort of like I've been hit by a truck."

"That's an improvement?"

"Over feeling like being run down by a train, yes!"

A man nearly side-swiped Miguel with a tall bar stool. "Sorry," he gruffed.

"Maybe I should get out of the way," Miguel said. "People are trying to work."

"Shall we lunch upstairs?"

Miguel rubbed together his palms. "I'm starving."

"Another good sign," Don Luis said. "Please ask Barbara to prepare a check to David's Perfect Parties. Tell her that I'll fill in the amount and sign it." He winked. "If I'm going to dance this evening, I'm going to need a bit of rest, myself."

"I'm looking forward to seeing that."

Don Luis stamped his stick on the oaken floor and tottered away.

Miguel rotated full circle, his eyes widening, seeing the imagery of his country. The bare studio had been transformed. Rows of chairs on either side of the floor faced so that single men and women could more easily see each other. The men would be able to aim their invitations to dance, *cabeceos*, with better precision. Enormous rolls of black cloth were secured near the ceiling on either end of the studio. Similarly, the glass-walled fishbowl had been festooned by heavy black cloth with deep gathers and wave-like undulations from ceiling to floor. The light, airy studio had become a mysterious, macabre *tanqueria* from bygone days. Don Luis was fortifying his crucible of tango.

Miguel knocked on Barbara's office door, but there was no response. He turned the knob and entered. It was a smallish space with wooden chairs and cabinetry coordinating well with the lightly stained floor. Miguel eyed the desk for a notepad. He observed an open folder, detailing company personnel and their personal data. Candice Borakowski was first, Charles Christianson second. Ah, ha, Candy's personal data. His eyes narrowed. He'd never before heard Chaz's last name, or his given name for that matter. There was a lot he didn't know about his colleagues. But he was about to learn a few things. Miguel eyed the open portal, before bending toward the folder and flipping to the last page. He observed data for Ernest Wagner of Pelham Bay Park, New York. Miguel scooped up the pages and rolled them into a cylinder. He exited the office and made for the elevator. He would photocopy them in Don Luis's office and return them in moments.

"Miguel, Miguel," Don Luis called out.

He approached with the sheaf at his side, slightly behind his leg.

"Do you suppose when old Cachafaz was dancing away the night, he would have preferred the bar on his side of the room or would he have liked to use it as an excuse to circulate about the room nearer to the ladies?" He smiled devilishly.

"I think that is—"

"Excuse me, sir," roared a stump of a man in an ill-fitting suit, his eyes darting everywhere, "I'm looking for a Luis de Granada."

"Who should I say is calling on him, please?" Don Luis asked in clipped speech.

"Detective McGarrick of the NYPD." He flashed his shield with a flourish at odds with everything about him.

Miguel felt his heart sink.

"I am Luis de Granada. How may I be of assistance, Detective?"

"I understand that you are the employer of one Miguel Zanotto, a tango dancer from Buenos Aires, Argentina."

"Quite noisy in here. I can hardly hear you, Detective." Don Luis turned toward Miguel. "Juan, what are you waiting for? I needed that music yesterday!"

"*Sí señor, perdóneme*," Miguel said, rushing away, clutching the sheaf. He had to hold himself back to keep from running toward the elevator, though his leg had stiffened and every heel strike sent a painful jolt up to his shoulder.

Hours later, Miguel assessed himself in his bedroom's full-length mirror. Luxurious sport coat, perfectly pressed shirt, he was perfect, a perfect imposter. He had never before felt more worthless, hiding out from the cops in Don Luis's posh flop house. And his body ached from head to toe. The last thing he wanted to do was dude up and put on a fake face at a dance party. The milonga should be a place where you could nurse your sorrows, bind your wounds to melancholy music and a stranger's embrace. You could express the depths of your feelings, your sorrow—*tanguidad*—to another person without clumsy words. Your body could tell her body exactly how you felt.

Five minutes later, Miguel had on a pair of his basic black pants and an inexpensive white cotton button-up shirt. His favorite black dancing coat, lightweight wool, a bit frayed at the cuffs but beautifully pressed, hung at hand. He searched for his patent leather dancing shoes. He bent to his carpincho-hide sundry bag and thrust in his hand. He grasped one shoe, rummaged for its mate. An unfamiliar object. Miguel withdrew a cell phone and stared at it. Opened the sticky cover and rubbed together his fingers, finding them smeared with blood.

Miguel was boomeranged back in time, the scene so very vivid. He relived gunfire, exploding glass, and El Primitivo's cries, including his last words: the dangerous studio and the deadly *masha*. What was he saying? Why did he offer up this phone? Miguel started to wipe the blood on his pants, but he was going to a milonga. He must respect the ritual although he desperately wanted no part of it. Miguel made for the washroom, where he washed his hands and dried his eyes.

CHAPTER 60

ON THE INSIDE LOOKING OUT for a change, Miguel descended in the glass elevator, struck by the studio's transformation. He approached a floor-side table where Don Luis laughed with Dr. Wagner, both of whom wore tuxedos. Chaz stood nearby, sporting high-rise black trousers and braces. His gold lamé-look shirt, with its blousy three-quarter-length sleeves, was unbuttoned to mid-chest. Miguel assumed Chaz had a ballroom dancing throwback moment in his dressing room, a Blackpool blackout. His bleached *do* contrasted his scraggly dark beard. It appeared that he used his shaving time—for the past few weeks—spiking up every hair on his head. Miguel supposed this was speculation. But one thing was clear: the room was not the only thing transformed.

Miguel heard Wagner say, "Here's a fine medical term," as he scratched on a paper pad. Miguel leaned over to see the scribble: *Inoculatte.*

Don Luis said, "I haven't the foggiest."

"*Inoculatte* is taking coffee intravenously." Wagner giggled, his spirits high.

Miguel watched as Don Luis took up the pen.

"I can do better with your tedious medical vocabulary," Don Luis said, scribbling: *Osteopornosis.*

Wagner shrugged.

"*Osteopornosis* is a degenerate's disease."

Chaz guffawed. "That's great, Don Luis, you letch."

Miguel eyed Aggie and MoJo on the floor, dancing a huge international-style tango, anathema at a milonga. Despite the distress emblazoned on her face, Aggie was lovely in a strapless black dress, cut well up the thigh. A simple red choker at her neck completed a classic tango color scheme. MoJo, in all black, looked like Darth Vader.

Wagner said, "Take a look at this one, Chaz." He had written: *Glibido.*

"Is this what you learned in years of medical school?" Chaz asked, annoyed.

"No, but I can tell when someone is *glibidinous*: All talk and no action!"

Miguel didn't understand the jest completely, but it seemed as though Dr. Wagner had belittled Chaz's masculinity. Everyone laughed, everyone except Chaz.

"Oh, that's bad, Ernest," Don Luis said, smiling. "Please don't be an *Ignoranus*."

Chaz said, "Lemme guess: not only stupid, but also an asshole!" He nearly burst his side. Chaz literally doubled over as Dr. Wagner stormed from the table.

"It's impossible not to tease him a bit," Don Luis said. "So brilliant and all."

Miguel replied, "Someone might think you were trying to push him closer to the edge. See what he's really capable of."

"Ah-hum," Don Luis cleared his throat loudly. "It is time for some dancing."

"Indeed," Chaz said in an affected English brogue, "as soon as I find Aggie."

"Aggie told me she could hardly wait to experience Dr. Wagner's embrace."

"Bullshooot," Chaz mocked, making his way toward the floor.

Miguel shot Don Luis a curious look. He responded with a gentle downward tamping motion with his palms. Mischief was afoot, as usual.

Time raced by. Miguel retreated to the cantina after eleven. He hummed "New York, New York," having just heard it used as a *cortina*, the demarcation between musical sets. His favorite line was the same one all immigrants adored, "If I can make it there. . . ." He slammed down a *café cortado* and returned to the milonga, finding the overhead streamers unfurled. They were wafting in an air-conditioning-generated breeze. Spotlights illuminated the ominous black-cloth banners, and their chilling crimson characters. They seemed to drip dread, advertising the new show. At one end was '*¡Muerto por el Tango!*' at the other, 'Murder by Tango!'

CHAPTER 61

THE AIR WAS ELECTRIC WITH BUZZ about the new show. Miguel assumed that Don Luis found the evening to be a whopping success. It appeared that the one hundred exceptionally turned-out New Yorkers, arrayed in black tie, double-breasted suits, rakishly slanted fedoras, provocative dancing dresses, cut up to there, and impossibly tall shoes, were all knocked out.

Miguel, himself, was impressed, but had no desire to dance. He couldn't feel it, wasn't in it. His shoulder hurt, making embracing uncomfortable, and his mind was a tumult of questions and indecision. He rejoined Don Luis's table where Dr. Wagner, who had apparently gotten over his upset, was once again playing word games. Jean-Luc had arrived and was sitting at the adjacent table, his back to Don Luis.

MoJo bounded up and greeted Miguel warmly. He intimated that Ruthie was too intimidated to come along. Miguel nodded understanding. They noticed Dr. Wagner had written something that he seemed to think was of great import: *Reintarnation*."

Don Luis shrugged.

Wagner arched his eyebrows. "*Reintarnation* is being reborn a hillbilly!"

A waiter passed carrying an hors d'oeuvre tray. MoJo asked, "You smell that?"

Wagner sniffed the air and replied a disdainful "No."

"Reminds me of Bubbe's fresh-baked *rugelach*." MoJo scribbled: *Noshtalgia*!

Wagner sat stone-faced.

"Very good, indeed!" Don Luis enthused, reading the invented Yiddish word. Just then, Don Luis's gaze was captured by a striking woman who approached the table. Miguel surveyed her carefully. Buff arm muscles shone from below her silk sleeveless dress. It was adorned with a red diagonal stripe across the bust, continuing down one side, vanishing just past her hip, where the side seam opened. She wore a polished stone around her elegant neck. There were no vampish—ripped to perfection—fishnet stockings, worn by so many others. Her unimaginably sheer hose accentuated curvaceous thighs, taut calves, and slender ankles. Her modest four-inch heels were black peep-toes with red and white polka dots.

Don Luis stood and, constantly holding the woman's gaze, strutted around the table leaving behind his walking stick. He took her hand and kissed it, bowing slightly at the waist. Miguel couldn't help but think of Kemal, and his deep bow before slicing into him. Miguel rubbed the white trace on the back of his hand, wondering just how much Don Luis and Kemal were birds of a feather.

The music mounted, strains of Carlos Gardel's tango classic "Cuesta Abajo" filled the air. Miguel was moved by the syrupy strings. And then, to his amazement, Don Luis jerked his head toward the crowded floor, a *cabeceo*! The lady beamed. Miguel's jaw dropped when they approached the floor, arm in arm, Don Luis's gait as steady as an Arab charger's. Miguel plopped into a chair and watched dumbfounded as they danced. Don Luis's lead was commanding, her follow effortless. A moment later, Aggie sidled up to Miguel and looked into his eyes. She jerked her head toward the floor in a macho *cabeceo*. He feigned surprise, thrusting an index finger into his chest, mouth agape.

On the floor, Miguel felt his forearm quiver slightly as he embraced Aggie's back. She leaned into him, her lean torso finding his pectorals. He was nervous. Not because his shoulder hurt or because his arm was uncomfortable; he didn't know exactly why. It was a new, disagreeable sensation, as though his confidence had deserted him. His thoughts time-warped back to when he was unable to save El Primitivo. He wasn't even certain how he'd saved himself. Did he really take out Gordo? The police apparently thought so. Miguel couldn't wait to talk to Don Luis about their visit earlier in the day. Ah, he had to turn off his mind and concentrate on the lilting music. No use.

Eyes open, to get the lay of the floor around them, Miguel struggled with how to begin the dance. Amid his indecision, he met Chaz's intent gaze. Miguel felt completely exposed. It was as though Chaz could read his pathetic thoughts, and was laughing inside. He searched Chaz's face, to see his upturned lips, but all he could see were his sparkling blue eyes, boring into him. Marble-hard eyes, staring a hole all the way through him.

Miguel increased the pressure of his embrace and lunged left, colliding with Don Luis, who smiled kindly and moved along. He began to feel sick to his stomach. It was as though his feet were cast in concrete. Chaz glared. Miguel lurched forward without conveying his intentions clearly to Aggie. She nearly stumbled stepping backward. He sucked in his breath and held it, like a rank beginner. After only a moment, he was suffocating and understood much better the concept of death by embarrassment.

After a nearly insufferable *tanda* of three beautiful tangos, complete with fits and false starts, bumps and bungled steps, Miguel thanked Aggie for the pleasure of dancing. It was as false as the first time he'd danced the milonga at the company audition. Mired in shame, he added, "I'm sorry."

Miguel escorted Aggie to her seat and walked slowly, patting his brow with a handkerchief, back to the table where Don Luis sat and Chaz stood, draining another drink. Miguel avoided Chaz's probing eyes, but couldn't skirt his insulting remark, "Can't say that *tanda* was no sweat, huh, Miguel."

Don Luis said, "The music is marvelous, Chaz. Perhaps you should dance."

"I'd rather play word games," he replied. "What do you get when you cross a gay *tanguero* and a gangster?"

Silence.

"A stiffy." He laughed loudly.

"Get it, Miguel?" He screeched, "Oh, my God, did you *get it*—"

Miguel took the comment as an offense to El Primitivo's death. He lunged at Chaz, grabbing him by the shoulders. He shook him forcefully, yelling, "*Basta*!"

Chaz squirmed, his arms flailing and his torso twisting until he freed himself. He stood rigidly, a wild glare dominating his fiery eyes. Miguel met the intensity and upped it a notch before turning to walk away. Chaz raised his glass and smashed it into the side of Miguel's head. The glass rang. Ice and water shot outward, spraying Miguel's face. He turned and ducked Chaz's right hook. Miguel landed a blow to Chaz's head, addling him. He prepared to hit him again, but suddenly his arms were constrained, as though by metal bands. He threw back a glance to find Jean-Luc holding him fast. Chaz grimaced and readied his fist. Miguel writhed against Jean-Luc's power. Chaz was swinging, putting all his weight behind the blow. Miguel twisted to the left and ducked. The blow connected with his shoulder. It seared with pain.

Miguel tried to rotate his body, but Jean-Luc's arms were like bulky steel. What did he do for training, Miguel wondered. Whatever it was, it was time to focus on him, not Chaz, who was holding his hand as though it were broken. Miguel made a feint to the left and then rotated right, gouging his elbow into Jean-Luc's ribs. The metal fetters relaxed. Miguel turned, but in an instant Jean-Luc had him in a headlock, applying suffocating pressure. He struck Jean-Luc's kidneys from behind, but his punch had no heft.

Miguel let his weight sag; he fell to the floor, landing atop Jean-Luc, the choke-hold broken. Miguel tried to pin him to the floor, but he scrambled and reached down toward his ankle. A knife? This was turning into a real Argentine milonga, La Boca style. With his fist, Miguel struck downward, landing a crushing blow to Jean-Luc's wrist, causing him to release the weapon with a shriek. It skittered with the clunk of a gun toward Chaz, who stood watching. Miguel rolled away from Jean-Luc, popped up to his knees, and then crouched, ready to counter a charge. It never came. Jean-Luc fell to his knees, searching the floor frantically.

Don Luis commanded, "Cease and desist this instant." He stood tall, glaring at Miguel, Jean-Luc, and Chaz. He said, "Chaz, go home and sleep it off; Jean-Luc, thank you for coming, good night; Miguel, feel free to retire and get some rest."

The room was quiet, except for the lovely lilt of Gardel's heartbreaking classic, "El Diá Que Me Quieras." Miguel saw Aggie watching from the floor's margin, mouth quivering, hands to her head. He thought that the last thing she should be dreaming of was the day when he would love her. He was cursed!

CHAPTER 62

SUNDAY GLOOM, not even the happy squeak of a mouse could be heard in the halls of Don Luis's palace. Rain pelted the large glass panes of Miguel's bedroom windows, producing a perfect soundtrack for skullduggery. An ominous clap of thunder rattled the door as wearily he stalked his room, having hardly slept, reliving the previous night's disastrous milonga. Nothing was right, not with him and certainly not with the company members. His stomach churned and boiled. The shoulder was more wrenched than it had been after his death-defying escape from Gordo. He was determined to get to the bottom of that, too.

Dressed in black, trousers and a pullover, Miguel tied on sports shoes and bounced from foot to foot. Today of all days, he needed to feel like the man he used to be. But it was tough, having become mired in a posh den of weirdness. He looked around at the cream-colored this and the gold-embossed that; who the hell did Don Luis think he was, Louis Quatorze?

Miguel did not need luxury; he needed to regain his nerve. The first step was clear. He secured his bedroom door and accessed his locked case, stowed in a cavernous walk-in closet. He opened the case and removed the sheaf of papers he'd stashed there the previous day. Miguel took a deep breath and plumbed the suitcase's bottom, fetching up the photo. Broken glass in the frame obscured his face, but it was their faces he needed to see. He met their eyes: clear, vital, alive, now dead. Natalia's anyway. His mother, lying in a stupor in BA, was not far behind. Steeling himself, Miguel carefully replaced the photo, secured the case, and shoved it back into the closet's recesses.

A couple of quick, short breaths. Miguel sensed the blood coursing through his body. He felt worse and better, accessing the banged-up travel bag, withdrawing El Primitivo's cell phone. Not wanting to soil the elegant washroom towels, he used tissue paper to wipe it clean. He rinsed his hand under warm water and watched the sanguine-tinged stream spiral down the drain. Like a wasted life. El Primitivo's life.

On the floor, back against his bed, Miguel energized the phone. The screen displayed a background of what appeared to be beautiful women. On closer inspection Miguel determined that the second one from the right was El Primitivo in drag. They were all men. He focused on the blinking cursor, stationary in a password field. Now the work begins, he thought. He typed the names of tango composers, milongas in BA, the few gay tango dancers that he knew. *Nada.* After a short while—that seemed like a long while—he dropped the phone to the floor.

Miguel paced, wringing his mind for ideas for El Primitivo's password. Caffeine could bolster his brainpower. He stuffed the phone in his pocket. Sure enough, within a minute of tasting the super-potent brew, not a calming *café cortado* but a *doppio ristretto*, Miguel realized that he might actually have access to at least one of El Primitivo's passwords. He hustled toward the computer cubbyhole.

The computer kiosk achieved, the first order of business was to disconnect the unknown keylogger to not leave a keystroke trail. Miguel traced the cable to the CPU and found nothing. Having no time to obsess, quickly he inspected the opposing side of the keyboard and found that the cable he had installed and embedded in the plastic cable runner had been untouched. He followed the guide to the heavy screen, providing a backdrop for the space, and located his keylogger, still jammed between the screen and tabletop. He felt relieved.

He used an adapter he found underneath the workstation, in the cable snake pit, to connect the keylogger to a USB port. He searched on El Primitivo and located a recent login script with a password unassociated with tango and milongas, but reflecting his own name and probably his birth year: 19Perseus94. So, he wasn't too turned off by his name, thinking that Miguel had never chosen a password he hated. While he was at it, Miguel rooted around in Chaz and Candy's folders. His contained oodles of videos of his tango performances, loads of both old and new Argentine tango music, and a bunch of emo music. Hers was a mishmash of unfinished letters, poetry, tango music, and *risqué* selfies.

Alert and processing everything at once, Miguel recalled encountering Jean-Luc in the kiosk. He had typed furiously. He searched for the man's name, an unfinished letter of no significance was displayed among Candy's files. Miguel read it and understood her dilemma. He wondered the same thing she did, was Jean-Luc serious or was he using her for something other than sex? He searched again, simply using, Jean, and then merely, Luc, nothing. He had no account and had not logged his name anywhere. Then why was he in here, Miguel pondered, replacing his little device and exiting? Another mystery.

Burrowed in his bedroom, Miguel accessed the phone using the pilfered password. He went for the contacts directory. Lots of funny names—mostly code, he suspected. He looked for Gordo. Absent. He accessed the log of recent calls. Numbers from all over the place: New York, Argentina, even Italy. It appeared to be a lot of worthless info. But he had thought it useful for Miguel to have it. Why?

Miguel sat pondering all of these questions. He picked up the sheaf of papers bearing company personnel info. He engaged NYroute.com on his phone to determine the easiest subway routing to Dr. Wagner's Pelham Bay Park home on Roosevelt Avenue. The man was definitely a bundle of raw nerves. Had he done it, Don Luis believed so. Miguel didn't know, but he intended to find out.

A crack of lightning illuminated the room with blinding intensity. Thunder pealed, its deep voice rattling the windows and doors. Horrible weather, but it was Sunday and Wagner would likely be at home. Miguel would wait a while, closer to dark, to take a secret look at the man who may have robbed Natalia of her life. Miguel patted his hip pocket, finding his weapon ready, just as his hand was willing.

On the Pelham Number 6 train, Miguel was anonymous. He didn't feel the sense of menace that had accompanied him on his foray to the spyware shop. It was a long way from the Upper East Side, in more than one way. There were few riders. Young kids stared aimlessly out the windows, their mother's listless, inert. Miguel recalled his happy childhood, a time of little supervision, roaming wild on their Rosario property. Later, there had been plenty of opportunity to act out when visiting his cousins in La Boca. His mother had loved him intensely, and imparted her sense of self-respect and her work ethic to Miguel. He glanced at a cute little boy sitting in the dirty aisle, no parent in sight, not even a surly Gordo to urge him into a seat. Miguel's heart ached, thinking of Hector.

Miguel prowled the exterior of Dr. Wagner's park view home, seeking a lighted room. He found one in back, far from the impressive front façade. The rain had stopped. A window was open and Argentine tango wafted on the pregnant night air. Miguel waded into the greenery, slowly, quietly, ignoring the pricks of thorns and the splatter of rainwater from wet leaves into his face. The scent of moist dirt permeated the place. He stepped up onto an overturned gardening bucket and peered in at Wagner. Miguel couldn't believe his eyes or ears. The tango music blared inside the unusual room, filled with instruments, specimens, antiseptic-looking metal cupboards, and large metal bins with gleaming faucets. Dr. Wagner seemed to stumble toward a cutting board of sorts, bearing a large hunk of flesh. Miguel recoiled. It looked like a chunk of human flesh, a thigh maybe. Wager began to slice into the meaty chunk. He smiled with relish. Miguel had not smiled once during years of work at a meat packing plant. His stomach turned. What was Wagner doing? This man was crazy, and no doubt a killer of something. Miguel considered offing him on general principles, but he wanted concrete evidence.

Wagner appeared to be distressed, examining his incisions. He wiped his eyes on his sleeve and dropped his instrument. He rushed for a bottle of a recognizable brand of vodka. Put it to his lips and slugged hard.

Miguel recalled that Wagner had drunk only water at the milonga. He also remembered Candy's revelation to Jean-Luc, about Wagner's little problem. Obviously, the man could not live with the thoughts of his deeds. Miguel climbed down and withdrew. An adjacent room with an open window became his target. He muttered to himself, "Wagner is half drunk, he'll never know what hit him. Still, I will stare him in the eyes as I spill his blood."

Miguel pulled on nylon gloves, approaching the window of what appeared to be a guest bedroom. He withdrew his knife and hooded the blade as it arced open silently. He inserted the blade in the screen and sawed. The synthetic material cut like warm butter. Finally, he would accomplish his noble goal. Slowly and quietly Miguel proceeded, sawing evenly in short strokes until, "*Riiing*! *Riiing*! *Riiing*!"

sounded an external intrusion alarm. The screen possessed signal-conducting strands connected to an intrusion detection system, and he had severed one. Miguel hopped from his perch, his head snapping side to side. A thicket extended to the house from a tall fence behind him. The only path to the street was past the open window of Wagner's gruesome lab. "*Riiing*! *Riiing*! *Riiing*!" the alarm screamed and floodlights illuminated the landscape.

Miguel ducked his head and tore across the open area. He heard Wagner scream. He kept running, as the neighbor's porch lights were switched on. In a moment he was on the roadside, making tracks down the hill.

CHAPTER 63

THE PELHAM NUMBER 6 TRAIN clanged away from Dr. Wagner's Park, heading toward Manhattan's Lexington line. Miguel had cooled down. He had to admit that the alarm had been a blessing. He couldn't say for sure that Wagner had killed anyone, let alone Natalia. But from now on, in his mind, Wagner was guilty until proven innocent.

From his backpack, Miguel removed El Primitivo's phone. He energized it, entered the password and stared at the screen. What could he do with it that was meaningful? "Bang! Bang!" Miguel's hand jerked to his hip pocket. "Got you right in the head," a little boy pointing a toy pistol at his friend said. "You're dead!" Miguel cringed, hating the culture of violence more than ever. Suddenly he knew something meaningful to try with the phone.

Heather called El Primitivo, he had said. But really it was Lexi Lexus, Heather's hooker friend. She probably knew where Hector was staying, now that both of his parents were dead. While his mother had denied it, now Hector was truly a pitiable child. Miguel believed that he could comfort him, if they could just talk.

Tentatively Miguel redialed the last number that had called the phone. It was from New York area code 212 and was listed as phone contact VRE. Miguel chewed a fingernail waiting. A man said, "Yeah?" and Miguel froze. He heard commotion in the background. Someone said in a heavy Brooklyn brogue, "Hey, Vinnie, your shot."

Miguel could swear he heard billiard balls clacking, men cursing.

"Who is this?" the man asked. "Fuck you, pal." He hung up.

Miguel's pulse throbbed in his shoulder. What had he expected? He took a deep breath and tried the penultimate number, another local call.

"Hello," a man said.

A sad thought crossed Miguel's mind: what if El Primitivo had been lying about getting a call from a woman using Heather's phone? But why would he do that? What could he possibly gain from it? Whether Gordo had something to gain was a more intriguing question. But Gordo was history. Then it occurred to him, maybe this was Lexi Lexus's new Gordo.

"I want to talk to Lexi," Miguel said, with all the intensity he could muster.

"Lexi who?"

"I'm a friend, a customer friend."

"Gotta name?"

"Joe."

"Hold on, Joe."

Miguel terminated the call. He had the contact info he wanted.

Once back at Don Luis's tango circus, Miguel showered in scalding hot water to try and wash away the disgust he felt oozing from every pore. No luck. He mourned the unfortunate children of the world. But what could he do? He could save no one. He was wanted by the police for a murder he didn't commit. Sooner rather than later they would want him for one he committed with relish. Miguel ran his fingers though his still-damp hair. The world had always been a tough place, seemingly it was getting tougher. He needed to cool down. Maybe it would help to have something cold to drink. Dr. Wagner crossed his mind. He was probably passed out by now. Such a waste.

Miguel took the internal elevator down to the mezzanine. He heard a noise just around the corner. Peeking, he saw Don Luis securing his office door. Not in the mood to chat, Miguel held his position. His scuffle the previous night was fresh in his mind. Miguel assumed the same of Don Luis. But as a guest in the house, Miguel was bound to greet his host. He manned up and turned the corner. "Good evening, Don Luis."

"Miguel, how are you?"

"A bit thirsty. I'm going to the cantina for water. Is everything okay?"

"Yes, just checking a couple of things." Don Luis asked haltingly, "Company?"

"It would be my pleasure."

On the studio level, they admired the remarkable job the cleanup crew had done. Miguel turned his gaze from the over-the-top banners, now hanging dormant in the stillness of midnight. Although he had attempted it earlier in the evening, at the moment, murder by any means seemed to him a waste, a perversion of life's plan.

In the cozy cantina, Miguel drank water from the water cooler and Don Luis drank Perrier. It was a bitter pill for Miguel when he said, "I must apologize for my terrible conduct last night."

"Let's not speak of it. There are reasons for everything, even unpleasant things, especially them. We were both at fault."

"It was a fantastic milonga. Congratulations."

"To all of us," Don Luis replied, admiring his bubbly beverage. "I, too, must make an apology for ignoring you yesterday afternoon."

"Oh, is nothing," Miguel said, half-embarrassed.

Don Luis rocked in his chair and clucked his tongue. Deep thoughts. Slowly, he said, "You know, there is a story that I owe you."

Miguel seized the opportunity to move on, blurting, "Oh, yes, the green-eyed man. The descendant of our hero-villain, *villero*."

Don Luis seemed distracted, replying, "Oh, yes, of course, the green-eyed son of the rabbi who married Torquemada's cousin, Augustina de Leòn. Right you are."

Miguel sipped water, trying to relax his mind.

"He narrowly escaped burning at the stake in 1490. Afterwards, he carried on whole hog as a *marrano*."

"Sorry to hear that."

Don Luis shook off the revelation. "He told only one of his five offspring about the sham and shame under which they managed to survive."

"So, he died young?"

"He was not so lucky: he lived to be old."

Miguel's finger flew to his lips, his front teeth clamping a fine line of flesh.

"But his influence on the line was profound," Don Luis said. "Through the slings and arrows of outrageous fortunes they suffered for five hundred years, they were as quiet as mice about their heritage and their sacred book, which was scrupulously retained."

"That's something. It was not completely bad."

"But it was not so good, either. The secret diaries of many men and later of many women tell of their self-loathing, revulsion at their own lifestyles, and their impotence in acting against tradition that had bound them for almost six hundred and fifty years. Their stories are like vampire tales: deceit, death, suffering, self-revulsion, and inability to change anything constructively. These were the cornerstones of their lives."

"What did they do?"

"They worked, traded, developed political influence, and built lasting wealth. Used their money to try and insulate themselves from harm. The number who actually practiced Judaism diminished over the years and by the dawn of the twentieth century the family was a well-behaved, well-concealed Catholic clan."

Miguel hesitated, but said, "I'm not sure I blame them."

"And neither do I sit in judgment," said Don Luis. "To their credit, however, in the 1940s, some helped European Jews transit to Portugal and Morocco. Again a handsome, green-eyed boy who grew up to be defiant and wild. He led his clan in a resistance movement against Granada. They were found out, tortured, and hanged. Their bodies were tossed in the field near *La Alhambra de Granada*." Don Luis's chest heaved. "The same *vega* that inspired twentieth-century poetry by Lord Latymer and the classical guitar composition "La Vega" of Isaac Albéniz." His head drooped, eyelids closed.

"Is okay if you don't want to talk more," Miguel said, sensing the depth of pain. "This history is a bit too difficult to speak, perhaps."

"No, no. It's just that his brother took control of the family's resources and did a reasonable job of carrying on, knowing that he had been inferior in every way to his brave, dead sibling." His voice faltered.

"I understand exactly," Miguel replied, tears welling in his own eyes.

"Do you really?" Don Luis asked.

"I have only a sister, but the situation is the same." He paused. "So what did his family do? You say they were wealthy now, politically connected."

His voice quavered, saying, "There are so many similar stories, tales of heart-crushing grief." He tried to compose himself. "His family did what their family and so many others had done through the ages: they begged and cried for mercy from a deaf or unyielding or nonexistent Creator."

"So which is it?" Miguel asked solemnly.

"Who knows?" Don Luis paused. He stared intently as though trying to extract from the void the answer to the most monumental question that has ever confronted mankind. Haltingly, he spoke. "As I've said before, if there's any chance whatsoever that the designer of this magnificent universe is willing to interact with humanity, any person who would not dedicate his life to doing so would be a fool."

"Is that why you became a professor of religion, to interact with It?"

Don Luis clucked his tongue. "I wanted to prove that *It* didn't exist. That life is simply a craps game. Tumble the dice; see how they fall. I spent decades drilling my disbelief into impressionable young people. Demanding they regurgitate the *drek* I fed them week-in and week-out." He threw back his head. "My spirit was dead. The weight of my family's sin, of my own sin, was great. It seemed that I had to try and kill the students' spiritual instincts, too."

"I'm sure this was not intentional. You are not cruel."

"I was helpless," he said, adding, "and as frustrated as everyone else had been for the past six and a half centuries." Don Luis paused before saying, "But I have a plan that could alter the course of world history."

Miguel sat upright. "Did I hear you—"

"Indubitably, you did hear me correctly. This plan will redeem myself and a long line of unfortunates, who have suffered for centuries under the weight of unimaginable fear and anxiety. We shall all be redeemed before it is too late."

"I think I need a bit more water for this one," Miguel said.

"Oh, it's quite late, my boy," said Don Luis. "Let's get some rest now."

Miguel made his way to the counter, thinking what a cliffhanger. But, as usual, the conversation was turning weird. The idea of changing the course of history, what was that about? He ached to help just one person, a poor little boy, and couldn't. Miguel's head became heavy, thinking of hundreds of years of abuse, suffering, and death of so many. All because of a book, Codex, whatever. But was the Codex powerful enough to do what Don Luis claimed, to change the course of the world? And if Don Luis succeeded, would it really justify all the suffering? Could anything?

CHAPTER 64

FIGHT OR FLIGHT, Miguel couldn't determine which had the more negative impact on his body and spirit. Had he not experienced both during the weekend, perhaps he would not be wiped out after rehearsal on Monday evening. But the day had not been a total loss. Don Luis had come through with a nice surprise, two in fact. A banking associate of his had acquired box seats to the US Open Tennis Tournament's men's final for him the coming Sunday. Don Luis had asked Miguel if he cared to take Aggie, in appreciation for inviting them to her birthday dinner. Miguel relished the opportunity to witness the greatest spectacle of tennis in the world, the US Open final. He loved the athleticism and elegance of the game, although he knew little of it. And every Argentine knew the name and rugged features of former US Open tennis champ Juan Martin del Potro. He was an Argentine national treasure.

When Don Luis suggested that Kemal chauffeur them, Miguel had frowned. Don Luis then explained that getting to the National Tennis Center from Grand Central Station was easy. The Number 7 train of the Long Island Rail Road stopped two minutes away. But when he asked if Miguel felt secure driving a car in and out of the city and Miguel said with certainty that he did, Don Luis smiled broadly. There was a third option that was, ". . . quite exhilarating," but they would have to wait for the morning to explore it.

Miguel had stuffed the claim, as he had most of Don Luis's mysterious revelations. There was no telling what was to come. He did, however, manage to find the nerve to question Don Luis about the NYPD's visit to the studio. Don Luis had claimed that it was his fault and he would deal with it. Miguel saw no reason to pursue it further for the time being. It was sad that Don Luis's crushing burden of guilt and shame had colored his perception to the point that he assumed everything was his fault.

The best was yet to come. On Tuesday morning, Don Luis had escorted Miguel to the garage. The automobile caretaker and mechanic had dusted off a beauty for Miguel's inspection. Don Luis had patted the fender and said, "It's a Ferrari 575M." He pointed to the grill's *cavallino rampante* and joked, "It's an aging stallion, like me." Miguel had said only, "Wow!"

The technician fired up the engine and flicked the throttle. The cavernous concrete corridors resounded with the engine's throaty growl. It resonated in Miguel's chest, producing a broad grin on his face. Miguel took a brief tutorial on the car, which included explaining its electronic paddle shifting. The man had said, "In Automatic mode it's as docile as a pup. In Race mode," he tapped a red button on the steering wheel, "it's a beast."

CHAPTER 65

Miguel was stoked, and awake well before seven on Sunday morning. He was delighted that during their chats about the adventure, Aggie had suggested leaving early Sunday. After a hurried breakfast he made his way to the garage to ensure the Ferrari was full of gas, all shiny, and had not been stolen overnight by aliens—or whoever had recently circumvented Don Luis's security system. He bent and caressed with his hand a front tire. Slipped his fingers between tread rows, finding a canyon of rubber. Dug in his nails, deflecting the soft compound of sticky competition tires. Miguel considered that these were the car's tango shoes, the mediators of its dance with the roadway. They determined how much of the engine's muscle could be transmitted to the surface by the *tanguero* at the wheel.

Miguel looked down the vehicle's muscular yet taut fender, admiring the silvery, wet look of its titano paint and the perfection of its Pininfarina design. He opened the door and the smell of fresh leather wafted into his face from Bordeaux-colored, hand-sewn hides. He lowered himself into the seat and fired her up. The powerful V12 purred rather than growled at idle. The seatbelt clicked closed with surety.

The vehicle had no GPS, so Miguel's phone was a lifesaver motoring to Aggie's house in Morningside Heights. He departed Manhattan pulling away from traffic and an annoying purple land yacht that wove between lanes and always seemed too near to him. All in all, Sunday traffic was light and the car's handling magnificent.

True to her word, Aggie lived in an actual house, with a fence, and shrubbery, even a small lawn. Miguel had worn nylon training pants, a light-blue-and-white Argentine *fútbol* jersey, and sneakers, perfect attire for a stadium full of screaming tennis fans, he assumed. Aggie answered the door looking as though she were going to tea with the Queen, or at least a princess. She wore a knee-length, antique white dress with a thin periwinkle belt and mid-heeled periwinkle shoes. A matching bag and jaunty cream-colored hat with a turquoise-studded beige ribbon were perched near the door.

"Are we, um, going to the same place?" Miguel asked shyly.

"Absolutely, and we're color coordinated."

He smiled, only slightly confused by her reply.

In no time, the Grand Central Parkway East made a bowtie-shaped U-turn over the Long Island Expressway and became Grand Central Parkway West. They exited toward Flushing Meadows/Corona Park. It was thrilling when they flashed their parking pass at attendants, who gave them a thumbs-up and ushered them ever nearer the stadium.

Miguel and Aggie arrived at the investment banking company's box as the players took the court. The tennis stars were received warmly, Miguel and Aggie not so much. Everyone in the box, except Miguel, was well, if not superbly, dressed in linen or silk jackets, alligator shoes, Rolex watches, and every manner of chic eye- and head-wear.

After a so-so first set, they bolted and made for a foot-long hot dog vendor. Miguel was amazed that the dogs and beers were actually worth the astronomical price he paid. They ate leaning against a wall leading to excellent seating. At the first opportunity to sneak past the gate guard, they scampered to empty seats and enjoyed the match.

* * *

Big Benny could hardly hear the caller over the racket of big-screen TVs in the game room and the soldiers cursing at the tops of their lungs. Phil's Gentlemen's Club, down on the waterfront of the East River in Brooklyn, was hopping. Benny eyed Phil, pouring drinks, taking bets on the tennis match, showing pictures of hookers to horny soldiers. He was as happy as a druggie working in a pharmacy. Even Vinnie Rabbit Ears was drinking and smiling, now that he'd got his way.

"Pipe down, will ya!" Benny shouted at no one in particular. "Okay," he said into the grimy flip phone, "where's that thing."

The garbled reply sounded like the man had said they had lost it.

Benny cut his eyes to the odd pair not drinking, not glued to the tennis match. They were his guests but were getting on everybody's nerves, especially the soldiers. One was a local kid, fancying himself a deal maker. After his deadbeat dad gave him a tip about making big money buying and selling an old book, he'd gone halfway around the world to make contact with a badass and set up a deal. Benny assumed the kid was a chip off the old block and would sell his mother for a fist full of shekels. The other guy, superspy, Benny liked even less. He was too tightly wound. The crew didn't understand or didn't care that the guy meant serious bucks for the family. Benny understood and that was why he hadn't already sent him back to the Holy Land.

Benny could tell the guests were listening in on his conversation. They pretended to be using a notebook computer to develop a new plan, awaiting the afternoon's big event. Secure computers, *sheesh*, Benny thought. About as secure as keeping money in a shoebox under the bed. Why not just sign a confession and leave it on the fucking kitchen table in case the feds had trouble proving their case against you.

Even more ridiculous, these guys were supposed to be breaking into Interpol's International Criminal Database, using something called a back door. Benny remembered when it was the cops who broke into your back door!

He lowered his voice; it was a bit embarrassing. "We, uh, need the thing; we're waiting to have a little talk," Benny said.

The muffled reply suggested there had been a problem with a vehicle. The man apparently wanted Vinnie to drive out to Flushing Meadows and help.

"Goddamnit, I can't hear you," Benny said. "I'll tell Vinnie to get over there."

He snapped the antiquated phone shut and yelled, "Vinnie!"

Big Benny slammed down hard on the rickety table; drinks and munchies flew everywhere. Vinnie was only a group boss, *capodecina*, but he wanted to move up to *sotto capo*; that's what this whole thing was about. Vinnie didn't want to lose the hood Gordo had worked and he sure didn't want to look weak.

Benny pushed his buttons a little, saying, "Get your ass over there. This is your deal, *Signore Sotto Capo*."

Vinnie had cursed, but he headed for his coat, and his heater.

"Problem?" the bearded man inquired, looking up from his laptop.

"You sure they're there?" Benny asked.

"You kidding? She told everyone at the tango studio at least twice. She was as proud as if she was getting a boob job."

"Could use one," the younger man snapped.

"Sour grapes?" asked the elder. He added, "I think I should go with that *schmuck*, Vinnie. If Miguel ends up dead, it destroys my new plan." He stood.

Benny's eyes narrowed, even the man's voice grated on him now. And Benny recalled how both the 'infiltration plan' and the 'heist plan' had failed. The new 'divide and conquer plan' didn't sound great, but at least it wouldn't fill body bags. That, as always, was his plan of last resort. Death was splashy in the papers; the press loved it. And the cops had to pin it on somebody, fast. Usually somebody like one of Benny's soldiers, lifetime criminals with histories of violence. Benny said, "If he heard you say that, all of the angels in heaven and demons in hell couldn't keep him from tearing your throat out. So, please sit down and shut up!"

CHAPTER 66

GAME, SET, MATCH! The Serbian star vanquished his opponent handily. The final vestiges of a perfect Indian summer afternoon lingered over Flushing Meadows–Corona Park. Miguel appreciated the dry air after the excessive rainfall of what had been called the dog days of summer. The pair neared the stadium exit closest to their exalted parking place, feeling a tad let down by absence of drama in the match, yet thrilled to be part of a spectacle not involving tango.

The 575M roared to life. Miguel engaged automatic mode and the stability control feature that was essential for casual driving. They rumbled toward the highway, chatting and reliving the experience. Entering the Parkway, Miguel noticed a shiny new vehicle lagging behind them. Its lights were penetratingly bright and low to the pavement. He assumed its driver was just as concerned with taking care of his baby as was Miguel. Don Luis's stereo station of choice played his new favorite old tune, "New York, New York." He gripped the girthy wheel confidently, thinking he was making it there, by the skin of his teeth and with a little help from his friends.

Suddenly the fancy car that had trailed switched lanes and accelerated. Soon its front bumper was even with the Ferrari. Miguel glanced over, smiling, but the car's darkly tinted windows hid its occupants. Nearing an exit, the car crowded Miguel's lane. Miguel dodged it by moving to the outermost lane, but it kept coming, forcing him first onto the shoulder and then to exit onto the Brooklyn-Queens Expressway.

Miguel spit a curse and accelerated. He felt the V12's power; the speedo registered 145 kilometers per hour, and climbing. It was near the speed of the tennis pros' weak second serves, about ninety miles per hour. Aggie used her phone to find an alternate route back to the city. The aggressive sports car followed at a safe distance, but both moved at a fast clip, 160 kilometers per hour. Miguel searched for an exit, any place to shake the pursuer. He saw a sign for an unpronounceable bridge, the Kosciuszko Bridge, but no exits. They rocketed over the bridge at 180 kilometers per hour, the speed of a pro's aggressive second serve, 110 miles per hour. The car handled like a dream, but the speed was too much for traffic. Aggie said to take the McGuinnesse Boulevard exit and head toward the Queens Midtown Tunnel. Miguel did so without hindrance. This was almost as worrisome as if the pursuer had tried to intercede. Was he bored with his little game or was Miguel playing into his hand?

Miguel's eyes were everywhere. Aggie seemed to sense his nervousness. She chatted idly, trying to calm him. He observed the exit for Greenpoint Avenue. A vehicle pulled rudely from the shoulder out into traffic. Miguel's luck, it lodged itself ahead of him. He hit the brakes, slowing to 100 kilometers per hour. And then out of nowhere the sports car was beside him, nosing into Miguel's lane, about to dent the 575M's front fender. Miguel yanked the wheel, avoiding a collision, but then the pokey vehicle cut over in front again. He was being forced toward another exit. The sports car made a dig toward the Ferrari's nose, forcing Miguel and Aggie to exit onto Greenpoint and head toward the East River.

"Oh God, what's he doing?" Aggie shrieked.

"This is worse than Napoli," Miguel replied.

The pokey car's brake lights shone. They reflected from its purple paint, sending a chill up Miguel's spine, as he recalled the barge of a car from earlier in the day. Miguel accelerated, cornering randomly, trying to lose the pursuer. No use, the other car appeared to be made for racing. Miguel cut his eyes from the road for an instant, just long enough to see the abandoned warehouses, gutted buildings, and trash-laden sidewalks. Miguel's spine went from cold to hot. He told Aggie to hold on.

Michael shifted from automatic to F1 paddle-shift mode. Now, he would be in charge of the transmission's changes. He depressed the accelerator and hauled back on the right-side paddle for a downshift. The tach jetted to 8,000 rpms and the big V12 howled. The car didn't hesitate or squat before scalding rubber and rocketing forward, crushing Miguel and Aggie into their seats. Miguel stole a glimpse of Aggie, sitting with her hands clenched into fists, blood drained from her face. He couldn't stop the grin that spread across his face as the lights of the sports car trailed further behind and the speedo hit 220.

Miguel crushed the brakes and made a hard left, the rear cried making the turn. He punched the accelerator, trying to further his lead, but the engine failed to respond. A beacon with squiggly lines blinked on the dash. The automatic stability control was working, and had temporarily cut the engine's fuel flow. The sports car flew up behind them. Miguel saw the passenger hanging out of his window. There was a flash and then another. Was the pursuer shooting at them? Miguel mashed the gas. The vehicle's rear end cut loose from the pavement and slewed toward the curb. And then it boomeranged around in front, as Miguel counter-steered and locked up the brakes. They were in a spiral. A death spiral? Miguel knew what to do, but could he make himself?

He released the brake and jammed on the gas, continuing to steer into the spin, and as suddenly as it began the skid was over and the car leapt forward in the middle of the roadway. Miguel took a breath and flicked on the high beams. Now he could see clearly where they were heading . . . straight toward a concrete barrier! Aggie emitted something like a squeak and covered her face with blanched hands. Miguel covered the brake, but observed the fancy car storming up on his bumper. Flashes—and bullets—erupted from the passenger's side. They were going to shoot them or rear-end them at high speed, or both. The barrier loomed. Miguel stole a glimpse of the ominous red button screaming to him from the steering wheel. It was time to be a *mensch* or die.

* * *

Don Luis reluctantly invited Detective McGarrick and his partner to step inside. He encouraged them to sit on the uncomfortable *bancos* beside the studio's main dance floor.

"Just a few routine questions," the detective had said.

A half-hour later Don Luis was smiling, admitting nothing, recalling little. The detective appeared unhappy. He squirmed and reached for his back. Forty-five minutes into the interrogation, the detective stood and stretched out his back. He indicated that on his next visit, he would bring a search warrant for the entire building. As a parting shot he said, "Mr. Granada, these are serious charges. And, off the record, we have the murder weapon in our possession."

* * *

Miguel and Aggie limped up to the studio in the 575M. Their nerves were frayed. And while he had defied death, avoiding a hail of bullets in a choking cloud of smoke, Miguel couldn't be sure if the occupants of the sports car had survived their collision with the barrier. He had summoned his courage and hit the red button, engaging Beast mode, before punching the accelerator. The tach redlined and speedo whirled as Miguel whipped the Ferrari's steering wheel violently, inducing a 180-degree power slide. The car recovered instantly and squatted for a microsecond before accelerating away from the barricade, averting disaster by a hair.

A cognac to settle their nerves seemed like an excellent idea. Miguel could not find a garage door opener so he decided to go through the studio and open the garage from the inside. He parked on the street and turned on the emergency flashers. Aggie warned the ticket would be huge. Miguel hopped out and hustled to the studio street entrance. He reached for the keypad when from behind him a man said in a gruff voice, "Miguel Angel Zanotto, you are under arrest." Miguel started to whip around but suddenly his arm was behind his back and his face was smashed into the rough wall. He could hear Aggie screaming to him in the background, "Say you demand a lawyer!" Her cries were drowned out by the detective's somber chant, "You have the right to remain silent. . . ."

CHAPTER 67

Aggie awoke feeling miserable. Her uncle Dan had been wonderful to take up on a Sunday night the fight for Miguel. She couldn't wait for an update. What and how to tell her parents was an issue. If she controlled the information exchange from the start, she could hopefully avoid massive damage control later.

In the kitchen, the Nespresso machine vibrated softly, dispensing a thick stream of mind- and attitude-enhancing java. Aggie added hot milk and raised the cup to her lips, thinking this was really going to help. She glanced over the rim and saw MoJo frowning, clutching a cordless phone.

"Put that down," he said. "We got to talk."

"I can drink coffee and talk."

"Listen to me. It's time you start doing exactly what I say or there's going to be trouble." He thrust up the phone. "Even more trouble."

"More trouble?"

"Don't bullshit me, young lady. Just talked to Danny."

"That's private."

"There's no attorney-client privilege in my house, not while I pay the bills."

Aggie knew she needed to keep it light. Maybe if he vented a bit then he would tell her what Uncle Dan had said. "I'm sure this is all a big misunderstanding. You'll see." She fake-smiled.

"What Danny sees is that Miguel, or whatever his real name, is looking at deportation at best, maybe a murder wrap for killing a hooker."

Aggie put down the cup. She just wanted to disappear into the teeny-tiniest crack in the floor. She actually held her breath and closed her eyes, but it didn't help. When she opened them, she was still standing there, feeling like shit. "It's a mistake," she said.

"The DA don't think so. He has the murder weapon with Miguel's fingerprints, and his prints inside the dead girl's apartment. Same lovely Flatbush joint as him."

"You know how the cops fib; they probably got *bupkis*. Is he still in jail?"

"No, the cavalry rushed in just in the nick a time. Good ol' Don Luis, the puppeteer, got a big-shot lawyer to go down to the courthouse and dance and sing and pull some strings. Wallá, Miguel's out on bail."

Aggie kept a straight face somehow, although she wanted to dance a jig.

"But I'm telling you to stay away from him, from the lot." MoJo wagged a finger. "The voice of experience says there's something fishy about the whole setup."

"Pops, that's so unfair."

"Word on the street is the Don is trafficking in stolen artifacts. Sacred stuff, a ancient Bible or some damn thing."

"How could you possibly know?"

"I got sources," MoJo said, his head nodding as though spring-loaded.

"If that Seth Snakeberg has trumped this stuff up. I'll, I'll—"

"Here's the deal: you're not going back to that studio no more."

Aggie gasped. Her vision blurred. She was going to faint. No she was not.

One of MoJo's fingers popped up: "Call the Don, tell him it's *finito* for you." Second finger: "Call the NYU registrar or bursar or pursar or whichever -sar you need to and enroll for the winter term."

Aggie moaned.

MoJo spread open his hands. "I'm just trying to save you more heartache. I've seen it with my family. I had to cut them off." He chopped, sighed heavily. "Was the hardest thing I ever did, but I refused to have a bunch a criminals influencing my kids. And I'm not going to have a bad apple and some rich whatever-he-is corrupting you."

MoJo stormed out. Aggie slumped to the floor, sobbing, wondering if this could really be the end with Miguel. And did he say, ". . . killing a hooker?"

CHAPTER 68

MIGUEL HAD ALREADY ADOPTED a more optimistic view of his future when he made bail from Lower Manhattan's White Street lockup. A long night. At first, the cops had tried to rattle him by telling him he was facing deportation and or a capital murder charge. Given the possibilities, deportation didn't sound bad. They had asked repeatedly who Miguel worked for, CIA, Mossad, Cremora? And his accomplice? Initially, he thought they meant El Primitivo. They said, no, the marksman. Was the killing for revenge against Mob Boss Big Benny, they had asked. Miguel got the idea that would mean big trouble. He'd been confused, but said nothing other than, "I demand a lawyer." Miguel had Aggie to thank for that.

Once they realized that Miguel wasn't going to talk and Aggie's uncle Dan called to say he represented him, they just left him alone for hours in an interrogation cell. Time had crawled. At least he didn't have to fight a bunch of drunks or punks to keep his shirt and shoes, as he might have had to do in a Buenos Aires lockup.

Dan Jacobs seemed to be a fine gentleman and an excellent lawyer. He told Miguel exactly what to say during the interrogation. He hammered the cops, demanding that they immediately run Miguel's fingerprints and disclose if they were on the weapon with which Heather was killed. Turned out, they didn't even have that murder weapon. They had made Miguel's prints on a glass in her bedroom and on a .357 magnum pistol used to shoot Gordo in his right shoulder. The fatal bullets, Miguel had learned, were fired from a small handgun, .22 caliber. Ballistics suspected it was a Baretta model 70, using a low-powdered round, because of the shallow depth of penetration into Gordo's head. Possibly from something called an Aelph Weapon, whatever that was.

And then in the morning when Solomon Rubenstein, Don Luis's attorney, had shown up the worm turned. He entered the interrogation cell and Miguel thought the cops were going to genuflect. Suddenly "Wetback son-of-a-bitch," and "Tango dancing cock sucker," became "Mr. Zanotto."

To Miguel's amazement, Mr. Rubenstein produced pages of Miguel's immigration documents. A work visa application was among them, and a stamped tourist visa application. Miguel was no less than floored when he saw that even his correct Argentine Documento Nacional de Identidad appeared on every page. And he had entered the country using his cousin's passport! Don Luis had obviously come to the rescue. He'd known all along and said nothing. He talked all the time, couldn't shut him up about the cursed family, but he had said nothing about understanding Miguel's correct identity. Who knew, maybe he was also aware of Miguel's mission of revenge?

When the three men walked slowly down the lockup's rough concrete steps, Miguel hoped that the disgrace of prison was being scraped away little by little from his shoes and soul. After shaking both lawyers' hands and thanking them, Miguel saw a black Mercedes Benz limo pull up. A moment later, Kemal sprang out and rushed to open Miguel's door. It was the first time in a while the little man was a welcomed sight.

CHAPTER 69

MIGUEL ADMIRED THE TERRACE at Palazzo de Granada, overlooking a sliver of Central Park greenery in the distance. He enjoyed the aroma of *café* and freshly baked bread, emanating from the kitchen where Don Luis and he had chatted about family tragedy. Seemed a long time ago, although recent. Since that time, El Primitivo had died in Miguel's arms and Miguel had been imprisoned. He had changed. Some of his bitterness had been melted away by the kindness of others, some had been worn away by time and tides.

Don Luis wheeled himself onto the terrace. "Come now, my boy, do take a seat."

"I'm sorry, but I must stand while thanking you for everything you've done for me, Don Luis." Miguel extended his hand. "I don't know what I would have done."

Don Luis waved him off. He looked up with eyes more swollen and cheeks saggier than usual, from a sleepless night.

Miguel believed that slumped in his chair, Don Luis looked like a punctured inflatable superhero. His wiry hair was combed, but stood out on one side, as though from static electricity. It was Miguel's fault he had landed in jail and had needed to be rescued.

"Let's try again. Good morning, Miguel, ready for breakfast?" Don Luis took Miguel's hand and pressed it lightly to his whiskered cheek.

Miguel self-consciously withdrew his hand. "Sorry that I upset your sleep."

"Ah, old people don't require very much sleep, you know."

"You didn't seem old, dancing at the milonga," Miguel said. "*¡El toro vive!*"

"The bull lives, yes. Such good fun," Don Luis remarked in almost a whisper. "Miguel," he continued, "pardon my American manners, but I hope to have a meaningful chat over breakfast, even before it."

"I know this habit of Americans. Clear the air and then enjoy your meal."

"Um, it would appear that we haven't been perfectly straight with one another," Don Luis said. "I was hoping we might true up a few things."

Miguel cast down his eyes.

"I'm not necessarily talking about falsehoods, but also half-truths." Don Luis added, "And I'm at least as guilty as you. For example, I was concerned you might run afoul of the immigration authorities had you not been entirely truthful upon entering the United States. So I made an effort to head off difficulty by helping you to apply for a green card." He smiled sweetly.

"And so you investigated me and my family?"

"I did not."

Miguel looked into the sedate eyes of a brilliant man. They gave away nothing. He determined to do the same, at least until he understood better Don Luis's real game. "Okay, so you asked a few questions here and there."

"That I did." Don Luis's façade seemed to crack somewhat. "You could have been deported, imprisoned in a foreign country." He paused. "I know what that's like."

"Oh, it was all for me." Miguel said slowly, "Your tango company and its new show did not figure into the equation?"

"Well," he exhaled forcefully, "yes and no."

With this comment Miguel's guard was up again. "So why did you pick me for the show anyway? There are fantastic *tangueros* in the US and even more in BA."

"Ahem, your dancing has a special, um, intensity."

"Please, don't insult me. We are friends, yes."

The door separating the intimate dining terrace from the house swung open. Kemal exited, pushing his gleaming metal cart. "Gentlemen, breakfast is served."

Miguel drilled the little man with his eyes, thinking Don Luis was on the ropes at last, but saved by the cart. He said, "I have questions of my own, you must know."

"In time," Don Luis replied, "all shall be revealed."

After breakfast, Miguel trailed Don Luis en route to his office. Don Luis wheeled himself toward the door's numeric keypad. Miguel turned away. To his surprise, Don Luis asked him to look. "The code is 12-18-64." He tapped the pad, adding, "This is the most joyful birthday for me."

Miguel was confused. Don Luis was surely born before 1964. He asked, "Was it your favorite birthday?"

"My birthday is in May, not December," he replied, forging through the door.

Miguel emblazoned the numbers in his mind, 12-18-64. The digits were familiar, but something was wrong. For starters, the month was first in the sequence.

Don Luis blurted, "I loved my wife Carolina very much. Sensitive, and a talented opera singer. She passed more than a year ago."

"I'm sorry."

"I was faithful to her, strictly speaking, but unfaithful, barbaric at the same time."

Miguel remained silent.

"You know, Miguel, opera is much different from tango. Enjoying *belle canto* opera, one watches others play out their fantasies. They experience ecstasy and descend into their hells, singing rapturously all the while." Don Luis drew with his hand a clear dividing line. "Whereas in *el tango Argentino*, one is the star of his or her dances, with the partner as costar. In tango, we enact our own painful dramas and pleasurable trysts right there on the floor."

"Interesting."

Don Luis clenched a fist. "We dive headlong into deep, sometimes impenetrable passions and torture ourselves. That was my experience as a young *tanguero* in Buenos Aires. And that of my younger brother, before me, God rest him."

"You had also sisters?"

"A single sister who, as a teenager, simply failed to wake one morning."

Miguel shook his head.

"It was accepted with a fatalistic attitude. And then there was the special boy."

"Your brother, who passed recently."

"Yes, his name was Jesus Maria Carlos de Granada. He was the apple of our parents' eyes." He torqued the beard. "Born late in their lives, decades after me."

Miguel smiled. He could not imagine anything better than fathering a child in his maturity, after he, himself, had really grown to manhood.

"He was sparkling, talented, handsome, and clever. Oh," Don Luis chuckled, "and, for better or worse, he did everything that he pleased. You see, I was more serious and our sister somewhat shy and plain."

Miguel laughed. "I have a cousin who is this way."

"I know."

"Excuse me?"

"Ahem, my brother, in his early twenties, found a spot of bother in Spain. He fell in love in Andalusia with a beautiful Roma. So our father sent him to Argentina."

"There are some gorgeous gypsies there, too."

"Ah, there you go, playing straight man again," Don Luis said. "Well, in no time he was a master of the tango and neglecting his work at our company." He looked away thoughtfully. "That troubled our father a good bit. More than a bit, I'm afraid."

"Was your father in the wrong?"

"Not in the least, I believe." He put forth a dithering hand. "Now, in my mother's mind, perhaps, yes. I know that looking at me it may be hard to imagine that she was also a languid beauty, but she was indeed, and proud. Jesus Maria could do no wrong."

"Of course not."

"My father was the son of prosperous merchants, land developers, exporters, people who had worked hard to amass their fortune. And he, too, worked diligently. As a young man our father was not having love affairs and fathering children out of wedlock. He studied seriously at the University of Granada, my undergraduate alma mater."

Miguel nodded. "I am understanding the scenario."

"So, father sent for Jesus Maria to return home to Spain. He refused, having fallen deeply in love with an Argentine woman, also of unquantifiable background, shall we say." A nod of the head; a wry smile. "He wrote to me of her charm, strength of character, lust for life, and passion."

"Definitely, how do you say, *locamente enamorado.*"

"Madly in love! But Jesus Maria had courted many women and never before had he said much at all about them. Nothing like this marvel of a woman in Buenos Aires.

"A *porteña*?"

"Yes." Don Luis hands fell inert in his lap. "Time passed and his expenses grew; our father was alarmed at the decline of the family business, so he demanded Jesus Maria return home or face disinheritance."

Miguel bit his index finger sidewise, raised his eyebrows.

"Our mother interceded and father instructed me to leave school, where I was taking doctoral classes at Oxford, and go talk sense to my brother. Dutifully, I went."

"What else could you do?"

"Precisely. And what I found was shocking. Yet the longer I stayed, the more natural it all seemed."

He fell silent, lost in the past. This was really a more tenable story, Miguel found, than the grief-ridden tale of the unfortunate Jewish family. He could even relate to the high passions of the characters and the high-handed, often selfish behavior of the rich. If only he had a father or a brother to help him, his life would have been so much easier.

Don Luis interrupted Miguel's thoughts with an observation. "Sometimes I think of my experience there as a manifestation of the Law of Human Relativity."

"I don't understand," Miguel replied.

"Just keep living, my boy," Don Luis smirked. "You'll see that man has an amazing capability to meld and contort and deform until whatever position he is forced to assume seems quite normal, even comfortable. I admit that I followed right in my brother's footsteps. Never as elegantly or as effortless as he, but finding identical vices and even the same object of my affection."

"You were brothers."

"But we were so very different, Jesus Maria and I." Don Luis sighed. "Yet that first time going to dance tango on Avenida Corrientes, at the intersection with Suipacha," his voice quavered and he paused to wipe a tear filling his eye, "that night at La Confiteria Ideal changed my life forever."

Miguel watched the former bull of a man—now crippled, broken, and defenseless—sob, slumped in his wheeled chair. The heart offers warmth and vitality, while stripping away our dignity and will at its whim. Tears flowed down the spotted skin of Don Luis's cheeks and disappeared into the gnarled beard. And Miguel's heart melted.

CHAPTER 70

"YOO-HOO! OH, YOO-HOO, are you love-birds still up there chatting away?" Chaz called out from the studio below.

Don Luis composed himself briefly, before wheeling out of the office and onto the mezzanine's landing. He asked, "Chaz, is that you?"

"Oh yes, Donny boy, it is I," Chaz replied in a plummy English accent.

Miguel heard a great laugh from below. He hoped that Chaz didn't have a drinking problem, too. He wondered if the company was doomed.

"You're not the only one who can speak the King's English," Chaz cried loudly.

Miguel inched toward the anteroom. From around the corner he saw Chaz swinging around one of the support pillars, à la "Singing in the Rain."

"Really, Chaz, this is quite rude," Don Luis said. "What do you mean?"

"You never talk to me anymore, Uncle Donny."

"I am absolutely avuncular towards you, but acting this way you're making me question my commitment to you."

"Oh, but this is serious."

"Please go and tweet to your millions of followers, or something equally useful. Where will I find you, when I'm done here?"

Chaz swung around and stopped. He pointed his arm, lance straight, at Don Luis and then slewed it toward Miguel's concealing corner. "I'll find you, both of you, all of you!" he screamed.

Miguel was shocked. He stole a look around the corner to find Chaz skipping off toward the cantina. Hopefully Chaz would have an espresso and then a handful of tranquilizers before rehearsal.

"Divas," Don Luis snorted, rolling back toward the office.

Miguel's mind was muddled, wondering why Don Luis was baiting Chaz and Dr. Wagner. Chaz was clearly near breaking. "Perhaps you should speak to him now. He seems quite upset," Miguel said.

Don Luis's expression brightened. "Yes, he does."

* * *

Miguel watched unctuous espresso spill into a little cup, its smell invigorating, when he heard Don Luis call out, "Chaz, please come up to my office." The furious typing in the computer kiosk stopped suddenly. In silence, Miguel slammed down the *café* and headed straight for the computer kiosk.

Underneath the computer table the mystery keylogger was still missing. Good, Miguel thought, he wouldn't have to disable it before proceeding. He assumed the person who had removed it had either snagged the info they wanted or gotten cold feet. Miguel accessed the hidden file where his keylogger's data was stored. Chaz's clickstream was the latest in the long list.

He scanned hurriedly through the document that Chaz was creating, a cutter's manifesto of sorts. Miguel didn't care to understand the details of the rambling rant, but the gist seemed to be that you are born, you are abused, and then you die, so why not use any means available to get through it, including mutilating your flesh. A gruesome take on the beauty of life, Miguel thought, scrolling down to find Chaz's other entries.

Chaz had accessed an account associated with user Barbara Reed, the company's stern-faced bookkeeper and computer commandant. He had navigated to a folder called Security and then to its subfolder, Surveillance Video. This was getting strange. Miguel copied the video stream of camera 3 from the clickstream and dropped it into his own account, into a folder called Old Tango Stuff. Miguel was dying to see the placement in the building of camera 3, but he took his time and carefully replaced his spyware. After closing the keylogger's hidden file, he double clicked his Old Tango Stuff folder.

He heard Candy, from around the corner, ask Chaz, "And what did he say?" Miguel couldn't believe how quickly time had passed. He should logout and leave, without replacing his little friend. No, there was time, if he rushed.

Chaz said, "He denied it. Said not to get paranoid in my *maturity*. I could've smacked his fat face right then."

"Wagner tells a different story," Candy said. "Suppose Don Luis is playing one of his weird games, just trying to piss off both of you."

"I've been played with enough in my life," Chaz confided. "With my mother, I was lucky to live to my second birthday." He jested, "Then she found ballroom dancing and a new husband. It got better for a while. But by five, I knew better than to walk down the stairs in front of her." His sardonic laugh reinforced the gallows humor.

Miguel nodded incomprehension as he moved the cursor onto the icon labeled Camera 3 and clicked. He saw the image and gasped—

"What have we here?" Chaz questioned, craning his neck, extending his head around the cubbyhole's entry.

Miguel felt like a little boy caught with his hand buried deep in the cookie jar.

CHAPTER 71

REHEARSAL WAS A NIGHTMARE. Don Luis played the role of provocateur and poltergeist. One minute he was everywhere on the floor, demanding excellence, urging on passions, and criticizing anything short of perfection. Miguel was embarrassed to see Chaz and worried about Aggie's absence. He had jerked the computer monitor around just in time to avoid having Chaz observe the video Miguel had culled from his personal file space. There was a price to pay. Chaz had ribbed him unmercifully about watching porn, to get *up* for rehearsal. Miguel had smiled thinly. And when Candy came over to the kiosk to reinforce Chaz's joke, Miguel had covered his private parts, in mock shame.

Miguel had watched the door at every opportunity, hoping to see Aggie's smiling face. He wanted to thank her for everything. Maybe tell her, at last, how he really felt. Chaz seemed also to keep a roving eye on the door. Miguel wondered who he was expecting. The dancers cleared the studio in record time after rehearsal. Miguel saw Dr. Wagner exit the floor immediately, failing to admire the perfection of his footwork in the mirror, his custom.

Back rest, shoulder massage, or sleep? Miguel was trying to determine which had the highest priority when he heard a muffled but life-threatening cry from the backmost reaches of the studio. He raced toward the rear exit. He heard sobs and burst through the metal door to find Stephanie lying on the ground in a rain puddle, grimacing.

"Did you fall?" Miguel asked.

"He hit me, took my purse," she whimpered.

Searching left and right, he asked, "Which way did he go?"

"He's gone. He was fast."

"Who's gone?" Candy asked, from the open door.

"*El bastardo* smashed my knee and stole my purse."

"Call an ambulance, Candy," Miguel snapped, eyeing the swelling joint, bloodied and bruised. He bent down to Stephanie and cradled her in his arms.

"It didn't have any," she sucked back a tear, "there was no money."

"That's good," Miguel intoned.

"My knee is numb," she wailed, and flung herself onto Miguel's chest.

"It's going to be okay," he said softly, his heart wrenching. "I'll carry you inside." He added, forcing a smile, "We'll clean you up."

"*Gracias*," she whispered.

"Good heavens, Stephanie," Don Luis said, "what the deuce has happened?"

"She was mugged," Miguel replied.

"Kemal! Kemal!" Don Luis called.

Kemal didn't respond. He was usually close at hand during the rehearsals and immediately afterward. Miguel wondered where was he now?

"An ambulance is on the way," Candy said. "I'll get a cloth for her knee."

"Perhaps some ice would be good," Don Luis said, "to minimize swelling."

Miguel looked anxiously at the knee, twice its normal size. This could be the end of her career. His unhappy thoughts were broken by Kemal's entrance. He wore a white shirt and dusty black trousers. His face was flushed and he appeared to be out of breath.

"There you are, Kemal," Don Luis huffed.

"Sorry, sir, I was wiping down the Mercedes."

"Please fetch some peroxide and ointment immediately."

Miguel eyed Kemal's exit. He asked Stephanie, "What did he look like?"

"He hit my knee from behind and knocked me face down." Stephanie paused. "I could only see that his pants were black."

* * *

Aggie had not eaten anything all day, other than half a bagel hull. On the train ride home her tiny tummy had growled. But now, peering into the refrigerator at a selection of healthy food, nothing looked appetizing. She poured a glass of orange juice, hoping to get up to her room quietly and collapse into bed. She turned to find her father standing on the far side of the kitchen, arms crossed.

"Hi, Pops," she said, praying to slide by.

"Hi, Pops . . . that's it?"

"I've had a really bad day and just need to go lie down."

"I spoke to Danny again this afternoon," he said, scrunching his brow low.

"Me, too. Said it looks good for Miguel."

"Yeah, Miguel and his phony papers."

Aggie cut her eyes at him with a glare she'd seldom used. She saw her father's pupils widen with incomprehension. He was about to blow, but so was she.

"He still may end up back in the hoosegow, Danny says." MoJo softened his tone. "Naomi girl, why do you think I worked so hard to keep you away from this kinda ugliness? I told you, I disowned members of my own family." He ran his fingers through his thinning hair. "Christ, cousin Benny—"

"Hardly time for a joke, Dad."

"I ain't joking. You've been so sheltered. What you need is to finish your education, get a real job, marry a decent guy, and raise some kids."

A tsunami of pent-up frustration welled in Aggie's brain. She pushed back hard against it. It mounted. She had never taken on her parents, hardly ever had they not been in one accord. But she couldn't handle the insolence of her father, who knew little of the pain she experienced on her return from Argentina and nothing of her sexual frustration.

"Dad, you couldn't be more wrong," she said, trying to squeeze through the doorway, and get to her room before falling to pieces.

"Where do you think you're going?" He paused. "You know, this tango playground, this could get some dirt on you that won't wash off so easy."

Aggie looked straight into her father's narrowed eyes and said, "No need to worry about that. I tried to give it away and got no takers."

"Watch your mouth. Imagine if your mother heard you talk like that."

"Is my mouth only valued when it's saying what you and Mom want to hear?"

"Just call the Don and tell him you're through. And, for your information, he ain't so squeaky clean either. Word is there's a murder wrap hanging over his head."

"*Feh.*"

"And he's got some kind a dungeon in that fancy-schmancy building." MoJo paced the floor. "And believe me, there's something funny with him and Miguel, too." He tapped his nose. "This *schnoz* knows."

"All that bull about being strong, paying dues, that's all bogus," Aggie retorted. "You just want me to color inside the lines real nice. Make pretty pictures, get degrees, be Docta Jacobs." Aggie's face darkened, adding, "You're dying for me to lend you legitimacy. I am not going to medical school. And I don't give a shit if I'm a lunch lady at Mother Hale Academy."

"Sheese, wait until Seth hears about this. What am I going to say to him?"

"From me, you can say, Fuck off!"

MoJo's knees buckled. He slumped into the doorjamb and clutched his heart with both hands, before his head thudded on the floor.

CHAPTER 72

DR. WAGNER'S MIDSUMMER night's dream persisted in the temperate Indian summer. He moved about his home laboratory, using tango steps. A fresh breeze wafted in from an open window. It was as though he were dancing on a cloud, a cloud atop a finely polished, hardwood floor. A tango gem from the '40s perfumed the air. Ernest loved most the old-time numbers with regular rhythms and predictable breaks. He could execute his flawless footwork with precision. His patterns were set in granite. Nothing boring about that, a matter of preference.

Those who over-improvised muddied technique and sacrificed balance. Chaz crossed his mind. Poor Chaz, he seemed to have lost yet another partner, Wagner lamented to himself, kicking up a high *sacada* to his coat rack. An impossibly large grin extended from one pallid cheek to the other. Ernest turned around in a complete circle leading a ghost partner in a circle around him, the *molinete.* He guided her steps carefully: back, side, forward, side; back, side, forward, side.

Dr. Wagner reflected on his near-perfect day. The call from Profundum Medicus's Dr. Powers suggested that their investment in his new, all-ceramic scalpel was essentially a done deal. Wagner believed that his little demonstration to Dr. Thornblad had done the trick. Powers had said it would be, "a couple of weeks, tops."

Ernest gloated. He muttered, "And I shall be *primero bailarino* by this time next week. What is Chaz compared to me?" His ridiculous stunts belonged in a circus. And it was too bad that he had so much difficulty keeping a partner. Just his bad luck, I suppose, Wagner smirked to himself.

CHAPTER 73

MIGUEL SLASHED HUMAN FLESH, felt its drag on his blade. The spray of blood warmed his hand. The man winced with pain, grabbed his arm. Miguel lunged at him again, the steely point of his shiv driving toward the abdomen. The man parried Miguel's thrust, kneed him in the balls. Bent double, Miguel watched from the corner of his eye: the man readied his knife high, this time going for Miguel's jugular.

It was a payday ritual in La Boca, a thief seeking to collect another's honestly earned wages. Doing whatever was demanded. Miguel had been unwilling to surrender his paltry pay, the money needed back home for necessities, for food.

Low, like the stance of dancing milonga, Miguel kept his body's center near the earth, grounded. The man sprang forward, already carving with his blade. Miguel rotated his core out of the way in a *giro,* leaving behind the dulled point of his scarred shiv to find the man's belly. The blade was like an extension of Miguel's hand, used all day at the plant, stabbing and slicing the flesh and sinew of dead animals. Now, he felt the stab into human bowels, felt the warmth of the man's blood pouring over his hand. His nails, already darkened by animal gore, were dirtier and even more profaned by the blood of a desperado. The man collapsed to the ground, moaning in agony, as Miguel made his way quickly into the inky night.

But now, the screaming of sirens. Their doleful wail seeming to surround him. Miguel was caught. How could he explain the stench of death about him, the fresh blood of an unknown man soiling his hands and clothes? The sirens shrieked louder, until Miguel awoke. He panicked, although he had known the night for this call would come. In his heart he knew that he was a failed son. He had left his mother on her deathbed to come to North America on a blood quest. And here he was in the very bosom of opulence, doing whatever this was, playing a bit part in a charade, a macabre masquerade. He was trying to recall Saint Ignatius of Antioch's Prayer for the Dead and to steel himself for the news of his mother's death when he grasped his cell.

"*Hola*."

"Miguel, did I wake you?"

"Aggie, it's you."

"Were you expecting someone else?"

"No," he said catching his breath. "I was reliving a moment from the past."

"Dancing in BA?" she asked softly.

"The La Boca tango, we sometimes call it." He rubbed his eyes, asking, "Are you okay? I missed you today. I wanted to thank you for every—"

"Don't. I'm so glad to have helped."

"I guess we all need help now and then."

"It's crazy the way life suddenly goes out of control." She sighed. "It's like my life has been taken over by some vengeful puppet master."

Miguel had not felt as though he and Aggie were soul mates, but they were on exactly the same page. "Really? I'm sorry. But there is even worse news for others."

"Who? What?"

"Stephanie was mugged behind the studio. I think her dancing is over."

"Oh, my God, that's terrible. Did they catch him?"

Miguel held his reply, uncertain which thoughts to reveal. He didn't want to scare Aggie. "No, she didn't see him well."

"Things are terrible for me. I had the most horrible argument with my dad."

Miguel heard her voice crack. He longed to hold her and comfort her. "Is okay," he said. "Just take a minute."

"I can't believe what really hurtful things I said to him." She sucked back tears. "He fell to the floor. I thought he was dead."

"Why did you do it?"

"He, you know, said some pretty bad things to me, too."

"About what?"

Miguel's mind raced. Did MoJo have a mistress and was leaving the family for her? Miguel wanted to help, but couldn't see how. "It's okay if you can't talk about it."

"About you," she stammered.

"*¡Ay, caramba!*"

Through sobs, she said, "He claimed you had an affair with a prostitute and the cops think you killed her and that she has a son by a drug dealer and you were implicated in his death too; and that your name is not Miguel Andro Zanotto and that you entered the country illegally and that ICE may pick you up and deport you any time; and Don Luis is wanted for murder and he has a torture chamber in the basement of the studio; and—"

"Whoa, let's take one thing at a time." Miguel ran his fingers through his hair. He had received some late night calls from women, but not like this. He spoke slowly, "Some of the things you are saying are true, but there are reasonable explanations for all of them, if only unfortunate timing."

Aggie wept quietly.

"I did not kill anybody. The cops have a couple of dead people and they need to pin it on someone. The truth is the drug dealer killed the former prostitute. Together they had a child who is still barely alive." He paused for the info to sink in, imagining that for Aggie it was like *caca* soaking into her dinner napkin. "I did try to kill the drug dealer because he was firing a machine gun at me. I barely hit him, but someone else, a marksman, shot him dead. Is very mysterious, believe me." Miguel took a deep breath, this was getting harder. "And to get into this country, I used my cousin's passport and name because I had no work visa for the US any longer, but he did. For any Argentine to visit here, you have to be a millionaire or the US government will not let you in." He explained, "The economy is very bad in my country."

Aggie whimpered, "This prostitute—"

"Former prostitute, one day we may talk about that one. First, what is this about Don Luis killing in his dungeon?" He held his tongue to keep from cursing MoJo in the foulest terms. "Your father is saying these things; how would he know?"

"My dad grew up poor, not exactly on the streets, but some of his cousins were bad people. Dad still knows some bad people; he hears things from them."

"This is my mother's story, too, except we support her pitiful family."

"Dad keeps this part of our family secret. He's embarrassed and hurt, I think. He tells stories, says he's joking. But I believe they really exist somewhere."

"He must have some decent sources. He got some things right, but he doesn't care for the whole story, just the damning part."

"He has a motive," she said.

Miguel heard Aggie's powerful exhalation, felt its weight hit him in the face like a side of beef, swinging on a hook. "I thought so."

"Lots of fathers think they know best for their daughters their entire lives." She paused before adding, "One day we may talk more about this one."

Miguel smiled, hearing his own defense quoted back to him. He decided to open up a bit more. "I know your father thinks Seth is great and might be great for you. But Seth is mixed up with some really bad people."

"How could you know that?"

"I saw him in a back room at Junior's Deli with some Mafia-looking types."

"You swear it?"

"Yes. He saw me, too. I mentioned it to him at your party, while you were away from the table. About Don Luis and murder and dungeons, this is a serious accusation."

"I don't know. But he was so mean to me and everyone, really, at rehearsal. He's getting weird. And that gruesome name for our show. Who will come to watch *Murder by Tango*?"

Miguel could hear Aggie's heavy breathing. It was as though he could read her thoughts over the airwaves. He dreaded her next utterance.

"So, what's really up between you and him?"

"I, truthfully, um, don't know for sure." There. He had spoken the truth.

"He lets you live in his mansion for free and drive his Ferrari."

Kaboom! He thought perhaps it wouldn't hurt, but it stung deep. Maybe it would even help to clarify his thinking to say more. He knew he could trust Aggie. She was the only trustworthy person he knew in this whole damn country. "Don Luis has been telling me things about a family, a cursed family. His own family, he says."

"Why is he so nasty at rehearsal?"

These were the same questions that haunted Miguel day and night. "He antagonized Chaz earlier today. They were shouting at one another before rehearsal. He did the same thing with Dr. Wagner a few weeks ago." He sucked air between his teeth. "Seems like he's turning up the heat in the tango crucible. Trying to trigger something."

"He triggered something okay; Stephanie's life is over."

"What makes you think he was involved?"

"I know that's unfair. It's just . . . where was that little man, Kimmel?"

Miguel shuddered. "Funny you should ask. He showed up immediately after."

"I knew it."

"Don Luis called him and he appeared with dusty black pants, like the mugger wore, Stephanie said. And, he looked a bit nervous." Miguel wondered how much to tell her? "I don't like him either," he said. "We had a kind of misunderstanding when I first arrived. A matter of his dagger nicking my hand on purpose."

Aggie fired, "And Don Luis, the cripple, danced amazing at the milonga!"

Miguel's mouth was open wide and his thoughts running wild. He managed to say, "All of which means *nada*!"

"You're right." She paused. "I'm glad you have faith in me; my dad's lost his."

Miguel felt her pain. "Just be glad you have a dad who cares for you." Thinking of Hector and himself, he added, "Some people never have one at all."

"I think I needed that," she replied. "But one night when I left rehearsal, a man was sitting in a rental car watching the studio. He hid his face, but I thought I had seen him before. I photographed him with my phone."

"You be careful!"

"Yeah, I was scared, but he sped away, tossing out a cigarette. I kept it."

"You are too much."

"Stunk up my purse, like crap. It's called Noblesse."

"Odd thing, El Primitivo gave me his phone before he died. He said to watch out for *masha* at the studio. Said it's very dangerous." He lowered his voice. "I'm sorry to cause you so much trouble, like Sunday on the road. Sometimes I think you shouldn't—"

"Well, don't think about that." Her voice was resolute. "They weren't cops. The cops were waiting at the studio. But who could they've been?"

"Lots of questions, not many answers."

Aggie added with animation, "And how did the cops know to stake out the studio just then looking for you? There's some creepy stuff going on, and I'm worried for you."

"I may be a dumb *milonguero*, but I'm on high alert all the time. I have a feeling that soon something is going to give."

"Please be careful." She sighed, adding, "It's getting late, huh."

"I'm glad you called. I feel better."

Aggie's voice was hardly audible. "I, I really care for you, deeply."

"Me, too," he said, unraveling the simple code.

"Good night, and sleep well."

Lying in bed, Miguel wondered just how much he should press, and how. If there were forces at work, doing heaven only knew what, he should beat them at their own game. But was playing this game worth it? He considered Don Luis's collapse into sobs from the crushing burden of sorrow and recriminations for his cursed family. His pain could not save even one of his tortured relatives. Did it make sense for Miguel to stiff-arm the love of a wonderful woman for a blood quest? Would it revive his mother to end the life of his sister's killer? Absolutely not. And would it restore his sister's lost life? In short, accomplishing his quest would really accomplish nothing, except to guarantee Miguel's separation from the one he could love, possibly forever.

Miguel turned over and tried to blank his mind. Too many thoughts. Thoughts of love, hate, revenge, atonement. Soon, he was going to have to make a decision to choose life or death.

CHAPTER 74

Miguel and Aggie embraced like lovers at the studio, but no one seemed to notice. Stephanie's mugging had people on edge. The extent of her injuries was still unknown. Miguel could not help but notice that Chaz, her erstwhile partner, who was now in need of a partner, was remarkably calm. And Dr. Wagner was downright chipper.

Don Luis rolled in, walking stick across his lap, a scowl dominating his face. Did he plan to beat the dancers into submission? Everyone greeted him warmly. He gruffed a "Good afternoon" and then clapped his hands. "Candy, queue the music for the first ensemble, if you please. Places, everyone."

Miguel liked the spirited tango by Maestro de Angelis. He smiled to Aggie, who stood close beside him. In his peripheral vision, Miguel observed Dr. Wagner leading his partner Adriana toward the center of the floor, the usual starting spot for Chaz and Stephanie. Miguel's mind raced, trying to recall where Dr. Wagner had been when Stephanie was injured. He looked panicky at Aggie, who regarded him quizzically. Miguel made a quick chop with his hand. Aggie blanched.

Chaz moved toward the center. Soon he and Wagner were occupying nearly the same physical space. Miguel glanced quickly at Don Luis, whose breaking smile suggested that he was amused.

Don Luis said, "Are we going to have one of those awful two-men-on-one-woman tango farces? Simply the bane of modern tango shows."

"This is my rightful place, under the circumstances," said Wagner.

"And what circumstances would those be?" inquired Don Luis.

"Chaz has no partner, for starters."

"Quite right," Don Luis replied. He pointed the stick straight at Aggie. "Do be a dear, Aggie, and partner with Chaz."

Miguel's expression turned gloomy, watching Aggie walk away from him. She appeared to be in shock, about to play *primera bailarina*, surpassing all of the more experienced girls. She looked sheepish walking to center floor. Chaz leered as Aggie made her way toward him. His slovenly dress and scraggly beard were unattractive, but it was the video footage of Aggie he had pilfered that made Miguel look at him as a degenerate. Chaz swelled out his chest, bulbous and firm from agonizing workouts. Since they had first met, Chaz seemed to have undergone a metamorphosis. Miguel hoped, for Aggie's sake and against all intuition, it would prove positive.

Jean-Luc had slipped in and taken a seat on a *banco*. He was attentive. And his spirits seemed to lift just when Miguel's fell. Where had Jean-Luc been during the calamity of the previous day? Nowhere to be found. His lesson with Candy had been conveniently cancelled, perhaps. Miguel would inquire, subtly, about that. Jean-Luc glanced back and forth from Aggie to Miguel, their faces darkened with anguish. He appeared to be as happy as a man experiencing schadenfreude possibly could.

"I beg your pardon," Wagner fumed, "she doesn't know the choreography for this area of the floor. And I don't believe she's fit for the part." He stood tall, like a brittle statue. "It's a challenging ensemble, and Adriana and I have practiced the leading position many times."

"I'm quite sure you have, Dr. Wagner. Please assume your usual position."

"I will not." He stammered, "We, we have an understanding, you and I."

"We do," Don Luis allowed.

Miguel's, everyone's ears were on fire now. Would the politics of tango be laid bare for all to see and smell, odious as they were, no doubt?

Don Luis cut though the drama. "Dr. Wagner, you shall be *primero bailarino* of this company beginning the day you deserve to be, and not one day earlier."

Miguel caught his breath. He watched Wagner's face change shades of color, beginning with rosy pink, ending in fiery red.

Wagner spoke quietly, but with the sear of fury. "You will regret this. I swear, if it's the last thing I do, I'll make you," and then he gestured toward Chaz, "and you, sorry." He stormed from the floor.

"Excellent performance, Dr. Wagner! You may be a principal on the theater stage before you achieve it on this floor," said Don Luis, chuckling.

Miguel remained detached. His life was too full of drama. He noted that Chaz had moved close to Aggie. They smiled at each other. He held her hand and whispered into her ear, oblivious to Wagner's dramatic exit.

Don Luis cleared his throat and said, "*Adriana, sola, por favor.*" He aimed the walking stick, cum wand, toward Candy. "Dance with Miguel, please. And try not to be too rough."

Candy smiled seductively. Aggie jerked around her head to see.

Don Luis clapped his hands. "*Musica.*"

A moment later, lilting strains of tango music wafted onto the swirling collection of talent, frailty, ego, bone, muscle, and mania that is a dance company. The ensemble moved silkily across the finely polished floor, as a single self-defeating and yet symbiotic organism.

Chat time at the five o'clock break was brief. Aggie mentioned to Miguel that Chaz wanted to work with her in the fishbowl on a particular position. He had raised his eyebrows, silently querying which position Chaz had in mind.

* * *

In Chaz's posh apartment he dismissed Regina's call as an old woman's handwringing. It was true that he hadn't called his mother since . . . well, there was no way he was calling back now. The last time they spoke, it was like, "I can tell you're off your medication." And then, "No, I'm not. You're off *your* medication." Chaz believed the entire country was on medication. He fingered the little firearm, his new toy. Twirling it, he imagined taking aim at everyone who'd hurt him, and Regina would top that list.

Chaz blinked twice and focused on the living room. He was anxious to get comfortable and to see the latest installment of video camera 3, starring none other than himself and Aggie. This was hot off the press, as they used to say, back when presses ruled the world. A pen might have been mightier than a sword, but these days, to do real damage required a video camera. He couldn't wait to see her face contorted in *tangasm*, the way it was in the video with Miguel. Chaz was sure that with him, Aggie was bound to be multi-*tangasmic*!

He poked the thumb drive into the plasma TV's USB port. He'd copied the captured feed onto the drive after rehearsal. The video of the main dance floor from camera 3 was streamed and stored on disk in Barbara's account. Accessing it was no problem, now that he possessed her user ID and password.

Chaz shed his clothes and fell to the sofa, joystick in hand. He scrolled through his favorite feeds and miscellaneous videos. He observed a video featuring Natalia. He was nearly moved to tears, recalling the way she commanded her body on the floor, using those gorgeous feet, rooted in the wood. She entertained a love affair with the floor, but not with him. He couldn't believe what had happened to her. Must have been an accident, possibly by a normal, sensitive person, a little unhinged at the time. A scary thought.

Concentration *interruptus* . . . his cell pinged, alerting Chaz to an incoming tweet. Christ, who was it? He yanked up the phone and glanced at the screen.

@cut00: "BIG prob. 10 ambien + ½ bottle vodka. sick n sleepy. pls twt soo"

Chaz tossed away the phone, thinking, *Jeez, Cindy, get a life.* He scrolled to the last of video files on the drive. *Pure, chaste Aggie Jacobs, here I come.* Sounded too good to be true. Yes, why hadn't he seen it earlier? He worried for her, though. She was like a flower, too delicate to last in this abusive world. Chaz's heart ached, but at long last, his passion grew.

CHAPTER 75

THE DAYS WERE SHORTER and the nights cooler by early October. Over the preceding couple of weeks Don Luis's bile seemed to have diminished somewhat. Perhaps because the sloppy new show had become a real Argentine tango *espectáculo*! Miguel was still not up to his standard of dance. But he managed to deal with Candy's sexual advances, wardrobe malfunctions, odious cigarette breath, and acerbic wit.

Miguel and Aggie hardly practiced together. One rehearsal had been cancelled earlier in the week for Yom Kippur. And she usually worked before and after rehearsal with Chaz, her new guru. His persona was a mélange of his previous affectations: prima donna attitude, capriciousness, and newly cultivated ones: disheveled appearance, wild wardrobe, and sudden outbursts, both manic and depressive. Dr. Wagner had returned, tail between his legs. He and Adriana danced second fiddle to Chaz and Aggie. Jean-Luc was rarely seen at the studio, which was fine by Miguel. He had never trusted him.

On a crisp Thursday morning, the landline in Miguel's room rang, the distinctive ring allocated to him. Don Luis asked him to come down to his office for a chat. Moments later, Miguel approached the anteroom's open door.

"Do come in, Miguel," Don Luis said animatedly.

Miguel watched Don Luis's hand shoot to his beard. A tell. Something stressful or at least complex needed to be plumbed. Miguel braced himself.

"Tell me, Miguel, how are you holding up?"

"My body is much better. But my mind is, um, still a bit raw."

"Perhaps you need more time away from this place. Opportunities to explore the city, to be more comfortable here."

"I'm sorry to say that I have no plans to stay in this city. I am happy to dance in your company. But when that is finished, I will go back to my city, with the *porteños*."

"Oh, yes, your vision of the future, your plan. I had one—both actually. What folly." Don Luis thrust back his head accentuating the point before saying, "If there were a God, do you know how you could make him laugh?"

Miguel shook his head.

"Tell him about your plans."

Miguel crossed his arms, feeling spiked.

"You've already been there and seen behind BA's curtain." Don Luis removed his spectacles. "After New York, nothing there will be as grand as it used to be for you."

"If we went to Buenos Aires, I would show you my unforgettable city."

"I have not been for twenty-five years, but recall it vividly." He closed his eyes, his expression betraying a cinema from the past playing in his head.

"Why so long?"

"It's a complicated story," he said. "But I have agents there, business associates."

"Oh."

"What about you? What will you do there, become Chaz in ten years' time?"

Miguel tried not to react, but the suggestion pricked him again.

"Even should you become Gavito, a tango god, what then?"

"I want to help," Miguel replied, rapidly adding, "disadvantaged kids, who never had a chance in life."

"Look around you: no shortage of them in your former hood," Don Luis said.

Hector crossed Miguel's mind. He wondered if the child were still alive. How long could he survive in the *care* of Lexi Lexus?

"You seek to be among your own kind. Thinking, there you can find the heights of comfort and depths of belonging. Right? But also one can reach the depths of pain and disenfranchisement among one's peers, like feeling alone in a crowd."

"Is possible, I suppose."

"But what if your kind were everywhere? And you could find them if you pay a bit of attention. How would that be?"

Miguel wasn't certain at what Don Luis was hinting, but this was typical. He said, "It is affirming to be with one's *amigos*, compatriots."

"Ah, but you have been critical of those who are, in your view, cliquish, to use a term," Don Luis retorted. "Those whose ranks are exclusive rather than inclusive."

"Possibly."

"No, definitely, Miguel." Don Luis tented his fingers. "Imagine being a member of a controversial minority and you have the opportunity to interact with and enrich one of your own stripe or another who, once enriched, might use the resources to try and destroy you. Which would you seek as your friend? Which would you prefer to enrich?"

"Is clear."

"There are reasons for everything, sometimes bad reasons. Nothing gets better if the status quo is always maintained. But can you understand the deep-seated fears and programming that must be overcome to realize a brotherhood of man. A world where you and others, similar and dissimilar, can display your true stripes without fear."

"Ah, your dream of world peace."

"For the moment, a dream, perhaps," Don Luis allowed. "But I know of a time when the people who now fight most furiously lived together in harmony. It was a golden era of prosperity and tolerance. It was in my adopted country, centuries ago."

"Really?"

"This place of peace, scholarship, and prosperity was Córdoba and, in fact, much of Andalusia, during the Golden Age of the Umayyads. That is the Sons of Umayya, originally descended from Damascus, longtime governors of Syria. Ultimately, their empire stretched from the Middle East to North Africa and to Europe, encompassing the Iberian Peninsula." He wagged a finger. "For one hundred years, from 929 until 1031, the Caliphate of Córdoba flourished like no other place on Earth."

"Fantastic," Miguel replied, appreciating the momentary lapse in intensity.

"I am not partial to them because they were Syrian, although there are Syrians in my line. They are a very special breed, the Mizrahi Syrians especially, think Paula Abdul and Jerry Seinfeld." He grinned devilishly.

"In Spain or Iberia, as we call it, they follow a so-called Sephardic Jewish tradition. In Israel, the Arab Jews, Mizrahi, are classified as Sephardi and are under the purview of the Sephardic rabbinate. They have no chief rabbi of their own. And although Mizrahi Jews are descended from ancient Babylon, Syria, Iraq, Iran, Lebanon, and so on, they are now fewer than 50 percent of the Israeli population and have much less political and even religious influence in the country than ever before."

"That's a shame."

"Exactly. But it was not always this way and I believe there is a means to restore some power of the Mizrahim, so they are not completely marginalized. It will be a weighty decision when the time comes. And you may be required to make it." Don Luis fell silent; his fingers delved deep into his beard; his gaze fell heavily on Miguel.

What had he done to get in the middle of this, Miguel wondered?

Don Luis continued, "The Umayyads were more just than other rulers. Although Muslims, counted among free peoples were Christians, Jews, and Zoroastrians, all protected by law."

"I didn't know," Miguel said.

Don Luis replaced his glasses and added, "Perhaps you can better understand why a family of troubled Syrian Jews sought to leave their own stripe in Palestine and find a new, better place for their growth and development." Don Luis smiled kindly. "You, too, may find there is a better place than La Boca for your continued development."

Miguel's eyes were narrow when he said, "Now, I understand your plotting." This man had the power to twist and color and manipulate every topic of conversation. It was exactly as he had described on the first night they talked. Words are powerful!

"Yet, you remain unconvinced." Don Luis shifted his bulk. His chair groaned. "How about a practical consideration. If you controlled a great deal of wealth, hundreds of millions of dollars, would you want the Argentine government to have access to it? Think about the annexed pension funds, devaluations."

Miguel laughed. “This is the second time you accuse me of buying lottery tickets. I don’t buy them. I work too hard for my little money.”

“Neither do I. But I will suggest that when you buy a straw hat, do so in the fall.”

“This wisdom I can accept,” Miguel said with a smile.

CHAPTER 76

Miguel awoke feeling hopeful about forsaking his bloody quest. The opportunity to pursue love and happiness was right in front of him. His cell phone's email chime interrupted the pleasant thoughts. Miguel rarely received meaningful messages, so he ignored it in favor of continuing to bask in his positive emotions. When the chime sounded again, he grabbed the phone. The first message was from 'your.friend,' sent from some meaningless domain. The subject: 'Talk?' Graphics of two common carrier first-class airline tickets and a news article clipping were attached. The tickets were in the names of Mr. Louis de Granada and Mr. Selim Attallah. They were round trips from New York's La Guardia to Los Angeles's LAX. The newspaper clipping was from the *Los Angeles Times*, an article entitled "Assassination Tango?" dated two days after that of the flights from New York to LA.

Miguel's hand quaked. He didn't need to read the excerpt; he almost knew the article by heart. It was a pathetic, sensationalized account of Natalia Prafil's murder, months earlier in California. Miguel's head spun. He clicked the next message, identical sender and subject. More tickets, another article. This article detailed another *tanguera's* murder. Ms. Angelina Gonzales had been strangled and slashed à la Natalia. She had been found desecrated twelve years earlier outside the Buenos Aires *tangueria* called Club Español. The airline tickets for Mr. Abraham Carlos de Granada and Mr. Kemal Attallah encompassed the murder date from the clipping from BA's daily newspaper, *Clarín*. Miguel's fury waxed as he read the excerpt. The unsolved crime's gruesomeness was akin to Natalia's death. And then the final blow, a fate-sealing graphic. To Miguel's astonishment, an International Criminal Police Organization banner appeared on a graphic of an arrest warrant naming Luis Lopez Carlos de Granada as a murder suspect. It was dated the week following the murder! Miguel gasped; his phone hit the floor.

Miguel had no idea how long he was in shock. He stared blankly at a wall for what seemed hours. Fluttering noises, like small birds winging around under his bed, drew his attention. He ignored them. Stared. The birds fluttered again, but Miguel had no will to examine their plights. He stared. Miguel's head began to ache so badly it seemed as though it would explode. He forced his hands to his temples, sat, and staring into space. The birds fluttered once more and Miguel glanced at the floor. He saw his illuminated cell phone indicating an incoming call. The ringer was apparently damaged from its fall.

The caller's ID was blocked. The emails' subject lines, 'Talk?' flashed into his head. I suppose now it's time.

"Yes?" he said.

"Thank God!"

"Don Luis, is that you?"

"Miguel, listen carefully," Don Luis said, straining, sounding out of breath, possibly out of hope. "I've had an accident. I need your help. Are you free?"

"What's wrong?" Miguel asked, every cell in his body screaming, no!

"Listen carefully, this may sound a bit queer." He paused and breathed noisily. "Go to my office, open the door, and close it securely behind you. The combination is—"

"Twelve-18-64."

"You figured it out. You understand."

Miguel didn't understand anything other than the fact that Don Luis was probably a crazy serial killer and was toying with him for some perverse reason. Don Luis sounded panicked and helpless, but was it true? Or was it a game, like his wheelchair and his feigned paralysis?

"Miguel, are you there?" he asked, his voice trembling with distress.

"Yes. I'm here."

"Thank heavens. Go to the bookshelf behind my desk. Reach inside the paneling of the second shelf from the bottom, near the middle, and feel along the surface until you find a rocker switch. Press the switch and stand back. The bookcase will move and reveal a small elevator. Call for the elevator and take it down to the bottom. I'll be waiting."

Miguel shivered. He could hardly believe his ears. MoJo had been right. The house had a secret dungeon! How could he free himself without revealing that he knew? Miguel asked, "Is this, um, the number from where you are located, physically?"

"Yes, it is."

"And can I call you there if I have a problem?"

"Good thinking. Yes, you can." Don Luis groaned. "Hurry, please."

Miguel cut the connection and sprang from his bed. He was out the door in seconds flat, heading down to the second floor, his heart beating wildly. He repeated the combo to himself as a mantra. It was not really necessary. He could recall his mother's birthday, using the American system of month/day/year. The South American and European standard of day/month/year had hidden the combo's weight for a while. Don Luis said that it was the most meaningful birthday to him. His heart pounded ever louder.

Miguel took the stairs, two at a time, grazing the polished handrail for balance. He raced around the mezzanine to the keypad and tried to enter the code, but his hand shook terribly. Miguel held his left index finger in his right hand and slowly entered the code. The door lock buzzed and he pushed into the office. He flew past Don Luis's desk, accessed the bookcase, and began to grope.

Dusty tomes. Weighty words. But the bookcase's paneling was smooth and cool. Miguel supposed Don Luis discouraged the housekeepers from working there. He slid his hand up and down the middle panel. Nothing. He hoped that Don Luis was not badly injured in his accident because Miguel now had questions that demanded answers. Yes! The rocker switch was there, cleverly hidden alongside a wooden reinforcement strip. He pressed it.

The entire bookcase began to shift to his right. Miguel jumped back, startled. To his left stood an antiquated elevator shaft, covered by a metallic cage-type door. The shaft was slender, like the ones in cheap European hotels, even smaller than in his former Brooklyn hellhole, but equally stinky. He hit the call button and the sound of churning motors erupted. The dimly lit carriage ascended and stopped with a dull clunk beside the bookcase. It looked like an upright coffin. Miguel opened the cage-style door and tried to step in, but his feet wouldn't budge.

Now was the time to be clever. He had verified that Don Luis was at a phone number associated with this place. If he called back and got no response, he would know he was descending to certain death. But why hadn't Don Luis called Kemal, if he had tried to reach Miguel repeatedly and could not? Something fishy was afoot. What if Don Luis were not even there? Miguel produced his phone, hit redial. The number was busy. He strained trying to hear anything from below. Silence.

The little coffin of an elevator car awaited. He muttered, "No way," and turned around. He reached inside the bookcase, seeking the switch to close the hidden portal. He supposed his next move would be to collect his things and get away from the spooky house pronto. But why was it necessary to kill him now? So many questions. No answers. Miguel realized that he needed to be cautious or his death would be someone else's quandary. He relocated the switch, gave it a flick.

What was that? Miguel listened but the case was grinding across the wall. He flipped the switch again. It stopped. He listened. "Miguel," came a feeble cry from below. He flipped the switch once more and the case opened fully. "Help me," was the desperate plea. He eyed the coffin, its metal cage exactly like the one at Buenos Aires's Club Español, where the *tanguera* had been murdered more than a decade ago. The cage's rusted, black, diamond-shaped metalwork seemed to dare Miguel to enter and seal his fate. Full of dread, he snatched open the door, leapt in, pulled it shut, and hit the button. He shuffled his feet in dirty sand on the compartment's bottom and almost had to hold his nose against its stench. When the coffin jolted harshly, Miguel clutched the cage lattice and reached for his blade as he descended into darkness.

* * *

The gang had gathered upstairs at Junior's Deli for Vinnie Rabbit Ears's homecoming from the hospital. Mangled streamers wilted from the ceiling and a few helium-filled, Bugs Bunny balloons floated near the floor. The auto accident after the Open tournament had altered Vinnie physically. He walked with a limp, using a cane, and one of his large ears had been severed. Big Benny had warned the soldiers that several surgeries would be required to restore Vinnie's ear. No one should poke fun at the temporary. Benny had added that Vinnie's shooting hand was unharmed.

Big Benny sat at the table's head, polishing off his third piece of cheesecake, swilling the last of his second bottle of wine. He had asked Vinnie to sit beside him. Big Benny was a bit unnerved looking constantly at the plastic placeholder ear the doc at Brooklyn's Maimonides Medical Center had installed. It was way too pink, and much smaller than Vinnie's real rabbit ear.

It was time to let Vinnie express his appreciation for the nice lunch and then split. Benny stood and over the din said, "Hey, hey, pipe down! Vinnie, here, is going say a few words, then we're going to hit the road." Benny urged up Vinnie, who was glassy eyed, so drunk on 7&7s he could hardly stand. He leaned heavily on the table and said, "I just got one thing to say." Vinnie hiccupped loudly.

A soldier snickered. Big Benny gave him the stink eye.

"I want all of you to know," Vinnie slurred, spreading his hand in a wide arc, nearly falling back into his chair, "the man who did this to me will be punished."

Benny applauded loudly. "Thank you, Vinnie. Now, go home and sleep it off."

Vinnie pushed Big Benny aside. "Ain't fucking finished yet." He wagged a finger toward Mr. Beard and his young cohort. "I know you got other ideas." He screamed, "But don't fucking get in my way, you jerk wad, son-of—"

Big Benny stemmed the tirade with a right hook to Vinnie's jaw, felling him.

"Hey, Yoda, put a sock in it," a drunken soldier on the back wall called out.

Vinnie's goons stood, searched for the heckler, hands inside their coats.

"Sit down and shut up!" Big Benny said, ripping away his napkin from inside his shirt collar. He threw it onto the table, declaring, "This meeting is adjourned."

CHAPTER 77

THE SIREN SCREAMED; the ambulance sped down Second Avenue toward Beth Israel Hospital. Miguel crouched beside Don Luis, who breathed more easily with the aid of oxygen. He was paler than usual, but his cheeks showed more color than when Miguel had found him lying on the dungeon's floor. Although the gash on his head no longer bled, the EMTs said it would be touch and go for a while. Miguel held Don Luis's hand, intently looking at him, wondering exactly what to believe about him.

When he had found Don Luis sprawled on the filthy floor of his dank cell, Miguel had panicked. He observed the ramshackle little writing desk askew, and the phone, its receiver off the hook, lying beside him. There were no signs of a struggle, but a large takeout bag from Jake's Bar-B-Que, filled with old newspapers, was overturned beside the desk. The lighting was so poor Miguel could hardly see. Don Luis must have fallen trying to fill the bag or dislodging his wheelchair from the confining desk.

The claustrophobic basement was watermarked, about two feet up the side of everything. A closed book whose title included the word "Kabbalah" rested on the table. An open book was covered by a dingy linen cloth. Threadbare white cotton gloves, with ink-stained fingertips rested beside. Miguel had pulled back the cloth and observed ancient-looking rows of blackish script. Three solemn rows per page. Asian-looking characters. Hebrew characters, Miguel deduced. With so many dots and slash marks all over the words. And the pages' margins were annotated heavily by a different hand from the text. When Miguel touched the frail parchment, soiled at the upper corners, it was as though he experienced a shock. He jerked back his hands, thoughts spinning faster and faster. Could this be it, the Aleppo Codex? Miguel wondered if he should kneel, take off his shoes, both?

Miguel had cradled Don Luis's head in his arms, recognizing it was a painful wound. There was no water and certainly no medical supplies. He had to get Don Luis out of the unhealthy air, but how? The elevator had hardly room enough for one person. Miguel had patted Don Luis's cheek, trying to revive him.

Don Luis half-opened his eyes and said, "The *Keter*: save the *Keter*."

"I will save you both," Miguel replied. "Where is the emergency exit?"

"Chained."

"You have the key?"

He shook his head feebly. "Save the *Keter*; it's all that matters."

Miguel loaded Don Luis in his wheelchair and rolled him, listless, into the elevator compartment. Miguel climbed inside, feeling like a contortionist, and depressed the up button. The coffin jerked and stuttered and began to rise.

As the ambulance barreled down Second Avenue, ignoring traffic signals and veering from lane to lane, Miguel considered their chat in the cantina, where he had given Don Luis water. He had asked if it was true that Don Luis had a murder warrant from Argentina. He had nodded yes. In a few labored words, he had said that he had dueled a racist count who had insulted his brother and his brother's wife. He claimed the count had fired first and missed. Don Luis shot him fatally in the back as he fled. Don Luis was branded a murderer and forced to leave Argentina. That was when he returned to England to finish his Ph.D. Afterward, he moved to New York to being life anew.

Miguel had found the claim interesting. And while Don Luis's stories were usually riveting, now he had a higher standard for what he actually might believe as truth. The Codex was real. He had seen it, touched a sacred page. But dueling with a racist over his brother's wife, Miguel found that a stretch. And when Miguel had asked about his mother's locket reflecting the Carlos de Granada coat of arms, Don Luis had waved away the question, too exhausted to continue. Once at the emergency room the EMTs lifted the stretcher to the curb. Don Luis tore the oxygen mask from his face. His expression dark, he huffed out, "Beware Jean-Luc—"

* * *

Miguel walked the half-dozen kilometers from the hospital back to the studio. It was a brilliant fall day and he hoped the clear skies and fresh breeze would help to clarify his thoughts. There was new information to process. Decisions to make in this deadly chess match. He phoned Aggie and they agreed to share lunch and intelligence. He also phoned the house's main number and left a message, presumably for Kemal. He indicated that Don Luis was in the Beth Israel Hospital and might stay for a few days. Hanging up, he wondered where Kemal had been all morning. Then he realized that he'd seen little of him during the weekend. What had the imp been up to? Miguel determined to search the house to see if his handiwork was visible.

Miguel and Aggie ate leftovers on the balcony, overlooking Central Park. She was as natural and perfect as a woman could be. He swirled Merlot in a hand-blown balloon, admiring her. Their eyes met and locked. She blushed a deep pink.

Later, the pair settled onto Miguel's bed. Creamy walls, creamy covers, soft lighting, and marvelous merlot banished the awkwardness of recalling the last time they were in his room together.

Aggie said, "Something's missing."

"Yeah, lots of puzzle pieces are missing," Miguel obsessed.

"No, I mean here," she laughed. "We need some tango tunage."

Miguel shrugged. "We can go down to the studio."

"No way," she said, opening her dainty purse and grasping her phone. "Oh, that cigarette stinks, even in this plastic bag."

"The one the man dropped outside the studio? Let me see it." Miguel sniffed the wrinkled baggie and frowned. "I Googled Noblesse; it's Israeli."

Aggie put some sultry tango on the speaker. "Really? I took his photo."

She scrolled through the picture roll. "Here it is, not too clear. He had a bushy beard."

"That's him! Don Luis said, today at the hospital, to watch out for Jean-Luc." Miguel sprang up. He paced the floor. "Remember I told you I saw your sweetheart Seth at lunch with a bunch of gangsters."

"Are you totally sure about that?"

"He didn't deny it at your party. He threatened me instead. What do you think?"

Aggie enlarged the man's face. She turned the camera upside down, tilted it sideways. "I don't think it's Jean-Luc," she said, crinkling her brow.

"But I saw him walk. You know Jean-Luc has a funny, um, stride, you say?" Miguel paused. "And so the guys following us and shooting must be the Mafia."

"I hope not," Aggie said, her brow scrunching lower.

Miguel sniffed the baggie again. He cried, "Candy!"

"Smells more like *caca* than candy."

"Candy Borakowski. She smokes these. At least her breath often smells like this."

"She's pretty harmless, other than being a sexual predator, don't you think?

Miguel creased his forehead. "Maybe you should be wary of her."

"Well, she's your dancing partner. Is there something you know that I don't?" Aggie *enganched* Miguel's arm with hers, pulling him onto the bed.

"A lot," he teased, finding the warmth of her thigh with his hand.

Aggie said softly, "Wanna teach me, Maestro?"

The music swelled, sending a dizzying sensation throughout his body. Miguel caressed firmly the apex of Aggie's slender legs, pressing his mouth onto hers. He looked achingly forward to their long-awaited crescendo.

CHAPTER 78

"A zoo, run by Nazis!" Don Luis boomed over the phone to Miguel, castigating his hospital ward. Miguel had taken the unkind comment to mean that Don Luis had not been permitted to do exactly as he pleased. Miguel had tried, to little avail, to soothe him. Don Luis had said that his MRI results would not be available until the following day. He had urged Miguel to wait and visit then. Miguel had conveyed his wishes for a speedy recovery, and vowed to say a prayer for him. Don Luis had thanked him sincerely and reminded him to switch off all of the lights in the studio and cantina after rehearsal.

Miguel mulled Don Luis's final revelation in their conversation. There was going to be a press teaser at the studio on Thursday. Miguel had stated, in the most delicate terms, that in his opinion the show was not ready. He feared that the company would fail to impress. Quizzically, Don Luis had agreed, but had forced Miguel to promise not to cancel the event. He instructed Miguel to tell the company at rehearsal on Monday to be prepared to rehearse from three until five P.M. on Thursday and then to perform a mini-show for members of select press outlets at seven.

And the final remarks, talk about incredible. Don Luis had charged him to take his place running the company. He made Miguel promise to be stern and watchful. But the biggest shock was his parting comment: “We may yet have a murder by tango!”

CHAPTER 79

MIGUEL CAUGHT HIS BREATH. Just hearing the tone indicating an incoming email jangled his nerves. He assured himself it was Aggie checking in. Maybe planning to tell him once more how magical their night together was and how happy he had made her. He had hedged a bit when earlier they spoke. But the night was quite special for him, too. No matter how much he tried to convince himself it was only consensual sex.

No luck. A new message from 'your.friend,' subject: 'Talk?' confronted Miguel. He nearly had to rush for the bathroom when he observed the image of Don Luis and Natalia, smiling broadly, arms interlocking at the Dorothy Chandler Pavilion on the day of her murder. The caption: 'Believe me now?'

Why had Don Luis never said that he was there? And if he hadn't owned the company until later, why were they so intimate? Natalia was a bit of a firecracker, Miguel knew, but when she had spoken to him for the last time, she said nothing of Don Luis or his midget. But she had begged Miguel to come to California to see her. She had a fantastic secret to share. So he had made the trip, but Natalia was murdered before he could embrace her. A tear filled his eye. And then the rush of anger overwhelmed his mind. He would avenge her murder, if it took every ounce of his strength, even his life.

Miguel hit the reply icon and began to carefully tap in his cell phone number. He halted, believing that the sender already knew it. Miguel cut the crap and typed, 'call me,' then waited. A minute later, there was an incoming call from an unidentified caller. Miguel touched the talk icon and said, "*Que pasa*, Jean-Luc."

* * *

Dr. Wagner perused his copious notes, visions of authorship in his emeritus years dancing in his head. He was ensconced in his favorite easy chair in his home's den. Iced tea at hand. Feeling much better. Life was going his way. Oh, the fascinating remembrances he would reveal in his memoir: saving lives, erudition and sesquipedalianism, erotic tango exploits, exoneration from charges of murdering his wife—He grasped the glass and gulped. It was a difficult experience to relive, even his sanitized version. No, he would focus on his upcoming exploits as *primero bailarino* for New York's, perhaps the world's, premier tango dance company. Riveting material.

Tuesday afternoon at two, he would be signing the papers to license his line of Wagner Super Sharp Scalpel™ products to Profundum Medicus AB. He was gratified to learn that the company didn't want his products for a specialty scalpel market. They wanted to dominate the international scalpel market. He would be signing for enough millions to set him free, free indeed. Ernest was certain that the truth would not set him free, might do him a good deal of harm, in fact, but money would.

* * *

Miguel headed straight to the gym's elliptical trainer after the brief conversation with 'your.friend.' The caller had refused to confirm or deny that he was Jean-Luc Renaud, and he refused to disengage his voice-alteration software. He needed Miguel's assistance to avoid an international disaster, he claimed. Miguel assaulted the training machine savagely, his mind in hyperdrive. Within minutes his pulse rate was near 180 beats per minute, aerobic and pumping lots of oxygen into his brain. If he was ever going to connect all of these dots, it had to be now.

The man knew that Don Luis was in the hospital, said Kemal had told him. Miguel had cursed Kemal under his breath. When Miguel questioned their connection, the man refuted Don Luis's lifelong servant story, claiming that being Don Luis's lackey was Kemal's cover. He was an agent of the Mossad, and was supposed to be helping Don Luis guard the priceless Aleppo Codex until it was returned to Israel. But Don Luis was in financial trouble and was withholding it. That's why he was so fanatical about turning off the lights, wasting money. Miguel had gasped. It was all true. Even El Primitivo had told him to watch out for *masha* at the studio! And Don Luis's heart-wrenching quandary was whether to sell the precious Codex to the highest bidder or face life on the streets, the man had said.

The caller spoke of an evil twist. Kemal was now running open loop, out for his own gain. Miguel swallowed hard, rubbing the faint white scar on his olive skin. Mixing and matching info, Miguel had hoped to expose the caller's claims as false. But nothing he had said contradicted Miguel's beliefs or fears; it only heightened them.

The man claimed to have helped establish Kemal in the household, because he worked for Israel's Ministry of Foreign Affairs, a department closely allied with the Mossad. Miguel recalled Don Luis's last mention of Jean-Luc in the ambulance. The man was definitely on Don Luis's mind. The caller said that retrieving the Codex and restoring it to its rightful Israeli owners was his mission. He said Kemal had gotten other ideas once he realized that the original Codex was worth hundreds of millions of dollars. Miguel had raised Don Luis's claims that he believed using the Codex he could motivate Israel to establish a peace accord with its neighbors, a priceless accomplishment. The man downplayed its importance for peace, said it was solely of cultural significance. He had asked Miguel if he, personally, believed that an old book could motivate political stalwarts to make a deal with their bitterest enemies when death and destruction had failed? Miguel refused to answer, although he could not believe it himself. Deploring the skullduggery of Kemal and perhaps of Jean-Luc, Miguel quickened his pace. His muscles burned and his lungs strained to supply his brain sufficient oxygen.

Miguel asked for the caller's version of how Don Luis came to possess the relic. He explained that a member of Don Luis's Syrian Jewish family had agreed in 1958 to transport the Codex from Aleppo to Jerusalem. In transit, he switched the original for a copy he had made over years. Further, the courier destroyed the initial folios of the copy, including the Torah, its most important part, to inflate the value of the original he kept. Sadly, the man delivered a bogus Codex missing more than two hundred leaves, about 40 percent. Of course, he had ginned up a fantastic tale of having been robbed of the Codex and having retrieved only part of it. He had even gone so far as to implicate Israel's security services in the theft: Shin Bet, *the Unseen Shield*, and the Mossad, *the Institute*. The loss had been a huge embarrassment for the newly formed state and was quashed.

Sweat poured from every pore of Miguel's body. The machine's heart rate monitor was beeping loudly and flashing 247 beats per minute! He was anaerobic, his body and mind starved of oxygen. Miguel's concentration was broken and he began to feel dizzy. He was confounded, not enlightened by the new info. His heart ached. Was it possible that Don Luis's beautiful dream of peace for his people would be destroyed by a heartless spy?

Light head, loose grip, Miguel reached for the water bottle from which he'd been drinking. His vision blurred and his grip failed altogether. The bottle crashed to floor, splattering its pretty parquet pattern. It was as though he had been drugged. Miguel scanned the space for Kemal, found no one near. A shroud of darkness hovered over Miguel's head, as he recalled the man's final words. "You must help me retrieve the Codex now. Otherwise, Kemal will kill Don Luis when he returns home and steal it."

Head as big as a beach ball, that's how Miguel felt when he awoke dressed in workout gear, missing a single shoe. He reached for the back of his head. "Ay!" he said, fingering a knot. He struggled to open his eyes and found himself enveloped in total darkness. A tide of dread washed over him, realizing that he was unaware of where he was or how he had gotten there. And then his nose crinkled at an overpowering, sickly-sweet odor. But was it lethal?

CHAPTER 80

CRUNCHING POPPYSEEDS between her teeth, Aggie sat alone in the Brooklyn dry cleaning location's modest break room. She might as well get back to her desk for another hour or so, before heading to rehearsal. Aggie heard the rattle of mucous and heavy footsteps outside the break room's door. An instant later, she sat looking up into Sammy's grease-splattered face.

"Hey there, Aggie," he said smiling.

In her finest Flatbush elocution, she replied, "Sammy, how's it goin'?"

"Pretty good, girley. What's the latest?"

There was the standard reply and then there was one a bit more truthful. "I've been thinking about a few things. You know my family's history pretty well, huh."

"I'll say. Me and Moe goes way back to the neighborhood." He waved his grimy coffee cup for emphasis.

"Uh-huh." She paused. "Got a minute? Join me for a cup of coffee?"

She watched as he tapped up blackish-colored liquid from a dented urn in the corner. She couldn't help making a face.

"Want some?" He reached for her empty cup. "I'll get it for ya."

"You know," Aggie said, "sometimes I think about all the good times we had when I was a kid. But I can't recall everyone so well."

"Happens to all of us," he said, nodding.

"I recall Cousin Michael; he was a lot older than me, though."

"Called him Mikey, back in the day. Good kid."

"And, um, Cousin Benny. He was older than Dad, right?"

"Ah-hum," Sammy glanced at his wrist. "Look at that, would you? Time sure flies." He jumped to his feet.

"Come on, Sammy, sit down."

Aggie watched the tough guy dither. A sign of respect. He would walk out on anybody he chose. She said, "Pleeease."

Sammy cast glances everywhere before retaking his chair. It was like he was about to squeal and didn't want any witnesses.

"Tell me about him. How well did you know Cousin Benny?"

"Uhh, Aggie, your pop would be upset if he knew we was talking about this."

She smiled full-face. "Then we just won't tell him, will we."

"Well, I know Benny pretty good," he said, grinning. "We was in Sing-Sing together, him and me."

That was quite a lead-in. Aggie reeled, but kept her face straight. "What for?"

"Normal stuff, racketeering, B&E, running broads." He blushed, rolled a hand, saying, "Ladies of the evening kind of thing."

"When was this?"

He leaned back, skewed his head. "I went up about twenty years ago; a little more for him, maybe." He surveyed the room again, adding, "You know, he wasn't Big Benny yet, he was just a *sotto capo*." Sammy gestured, "Called him Benny Long Schl—"

"Got it. Um, what happened with Dad and him?"

The man shook his head. "Not good."

"All the more reason I should know," Aggie said, bracing for the worst.

"Long story short, your dad refused to testify for Benny. Not even at the sentencing hearing. After all Benny had done, sharing money from his heists, pinched food. Moe told him never to show his face around his family again. Ripped the pocket clean off his coat, your dad did." He nodded, gestured, "Clean off."

Aggie knew her dad had strong principles, but not supporting family didn't sound like him. She asked, "Why do you suppose Dad did that?"

"Benny got Little Joey in on a job, see." He sighed heavily. "Joey was supposed to be away from the real action, kind of a decoy. But he ended up dead."

"Dad has mentioned Joey before. Never said how he died."

"Moe never forgave Benny. Severed ties with him forever."

Absentmindedly, Aggie gulped down some bitter brew. She shook her head like a horse shooing flies.

"So where's Cousin Benny, now? Dad jokes that he moved to South Beach."

"Still right here."

"Brooklyn?"

Sammy stood. "I, uh, really got to get going." He looked both ways. "Don't rat me out with your dad, okay?" He jammed a finger across his lips. "*Omertá!*"

CHAPTER 81

MIGUEL GROPED THE WALLS, seeking a light switch, an exit. His stomach churned at the odor pervading the space. If he didn't get out of there soon he was going to be sick. Flicked a switch. Light nearly blinded him. Miguel looked around at the polished lockers, tango stars' large-scale posters, makeup mirrors, full-length mirrors and realized it must be the *tangueras'* lounge. The discord of all their fragrances, interacting over the weekend without fresh air, was overwhelming. He lunged for the door.

The missing sneaker he found near the entrance to the *tangueros'* lounge. His stomach calmed. Then came the memory of the phone call. It churned anew, more viciously with the memory of his workout's dolorous inner dialogue. Miguel vowed to scour the mansion from top to, well almost to, its very bottom, seeking Kemal. They must talk. Miguel searched for over an hour, but found him nowhere. So many floors with drawing and sitting rooms, bedrooms, various kitchens, the ballroom, music room, theater-equipped media room, Miguel's hand had been on his hip at every turn. He feared gouging Kemal first and questioning him later. But if he was even half as dangerous as Miguel suspected, Kemal was a man not to be underestimated.

Crashing down onto a *banco* in the studio, Miguel forced opened his mind more completely. What if the caller were not Jean-Luc? And what if he were lying and trying to steal the Codex for himself? But how could he know that Don Luis was in the hospital? Only Miguel and Kemal had known, unless he or his Mob connections monitored the house constantly. Aggie had witnessed Jean-Luc—surely it was he—staking out the studio's front door. Miguel sprang up and raced to the entry. He stood aside, burying himself in the jamb, peering, straining his eyes at the street and beyond. Nothing.

He turned and hustled across the main floor past the lounges to the back door. He thrust it open. Couldn't help sighing to himself, seeing the spot where Stephanie's tango dancing career had been terminated. He panned the enclosed area, let his eyes follow the concrete drive from the building to the end of the alley. Don Luis had chained and locked the high wooden gate adjacent to the street, ditto his inner sanctum. Miguel recalled Stephanie's claim that her attacker was fast and that he had fled on foot. There was no other escape from the alley other than scaling the gate's solid wooden planking. Striding toward it, Miguel considered how tall and strong a man would need to be to get himself over. Could he even do it? Miguel approached the gate and halted suddenly, his eyes perceiving movement in the shrubbery.

Miguel whisked the blade from his pocket. Depressed the stud. Its blade hungrily snapped open. He approached the hedge, low, like dancing milonga, his arm relaxed, extended away from his body, ready to strike. Miguel peered into the greenery, seeking his foe. And then, among a thicket of gnarled vines and lush leaves, he saw the outline of a man wearing a khaki-colored suit. He was neither big nor tall. He was Kemal.

"Come out from there," Miguel said. "I want to talk to you."

Kemal emerged slowly from the Nellie Stevens holly shrubs. He wore the uniform of a foot soldier, complete with a raspberry beret installed in the epaulet of his jacket and summer combat boots. He carried a two-meter-long pole to whose end was affixed a large gleaming blade of an odd geometry. He did not threaten Miguel, but rather faced the blade in the direction opposite him. Miguel closed his knife and stowed it, realizing that there are times when size matters.

Overcome by curiosity, pointing, Miguel asked, "What is that thing?"

"Halberd, Mr. Zanotto." Kemal smiled broadly.

Great, Miguel thought. But why does a guy who can shoot close groups at long range in the dark need a medieval weapon? He asked, "What are you doing here?"

"Guarding."

"Guarding what?"

"Mr. Don Luis said to guard the alley." He jerked his head toward the gate and made a quick thrust with the massive blade.

Miguel prepared to defend himself, to try and wrest away the weapon. He said, "I know about you, Kemal. Jean-Luc told me everything. I'm calling the cops now."

"No!" Kemal said.

"Why not?"

"Mr. Don Luis said call him first. No police, he said."

Miguel was stumped. Kemal was not giving away anything. Was it possible there was nothing to give?

It was getting to be time for rehearsal and there was another angle Miguel wanted to work, before completely tipping his hand. At least he had found Kemal, playing to perfection the part of loyal servant.

At the beginning of rehearsal, Miguel informed the company of Don Luis's unfortunate fall and the coming press gig. Chaz practiced *giros*, turning around and around in circles, as Miguel spoke. Outwardly, he had ignored Chaz's dervish-like display, but Miguel thought he and Kemal would be quite a pair in long white dresses with cinched waists and enormous bellowed hemlines, grinning, spinning, slashing. Miguel wiped the thought when Dr. Wagner spoke.

"I have no intention of dancing for the press or any other entity until I have been elevated to my proper place in the company."

Miguel observed Wagner cut his eyes vengefully toward Aggie. He didn't understand the problem, but there definitely was one.

"And, her," Wagner scoffed, "pfff, she's nothing compared to Adriana."

Aggie closed her eyes. Miguel's heart ached for her. He straightened out his face and said, "Please warm up with your partner for the final ensemble." It was the show's most glaring weakness in his mind. But more importantly, he danced the number with Candy, and wanted a little face time with her.

Miguel embraced Candy, ignoring her Turkish cigarette breath, as he thought of it. Her spirits seemed sky high. He said, "Let's dance really slow. Feel every step, each position, for balance and comfort."

"I'm definitely built for comfort," she replied, opening her chest to him.

The lilt of an old standard inspired them. They did not dance to the *compass* of the music, but used the beat solely as a backdrop for their coordinated movement.

"I haven't seen Jean-Luc lately," Miguel said. "No more lessons?"

"He said his leg is bothering him again."

"How was it injured?"

"He fell or something last year. Called earlier today and cancelled." She moved slowly and sensuously to their self-defined timing.

"Did you know him then?"

"No," she beamed, "we met this past summer."

"Huh, I thought you were old friends," Miguel said, off-handedly. "So you picked him out of a line of admirers, eh?"

"Actually, he bought me a drink. Said I looked like a professional dancer."

Miguel smiled devilishly and said, "*Qué romántico.*"

"Better watch out, the English police will hear."

"The cat is away," he said. "Besides, he's not aware of many things."

"Yeah," she sneered. "But I thought you two are close."

"I need the job, for the moment."

"I hear that," she replied. "I'm pretty sick of the tango stewpot, or whatever he calls it. I'm glad the old fart's gone, at least for a while."

"Me, too," Miguel spit.

Candy rolled her hip into Miguel's groin. She said, "This exhibition is going to be a fucking disaster. I had high hopes for the show, but it could be over before it begins."

He equaled her pressure, asking, "But what will you do?"

"I've got a backup plan," she flashed her crystal eyes. "Got to, you know."

"Really?"

She inched closer, her bosom resting on his chest, and whispered, "Don't tell, but I may be moving north."

"Ohhh, when?"

"Could be sooner than later." She added, "If the press thing is a douche."

"Maybe I need a backup plan, too." He said, anxiously, "At the break, let's go outside and have a smoke."

"I didn't know you smoked. Have any cigarettes?"

"No, but you do."

She smiled sweetly. "I just smoked my last one on the way to the studio."

"We can ask around," Miguel said, wanting to ring her miserable neck.

The music ended. Miguel called for the number to be queued again. From the corner of his eye, he observed Chaz's rapid approach.

"Excuse me, Miguel, but in Don Luis's absence, I run this company."

"In the past maybe so. But according to Don Luis, speaking by phone this morning, he believes that your routines are most in jeopardy."

"Really?"

Miguel held Chaz's gaze. "You have lost yet another partner."

"I have an excellent partner," Chaz retorted.

"Don Luis tasked me to conduct the rehearsal and to watch you carefully." Miguel set his jaw. "Now, take your place on the floor." He clapped his hands. "*¡Musica!*"

Three starts later, he saw Aggie release Chaz's embrace and cry out, "*Este paso es miados por los gatos.*" Miguel wanted to snicker at the immodest Argentine expression for something being hexed, but kept a stern face. He asked, "Aggie, do you need a break?" Miguel's eyes burned when he saw Chaz stroke her hair, calming her.

Chaz said, "We're fine."

"From the top," Miguel commanded. "Remember, three days until we're ripped apart by New York's press. Time to step it up—now or never. Music, please."

He watched the expressions and movements of each individual in the company, as Don Luis had exhorted on the call. He had stated explicitly, "You must be my eyes and ears. Keep up the pressure, and tell me who is destined to break."

CHAPTER 82

MIGUEL WAS NOT TAKING NO for an answer! On Wednesday morning he had told Don Luis boldly that he was determined to visit. He hung up the phone and calculated a reasonable walking time. Dressed in his favorite casual clothes—training pants, Argentina national *fútbol* jersey, and sneakers—he prepared to hit the pavement. Miguel glimpsed himself in a studio mirror. He recalled his afternoon at the US Open and hurried upstairs where he changed into a crisp white button front shirt and black trousers. He exited the studio's massive back door and headed toward the tall alley gate.

Miguel gave Kemal a little wave. He returned the gesture from his post, embedded in the shrubbery, halberd at the ready. He felt Kemal's scheming eyes on him as he approached the gate and appraised how challenging it was going to be to surmount it. He might not make it over, but was determined to give it a go. With a running start of five paces, Miguel leapt up trying to grasp the top-most reinforcement from which he would have to swing himself upward and over another half meter of height. He failed and dropped to the ground, landing on his feet, using his knees as springs to absorb his weight. He heard a snicker from the bushes and spit a curse.

He looked up at the top margin of the gate, at least a meter beyond his extended hand. Maybe this was not possible. But Stephanie had said the man fled this way. Kemal was shorter and less leggy. And Dr. Wagner really was not in shape for this kind of maneuver. And if he'd fallen, his dancing career could be over, along with a little recuperation time in jail. He would not risk it. Jean-Luc was as solid as the gate itself, but jump over it, no way. Miguel puzzled over who would want to hurt Stephanie or Chaz, indirectly. Chaz could probably scale the gate, but he would not hurt his own partner and jeopardize his cherished position in the company, or would he?

He gritted his teeth and stepped back twenty feet from the gate. Miguel tore toward it at full speed. He neared and relaxed down into his legs, then he sprang up, like a jumping frog. The top beam attained, he hurled himself high into the air just grazing the gate's top margin with his hand as he flew over. He landed on his feet, but they slid from under him and onto his bottom he thudded. Wow! He would never try that again, he affirmed to himself, brushing away dirt from his trousers.

Miguel panned to see who he might have entertained with his antics. A purple land yacht was parked three-quarters of the way down the block on the roadside. He leapt back, flattening himself against the dirty gate. Had he been observed? His chest heaved, recalling the vehicle's role in his unfortunate diversion toward the waterfront. He recalled its chunky occupants, dead ringers for Junior's back room diners. Miguel's heart sank, thinking they were watching the place continually, observing every vehicle's exit and entry. Just waiting for a chance to make a move. Miguel hugged the wall and made his way around the property to the cross street and then set out for Second Avenue.

The visit with Don Luis was a downer. The great man's vitality had been stolen by his fall. And it seemed that drugs had addled his otherwise lucid, if not tormented, mind. He claimed that his bed was alarmed. If he got up, the Gestapo intruded on his privacy immediately. Miguel listened patiently as Don Luis babbled on about time running out to reverse the adverse mental and biological effects on his people from millennia of persecution. And the need to secure peace accords with their neighbors, before Iran went nuclear.

It was frustrating for Miguel because Don Luis had mixed up the characters in his family saga. Suddenly, he included Miguel in the line, and warned him of extreme danger when he negotiated the Codex's transfer, even to the fittest party with best of intentions. Forces of darkness were trying to intervene. He said they were merciless.

There was confusion surrounding who best would make use of the treasure. The poor war-torn Mizrahim, to whom the relic had belonged for centuries, or the mainstream members of the government in Jerusalem. He warned Miguel to be careful and shrewd. He said, "You are the last of my line. You must preserve yourself at all costs."

Poor old guy, Miguel thought, walking briskly toward the Upper East Side. It was odd that Don Luis seemed completely composed, except for his maniacal ravings. Miguel ran his fingers through his hair and exhaled forcefully. Don Luis had possessed such a fine mind. Goose bumps sprang up on Miguel's arm, imagining himself responsible for the disposition of the Codex. He wouldn't know where to begin.

Faint strains of a tango classic greeted him. Miguel entered and watched Aggie dancing with Chaz on the main floor. They were perfecting their routines for the press gig. Chaz appeared majestic, toweringly tall and perfectly erect. His concentration was profound. Aggie was willowy, graceful, and compliant. He could have been the master matador, she the colorful cape billowing effortlessly and intoxicatingly at his command. Or he could have been the puppet master, his puppet vital and arresting, stealing the show. They turned to see Miguel staring. Aggie's face communicated her spasm of tango ecstasy. Miguel's heart sank, and he quietly dragged himself up to his room.

At rehearsal, later that afternoon, the air was thick with tension. Miguel found Chaz completely manic, over-engaged, and hyper-supportive. Aggie seemed tense, although she had apparently mastered his routines in record time. Miguel tried to force himself to be warm to her but couldn't. He had been shaken by his time with Don Luis and crestfallen at the sight of Aggie's profound *tangasm* while in Chaz's embrace. It was a show, of course, but her expression had betrayed something deeper than showmanship. To Miguel, it appeared that she was completely under his power. Chaz was her Svengali; Aggie his Trilby.

The curiosity of that day was Dr. Wagner. He was a nervous tangle. And although he complied with Miguel's requests, strain was visible in his every step. Even his walk seemed to evince an internal struggle, body overcoming mind in an epic battle. On the surface, Wagner appeared to be performing without conviction or passion, but Miguel was disturbed, sensing a reservoir of furor welling up within the man.

After the break, Miguel encouraged the company to go all out, indicating that tomorrow they would either impress or be humiliated by the press. In the event of the latter, chances were the show would be cancelled. This was the final opportunity to achieve perfection, he had said, exhorting them to make the most of it.

* * *

Aggie lay in bed puzzling over what was up with Miguel. It was well past midnight, but she couldn't sleep. Something had happened to him, to them. She fluffed her covers and eyed the clock again. Tomorrow was going to be the biggest day of her dancing career. Sure, it wasn't a show debut, but it might as well be. If the press bothered to hype the show, it would be a foregone conclusion that it was wonderful and deserved to be a hit. If they ignored it, or worse, panned it, a lot of work was down the drain and maybe the entire company. Aggie sighed, realizing she had been holding her breath, like a neophyte dancer.

She turned over, stuffed the pillow on top of her head. What was wrong with Miguel anyway? He had better not jeopardize his life. And for what? Obviously there was more to the picture than she could see. Yes, he was definitely holding out on her, and that wasn't fair. She had shared her info—her entire self—with him. It was only right that he be forthcoming with her. Aggie kicked the covers to the floor and snatched up her cell.

"*Hola*," Miguel said.

"Hi, it's me. Wake you?"

"I wish."

"Yeah, me, too." She paused for an instant before blurting, "Oh, Miguel, I wish you'd tell me what's wrong."

"We don't have to be at the studio until three tomorrow; maybe that's enough time." He forced a chuckle.

"I'm serious. Why can't you tell me?"

"It's too weird, and I wouldn't know where to start," he confessed. "Seems as though we have a little problem not only with the Mafia, but also with the Mossad."

"You don't mean that. Why would Mossad care about a dance company?"

"When I figure it out, and what to do about it, I'll tell you."

Aggie tried to bite her tongue to keep the words from spilling out, but her teeth just weren't sharp or strong enough. "I love you, Miguel. I can't bear the thought of being without you. Please let me in."

"Aggie, I'm sorry to disappoint you, but I'm a lost cause."

Tears began to flow. Her heart pounded. "Do not say that, ever. You are strong and smart and talented. Don't give up." She sucked back the sobs. "You have to fight to stay alive." She added, "For Catholics, martyrdom is so eighteenth century!"

"Having said that, you had better go to sleep. Big day tomorrow."

"I'm stressed," Aggie admitted, "but at least dancing with Chaz has turned out better than I expected. He has a way of mesmerizing his partner."

"Uh-huh."

"Sometimes it flows and I'm lost in the moment."

"Aggie, let me tell you something. Keep your wits about you. Nothing at that studio is as it seems."

"You really believe that?"

"Sometimes I believe the show was developed just to provoke another murder."

"Oh, that's so creepy." Aggie cringed, felt the skin crawling up her back.

"You're smart. Keep your head. I couldn't bear it if anything happened to you."

Aggie fought her covers, reflecting on the call. It was intended to make her feel better, but now her system was on high alert. Could Miguel have been exaggerating? He really didn't seem to be a drama queen, but the Mossad, really? Just because Jean-Luc smoked Israeli cigarettes? It was a bit of a stretch. But she'd been in the car while the Mob chased and shot at them. That was real, and maybe a good place to start unraveling this mess. Israel, who had been there recently? Oh, no! Her mind on fire, Aggie scrolled through her phone's directory. She dialed the number as her pulse rate soared.

"Yeah?"

"Seth, what is going on?"

"Well, Aggie, I been waiting a long time for your bootie call." He coughed. "Come on over."

"Don't be daft," she said. "What have you got to do with the Mob, and why do they care about Miguel?"

"You wake me at three in the morning to talk about that *schmuck*? Betta forget him; he's toast."

"What do you mean?" Aggie roared, "So help me God, if they hurt him—"

"So help you God, what? It's Big Benny and his crew. He's the biggest Jew Mob boss, figuratively and physically, in New York. He does what he wants." He yawned. "Come over here and sit on my face. You'll forget all about what's his name."

"You disgust me. I want to puke every time I think about you."

"So, you think about me."

"Fuck you, Seth."

"Too bad, I could of put in a good word for your guy at lunch tomorrow. But fugetaboutit, it's over for him."

CHAPTER 83

THE DAY OF RECKONING had dawned. Miguel sprang from bed and planned his strategy. Mental connections forged, he believed there was a way to address two quandaries at once, leaving only a handful unresolved. Miguel called David's Perfect Parties and asked that in setting up the staging and delivering the costumes for the press gig that they park their truck in the back alley, not on the side street. He instructed David to be at the big gray gate at eleven A.M.

Miguel regarded himself in his bathroom's mirror. A scruffy, long-haired neotango wannabe stared back. He took scissors from a drawer and went to work on his hair. He removed the excessive length from the back, shortened the sides to be easily brushed behind the ears, and evened the front, making it amenable to combing straight back. His shave was a bit too close, with a nick at his dimpled chin from lack of practice. Once his sideburns were trimmed, the man was himself again. Miguel dressed in tango clothing, black pants, button-up shirt, and his new dark jacket. In some communities, it was still important to demonstrate respect. And in the old world, especially, wearing a white shirt with a collar and a dark coat was an excellent start.

Just before eleven, Miguel's phone rang. David? No, Aggie. He stared at the ringing phone, his heart thumping. He was about to take a giant step. It could be their last chance to talk. But what would he say? He refused to endanger her. Miguel sighed and stashed the phone in his pocket.

The 575M gleamed. Miguel pulled into the alleyway a few minutes after eleven. He saw Kemal at his post with his antique weapon. Miguel wondered if it could have been used as a pole for him to vault over the gate? He heard the grind of a truck's gears and the groan of its suspension. He needed to unlock the gate and give directions to David's crew to stay put for five minutes, blocking the alley. Under no circumstances were they to allow the purple land-yacht to pass. Miguel charged Kemal to relock the gate when David and his crew departed, a chore not in conflict with any of his potential goals, like slashing or stealing. Two minutes later, Miguel was home free. The alley was blocked so well he couldn't see a thing past David's enormous truck. Away he went, minimizing the Ferrari's revs and exhaust noise.

Miguel crept along FDR Drive South in lunchtime traffic. He listened to Aggie's tender message, but vowed not to return her call until this deed was done. When he gained sight of the Brooklyn Bridge, it hit him that something important was missing. He was boldly, if not foolishly, heading to the seamy side of the city. He needed to bolster his courage. He hit the stereo power switch. Not an Argentine classic, but an American classic filled the cabin with a sense of hopefulness and expectation. He improvised, "I can make it here. I can make it anywhere." He settled deeper into the luxurious leather seat, before glancing into the rearview. Miguel could not believe his eyes. One car length back there was a purple land-yacht piloted by two bulbous goons. From the looks of their grins, they were singing the same tune.

* * *

Aggie slumped at her dad's desk, bending a paperclip this way, then that. She used the act as a form of Zen meditation, anything to keep her mind off Miguel. Why hadn't he returned her call? And what was this mysterious plan he was contemplating? The clip snapped in what she perceived as art mimicking life.

She squirmed in the chair, it's worn fabric catching, but hopefully not pulling fibers from her black skirt, fitted at the hips, generous at the hem. Aggie was dressed to go straight to the studio after lunch to prepare for the big afternoon and evening ahead. She felt silly wearing heels and a silk blouse to the office. Everyone in the place had given her grief, of the nicest sort. Muttering under her breath, she reached for another clip. And then the quiet ring of her cell phone grabbed her full attention.

"Miguel, what a surprise," she chirped, her voice seemingly smiling.

"Aggie, stay calm," he said. "Please call your uncle Dan and ask him to call me right away on my cell."

"What for? Why don't you tell me?" She gulped. "Are you in trouble again?"

His voice was tense. "I couldn't stand around anymore. But my plan is a little messed up, I think."

"Please let me help. Tell me what to do," she pleaded.

"Tell your uncle I'm going to the big boss for a talk, to make him understand." Miguel added, "Dan is smart and he knows these people. He'll know what to do."

"I'm not calling him. You tell me exactly what's going on." She heard the screech of brakes. Aggie caught her breath. "Where are you?"

"Shit, I missed the Brooklyn-Queens Expressway exit."

"Brooklyn!" She was flabbergasted. "Come here, now. We'll talk this through."

"Just call—"

"Miguel. Miguel!"

Aggie's face contorted. She smacked her forehead with the palm of a hand. She was in shock. Miguel was in Brooklyn going to talk to the big boss. Oh, my God . . . Mafia Boss! They had tried to kill him a few weeks ago. Was he crazy?

Aggie leapt from the desk and raced toward the break room.

CHAPTER 84

MIGUEL FLICKED the Ferrari's throttle. He had overshot the entrance to Junior's Deli and had to dive into the parking space reserved for takeout. He fanned the back end of the supercar around in a 180, its engine growling, tires wailing. Whatever the cost of the ticket, it had to be cheaper than the alternative. He blew through the heavy glass doors and hustled toward the back rooms. In proximity, he saw a chunk of a man standing guard beside the door. Miguel scanned the wall, grabbed a tray from a stand, draped a used napkin over his arm, and strode forward. He had known that a dark coat and a white shirt were correct. He grasped the door handle. A ham-sized hand crushed down on his.

"Just where do ya think you're going?"

"I dunno," Miguel sneered. "Big Benny asked for me. I'll tell him you didn't lemme in." He turned on his heel to leave.

"Hey, don't be a dope." The man opened the door.

Miguel walked confidently into the dismal space. A man stood and glared at him. It was the guy with rabbit ears from Sarge's hellhole. He used a cane for support. Miguel's knees weakened.

He lifted the stick and jabbed it menacingly at Miguel. "You see what you did to me." He spit on the floor. "You going to pay for this."

Miguel summoned courage enough to speak quietly. "I'm sorry for your injury, but I did not do it."

The man's hand shot inside his coat.

A bull of a man, sitting at the head of the table said, "Vinnie, later."

"Big Benny, he's a liar. Look at them eyes. He drove that Ferrari like a maniac. Made me crash, he did."

Miguel looked at the big man called Benny and bowed slightly at the waist, à la Kemal. He said, "*Mio caro, signore Grande Benny.*" He hesitated. "Sorry, but I don't speak good Italian." Miguel wiped his palms down the sides of his pants, walked forward, and extended his hand. "I am Miguel Zanotto from Buenos Aires."

Benny shook his hand. He said, "English is fine."

Miguel dared a faint crack of his lips, delighted his death was not imminent.

"Where's Frankie and Louie?" Vinnie asked. "They brought you here, yes."

Miguel shook his head.

"No?" Vinnie pointed an index finger between his eyes. "Whack 'em on the way, did you?" He brandished a handgun, leveled it on Miguel.

"What's the matter with you?" Big Benny called out. "Put that thing away."

Miguel began, "I came here on my own. But I think the others are close."

Benny said, "You just came here, for what?"

"I think there has been a misunderstanding. I want to tell you the truth."

"Bullshit," Vinnie spewed, "he's a goddamn ATF mole, I say."

"So, Miguel," Big Benny asked, "did you or did you not force Vinnie, here, off the road when he was trying to get you to pull over for a chat?"

"We were driving very fast and it was night. Someone was shooting behind us. I thought they wanted to kill us, so I used a driving trick my cousin taught me to turn around quickly. But Vinnie couldn't stop and he hit a wall."

"Fucking *fugazi*. A driving trick he learned at the CIA farm," Vinnie said. "He lured me toward that wall and whammo."

"Your cousin taught you?" Benny asked.

"He was a cop in Buenos Aires, became a PI, you say. I worked for him a while," he said, his head dropping perceptibly, "I couldn't stand it."

"So you're from Argentina and you dance tango," Benny said. "Did you know Carlos Gavito?"

"He was a great man," Miguel said. He clinched a fist and looked directly into Benny's small, black eyes. "An authentic *milonguero*."

"*Eso*," Benny replied solemnly. "I saw *Forever Tango* at least a dozen times on Broadway in '97 and '98, at the Walter Kerr and then the Marquis Theatre." He patted his sizeable paunch. "I was a bit trimmer in them days and tried it, you know, as a lark." He thrust up his hand. "Sheesh, Argentine tango's impossible."

"I don't want to interrupt this stroll down memory lane," Vinnie sneered, "but this is the guy that tapped my man in cold blood. I got a beef with that."

Benny said, "A witness says he saw you whack Gordo. You knew Gordo, yes."

Miguel nodded.

"Says you nailed him between the eyes for no good reason."

"Gordo used an automatic weapon to kill my friend El Primitivo."

"Nice Greek kid."

"Yes, a nice guy," Miguel said, recalling his friend's reckless abandon.

Benny raised his eyes. "So, uh, just how gooda friends were you two?"

"Not like that." Miguel shook his head. "He was helping me with Gordo. But he shot him like a dog." He sucked back a tear. "Then he came for me."

"Oh, my heart's breaking," Vinnie Rabbit Ears moaned.

"Hey, keep outta there," the door guard warned.

Miguel and everyone else turned to see a lovely young woman, flanked by two neckless Mafia soldiers, pushing into the room.

Vinnie said, "Can yous keep it down? And what's this muffin doing here?" He yanked a thumb. "Bathroom's down the hall."

Big Benny stood and growled, "Watch your mouth. This here is a young lady." He smiled and asked, "Aggie, to what do we owe the pleasure?"

CHAPTER 85

Dr. Wagner hunkered at his desk in the bowels of Bellevue Hospital. A pettish frown disfigured his face and a cell phone rested precariously in an open hand. His head droned with a dirge of sorts, even more depressing than tango songs. He stared at the marine gray walls, trying to cope, but shell-shocked. He had managed finally to reach Dr. Rolf Thornblad to try and understand why Profundum Medicus was not returning his calls. After days of stalling, failing to meet to sign the licensing agreement, he feared the worst. Thornblad had been diplomatic. Said the company, whose directors were his chums, just needed a bit more time to perform more personal diligence. His tone had been more solemn than an undertaker's.

Diligence? Snooping is what they had done. And they didn't need more time; they had used much time finding some busybody who had squealed on him. Gleefully ratted him out, for faltering under a crushing load of pain and guilt. Were they all so strong, so upright that they could bury their mistakes and walk with heads held high? Of course, it was probably not one of his colleagues at the hospital. It was his dear tango company cohorts who had spoken out against him. The hospital interviews had been concluded earlier. People had whispered to him, given him thumbs-up. He suspected this was a new round of diligence from secondary sources. His face reddened as the culprit's ruby lips and crimson nails flashed into his mind. Big tits, bigger mouth. Ripping away his lab coat, throwing it to the ground, he swore, "Vengeance will be mine."

* * *

Don Luis phoned Kemal from the *lager*. His instructions must be obeyed scrupulously, he stressed. Kemal darted from his post in the alleyway, hiding his halberd among the Nellie Stevens holly. Quickly he changed into a grey suit and tie, fetched a handful of perfect rose buds from one of numerous arrangements supplied by David, and pulled from the garage in the Mercedes limo. He fought heavy traffic but arrived at Beth Israel Hospital shortly after one, Don Luis's target ETA.

Kemal presented himself, flowers in hand, at Don Luis's ward. He signed in and was waved along by a nurse who found the roses exquisite. He had smiled and bowed. Once in Don Luis's room, the flowers were tossed. Immediately, they removed Don Luis's inconvenient appendages. Next, Kemal lowered the side rails of his master's bed and carefully, on a count of three, rolled himself onto the mattress as Don Luis rolled off, circumventing the alarm.

CHAPTER 86

MIGUEL'S EYES POPPED when Aggie stepped forward into Junior's dismal private room. He was confident her arrival was unplanned. But to his surprise, she strode across the scuffed tile floor and faced the big man at the head of the table.

"So, Cousin Benny, you recognize me," she said.

"I know what goes on in this neighborhood, and across the bridge, too. You grown up nice and tall, like your ma, not like him."

She hugged his neck. The family reunion was quite surreal for Miguel, who felt as though he was on trial for his life.

Vinnie sprang to his feet. "I object to this here intrusion. How can we have a proper sit-down with strangers?" He pouted, "It ain't fair."

Aggie said, "Cousin Benny, I was there with Miguel that night when someone tried to run us down, shooting and everything. It was awful."

"We covered that," Benny said. He pointed to a chair. "Hey, you," he said to one of the goodfellas, "bring that over here. And Vinnie, sit down."

Miguel watched *el Conejo* grudgingly take his seat. Aggie sat primly, purse on her lap, beside Big Benny. This was looking better. Miguel said, "Big Benny, after Gordo killed El Primitivo, I tried to shoot him with a huge pistol that I had used earlier to scare away his *amigo*. But I can't shoot well and only grazed Gordo's shoulder."

Big Benny turned to Aggie and said, "Miguel was, um, having relations with Gordo's ex wife, you see, a hooker calling herself Heather."

Aggie nodded nonchalantly.

"Heather got dead and the cops were pretty sure it was Miguel." He tapped his temple, "But I knew better. This Gordo was angry and trigger happy."

Aggie sat unflinching, a neutral expression plastered on her face.

"Can you explain two bullets in Gordo's head?" Benny asked Miguel.

"There's another part of the story, involving two men I saw here, one from New York the other from Canada, he says, but I don't think so. Middle East probably."

"Uh-hum," Benny said, flashing his eyes to Vinnie. "And what's they got to do with anything?"

"One man is a professional killer. He may have a partner who is also quite lethal, but I didn't see him here." Miguel's palms turned upward when he said, "I think one of these men was there and shot Gordo to save me."

Vinnie Rabbit Ears asked, "Now why would they give a rat's ass about you?"

Big Benny nodded thoughtfully.

Miguel's belly flipped. "They want to use me later to steal a priceless relic."

"This guy Gavito's tango shoes?" Vinnie guffawed.

"Hey," Big Benny said, "show some respect, how about it."

"Is a sacred bible for Jews." Miguel added, "I think these men want to take it for themselves and sell it on the black market for a fortune. But they can't get it."

Benny glared at Vinnie, who had stopped smirking. Benny said, "This thing is at that place or the other place?"

Vinnie jabbed a finger toward Miguel. "He knows nothing, just words."

"But you told me the thing was safe and they were going to get it, no problem." Benny's volume rose, asking, "You bullshitting me, Vinnie?"

Vinnie yanked out a pistol. "I ought to whack this fuck right now."

Benny glared. In an instant weapons were drawn, trained on Vinnie.

Vinnie put down his pistol delicately. He said, "Now, let's not get excited." He continued, "This kid is after the thing to sell it for himself. He can't even dance tango."

Big Benny cast glances between Miguel and Vinnie. He rubbed his chubby chin. "Miguel," he said, "you told me you knew Carlos Gavito."

"Not well, but yes. I talked with him when I was young. His partner Marcela Durán is from my town, Rosario. They came there sometimes to visit and dance."

"I still watch them on YouTube."

"Me, too."

"Tell me about his tango. Why was it, uh, what was so special about it?"

Miguel heard Aggie gasp. It was known in tango circles that while Gavito talked a lot to students and to the press, he was somewhat of a mystery man. "I believe that as much as tango, in its essence, is the longing to be whole, Gavito exemplified this in the extreme. He was a man divided in his spirit, in his soul."

"He didn't live in Argentina for a long time, but in Europe and the Middle East."

Miguel nodded. "And this, too, was a bit of a problem for him in Buenos Aires. He was not a *porteño* by birth. And they didn't trust him after he had been away. He was famous in America before he was famous in BA!"

"Yeah," Benny said, "he had to import himself into his own country. He had left the neighborhood, and had to pay some big dues to return." Benny eyed Aggie.

Miguel was uncertain what the look meant. But Aggie nodded her understanding. The Big Apple was beginning to look like pretty small potatoes.

"His most famous *paso*—not a step, but a static position—is the Gavito Lean. Is like two people, embracing at the heart but, how do you say, splintered—" He made a chevron with his hands, adding, "They look like a human Eiffel Tower."

"I like that," Benny said. "A human Eiffel Tower."

"Is a metaphor for longing to be united, but separated by an impossible distance."

"Thank you very much, Miguel," Big Benny said.

"Hey, not so fast there!" Vinnie shouted.

"Lower your voice," Benny said. "We ain't deaf."

"More words. He's a con artist, I say." Vinnie crossed his arms. "I ain't buying it. He talks the talk, but can he walk the walk?" He grinned at his poetry.

Miguel asked, "Aggie, you have your phone?" She produced it from her purse. "Big Benny, should we dance for you?"

"*Fantastico*!" he said. "But you know what I want to hear."

Miguel asked Aggie, "Have you "A Evaristo Carriego" handy?"

"I think so." Lowering her eyes, she added, "But I've never danced to it."

"No problem, is very easy," Miguel replied, smiling. "Big Benny, we need to prepare for a minute. Is okay to go to the rear of the room?"

"Sure, take all the time you want." Big Benny laughed. "It's one of the hardest tangos in the world to interpret," he said. "But it's the biggest, thanks to the show *Forever Tango* and the greatest *milonguero* ever lived, Carlos Gavito."

CHAPTER 87

THE DRONE OF STALE AIR-CONDITIONING, the squeal of car brakes outside the paper-thin walls, and the stench of soured booze all faded when Miguel spoke to Aggie. He held her fast with his stare, the emerald flecks in his eyes softening, embracing her earnest gaze. He understood the enormous stakes of this game, but the first rule of playing it well was to forget them.

Miguel said, “This is nothing; we dance tango all the time, yes.”

She nodded.

Vinnie screeched, “Get the car ready. When this guy flops we’re going to take him for a little ride.”

Aggie shuddered. Miguel grasped her trembling hand.

“Listen,” he said, “Gavito made this dance special because he showed everything that *milonguero* dancing stands for in one song.”

“Okay.”

“The first time I saw you,” Miguel said, “and you explained your idea of the *milonguero*, his devotion to pitiful friends, to tango culture, and, most of all to his family, I knew you could understand me.” He looked away. “Is not so, um, easy for me to reveal myself. Tango is a way for me to show who I am, and to be intimate with another person. This was the basis for the painful thing I did that hurt you. I was afraid for us to be intimate, so, I. . . ."

Aggie bit her lip. She squeezed his hand and said, "I understand."

"Forget about all the tricks and fancy steps we do in the show." He shook his head. "And the over-hyped *tangasm* is nothing compared to the essence of *el tango Argentino*. It's a shame, but most professional dancers either never learn or forget the core of the dance."

"There's so much pressure to be beautiful, sexy," she said. "Maybe essence is subtly forced out."

He knit together his brows. "I try to explain how *milonguero* Gavito interpreted the music of "A Evaristo Carriego" and showed us that essence of tango."

"Great," she said, nodding bravely.

"The piano begins quietly. We are apart and alone in the world. We converge cautiously because we are afraid. I find the will to reach out for you, but you turn away. And then you encourage me to be with you. My mind is bent, and the eerie melody of the violin sings my twisted thoughts, the pain of my past and the hopelessness of my future."

"Then what?"

"I begin to dream of love and union with you. Something even greater, perhaps union with myself. But you cannot settle your mind, cannot overcome your wounds from the past, to be free and embrace with your whole being a new lover."

"I don't know if I can do this," she whispered. "My soul aches."

"All souls ache for love and union," he said. "Like the poorest *milonguero* who dances with a beautiful woman, but knows they will never be together when the dance is over. You must focus on the moment. Live for this moment, this dance, this union, now!" He sighed. "Damn the next. It may not exist for you, or more likely for me."

Aggie fought back a tear, her face crumbling.

"The music swells and you give yourself to me completely." Miguel continued, "We make the most beautiful love to the bandonéon. We are coming together at last, overcoming our fear of rejection, wounds from the past, and our human frailty. We are determined to be one with each other, and to be whole. At last we find a reason to live."

Aggie released her breath. She huffed, "Miguel, I can't possibly remember all of this." It was as though she was going to hyperventilate, saying, "What will I do?"

"Just relax. You will remember. In all of tango, the music tells you the story every time and your body follows."

"The end is the clearest of all," he said with detachment. "You cannot accept a beautiful reality. Only isolation is real to you, because you are human."

Aggie's head was swiveling subtly when she said, "No, Miguel, this will not be our story." She crushed her face into his coat and wept.

He held her tenderly and rued the day he had taken up his murderous quest.

Aggie turned her face up to Miguel's and looked deeply into his eyes. "Don't believe this. We'll be together and happy."

Miguel tried to mask his pain. But there was no step to dance, no tango music to interpret, not even the hollow sigh of a partner's *tangasm*. There was only a woman and him. He looked away. "In the end, the *milonguero* knows it's over," he said. "Desperately, you cling to me. Shamelessly, I drag you across the floor. The finale, we pose in the Gavito Lean, our hearts united, but our bodies and our paths far apart, as always they will be."

Aggie wept.

"Hey, what's he up to back there?" Miguel heard Vinnie Rabbit Ears ask.

"Aggie," Miguel said quietly, "tango is not a toy thing for everyone. For some people, it is more real than life."

CHAPTER 88

The piano's meandering melody wafted from the small phone, permeating Junior's secret upstairs dining room. Big Benny and the wise guys were deathly silent. Even *el Conejo* was quiet for a change. And then began the haunting phrase of the violin. Miguel faced Aggie. His mask was solemn; this was no time for smiles or winks, he was the embodiment of Gavito. Aggie appeared composed, yet so somber, looking at him. They were separated by only six feet of scuffed, sticky floor, although it felt like an abyss. This, thought Miguel, as he made his initial step toward her, is the real human experience, the real tango.

Miguel and Aggie embraced loosely and moved to the gut-wrenching melody. She was supple in his arms, but he could feel her heart pounding. And while she was balanced on her feet, he noted a slight shudder with each step. He did not lead over-the-top performance figures. Instead, Miguel danced as he had explained in the room's musty back corner. The simple figures and the intensity of the moment cast the impression they were executing the gravest of ceremonies. When Miguel walked to the music's cadence, their tenuous relationship was clear. They were taking fledgling steps toward something deeper.

And then the music waxed, even as its tempo waned. The violin and bandonéon sang of the lovers' newfound bliss. Miguel drew Aggie close to him and felt her clutch at his back. Her hand climbed slowly up to the nape of his neck and squeezed with the subtlest pressure. A dart of emotion fired down his spine and he responded by caressing her more closely to him. He closed his eyes and his chest welled with tenderness.

"Look at that," Big Benny said. "It's like they're really in love. I can feel it."

Miguel tried to ignore the man's remarks and focus on his movement, his intentions. But something was wrong. It was as though Miguel's brain had been short-circuited. As a professional, he had never faced a total block on the dance floor. But now, all he could experience was the pleasure and warmth of embracing Aggie. He just wanted to hold her close and show her how he really felt for her. Damn Benny and Vinnie and the fact this could be his last dance. Or maybe it was because it could be his last tango that he wanted to make it clear to Aggie how much he loved her and never wanted for them to part.

Vinnie Rabbit Ears cracked from across the room, "I think we're about to see a different kind of pole dancing. Shorter pole, but stiffer!"

Miguel was jolted out of his trance. He released his too-firm grip on Aggie and opened his eyes, blinking to clear his mind, to maintain his professional bearing. The melody had changed; again it was dark and foreboding. Miguel understood the portentous chords; trouble for the lovers was afoot. They were unable to overcome their past wounding and were beginning to be fearful of yet another romantic failure. Miguel led Aggie around him in circles of confusion, the *molinette.* He turned, watching her precess slowly around him in a perfect circle of doubt and despair. This was the torture of life and tango, being enacted in yet another smelly den. Only now, he hated this ritual. And he truly despised what must come next.

"Oh, it's about to get messy," Big Benny boomed from the head of the table. "The *milonguero*, he has to leave. Knows it's for the best."

Miguel summoned all of his emotional strength. He was a man whose mission—whose destiny—had been decided. Nothing must be allowed to keep him from accomplishing his goal. Neither satisfaction, nor happiness, nor the beguiling influence of love. He glared at Aggie and thrust her downward from his chest. She clung to him as he withdrew, dragging her along the soiled, splintered floor in *arrastre.* Now Miguel's mask was severe, but his heart was quaking. It was as though his chest would burst with the pain of loss and his desire to be with

Aggie. He took another step away from her, but could no longer exert control over his body. His arms trembled and his knees began to give way, under the weight of the lie his body dared tell.

Miguel was trying to mislead Aggie and himself into believing that he did not need her; he could make it without her. It was time for him to take another step, the music demanded a step, the ritual demanded him to step away from her. But Miguel realized he was like a Colossus with feet of clay. He looked into Aggie's face and saw there was no mask, no guile. She wore the compassionate expression of a woman who knows and understands a man's trials and his insecurities. She would be there with him to face them, until the end. His body quivered and he all but collapsed to the floor.

Miguel bent low and looked at Aggie through tear-filled eyes. He raised her up from the filthy floor toward him. And as the terrible demand for separation and isolation pounded out from the little phone, he embraced her intimately, with his entire body and soul.

The group murmured as the final strains built to a crescendo. It was as though the dancers had prematurely stopped dancing. Miguel tenderly caressed Aggie. His rounded torso caused her to arch her torso in sympathy. He took a small step backward, yet maintained the comfortable position they enjoyed, heart to heart. They remained balanced in harmony—rather than in torture—in Maestro Paiva's elegant Bridge. Big Benny's applause and the goons' whistles and shouts filled the room, but Miguel and Aggie were somewhere else. Somewhere beyond the grim reality of Junior's secret space, and far beyond the isolation they had endured for too long.

CHAPTER 89

AGGIE HELD HER HEAD IN HER HANDS all the way to the studio. The flash and fire of a Ferrari left her unimaginably cold. How completely exhausted she was from dancing one song was incomprehensible. She wasn't even sure she had done it. The entire dance had been a blur of longing for togetherness with Miguel, and fear of rejection, and an unfathomable sense of isolation. *Tanguidad* didn't even begin to describe the tsunami of dark emotions that rocked her, dancing with Miguel in front of a dozen mobsters.

The Ferrari roared and lugged alternatively, up Flatbush Avenue, across the Manhattan Bridge, and up Third Avenue toward the studio. Aggie could only relive the shock of the past couple of hours. She recalled Sammy whispering Big Benny's lunching joint to her, after a lot of begging. And her entrance and dancing in the backroom at Junior's was still like a dream, a first-class nightmare! But when it was over and the wild applause began, even Vinnie Rabbit Ears had clapped for them. And then when he dropped his pistol it discharged and shot a hole through his table. The thugs drew their guns and leveled them randomly. The door guard burst in, dragging Seth Sheinberg, who must have watched from a crack in the door. Cousin Benny was not happy.

And the way Benny talked to Miguel—like *mensch* to *mensch*. He had said, "Greed was the reason for the lie about Miguel offing Gordo. There was money to be made, promotions in the family's organization to be gained." Aggie recalled that he had stressed that part, staring at Vinnie. She remembered he'd said, "Superspy was supposed to show up and enable the inept family to do a certain deal. The family had cased a building earlier, but wasn't sure how to bust in and get out. Superspy was going to do the heavy lifting. He failed."

Benny had jabbed a fat finger toward Seth, calling him, "Our cybercrime master." He said that Seth had, ". . . played Boy Scout in Israel and caught a big, stinky fish." He added that Seth and the superspy most recently ". . . dreamed up a plan to hoodwink somebody into stealing the thing and giving it up to them." Benny had admitted, "I think that's busto, too."

Aggie was sure that Don Luis was the target. And it became clear that 'superspy' was Jean-Luc. How Miguel had known that he was a Mossad agent, Aggie didn't know. But she hoped that Miguel's fears concerning her safety at the studio were not equally well founded. How Seth could have gotten so mixed up in this was another quandary. Aggie watched him hang his head and occasionally nod objections as Cousin Benny had told the story. Seth was in big trouble for lying about Miguel. Aggie had to smile to herself.

CHAPTER 90

Don Luis's personal fantasy land was fully prepared when Miguel and Aggie arrived late for Thursday's brief rehearsal. Miguel panned his head from side to side, eyeing the elaborate setup. A huge rolling bar had been established for the edification of press elites. And David had strategically deployed wooden folding tables and chairs, bearing black tablecloths and chair covers. Each place setting was accented with a crimson napkin. The color scheme was perfectly tangoesque and macabre.

Miguel and Aggie approached the former fishbowl, now shrouded in opaque fabric, covering its glass walls and door. He examined a printed card placed on a nearby table. The card claimed it was a red-letter night for New York City. It went on to say that excerpts from an upcoming *El Tango Argentino Espectáculo* would be performed. The show merited a scarlet letter. Not an 'A,' but an 'M' for *Murder by Tango*!

"Oh, there you are," said Barbara, the company's business manager, handing Aggie and Miguel each a manila envelope. "I've been a nervous wreck waiting for you."

"Sorry," Miguel replied, "lunch took longer than expected." He eyed the envelope. Shook it. Mocked trying to peer through it.

"Those are your instructions from Don Luis. He says to follow them precisely."

"I hope mine begins with a shower, because that's where I'm headed," Miguel said, ripping away the top of the communiqué. He hugged Aggie and pecked both of her cheeks, whispering, "You were fantastic. Keep it up just a little while longer."

Aggie made a monster face.

"Please," he added, "for me."

She tore the end from her envelope and withdrew the lone page of instructions.

Miguel accessed his directions, but stopped reading when Aggie gasped.

"How could he?" Her hand flew to her mouth. "Is this a joke?"

"What?" Miguel asked.

"It says Dr. Wagner is going to be *primero bailarino* and I'm to dance with him." We have hardly ever, we never even—How can Don Luis do this?"

Miguel's sunny façade vanished. "Aggie, this is not a joke." His tone darkened. "You have to be on your guard tonight."

"I am so stressed. I can't take this," she said, her voice cracking.

Miguel turned to Barbara. "Is he here?"

"Um, no, he said he would be a little late."

He gave her a look of disgust, pulling Aggie aside. "We can do this; we're a good team." Miguel took her letter. "What else does it say?" He mumbled, "Three duo numbers, an ensemble, and then a break. Masks," he paused, "so we wear physical masks. That should help when you dance with Wagner."

Aggie did not smile.

Chaz and Candy neared. She appeared to be consoling him. Miguel expected that she painted a picture of how lovely Quebec is in winter. ". . . and only minus 30 Celsius."

Miguel continued to read aloud Aggie's info. "Meet Don Luis in his office immediately at intermission."

Aggie moaned, "Why is he doing this to me?"

Miguel bit his lip. "It's not about you," he said. "But be prepared for anything. There's no telling how he will try to terrorize Wagner and Chaz in the second half."

Her head tilted.

"Don't worry. I intend to beat him at his own game."

Miguel pecked Aggie's cheek and headed for the *tangueros'* lounge. He tore off his shirt and sharpened his eyes on his personal instructions and wardrobe calls.

Standard stuff. Obviously he was not a target. But in war, collateral damage was always possible. And Don Luis was using his tango theater as a combat theater, where he had struck the initial blow. Stripping, Miguel considered it was certain this woe would be repaid by all camps before the night was through. He glanced into a mirror. His variegated hazel and green eyes stared back at him. What was the fate of this generation's green-eyed boy, he wondered. Perhaps tonight would reveal his destiny. Miguel heard a whimper coming from a closed bathroom stall. It appeared Don Luis's tango caldron had been productive, and he was pretty sure who was overdone and over the edge. But what would he do next?

Miguel dressed for rehearsal in record time. He stashed his blade in his hip pocket and made for the door. Halfway there, something told him to take a quick look in that bathroom stall. He saw nothing unusual and turned to exit. But looking back, Miguel refocused on a tiny blood-red dot on the seat and a faint pink trace leading down into the bowl. He shuddered. His mind time-warped back six months. The feelings of revulsion and helplessness, they were taking hold of him again. He slammed the door shut and rushed from the lounge. It was time to have a man-to-man with the marionette master.

Miguel flew up the stairs, ignoring the circus elevator. He peered through the narrow glass panel of Don Luis's anteroom. Darkness. He tapped out his mother's birthday, American standard, and flung open the door. Didn't bother to hit the lights, but strode straight through and opened the main office door. He stared at Don Luis, who sat behind the grand desk, dressed in a black suit with a crimson necktie, and Kemal, in his Asiatic costume, edging on a whetstone the jeweled handled dagger.

"Miguel, I was just about to—"

"Call it off."

"Oh, you know bloody well I will not do that, my boy." He scrunched low his brow. "We want the same thing, don't we, to know who killed Natalia, to exact revenge."

"I'm not your boy. And call it off or else."

Don Luis lowered his eyes.

"It's not worth it. My sister is gone. And my heart aches for her, but more death will not bring her back. And I will not risk Aggie, and neither will you, to out her killer!"

"My precious goddaughter is dead, and I will not rest until personally I see her killer's life extinguished. I want to do it myself, at this performance, tonight."

Miguel cut his eyes to Kemal, who listened like an entranced dog, dagger now at the ready. "Tell him to put that thing away." Miguel withdrew his blade from his pocket. "Or he'll have the fight of his life on his hands."

Don Luis waved off Miguel. He said, "Kemal, please, take up your post downstairs. I shall be with you shortly."

Miguel watched on high alert as the little man smiled amiably and sheathed the weapon. He departed. In silence, Miguel eyed Don Luis.

"So, you are prepared to cast everything to the wind at the eleventh hour," Don Luis said. "All of your detective work, keen observation, your deceptions—"

"Playing your puppet," Miguel added with a sardonic smile.

"You have never been my puppet, although I have used you." He sighed. "I, too, am a fierce competitor, Miguel. Together we are stronger than if we are adversaries."

"I am not your adversary. I'm not your anything, and don't forget that."

Don Luis stood, on wobbly legs, and inched from behind the desk. "I can assure you that you are wrong about that."

Miguel's eyes burned on the man who played the pathetic cripple so well. The dueling sabers mounted on the wall were almost within Don Luis's grasp. Miguel flicked open the blade and raised it, saying, "Do not move another step."

It was an unexpected standoff. Miguel's emotions ran high. He refused to look at the splendid coat of arms, uncertain whether anything he had heard since he had shown up was true. He stepped back and bumped against the august dictionary, recalled having flipped through its pages. How far he believed he had come. Believed he was making it in this gritty city. But he was finding that the Big Apple was full of maggots.

"You had better get downstairs," Don Luis said. "You're tardy to rehearsal."

"I hope you've enjoyed manipulating me, because after tonight that's over."

Miguel stowed his knife and stormed from the room. The hollow echo of his shoes striking the floor reinforced the reality that he—any *tanguero*—controlling his destiny was an illusion. Nothing had changed from the ghettos of Buenos Aires to the Upper East Side of Manhattan. There was only survival, love, and death.

* * *

Dr. Wagner flashed a thin smile to Aggie. She noticed that he held his right hand slightly behind his leg when they met, hiding a flesh-colored Ace bandage wrapping his hand and wrist. She focused on it for an instant, prompting him to claim to have nicked it slightly in the lab. His eyes moved more slowly than usual when he spoke. And his speech was not his typical barbed repartée. Aggie was determined to make this a success, despite Wagner's injury and Miguel's morbid fears. She lived in Morningside Heights, but she was a Brooklyn girl at heart. It would take a solid punch to knock her out.

When Wagner showed Aggie his preferred lines for the opening steps of the ensemble they were to dance together, she caught her breath when he nearly fell from each static position. He became agitated after trying several times with the same result. Aggie reassured him that she understood and that together they could maintain better balance. He had sneered, "Oh, really, with you, better balance," and turned away. He seemed mad at the world. Aggie thought that if his balance were completely gone, at least his barbed tongue was back.

Aggie stood in the present with her mind fixed on the recent past. Of all the drama and stress of the meeting with Cousin Benny and his moronic minions, the thing that had amazed her was Miguel's reply to Cousin Benny's invitation for lunch. Miguel had said solemnly, "I expect to avenge the murder of my sister before the day is over." It had been mind blowing. Why hadn't he told her? Did she really know anything about him? Yes, she did know one thing for certain about Miguel. She was not giving him up for anything in the world.

CHAPTER 91

"SHOW TIME, FOLKS," was the line buzzing in Miguel's head when he eyed his phone at 6:45. He recalled the man in a famous American dance film who repeatedly popped pills, checked his pulse, and sprang the line. The handsome guy had courted death, who appeared to him as a beauty, finally seducing his own demise. It was time for Miguel's final act, and he was up for the performance of his lifetime.

The studio was filling with bodies of all shapes and sizes, modes of dress, and interpretations of what was in the offing. They had brought along boxes of equipment, lights, cameras and, as far as Miguel could tell, a good deal of attitude. He had overheard a distinguished-sounding man speaking to a photographer. He said, "Word is, forget Chaz, shoot the local girl." Near the main dance floor, Miguel heard a journalist speaking *sotto voce*, "D. L. says we can get an exclusive on Aggie. I want a million frames of her."

At the fishbowl—the former fishbowl, now the death-bowl cum costume department—Miguel ensured that his chalk-striped suit was prepared. Large racks of clothing consumed most of the small practice room's floor. A portable CD player languished in the corner. Miguel fingered a mask, a black job with raccoon eyes. It was the one he would wear for the program's finale. He traced its red lips with his finger, understanding drama was the ticket. All he wanted was for Aggie and himself to finish the gig and get the hell out of there.

Wagner and Aggie rehearsed on a nearby practice floor. Miguel noted that Wagner moved nervously on unsteady legs. His bandaged hand had bled through the fluffy, flesh-colored wrapping. Wagner looked up at Miguel, who pointed to his wrist. Nearly in shock, he ditched Aggie and headed for the *tangueros'* lounge. Miguel smiled, but Aggie's distress had never been more obvious. She flew to a ballet bar, perhaps to grip something stable.

Near the back exit, Miguel saw a long-haired photographer grappling with a bulky tripod. He walked over and asked, "Need help?" The man turned away nodding his rat's nest of hair and beard, continuing to hassle with his equipment. The guy seemed to be having a hard time all around. His press photo on his badge didn't look a thing like him. He'd aged twenty years just getting in the door. It was that kind of business, Miguel assumed. Photography, like tango, often meant late nights and low pay. A gong resounded throughout the studio. Miguel turned to see Kemal holding a giant mallet, grinning and bowing. Truly, it was show time when Don Luis boomed, "Places, please. *¡Musica!*"

The show began smoothly. The couples' routines had gone surprisingly well, given that every person was stressed to the absolute max. Even Wagner had managed to remain upright, doing a stiff salon tango bit with Adriana. Chaz had been a brooding dance genius in his over-the-top neotango routine with Aggie. As Miguel took his place on the floor for the first ensemble, he smiled within at the credible milonga Ingrid and he had just completed. With enough grueling practice, anyone can do just about anything.

The initial ensemble was based on a tried and true scenario: booze, broads, and bustle in a barroom. The men wore double-breasted, chalk-striped suits and the women, suggestive dresses cut up and down to there. Aggie was especially provocative in a red number with black lace trim at the chest. Elbow-length black gloves and a flowing shawl completed her persona as a tango vamp. Miguel had tried to catch her eye, but high-intensity camera lighting strobed her continually. It seemed the press had found their star.

A fine troupe. Solid professionals. Miguel had to admit it. But Don Luis was using these people, including him, wringing them out emotionally for his own ends. In his peripheral vision, Miguel saw Candy's back. She had turned away and was busily lifting and separating herself to be sure to overflow her shimmering sapphire-blue dress. But where was Chaz? Adriana, his partner for the number, stood alone off-center. When would he join her, banished from his coveted center stage placement?

Don Luis had wheeled himself in front of the floor and was introducing the bit to the press with a sense of pathetic flare. He urged them to feel the energy in the barroom where the mixture of women and tango would soon make for an explosive cocktail. He clapped his hands and commanded music.

Miguel followed Don Luis with his eyes as he rolled from the front of the makeshift stage to the side, near Kemal and the entry door. But who had entered during the spiel but Detective McGarrick. Miguel's pulse quickened. This was not an auspicious development. McGarrick was actually a homicide detective. Had he been summoned in advance by Don Luis? It did not appear so, given Don Luis's wagging finger and hyperextended neck, visible during their exchange.

The intro music began and Chaz slinked from behind the company to his place with Adriana. Miguel caressed Candy, per the script, and they began to dance. It was only during a *giro*, when Miguel rotated full circle, that he observed Chaz's facemask. It was a sinister devil mask, brick red with yellowish horns curled back toward the head. It seemed to ooze blood from lifelike pores. The momentum of the number built to the fight scene. Dr. Wagner would challenge Chaz, center stage, Chaz presumably having tried to steal away Aggie. Art imitating life, yet again. Candy would throw herself into the breach and seduce Wagner, dancing him away from the conflict.

Tension mounted, the sensuous swirl of tango pervaded the air. It was as though oxygen were being sucked from the room by the action. Suffocation was nigh. Miguel cut his eyes to the center and saw Wagner snatch Aggie's arm, pulling her away from Chaz, disturbing her delicate balance. He drew back for a swing at Chaz. The music's sinister vibe and the violin's crazed screeches complemented the wild action. Wagner swung. Chaz parried the punch. Wagner dogged him, lashing out wildly while screaming.

Camera flashes illuminated the action brighter than midday. Chaz emitted a cry and landed a punch to Wagner's cheek. The press went wild. Deafening applause filled the space. Candy rushed to break up the brawl, but was pushed aside by Chaz, who lunged at Wagner. He sidestepped the move and kneed Chaz in the groin. Chaz fell to the floor, humiliated. Wagner grabbed Candy's hair. He pulled her around the floor, yelling at the top of his lungs, "It's your fault, you slut. I'll kill you." The press corps wildly applauded the realism. The room resounded with catcalls and *esos* while cameras hungrily devoured the action.

Don Luis waved his arms violently to a stagehand. The lights went down and the curtain fell in front of the floor, like a black pall. The intermission music began, but the raucous press corps nearly drowned it out, confirming that Don Luis had created a production worthy of its sensational name.

The lights came up behind the curtain and Miguel saw Wagner manhandling Candy, her arm forced behind her back. She grimaced and cried as he mercilessly lifted her hand high above her head. He shouted, "You ruined my life. You told them I'm a drunk. Now I'm going to ruin yours!"

Miguel flew toward them. He rammed Wagner, crashing them to the floor hard. Wagner grabbed Miguel's coat. One potent punch to Wagner's jaw took him out. He lay still. Miguel stood and exercised his aching fist. He shook his head, half-unbelieving. Wagner was twisted and dangerous, but expressing his rage on a helpless *tanguera* was too low. Surely there had been other victims of his uncontrollable rage. Natalia! Miguel's mind snapped. Now was his chance. He dived atop Wagner and grasped his neck in both hands, squeezing with all his might.

McGarrick hooked his forearm around Miguel's neck. He hauled back, choking him, pulling him backward onto the floor. Miguel struggled to catch his breath. McGarrick said, "That's enough. I got him." He cuffed Wagner, who lay whimpering on the floor.

CHAPTER 92

THE LAST TANGO IN NEW YORK CITY: that's how Miguel felt when Detective McGarrick produced a plastic zip tie and told him to turn around. Wagner had gotten the sturdy metal cuffs. The studio was on fire with gawking press reps. Only moments earlier, McGarrick had led away Wagner, and now had it in for Miguel. It was a surreal moment begging illumination or at least the answers to a few fundamental questions. Miguel asked, "What have I done? Why here? Why now?"

"You've got a true friend," McGarrick answered. "Sent photos of you at the Dorothy Chandler Pavilion in LA, proving that you were at the crime scene. Claims he has proof that you killed one Natalia Prafil. Said you were going after another tango diva tonight, one Aggie Jacobs."

Miguel jerked away his wrists. "That's crazy. Natalia was my sister." He searched for Don Luis, for Aggie, to lend credibility to his claim. They were nowhere to be found.

In a measured tone McGarrick said, "I don't know about that. But I do know that you flew from Buenos Aires and arrived in LA on the day of her murder."

"That's a lie. This is all a farce, orchestrated by the Mossad."

"Right. Turn around."

Miguel exclaimed, "What about my rights?"

"What rights? You got lucky before. Don't make me use force; I won't hesitate."

"But Detective McGarrick—"

The detective thrust up one hand and covered his earpiece with the other. His scrunched features darkened, listening. After a brief silence, he said, "Roger that. Sure he came in here?" Hands to his sides, McGarrick surveyed the space with hungry eyes.

Miguel examined the crowd examining him, as they continued to stuff their faces with fancy hors d'oeuvres and stiff drinks. They seemed delighted by the show, both of them. McGarrick grunted, slewed his head from side to side. Something was amiss, but he couldn't see what it was. Miguel asked, "What's wrong?"

"You be quiet."

"I can help. Please tell me what you're looking for."

"Photographer for the *Village Voice* was mugged outside. Guy stole his camera, press pass, came in here."

"I saw someone odd," Miguel said. "Long grey hair, a patchy beard. His photo badge did not match his face at all."

"Where? When?"

"Near the back entrance before the show."

McGarrick squeezed Miguel's arm. "Stay put, you hear?"

Miguel nodded. He watched McGarrick plow through the throng of excited press elites. Miguel slewed his head back and forth searching the crowd. What was he going to do, wait around for McGarrick to prove his innocence? He forged a path in McGarrick's wake toward the rear exit. Then he suddenly tore away and ran up to the mezzanine for a better vantage point. Miguel found Don Luis there, looking pale, slumped in his wheelchair. His hands rested on a plaid blanket, draped across his lap. He stared down onto the bustle with a forlorn expression, like someone on an ocean voyage, sailing off the edge of the Earth.

Miguel regarded him carefully, wondering if he could be certain that the obvious killer, snatched up in Don Luis's dragnet, was in fact the real killer and not a scapegoat? The entire production had been constructed to pulverize people and then sift them, hoping that some fragile individual would repeat or try to commit a hideous act. While humans seemed to repeat their mistakes, who was to say that the whole charade was not a brilliant plan to cover the guilty puppeteer's tracks once and for all?

Miguel could let the dead bury the dead if only he could get out alive with Aggie. He asked, "Where's Aggie? Her instructions said to come here at intermission." Miguel's mind flashed. He raced toward Don Luis. Their faces separated by mere inches, Miguel demanded, "Where's Kemal?"

"At his post. And I'm afraid Aggie has stood me up. I wanted to save her from that." He gestured below, toward the din. "She's a star now."

"And who arranged it?" Miguel asked. He looked down and noticed a woman with a shock of brassy red hair, spilling a martini with one hand and dragging a man with several cameras around his neck with the other. She crawled over anyone in her way, her head switching back and forth as she beat a savage path. His mind was sharp, but Miguel was uncertain what he should be seeing. There was too much movement everywhere. He changed tack, thinking, what I am not seeing? Chaz!

* * *

The demon mask covering his face, Chaz embraced Aggie. They were on a tiny patch of floor behind the rows of costumes and boxes left behind by the decorator's crew. The ruse had worked. She hadn't recognized his handwriting and believed Don Luis had instructed her to meet Chaz there, in a last-minute change of plans. Chaz had written that she was to dance the final ensemble with him. An extemporaneous ending had to wow the press, securing the rave reviews Don Luis craved. The ending must be composed secretly during intermission, inside the fishbowl.

A neotango rant spewed from a small portable player, sitting on the floor in the rear of the curtained room. Chaz observed that Aggie was relieved to get away from the press crush. They had all wooed her. No one had asked him a single question. Not a solitary flash had brightened his face. A star had been born; and one had died. Chaz stood watching its genesis from off the floor, his arms folded, devil mask glowering at Aggie. She had smiled gracefully, nodded, and said, "Oh, thank you. Thank you very much," a hundred times. He, Cachafaz, had been ignored. And then he had shown her the note. He directed her away from the floor to this soundproof hideaway. Aggie had been nervous, but his embrace would calm her. He was a tango god, although a seeming Satan.

Chaz caressed Aggie intimately, savoring the moment. But his excitement was blunted, recalling how that bitch Natalia also had stolen his gravitas. Her footwork had been so spectacular, even he'd been spellbound. But in the end, his spell had been more powerful. And he had mutilated those pretty feet unmercifully. Now, history desperately wanted to repeat itself. And his little friend was handy. He'd used it on himself for the first time in a long while, in the bathroom, to overcome the anxiety of being humiliated by Don Luis. He planned to use it next on Aggie. He would mutilate her and by doing so pierce Don Luis. Yes, the old man loved these new kids. Why hadn't he cared that much for him, Chaz wondered? No matter, he would make Don Luis suffer for his sins.

More bombast raged quietly from the small CD player, Chaz fixed his focus on Aggie. Her black shawl hung over a shoulder. He held her eyes fast, reaching without releasing her from his demonic gaze to take hold of the shawl's fringed corner. He pulled it up slowly toward his face, just beneath eye level. He glared through his mask's hollow eyeholes at her as he became the focus, the epicentral axis about which he led her *giro.* Aggie encircled him, dancing a *molinette*: back, side, forward, side; back, side, forward, side, endlessly swirling toward an exquisite *tangasm* and ineluctable death.

* * *

Miguel scanned the entire morass of people from his mezzanine perch. Face by face, he searched. Aggie was nowhere among the crowd. How could he have lost her when she was closest to being his? Eyes straining, taking in everything at once: the honey-colored dance floor, bathed in purple stage light and the gloomy black gauze covering the once airy practice floor. The fishbowl's transformation seemed to reflect that of the entire company, light having been overcome by darkness. Yet, from above the opaque curtain, back at the fishbowl's farthest reaches, Miguel could see a couple. They were quite close, but not in dance position. The man lingered behind her, extending a scarf. The woman turned and Miguel saw Aggie's face.

Miguel bolted toward the stairs, leaving Don Luis calling after him. He took them three at a time and hit the landing hard with both feet. His eye caught the imposter, huddling aside the landing in the dark. Miguel paid him no heed, but forged ahead toppling serving trays and ramming a PA speaker cabinet that crashed loudly to the floor. A woman screamed when he swept past. A man pushed back when Miguel steamrolled by. Finally, Miguel burst through the fishbowl's door, nearly tearing it from its hinges. He flew past the clothing rack and boxes to find Chaz kneeling beside Aggie. She was unresponsive, and in his raised hand shone a gleaming blade.

CHAPTER 93

THE DEMOLITION OF A MAN is not achieved easily. Neither can his measure be taken simply. Don Luis believed that a man is a complex amalgam of hopes, fears, dreams, and deeds. Perhaps all too human ever to be completely deprived of his humanity, but quite capable of being deprived of life. He considered this, and more, as he descended from his second story office toward the mêlée.

How history would judge him or his cursed family he could not say. But all of the struggle and strife of a lifetime—of six hundred years worth of lifetimes—was playing out below. The last of his line was facing death to save a woman. For Don Luis, this was no *Götterdämmerung*; it was more the essence of *el tango*, of the lifecycle itself.

Don Luis felt that he had died a thousand deaths for one woman—a woman he had never held in his arms, never even kissed. And who now, by all accounts, lay dying far from him and her cherished son. Had her life been easier? He believed not. She had been a mother and a wife, albeit briefly and only according to the common law. But she had known the love of the man she wanted most, his brother. When the elevator door slid open and he propelled himself into the throng, Don Luis affirmed to himself that it was a far, far better thing he was about to do than to save his own, miserable life. He was saving his bloodline.

"Out of my way!" Don Luis shouted, his voice heavy above the din. "Hear me, I say, get out of my way!" he bellowed, steamrolling the crowd. He charged the brassy-haired witch, who cursed him as he passed. He flailed his arms, jabbed with his stick, making way, until he saw Miguel and Chaz on the floor locked in mortal combat. Miguel had ripped away Chaz's mask. Streaks of blood marked his face, slashed in self-mutilation. Miguel punched him with his fists, but Chaz withstood the pounding and sloughed him off with brute strength.

"Chaz, it's me you really want," Don Luis cried. "Come here. Do your worst!"

A chill shot through Don Luis when Chaz stood and leered. "Well, Uncle Donny, so you've come to die. Good, because this is all your fault!" Chaz shifted his weight and juggled his hands before pulling from his waistband a small handgun. He fired and fired again, striking Don Luis's strapping chest. The little pistol's quiet *pop, pop* mimicked a kid's plaything. It was as though Chaz was enacting a backyard massacre, using a toy cap gun. Don Luis absorbed the slugs, hardly moving. He seemed to fix his gaze on Chaz with greater intensity.

Don Luis saw Miguel charging and yelled, "Noooo!" He produced a dueling pistol from underneath his blanket. Unsteady, Don Luis fired at Chaz, who dodged the round and trained his weapon on Miguel. Chaz fired. Miguel clutched his chest and hit the floor. Don Luis was helpless as Chaz raced toward the rear exit, making his escape.

* * *

The pseudo-photographer crept quietly into Don Luis's open office. Now he knew about the elevator, hidden behind the bookcase. The security diagram his frenemies had helped him to access held more clues to Don Luis's lair than he had initially understood. The electrical feed to the office also powered a secret elevator. Even the switch's placement on the bookcase had been included on the drawing. He ran his fingers under the second shelf. Mid-span, he hit pay dirt and flicked the switch. The case groaned, translating.

The claustrophobic cage descended toward Don Luis's *sanctum sanctorum*. The man recalled the stench from his previous attempt to loot the priceless relic. He had ditched the stolen camera but gripped a very special tripod of his own making. A tripod, indeed, although two of its legs were decoys. The elevator clunked to a halt. He opened the cage door, the reek of mildew and sea-rot overpowering. Time was precious. He had to find the Codex and flee, before the place crawled with cops, other than the one he had summoned. Don Luis might be a shrewd Jew, but so was he. The Codex would be hiding in plain sight.

A cursory glance at the reading table yielded nothing of note. "Kabbalah," Jean-Luc sneered, "shit." What looked out of place, anything? He spied a rumpled takeout bag from Jake's Bar-B-Que, apparently filled with newspapers, and hefted it. It was not a used grocery shopping bag, as he had specified during their unheeded phone call, but close enough. He tore through the paper and found a massive book at the bottom, overwrapped with yellowed newsprint and heavily taped. He grabbed both of the bag's handles and scurried toward the emergency exit, around the corner to the left according to his memory. A moment later he attacked the metal exit door's girthy retaining chain with long-handled bolt cutters, their massive jaws hungry for steel. The links snapped like plastic and he eased the door open, thinking it'd be smooth sailing from here. And then he saw an apparition: a little Sinbad of the Sea, brandishing a big halberd.

* * *

Miguel pulled himself up from the floor. He thought to stem the flow of blood from his shoulder. But when he observed Chaz making for the exit, Miguel flew after him. He saw Chaz nearing the door, but he changed course to avoid Detective McGarrick, who snooped nearby. Miguel grimaced, but pushed ahead faster when Chaz mounted the landing of the hidden staircase. Chaz turned and fired a quick *pop* at Miguel, who ducked the round and followed faster. Should Chaz make the top, Miguel reckoned, he might easily escape through a lower-level bedroom window. Miguel's wounded shoulder burned. It was the one on which he had fallen in his death-defying escape from Gordo. He wasn't sure if he should praise or curse it. Miguel made a mad dash up the stairs and at the top grasped Chaz's trouser leg.

Chaz grunted as he kicked back and tore himself away, but Miguel outmaneuvered him and rammed Chaz into the balustrade above the throng. Chaz groaned and slumped to the floor. Miguel's momentum nearly pulled him over the railing. He heard a collective gasp from the crowd below. He saw their upturned faces anticipating horror. Cameras flashed and clicked as he willed himself upright.

Miguel turned to face Chaz, who braced himself on the banister. He leveled the pistol at Miguel's chest. Chaz grinned and squeezed the trigger. Miguel ducked. He stayed low, lunging into Chaz, banging him against the banister harder than before. Miguel stepped back and quickly slid his knife from his pocket. Preparing to finish the job, he flicked open its blade with an ominous whoosh. Chaz, backed against the railing, rolled his eyes and sneered, "Stupid *porteño*, a knife at a gun—"

Miguel struck like a viper, slashing Chaz's hand. Blood spurted onto the shiny brass railing. "Fuck!" Chaz screamed, cording one hand with the other. Miguel charged again. He thrust Chaz and himself violently into the balustrade. The glass exploded into a million shards. Onlookers screamed as Miguel and Chaz tumbled headlong toward them. They crashed into the crowd. Miguel recovered himself and rushed a few paces to Don Luis, who seemed to be defying death. Miguel grasped Don Luis's hand and squeezed. Don Luis opened his sad eyes. Miguel met his gaze. Just as Don Luis began to speak, someone shouted, "Look out!"

Miguel caught a glimpse of Chaz leaping toward him from the side. Miguel rolled away, leaving his arm outstretched and his blade upright. Chaz impaled himself and cried out in agony. The crowd gasped. Expecting Detective McGarrick, Miguel leapt up and raced to the practice area. He hoped that by some miracle Aggie would be alive.

Miguel burst into the room and found Aggie lying on the floor. Her face was pale and her eyes were shut. Emergency medical technicians, who had arrived to treat the mugged photographer, attended her. "Aggie!" he said. She opened her eyes and Miguel beamed at her. When she tried to sit up, a technician patted her shoulder, restraining her gently. Miguel blew Aggie a kiss before dragging the other tech to Don Luis. They approached, but Don Luis waved away the man with a surly grunt. Miguel bent down to the chair and said, "Let him help you."

"I'm going to be fine, my boy," he said, coughing quietly.

Anxiously, Miguel nodded agreement.

"I do have some right to call you that."

"Is fine."

"Although I am not your father, I am proud to be your uncle." He struggled to continue, but fell silent.

Miguel felt for Don Luis's pulse in his wrist. Nothing.

Still, Don Luis spoke. "Your mother and my brother, they were in love."

"I have figured out the truth. It will take time to accept it."

"Yes, Natalia was shocked when I told her. She insisted on contacting you, although I asked her to wait. You were precious to her."

Miguel bit his lip, but the pain was not nearly enough to overcome the ache in his heart. He whispered, "I'm sorry. I feel like everything is my fault."

"Heavens no."

Miguel's splendid eyes widened, watching Don Luis struggle to speak. The bullets had injured his lungs. He was fading fast.

Don Luis rallied to say, "Anyone to blame, let it be Moshe ben Avraham, our ancestor, the forger."

"Perhaps."

"Everything I have is yours, including the *Keter*. It is powerful. Use it." He drew a labored breath. "Break our family's curse. Help achieve peace for our people."

"I promise you, I will try."

Don Luis's hand fell limp. His head drooped to his motionless chest. Miguel felt numb as though his own breath had ceased. He threw back his head and cast up his eyes, as though questioning why. Detective McGarrick stared down at him. Miguel said, "Please don't take me away yet. This is my uncle, my father's only brother."

Aggie approached Miguel's side, slowly. He looked at her pale face, into her earnest eyes. She had been through hell, but to his surprise she said, "Your uncle, really?"

Miguel stood and threw his arms around her. He whispered, "*Te amo,*" and buried his face in her hair. And then he told her things he had never before said to a woman.

McGarrick growled to the encroaching crowd, "Give us a little air here." The gawkers stumbled backward. He surveyed the crime scene, scanning all directions. He stopped and said, "Lookie here, Zanotto."

Miguel observed the detective reaching down beside Chaz. Using a hanky, he grasped the small handgun. He looked it over. "Miguel, this may be your lucky day. I got five bucks says this is the pistol that killed Gordo." He added, "Never thought I'd see a tango guy with an Aelph .22." He glanced around suspiciously, before half-smiling. "Is this really a dance company or a Mossad front?"

"Mossad, Jean-Luc," Miguel said. Frantically, his eyes searched the room. "What happened to the guy who mugged the photographer, the fake photographer?"

McGarrick sucked air between his teeth. "Bad news." He shook his head, adding, "We got another stiff out back. A little guy in a clown suit: baggy pants, turban, got a hatchet of some kind buried in his chest."

"Kemal," Miguel gasped, glancing at Aggie. "Jean-Luc stole the Codex." Miguel slumped in disgust. Fire shot from his shoulder and he winced.

"But we're alive and free," Aggie said.

Miguel heard Don Luis chuckle. He snapped down his head and saw the yellowed front teeth bared between ashen lips. "Don Luis, you're alive! What is funny?"

Through labored breath, he said, "*Keter* is in my office. In plain sight."

Miguel flew up the stairs to the office. There, on the dictionary stand by his monumental desk, lay open the ancient relic. He ran his finger down the middle of three rows of sacred script, marveled at the marginalia, and bowed before the ultimate authority for text, vocalization, and cantillation of the Holy Jewish Scriptures. He rushed downstairs and found Aggie holding Don Luis's hand.

Miguel said, "Don Luis, the Codex is safe." He stared at his lifeless uncle and sighed. "Maybe you wanted it this way."

Aggie said, "He told me he loved you like the son he never had." She tried to withhold her tears, but they streamed down her face.

Miguel remained silent, thinking he had found the father for whom he had always longed. And had met the woman he wanted to share his life with. He was blessed. Only one thing remained for his life to be complete. Miguel must return the Codex to its rightful owners. Then perhaps it could become for them, and hopefully others, what it was meant to be: a guide for peaceful living.

ACKNOWLEDGMENTS

The author is grateful for the care and patience demonstrated during his instruction by his Argentine tango maestros. He deeply appreciates Miguel Zotto *y* Milena Plebs, Osvaldo Zotto *y* Lorena Ermocida, Vanina Bilous, and 'Flaco Dany' Hector, king of the *milonga*. He wishes to thank Michael Walker *y* Luren Bellucci for their painstaking instruction. Also, he would like to thank the *chicas* of Buenos Aires and Santa Fe, New Mexico, for thrilling dances and for kindly fostering his development as a *tanguero*, especially *la Reina del Tango de Santa Fe*. And finally, a *cabeceo* for his faithful *tanguera* Chérie.

www.ingramcontent.com/pod-product-compliance
Lightning Source LLC
Chambersburg PA
CBHW030812310726
48980CB00006B/472/J
9780692752289